Praises for *When The Dragon Roars*

"*When the Dragon Roars* is an absolutely riveting read, full of surprising twists and turns and brilliant writing. The chapters are short, the dialogue realistic, the characters believable, and the plot gripping."

—*Viga Boland, Readers' Favorite*

"With tight, crisp prose and realistic dialogue, the author keeps the pace of his tome moving at highway speed. His characters are finely etched both physically and emotionally. Clerge knows the story he wants to tell, and he tells it in a way that is both involving and entertaining."

—*Joe Kilgore, Pacific Book Review*

"Brimming with twists, turns, and non-stop drama, *When The Dragon Roars* by Nesly Clerge is a thriller ideal for any fan of prison-noir."

—*Veronica Alvarado, Bestseller's World*

WHEN THE
DRAGON
ROARS

WHEN THE DRAGON ROARS

NESLY CLERGE

"When the Dragon Roars"

This is a work of fiction. Names, characters, places, and incidents are the product of the author's imagination or are used fictitiously. Any resemblance to actual persons, living or dead, events, or locales is entirely coincidental.

(Print) ISBN-13: 978-0-9965017-4-3
(Electronic) ISBN-13: 978-0-9965017-3-6

Publisher: Clerge Books, LLC
Editor: Joyce L. Shafer (http://editmybookandmore.weebly.com)
Cover and Interior Book Design: Damonza.com

ALSO BY NESLY CLERGE

When the Serpent Bites (Book 1)

Acknowledgments

So many amazing people have supported me through this expedition of writing *When the Dragon Roars*. First, I would like to thank my editor, Joyce Shafer, for her expertise and help in creating a thing of beauty. I truly appreciate her patience, dedication, and the several months of preparation.

Special thanks to Goodreads fans, reviewers and beta readers, which includes Maxine Groves, Sue Ward, Sebolelo Lorraine Sithole, Petra Aylin, Lee Cooper, K. Morton, Dianne Bylo, Linda Strong, Brenda Telford, Sue Leonhardt, Veronica Joy, Kay Smillie, Amanda Jane, Tracy Campbell, Kimberlie Lashley, Irene Appleby, Gabriel Dedeic, Dawn P. Harrell, Torrie Angel, Lynn McCarthy, Yoana D. Ivanova, Dee Cherry, Anthony R. Parsons, Patricia Brooks, Laura Cerone, Russell Dent, Tracy Watson Fisher, Donna Bolton, as well as authors J. Kahele and C. P. Balois—I am certain several names were inadvertently left out. I am thankful to all the folks who took the time to review my book.

I am wholeheartedly grateful to the following people for purchasing my first novel, *When the Serpent Bites*, and their continued support and invaluable help and feedback for the completion of this second book: Professor Derrick Posey, Hensie Lapierre, Roberson Lapierre, Evans Clerge, Danenia Smith—thank you.

My sincerest gratitude to my significant other, Tierra Guy, whose passionate encouragement made it possible for me to navigate this journey.

And to conclude, I know myself a man,

Which is a proud, and yet a wretched thing.

—Sir John Davies (1569 – 1626)
Which Is a Proud, and Yet a Wretched Thing

CHAPTER 1

FREDERICK STARKS HAD no other option. A fresh start was needed, if there was such a thing in a place like this. It had taken only a moment for words strung together into a sentence, to scorch him and cause what he'd believed was the single, and perhaps last, solid aspect of his life to crumble to ash. He'd been blindsided—again, but this time he was going to manage his life like the intelligent businessman he was.

He was clear that nothing tangible around him had changed and likely wouldn't. Walls would remain unforgiving gray concrete. Each six by eight cell would remain inhabited by miscreants and lunatics who wasted away for years in a postage-stamp existence. The long, couple-inch-wide window in his cell in D-Block reminded him every day that a successful, wealthy life, and his position in it was now just as narrow. Sameness everywhere he looked. Yet, everything was different. Because he was.

The way he chose to start over was a one-eighty to how he would have done it outside these walls, and had involved enduring needle pricks for four straight hours while dulling as much of the pain as possible with hits from a contraband bottle of Rivers Rum. During those hours he devised his plan. Altering his appearance was the first step.

He was certain about his decision. Then why was a game of Twister playing in his gut?

The undesired answer flashed in his mind: Fear. He was so damn sick and tired of feeling afraid. Afraid of prison life. Of inmates. Of what kind of betrayal or turmoil might land on him with his next breath. He'd never been one to give up or give in, no matter how dire the circumstances. Initially, the idea of being *a* leader in this godforsaken place had motivated him. Not any more. He wasn't going to settle for less than being *the* leader. He'd never give anyone anywhere the opportunity to dump on him and get away with it ever again.

Before prison his life had been about possibilities. Now he was entrenched in a reality that was a walking nightmare. Except he was awake. That's why this change was imperative. He would do whatever it took to make him feel alive again. That's why he'd caused Steve, the barber, to sniffle and moan as his thick dark hair fell to the floor with each buzzing scrape of the electric razor. That's why he'd endured getting a dragon tattooed from the back of his right hand to his shoulder. It was his visual reminder to never again trust anyone, as much as a statement to others that he was taking back control of his life.

Betrayal was a bitch, and a label that had all but become his soon-to-be ex-wife Kayla's middle name. And every breath the *bitch* took was like a stiletto thrust into his heart.

Starks studied the finished tattoo. At least he'd have something to show for enduring this process. All he'd gotten as a result of Kayla's perfidy was fifteen years stolen from his life, restricted access to family and friends, loss of reputation and the luxuries his income had provided. And, most recently, the loss of his best friend since freshman year in high school, a wound too deep to fully comprehend as yet. Crushing rage and a number of other emotions he wasn't ready to drown in weighed on him, pressed the breath out of him. Each of these losses hurt like a sonofabitch, but none worse than what the outcome had done, was doing, and would do to his three young children.

There was no escape for any of them.

With his latest agenda kick-started, he left Joe "Tatman" Reynold's cell and made his way to the exit that would launch him onto this new path. This time, however, his presence in the yard would be radically different from when he'd arrived at Sands Correctional Facility. What a joke of a name, he thought. Little about the maximum security prison was correctional.

His altered appearance garnered attention as he passed through the gray corridors. Some of the incarcerated ignored the rule about staring at inmates. Some did double-takes, muttering expletives in their shock at the radical alteration. Starks searched for the word to describe what he was feeling and decided on *renewed*. But renewal was supposed to feel good. Maybe he'd feel that way later.

Springing his new appearance on inmates was the best way to make the statement that his former self no longer existed; that this new Starks meant business. It was especially poignant to do this on a Sunday morning, when the environment of the place was somewhat calmer. He *wanted* to shock inmates. So far, he was getting the desired result. He smothered his smirk.

Starks crossed the threshold of the double doors that led to the prison yard. July heat engulfed him as he stopped to do a visual assessment. He should have been lounging by his backyard pool, flip-flops hanging loose on his feet while his kids played and splashed just yards away. Instead, perspiration beaded on his skin and was already attracting dust from the mostly grassless ground. He ran a hand over his pale hairless scalp. Time in the sun every day would tan the skin soon enough.

The two o'clock glare and heat struck him like hot needles. He rubbed his right arm gingerly and squinted against the blazing sunlight as he surveyed the yard to see who was there.

One thought steeled him: every fucking person inside these walls and out was, from this moment on, going to hear the dragon roar.

CHAPTER 2

STARKS CUT A straight line across the dirt-packed yard. He stopped at almost the same spot where he'd stood the first day of his incarceration. Six months, and it already felt like a lifetime. He wound his fingers around a mesh segment of the chain-link fence. Rust stains trailed like old blood down the twenty-foot white wall positioned ten feet beyond where he stood. Multiple strands of razor and electrical wire glinted atop the fence and wall, blinking a Morse code-like SOS that would go unheeded.

He leaned against the fence with his arms crossed at his chest, and casually observed the inmates. Several bolder prisoners assumed postures that let him know they were this—they mistakenly believed—new fish's potential opposition. This included a few members of the Los Hermanos gang he'd recently aligned with. Hermanos leader, Hector Sanchez, flipped his black ponytail off his shoulder. He pointed to the single blue teardrops tattooed on each cheek as he engaged in a stare-down with Starks. Starks didn't suppress his amusement.

Perceiving this as a challenge, Sanchez took a few steps in Starks's direction, pumping his arms and chest to flash muscle used often. Then he halted, mouth open. Sanchez muttered something to his soldiers nearest him. Recognition registered. Starks's name carried in a whisper across the yard.

He was certain one question was at the top of any list his fellow inmates might create: why?

Because ultimate betrayal changes a person.

Starks fought hard not to laugh as he strolled around the perimeter of the yard. Just like Tendum Enterprises, the engineering company he'd taken over as CEO and turned into a huge success, this place needed a major shake-up. It needed to be restructured, at least as far as inmate hierarchy went, and he was the man to do it. Beyond these walls was his former empire; what existed inside them was about to become his kingdom.

He nodded at inmates as he sauntered toward the door that led into the prison, all the while reveling in the comments and obscenities uttered with stunned voices as he made his way to his painted-gray cell in this gray-toned existence he now called his life.

The tattoo hurt, but pain was something he was becoming all too familiar with. His former cellmate, Mike "Weasel" Lawson and asshole gang leader Boen "Big Bo" Jones, with assistance from some of Bo's soldiers, had seen to that. And he had seen to those two.

The dozen stab wounds Lawson inflicted on his torso had healed into thick scars that still pulled, itched, and throbbed. The two-month coma Jones put him into, though it had been, in its own way, a more pleasant few months away from Sands, was something he still resented. None of the inmates missed Lawson, but some of Bo's gang were more than pissed off that their leader's influence inside and outside the prison had been stripped from them.

Maybe they'd come after him. Maybe they wouldn't, especially if he could offer them a good enough incentive not to. All he had to do was figure out what that might be.

Prison officials wanted to pin Bo's murder on him but couldn't. The attack had been too clever. He'd had help, lots of it: The rubber magician's thumbs with toxic powders hidden in the tips, both created by brainy Lewis Mason in his lab; Jeffrey Davis' skilled transfer of the thumbs to him under guards' noses in the visitation room; and his cellmate, Ronald Jackson's intricate plan, down to the last man, including one of Bo's soldiers who was fed up with taking shit from the gang leader. One quick thrust of the prepped child-size knitting needle supplied by Jackson, and Big Bo had been in agony until he lost consciousness and died less than forty-eight hours later, the poison undetectable in his system.

There was no way to link him to Lawson's killing, either. Hector Sanchez still thought killing Lawson was his idea, and he'd never talk. No one who knew the truth would. Inmates didn't tolerate a blabbermouth, and the occasional person who failed to follow this code was shut up swiftly, brutally, permanently. Not even solitary confinement to protect a snitch was a guarantee of safety, which he had proven in Lawson's case.

Two fewer inmates in this Massachusetts prison didn't make much of a dent in the overpopulated enclosure. But there were a lot of weaker men here—and strong ones as well—who were glad those two were no longer breathing.

The two inmates' treachery had created something hard inside Starks. They weren't solely responsible for this, though: Others had started that solidifying effect ahead of them. One person in particular had forced him to look at his life and himself with different eyes. He bounced back and forth between rage and numbness about this latest betrayal. Finding a solution to the problem created as a result wasn't going to be easy.

CHAPTER 3

STARKS PAUSED AT the threshold of his empty cell. The walk-in closet in the mini-mansion he'd shared with Kayla and their children was four times this size. He shook his head as he glanced at his few possessions. Still, he was grateful for the moments of solitude that wouldn't last.

He hadn't spoken to Jackson since sometime prior to seeing his attorney, Michael Parker, the day before. After that god-awful meeting, he'd returned to his cell. Jackson, who considered himself a mentalist, didn't have to guess something was wrong. The smell and splatter of vomit on Starks's scrub set, as well as his dead-man-walking demeanor made it obvious. Starks's climbing into his bunk and facing the wall was another clear signal. Jackson had been prudent enough to leave Starks alone and not pry as he usually did. Nor did they speak when they got up this morning, or during the eight o'clock count.

Jackson's shift in the kitchen was only half a day on Sundays. He'd have to return soon for the count at three. In the meantime . . .

What to do about Jeffrey?

He was still reeling from what Parker told him. It was bad enough Kayla had humiliated him with her rampant, all-too-public cheating. It was bad enough that her three-year love affair with Ozy Hessinger had led him to attack her married "use-'em-then-lose-'em" lover in such a brutal fashion. Then there was all the crap that had happened since he got here. All of that was bad enough, or so he'd thought, until he learned what Jeffrey had done. So much for his so-said best friend and business partner.

The *bomb* Parker dropped on him had spun him out of his already unpredictable, tumultuous orbit. The betrayal made him feel like a serpent with skin grown so tight it was smothering him and had to be shed.

Maybe it was all a huge mistake. Maybe Parker got it wrong. No. Parker's key piece of evidence about Jeffrey was all too accurate.

How could you do that to me? To us?

While he was stuck here, Jeffrey ran the business, handled all his financial matters, took care of paying five Sands guards for extra protection. Jeffrey was the go-to person if his three young children needed help. And so much more. He'd entrusted Jeffrey with nearly every aspect of his life. It was his own fucking mistake to trust anyone, and he had to find a way to fix it.

Sweat beaded on his scalp. His right arm and the raised scars on his abdomen throbbed. He threw a book against the opposite wall. "Goddamn them!"

And damn Mathew Demory for taking a leave of absence. No way was he going to meet with Edward Townsend. He'd seen the young substitute counselor sitting at Demory's desk. The guy was maybe thirty, at least eight years younger than him. Correction—nine years younger. He'd forgotten about turning thirty-nine while in a coma back in May. Afterwards, there had been too many other things to think about, like the agonizing physical therapy, coping with pain without medication once back in prison since he couldn't afford to have his senses dulled, and how to get revenge against Lawson and Big Bo.

Starks picked up the book and checked it for damage, gently placing it back on his desk. At the small stainless-steel lavatory mounted atop the seat-less toilet, he studied as much of his face as he could see in the tiny mirror secured to the wall then rinsed his face and scalp with cold water. He wiped down the lavatory and toilet rim then unfolded and refolded his few articles of clothing. It was when he was reorganizing the items on his desk that Jackson entered the cell.

"Who the fuck are you and what the hell you doing in my cell?"

Starks straightened up and faced him. "You mean our cell."

Jackson's eyes opened wide. "Starks? What the hell, man?"

"What do you think?" Starks turned in a slow circle.

"If I wasn't such a beautiful black man, you'd see how pale I just turned."

"It's the new me."

"I liked the old you."

"That Starks is dead."

"You can be such a drama queen at times." Jackson plopped into the hard plastic chair on his side of the cell, keeping his gaze fixed on Starks. "This is about whatever the hell happened to you yesterday. You didn't even wash out the stink from your shirt. I had to do it; couldn't stand the smell. That ain't like you, man. You're Mr. Keep-It-Fucking-Clean. You gonna tell me about it, or what?"

A voice blared over the intercom, "On the count!" Starks and Jackson took their places outside their cell.

Jackson whispered, "I mean it, man. Why'd you do it?"

"I heard the dragon roar," Starks replied. "It gave me a clear message."

"Yeah? What'd it say?"

"Wake the fuck up, asshole."

CHAPTER 4

JACKSON SLOUCHED IN his chair and studied Starks. "Time to tell your partner what's going on."

"I don't have partners. Not anymore."

Jackson cocked his head. "You got rid of your memory, along with your hair?" Starks gave no reply. "You were able to take out Bo as easy as you did because of me. You think you'd've had the same success on your own? You asked me to help and I did. I did the legwork. I set everything up."

"I didn't ask. You offered and I accepted. Actually, you pushed your way into my business. But you can't forget there was outside assistance that made a significant difference. Your plan wouldn't have worked as well as it did without Lewis Mason's solution. Pun intended."

"Three fucking cheers for Mason. You can stick his rubber thumbs and poisonous powders up your ass, for all I care. Listen, all I've done is help you since you moved into my cell. I look out for you, man. Have from the start."

"Everybody uses everybody. Stop trying to make yourself out as my personal Good Samaritan."

"Man, you turned into some kind of prick overnight. You use me, too, and you know it. Only I don't call it using. I call it collaboration. You think you're gonna go solo inside these walls? You're off your fucking nut."

Starks walked to the mirror and stared at his reflection. "From now on I'm not helping anyone unless it helps me more."

"That philosophy's gonna bite your ass. Look, I can see something bad went down yesterday. But we're just getting some good stuff going for us in here. Your rep with the inmates, for one. You can talk to me, man. You don't want to tell me what happened, at least consider what this," Jackson gestured at Starks's appearance, "new you could lose."

"I've given up losing. It doesn't suit me."

"Neither does a coffin."

"You threatening me, Jackson?"

"Get it through your thick bald head: I'm not your damn enemy."

"Enemies are not always obvious about it. Especially the ones who pretend to be your friend."

Jackson's gaze met Starks's mirror-reflected one. "I'm beginning to see the light."

"You don't see shit."

"I see you better than you wish I did."

"Fuck you."

"I don't do dragons."

Starks climbed onto his bunk and faced the wall, wondering what it might actually take to get respect in this hellhole. It might not happen as automatically as he'd hoped.

CHAPTER 5

STARKS GLANCED AT the red digits on his clock and groaned. Recurring nightmares had once again interrupted his sleep. He dragged himself out of bed and began his morning routine: Push-ups and lunges despite the pain, washed his face, shaved, got dressed, made his bed. Two packaged cinnamon rolls served as breakfast as he waited for the eight o'clock count. The rolls were fattening, but he wasn't ready to go to the chow hall just yet. He'd avoided the communal sharing of tasteless crap erroneously called food the night before, relying on items from his commissary stash. The chow hall tended to be an explosive environment. With his tattooed arm as sore as it was, he wanted to avoid even minor altercations for a little while longer. His appearance was bound to draw negative engagement sooner or later. He preferred later.

After the count, he made his way to the library to begin his eight thirty shift early.

He grinned in anticipation of what Paco might say when he saw him.

Paco was already seated at his preferred computer in the library, the older inmate's intense focus on the screen obvious.

Starks stood next to the desk and asked, "How's the memoir going?"

"It'll be memorable, amigo. I'm telling it all, and there's a shitload to tell about this place." Paco stopped typing and sat back. With a slow shift in attention he said, "How's it going with—" Then he glanced up. "Jesus,

Maria, and Jose." Paco hesitated a moment then added, "I have one question for you?"

Starks smirked. "Yeah, I know: why?"

"No, amigo. My question is, What will your *niños* think?"

Starks's breath caught in his chest. He pivoted and went into the small office at the back of the library, lowered himself into the chair, and stared at the blank screen of the computer monitor. His hand shook as he reached for the On switch. Elbows on the desk, he cradled his face in his hands.

Paco was right, of course. His children would be shocked and appalled at his transformation. Blake would soon turn thirteen. Although his children had been taught to be respectful, his oldest son was the most outspoken of the three. He could imagine what the boy would say, or, worse, say only with his eyes. Nathan was a few months away from turning eleven. He'd draw back and wrap his arms protectively around his slight frame, losing himself in silence as he so often did when upset. Kaitlin, who'd recently turned seven, and who had yet to visit him in prison, would be horrified at how her daddy now looked and would probably burst into tears. It was possible all three would refuse to ever visit him again.

Maybe he should block their visitation rights as a way to protect them. But this would mean never seeing them. Fourteen and a half years was too long for him to be completely absent from their lives. No matter what reason was given for keeping them away, they'd take it personally, if not now, later on. They may never again want to have anything to do with him.

His gut tightened at the thought. They were the only genuine saving grace in a life that had gone wrong.

He decided that when they visited, he'd wear a long-underwear top under his scrub shirt to cover his arms. But that still left his right hand, where the dragon's head began. He'd have to make certain he kept it from sight. His shaved head was easy: An outbreak of lice—*now contained, of course*—had caused him to shave his hair off. Better safe than itchy, he'd tell them. And he could say he'd decided to keep it that way, just in case. It was a lie they'd choose to believe. These diversions would last only so long, though. He'd have to come up with an explanation, but not until they were older, if he could get away with it that long.

He shuddered at the thought of what his children were learning by example from their parents. This was *not* the life he'd dreamed of for them, had worked and sweated so long and hard for. The stable, secure, loving family and home he'd wanted to provide for them no longer existed. Who was he kidding? It had been a fallacy for years. They'd all just pretended it was better than it was.

There was nothing he could do about it now. His children were as safe as they could be in their nanny's care. Better nanny Anita minding them, tending to them, showing them affection, than Kayla's parasitic live-in boyfriend, Bret, getting too involved with them.

Kaitlin was going to be a beauty, and he hoped like hell Bret was long gone by the time she'd be considered old enough to . . . No, he couldn't allow himself to think about that now. It would make him insane.

He did regret that the nanny now also had to care for Bret's two young daughters, as well, but the girls were as innocent in this sordid mess as his own children. Thankfully, Anita had a big heart. The last thing he wanted was for any child to feel abandoned or as though they were insignificant.

Not like Kyle was by me.

But in Kyle's case it hadn't been complete abandonment. He'd supported his illegitimate son financially and had spent time with the boy, albeit brief and sporadic.

He shook off the thought, reminding himself that in a few months, Kayla would give birth to Bret's bastard.

The thought that followed sickened him even more: the child's paternity wasn't a given.

He couldn't afford to think about any of this now. There were plans to implement and closer enemies to deal with.

CHAPTER 6

A T 6 A.M., the lights brightened to full strength; the electronic cell doors clanged open. Starks yawned and stretched. Jackson was already getting ready for his breakfast shift in the kitchen.

Jackson slid his shirt over his head and said, "Damn, man, all that tossing and turning kept me up. You're doing a number on my beauty sleep."

Starks dangled his feet over the edge of his upper bunk and ran a hand over his scalp, momentarily surprised to feel skin instead of hair. "I don't think more sleep would help how you look."

"Oh *goodie*. You're in one of your better moods today."

"My moods aren't your concern."

"Funny, though, how they have a way of becoming my problem."

Starks glanced at the clock. "Jesus, Jackson, the sun's barely up and you're already ragging on me."

"It's just my two-cents, but when are you going back to the chow hall? Your absence is drawing attention."

"Not that it's your business but I'm going this morning."

Jackson slipped on his lace-less shoes. "About time. Speaking of time, I gotta go. Later."

Starks leapt down, grabbing his side when some of his internal scars resented the action. He followed his usual routine then waited for the eight o'clock count before heading to the chow hall.

The line for inmates to get pre-prepped trays from the slot in the wall moved at pace. Skullars Bailey stood four men ahead of him. The Jamaican's nearly waist-length dreadlocks stood out, as did the man's pronounced height and bulk. As though intuition was at work, Skullars glanced behind him.

Starks indicated his request to sit together with a jerk of his head toward a table. Skullars nodded.

Several minutes later, Starks did the required rapping on the table then sat across from Skullars. "How's it going?" he asked.

"Okay as it can go in here, mon."

"Anyone giving you any shit?"

"Nah, mon. When dem batty boys see me, they turn and go the other way. I think they passed the word that my *backdoor* is closed and locked. Ever since they saw you take up for me, they don' wan' to risk it."

Starks chuckled. He placed a forkful of rubbery fake scrambled eggs into his mouth and frowned. "I'd almost give my left nut for Eggs Benedict."

"Not worth a nut, in my opinion, mon. But a live chicken that lays eggs . . ."

Starks pointed his fork at his companion. "You've got common sense."

"And I got sense enough to see people staring at you."

"You didn't say anything about how I look."

"Not my business."

"Definitely have good sense."

The remainder of the meal was eaten in silence punctuated by periodic generic dialogue and under the stipulated ten minutes allowed. The two men knocked on the table to indicate they were finished, dumped their trays, and then parted at the door, Skullars going in one direction and Starks heading to the library for his shift.

The library had been left messy and disorganized by whoever had been there the evening before. He thought about printing new signs to put up but realized there was no point. The last time he'd posted directives about keeping the place in order, the notices had quickly become canvases for explicit graffiti about what he could do with his directives. The new Starks couldn't afford to ride inmates about neatness: They'd wonder why he'd put a dragon on his arm instead of a kitten. He couldn't do anything that would cost him the reputation he needed to establish in order to achieve his goal.

Starks was filing books back into their proper places on the shelves when Paco walked in and took his seat at his usual desk. Correctional Officer Luke Roberts entered seconds behind the old man. The CO jammed his hands into his pants pockets. "Gotta talk with you, Starks."

"Let's go into the office."

Starks closed the office door and took a seat in the chair behind the desk. "What can I do for you?"

"Spencer's coming after you. He's been chewing the investigative council's ears."

"What do you mean?"

"I overheard him talking about an investigation. He mentioned your name."

"Details."

"I don't have any."

"That's not what I want to hear, Roberts. What the hell am I paying you for?"

Roberts' cheeks flushed. "As I said, I overheard him, and that's all I heard. I don't have the rank to be included in some details. I get information on a need-to-know basis." He looked down at the floor and started moving up and down on the balls of his feet.

"What else?" Starks asked.

"Payment's a week late."

Starks's brow furrowed. He leaned back in the chair. "You called the contact?"

"No answer. Didn't return my calls, either."

"Don't worry about it. I'll take care of it. Anything else?"

"That's it. I'll see if I can find out what Spencer's planning."

"I'll be waiting to hear from you."

Starks kept his gaze fixed on Roberts until the CO exited the library. What the hell was going on? Realization of the extent Jeffrey's contribution was to his survival hit him like a blow: his life was literally in Jeffrey's hands. And, Jeffrey knew this.

What was the man up to?

All the money he'd told Jeffrey to pay out to others. Easy enough to get it started then keep the funds. But to what end?

It was more likely that some slip-up had occurred and could be easily straightened out with one phone call. After all, it wasn't Jeffrey making direct payments to the guards, or wasn't supposed to be. He'd instructed Jeffrey to involve Jim Rogers. The private investigator was to line up someone reliable to make the payments. The potential pitfalls for this arrangement were glaringly obvious now. He should have thought of them before.

It was Tuesday, which meant his shift ended at noon. He'd have the afternoon to think. This was a dilemma that needed a solution. Whatever was going on had him on the brink of falling into a massive cesspool with no way to escape.

No shaved head or big fucking tattoo, or any other affectation, would be effective without his plan being backed by money, and lots of it.

This was not good. Not good at all.

CHAPTER 7

THE DIGITS ON the monitor screen switched to 12:08. Starks scowled at his replacement for being late and ignored the inmate's hand gesture as he passed him. He hurried to the phones, relieved to see one of the six instruments mounted to the wall was available. He gave his pin number to the operator, who placed the collect call to Michael Parker's cell phone. With each unanswered ring, Starks's breathing quickened. Parker's voicemail picked up. He convinced the operator that his attorney *would* accept a voicemail message and left word that he'd call back the next day around the same time. Starks went to his cell and gathered what he'd need for a shower after hitting the gym.

Several members of the Los Hermanos gang, minus their leader, clustered in one corner of the exercise room. Two of them were on a mat, demonstrating impressive wrestling moves. A few of them nodded at Starks.

Starks found a clear space and began to push his body and mind. Fifty push-ups (*What am I going to do about Jeffrey?*). One hundred sit-ups (*I need to get my thoughts in order before I talk to Parker*). After forty-five minutes of weight training mingled with a number of interludes where, under his breath, he cursed everyone, he still wasn't sure how to eliminate the Jeffrey situation once and for all. It was all so damn complicated. And painful.

Dripping sweat, he made his way to the showers. Lukewarm water sprayed his back as he kept a watchful eye on the few inmates in there. A level of relief washed over him: He no longer feared being attacked in this room. It wasn't that it couldn't happen to him—it had, and still could, if someone had the balls to take the risk. But inmates believed he had a secret weapon, which he did: the prepped child-size knitting needle was close enough for him to grab and use, if the need arose.

A crash to his left caused Starks to snap his head around. An inmate he'd seen in the yard but had never spoken to picked himself up from the floor, leaving the plastic trashcan he'd knocked over where it was as he backed out of the shower room.

It was obvious: The man was afraid to be this near him so decided to shower later. Starks laughed with satisfaction.

Still laughing, he faced the showerhead. A sudden surge in pressure sent water into his nostrils and mouth. He choked. Gulping air, he placed a hand against the tiled wall. Tears started unexpectedly. He let them stream as he caught his breath.

Kyle hadn't been able to catch his breath. How long was his five-year-old son conscious under water? Was he terrified when no one jumped in to rescue him? Did he know he was going to die? Did his small heart stop beating before his lungs could fill with water?

This wasn't the first time Starks tortured himself with such questions. He tried not to visit these horrific thoughts but they crept up on him when he least expected it.

Kyle's mother, Cathy, had been gorgeous when they'd met. Not like now, after her own grief had wreaked havoc with her looks. What a stupid mistake he'd made. The woman was calculating. He'd told her, just as he always had told any woman he got involved with, that he would never leave his wife. She'd said she understood. As soon as Cathy told him she was pregnant with his child—and he'd known this was deliberate on her part—the more-than-generous monthly deposits to her account began. She'd threatened to tell Kayla if he didn't marry her. He'd threatened to cut her money off.

Five years later, she'd called him on his office phone and told him his son was dead.

God, he was sorry. Sorry Kyle died so young. Sorry he saw him only when he lied to Kayla about business trips out of town. Sorry he didn't give the boy the life his half-brothers and half-sister had. Sorry he wasn't the father his secreted son deserved.

He'd never be sorry enough. How could he be?

He shut the water off, dried himself, dressed then went to his cell.

Jackson lay on his bunk reading. Without looking up he said, "Enter the dragon."

"I'm not in the mood."

"I'd say it must be that time of the month again but you're like this more often than not lately."

Starks chose not to respond. He folded his dirty clothes and placed them neatly in the cardboard box used for that purpose then hoisted himself onto his bunk, pushing away every thought from his mind but the upcoming conversation with Parker. He pondered what order or orders he should give his attorney.

He'd think of something.

CHAPTER 8

AT SEVEN THE next morning, five COs crowded into Starks's cell, which was already too small for two people. The first guard in the procession barked, "Frederick Starks."

Starks kept doing his lunges. "How can I help you?"

The first guard looked back at the others and said, "Get a load of this guy. Wants to know how he can help us." The COs snickered.

The name label stitched to the shirt of the guard doing the talking read *Woodson.* "You're coming with us," he told Starks.

"What's the problem?" Starks asked. "And why five of you? One of you asking me nicely would be enough."

Woodson snorted. "And, he's a comedian."

Jackson got up from his chair and asked, "What's this about?"

Woodson said, "Your name Starks?"

"No."

"Then mind your fucking business."

Starks stood with his arms crossed. "I'm not going anywhere until I know what this is about and where you're taking me."

Woodson placed his right hand on his Taser. "You can go on your own two feet or we can carry your drooling, twitching body outta here."

"Fine," Starks said. "Give me a few minutes to get myself together."

"Sorry, princess," Woodson said, "you got ten seconds."

Starks slipped on his shirt, with the prepped knitting needle tucked into the hem. "Ready when you are." He swung his head around and said, "No worries, Jackson. I'll be back."

"Here's hoping," Jackson replied.

Skullars Bailey was on his bunk in the first cell on the right side of the entrance to Cell Block D. He made eye-contact with Starks. He raised his eyebrows in a silent question, a question to which Starks could only shrug and shake his head.

Heads turned to watch Starks and his five escorts as they proceeded down one corridor after another. On the surface, Starks appeared calm, confident. Inside was another matter.

The path they followed didn't give any clues to where they were taking him, until they made one particular turn that led to the Incidents Investigative Council room. Why hadn't Roberts warned him? No money, no service?

Damn Jeffrey. Was this the first Domino to fall and take out the rest, until there was nothing left to keep him safe in this godforsaken place? Only one thing stopped Starks from panicking: the guards hadn't put shackles on him.

Tony Spencer, head investigator, was seated at the long table in his usual spot at the center. Starks noted that the last time he'd been invited to this kind of *party* there had been five men at the table. This time there were three, and the other two were new faces. Nameplates were provided, another difference from the other time—correction, times—Starks reminded himself. The man to Spencer's right was John Bentley. To his left was James Kratz. Each man had the same size stack of papers in front of him.

Spencer motioned for Starks to sit in the chair directly across from him and a yard back from the table. Two of the five guards took positions at the door. Spencer glared at Starks over his wire-frame glasses. "Making a statement, are we? Why didn't you just put a heart with *Killer* written inside on your forehead or put the blue teardrops on your cheeks?"

"I'm not a killer."

"You're not a dragon, either, despite your erroneous estimation of yourself," Spencer said.

"What's this about?" Starks rested his elbows on his knees and leaned forward, waiting, wondering if the proverbial other shoe was about to drop.

"We have good—better than good—reason to believe you were directly involved in the Jones and Lawson deaths."

"You're wrong. I'm innocent," Starks said.

Bentley cleared his throat. "You wouldn't be at Sands if you were innocent. The only thing that stopped you from killing Ozy Hessinger was the police pulling you off him. If you went after your wife's lover, why wouldn't you go after someone who attacked you here?"

"Hessinger was a matter of self-defense," Starks replied. "He pulled a knife on me."

Bentley tapped his finger on the stack of papers. "No mention of a knife in the police report."

"It's in the trial transcription." Starks smiled at the man. "By the way, I like your name. That's the car I drive."

Bentley curled his upper lip. "Drove, Starks. Only thing you're driving in here is time." He picked up his pen and tapped it on the table. "Boen Jones. Mike Lawson. Start talking."

"What happened to them has nothing to do with me." Starks slouched in the chair, with his legs stretched out in front of him.

"Both men attacked you." Bentley pointed his pen at Starks. "And you want us to believe you had nothing to do with their deaths?"

Starks gave him a half-smile. "I'd like to say I have people in here who like me enough to take revenge on my behalf, but that's not the case. Those two had enemies. Lots of them. Are you interviewing them as well?"

Spencer broke in. "You're here to answer questions, not ask them."

"I'm here," Starks said, "because you're making assumptions."

Up to this point, Kratz had been a silent observer but now sat forward in his chair. "How would you explain the death of the two inmates who attacked you?"

"What makes you think they're the only two who attacked me since I got here?"

"You didn't report any other attacks," Kratz said.

"If you're paying any attention at all to what it's like in here, you know why I wouldn't." Some of the tension in Starks's body eased. He was certain now that this was nothing more than a baited fishhook. "Look," he said, "I had nothing to do with what happened to Jones and Lawson. That's all I can tell you about that."

Spencer slammed his palm against the tabletop. "We know you did it, Starks. We have an informant willing to testify against you for both deaths. It's better for you if you confess willingly."

"Better for me? Right. Either you're setting me up or someone else is. I'm not taking the fall for this. I'm letting my attorney know what you're doing. I know my rights."

The sound of chair legs scraping across flooring drew everyone's attention to Spencer, who was on his feet, red-faced, leaning forward with his fists pressed against the table. "All you've done is create chaos since the day you stepped foot into this prison. Two deaths." He pointed a finger at Starks. "I know you're involved. Don't talk to *me* about your rights." He smoothed his tie, pulled his chair into place, and resumed his seat.

"Yeah," Starks said, "six months. Two of them spent in a coma, with extra hospital time needed for recovery and physical therapy, thanks to the two inmates you're so concerned about. Really doing a great job, fellas."

Spencer shook his head. "We know you have some kind of special weapon."

The knitting needle, usually weightless in Starks's shirt hem, weighed heavy in his imagination. "You can't be serious. This entire," he waved a hand toward them, "procedure, for lack of a better word—though, *sham* comes to mind—is ridiculous. If I'm not being charged with anything, I'd like to go. I haven't had breakfast and I'm going to be late for work."

"Maybe we're not charging you with anything right now," Spencer said, "but you'll eventually be caught. Count on it."

"Then I'm free to leave."

"You leave when we say you can." Spencer signaled the two guards. "Get him out of here."

Starks stood, nodded at the three men and made his way to the door.

Bentley called to Starks, who turned around. "We're coming after you, Starks. We're not giving up until we have you."

Starks stopped himself from telling them not to hold their breath, or better yet, to stick their heads up their asses and do just that. Less than two weeks ago he would have had the confidence to make that sort of cocky comment. But things had changed. The arrangements and people he'd relied on had been in order then. Now he wasn't sure what was what anymore. His plan wasn't moving forward as smoothly as he'd anticipated.

It was a case of the weakest damn link in the chain:

Jeffrey.

CHAPTER 9

S TARKS HAD TO call Michael Parker exactly at noon. It wasn't that Parker wouldn't wait for his call if he was a few minutes late, but that he wanted to get the call done and behind him. He finished putting copies of the local newspapers into chronological order then glanced at the clock placed high on the back wall. It was five after eleven.

Since he'd left Spencer's office, each time Starks glanced at the clock, which had been often, his anxiety escalated. He was worried about Spencer, and that maybe someone from Hector Sanchez's gang had squealed on him. But that didn't seem likely, because telling on Starks would be the same as telling on Sanchez. That would be a bad mark against the gang leader. Sanchez's followers knew the rules, especially when your leader is called The Razor, a label Sanchez had earned and didn't hesitate to reinforce, including when he felt a need to discipline those under him.

Spencer had nothing concrete on him or he'd already be in the Secure Housing Unit, again, being abused by guards with personality disorders and fed the inedible nutraloaf—a true sin against man—for God only knew how long. Aside from the deliberate physical discomfort of those cells and the mental torture of extended isolation, any time spent in the SHU was the worst thing that could happen now.

Starks busied himself by reorganizing books and materials he'd already put into order that morning, glancing more and more frequently at the clock. At 11:45, he couldn't stand waiting any longer. It was imperative he get to the phones early. Other inmates might be waiting to make calls, which was usually the case. He exited the library, traveling down the corridors just fast enough to indicate he had a destination in mind and wasn't to be interrupted.

The digital clock above the phones read 11:57. Three minutes.

All the phones were in use, and there were lines behind the callers. One line had only two inmates waiting their turn. It was his best chance.

Starks stood behind the second guy in line and said, "I need to get ahead of you."

The man turned, sneered at Starks then faced forward again.

Starks said, "I'll give you four cartons of cigarettes, if you'll get behind me."

The inmate started to say something, but stopped when his gaze landed on the dragon tattoo. He raised his eyes to meet Starks's. "Works for me."

"I can't get to the commissary until after my work shift is over later this afternoon, but I'm good for it. Ask around."

"I know who you are." The inmate took his place behind Starks.

Starks told him, "Meet me by the weights in the exercise room at five." The man nodded.

The inmate now in front of Starks had paid attention. "If you offer the same deal to me, I'll take it."

"Good. Same place and time."

Starks reached to tap the back of the inmate using the phone, but the man hung up and walked away.

The collect call was placed. Parker answered on the first ring. "I wasn't sure when I'd hear from you again," he said, "considering how our last meeting affected you. How are you?"

"I don't have much time, so I'll get to the point. We need to do something about Jeffrey."

"Please be more specific."

"I want him out of the company. I don't want that traitor benefitting from my hard work one second longer than it takes to get rid of him."

"Not possible."

Starks gripped the phone. "Not what I want to hear, Parker."

"Look, Starks, you're no longer able to call the shots." Silence hung for a few moments between the two men. "About the company, I mean. The board of directors removed you after the attack on Hessinger. You signed your ownership over to your mother."

"And Jeffrey signed off on her being a silent partner in my absence."

"You know the arrangement. She has only forty percent of the shares. Jeffrey's the majority shareholder now."

"He's a fucking viper. I'd bet my life he and Kayla are in this together. I have to get control away from him."

"And give control to whom?" When no answer came, Parker cleared his throat. "I understand why you feel that way, especially now, but we don't have proof of a conspiracy. If there is one, it'll surface sooner than later. And we'll deal with it. If it happens that way.

"Speaking of Kayla, her lawyer contacted me yesterday afternoon about the divorce. I should say her primary lawyer was who called me. She has a team of lawyers lined up."

"Handle it."

"It's not that simple. Discoveries are in order and have been formally requested. You and I need to meet soon to discuss your assets and properties."

Starks pressed the phone hard against his ear, ignoring the discomfort. "Listen, that whore is entitled to what she gets now and not a fucking penny more. You hear me, Parker?"

"I know you'd like it to be that simple, but that's not the case. Your situation is an involved one."

"Damn woman." Starks sighed. "Protect my interests as best you can. I plan to get out of this place one day, early, if that's possible, and I don't want to have been stripped bare of everything my blood, sweat, and tears created. Make sure my kids are taken care of, but that bitch can crawl under a rock, for all I care."

"I understand your frustration. I'll arrange a meeting as soon as possible so you and I can discuss it further." Parker waited for a response, which didn't come. "Starks, are you still there?"

After a moment's hesitation, Starks said, "Parker, you're my only line of defense now. I know it's asking a lot but . . ."

"I'll help you however I can. Just understand that my schedule—"

"Rearrange your goddamned schedule." Starks took a deep breath. "I'm sorry, Parker. I don't mean to take it out on you. I know you'll do your best for me. Get here as soon as you can. And, thanks. For everything."

Starks placed the receiver into the cradle and wiped his sweaty palms on his pants. The possibility, if not probability, that he was about to lose everything sunk in.

Life was too quickly becoming like a tightrope he was forced to walk blindfolded, and he was certain that Kayla and Jeffery would do anything they had to, to remove the net set up to catch him if he fell. One or both of them would make sure he tumbled. His head began to throb, and he felt like he was being spun around and around by an amusement park ride.

As though said from the opposite end of a tunnel, he heard the inmate behind him ask if he was okay.

The world went black.

Starks didn't hear the thud when his head struck the concrete floor.

CHAPTER 10

A DULL ACHE FILLED every crevice in Starks's head. He ignored it. Because he was on a beach. How he'd gotten there, and even where *there* was, was unknown. Nor did he care. It was the most relaxed he'd felt in a long time, so was in no hurry to open his eyes. He was free to just *be*. Free from thinking about anything at all.

Each wave on the shore sounded like voices. The voices grew louder as the waves rushed toward him then diminished in volume as they receded. He struggled to focus on what the voices were saying. One voice began to stand out: Someone called his name over and over, but the person pronounced it as "Stocks." It was beginning to annoy him. He tried to tell whoever it was to shut up and leave him in peace but couldn't get his own voice to work right.

A cold wave splashed his face, causing him to sputter. He opened his eyes and saw a small crowd of indistinguishable forms standing in a semi-circle around him. Skullars Bailey, his face screwed tight with concern, knelt at his side.

"You scared the hell outta me, mon," Skullars said. "Can you sit up?"

Starks blinked several times then shifted to an upright position, placing his back against the wall. "What's going on?"

"That's the question, mon. I was passing through and saw you hit the floor. You should go to the infirmary."

"I don't need a doctor, unless it's a witch doctor that can put a curse on some people for me." Starks, with Skullars' assistance, got to his feet. "Why am I wet?"

Skullars held up an empty paper cup. "You weren't coming round, so I tried cold water. It worked."

Starks swiped water from his eyes and face. He glanced at the several inmates watching him. "Show's over," he said. Everyone, with the exception of Skullars, moved back to the phone lines or left the area.

Skullars said, "I still think you should go to the infirmary. Let the doctor check you."

"Maybe later. There's something else I need to do now." The lines at the phones were thinning fast. Some of the calls weren't being picked up. Those men sulked away angry or dispirited. "Phone lines are lifelines," Starks mused.

"If you lucky enough to have somebody to call."

Starks checked the time. He hadn't been out longer than a few minutes. "You go on, Skullars. I'm fine."

"If you need me . . ."

Starks shook Skullars' hand then watched for a few seconds as the hulk of a man walked away.

Only one phone had no one in line behind the inmate using it. Starks took his place and waited. Five minutes later, he heard Lynn Starks accept the call.

"What's wrong?" she asked.

"Hello, to you too, Mom."

"This is the first time you've called me since you've been in that damn place. I'm your mother. I know when something's wrong with my son."

"One day I'll be out of here, and I need to know I'll have money to rely on. How much do I have in what I put in your name?"

"A little over three million."

Starks ran a hand over his scalp. "Christ. That's all?"

"We only started this arrangement less than six months ago. Plus, the stocks took a dip. Even though they're coming back up, I moved some of what was in stocks into tax-free bonds. When I see the interest statements each month, I know I did the right thing. The other investments and accounts are doing what they're supposed to."

"Smart move. Thanks. Are you using any of it?"

"You know I'm not," she snapped. "I use my own money and what I inherited from your grandfather. It's plenty for my needs."

"Jeffrey's still putting my share of company profits into the account?"

"Of course. Why would you even ask such a thing?"

He wasn't ready to tell her the truth. "I'm used to overseeing everything. I guess paranoia is par for the course in my situation."

"It's more than that. What's going on?"

Starks rested his forehead on the wall. He sighed deeply then said, "Kayla's going forward with the divorce. I spoke with Parker just before I called you. We're meeting soon to discuss my assets, et cetera. Apparently, Kayla's hired a team of lawyers. She wants everything, if she can get it, and the lawyers are going to want their share of the kill. Considering where I am, and why, I don't know how this cluster-fuck is going to end. I may come out of here with nothing more than what you're taking care of for me. That's why I'm concerned. All the years of sacrifice to build what I did with my businesses, only to maybe lose it all and have to start from scratch." Starks heard something glass hit a wall and shatter.

He moved the receiver a few inches away when his mother screeched, "I hate that bitch. I hate what's she's done to you. She took you from your children, from your family. She ruined your reputation and life. Nothing bad enough can happen to her."

Starks was relieved his mother wasn't sitting across from him in the visitors' room, ranting as she had the last time she'd gone there. He was equally satisfied to hear her express what she felt on his behalf.

"Parker's going to handle everything," he told her. "He's got his own team of piranhas. Each of them has profited big-time from my annual retainer, alone. They'll fight for me. Parker knows he's better off taking care of my interests than not; that it'll pay off in the long-run."

"I'd like to do something vicious to her."

"Don't do anything at all. Not even a phone call, and definitely nothing in writing. No contact of any kind. Please. I need you to be able to take care of things for me. You get yourself into trouble, and I'm screwed. You alert her to what I'm doing, and I'm screwed. You hear me?"

"You need your mother. I'll set up a visit."

"I'd rather you wait."

"I want to see my son."

Starks could easily imagine how his mother would react if she saw how he looked now. That was an explosion he could live without. "There's so much I have to take care of right now. I'll let you know soon when it'll be a good time to come here."

"Let me know early enough. All that ridiculous paperwork to see my own son. And you know it's a couple-hours drive to get there. I have to make sure your cousin Hank is available to drive me."

"I will. In the meantime, you're doing great managing things for me. That means a lot." He heard his mother harrumph.

"That's what mothers do, at least good ones. Not like Kayla. To think my grandchildren have a used mattress for a mother. They have to live with her boyfriend and his two brats in their own home. And she's pregnant with his bastard. Every time I think of her I want to yank out every damn hair from her head. I want to claw her eyes out. Rip her goddamned heart from her chest."

He let his mother carry on, understanding her need to vent, until the automated recording announced they had one minute left. He ended the call before it was automatically ended for them. As usual, neither of them said "I love you." It wasn't done in their family. As a child, he'd always wondered about that practice. As a parent, it was a practice he'd changed. He knew his mother loved him, but it would have been nice to hear it from time to time. That's why he'd made a point of showing and telling it often to his children. Even Kyle, who'd been deliberately lied to about his father, a father who supposedly had to be away for business nearly all the time.

Guilty relief filled Starks. He didn't want to imagine what would happen, especially now the divorce was about to get brutal, if Kayla had ever known about Kyle.

Shame threatened to take over. He couldn't allow that. There were too many other pressing matters that needed his attention. Like the fact he should head straight for the infirmary to get checked out. He'd never passed out in his life, not without having been attacked and knocked unconscious. He couldn't afford to be physically weak or even appear as such to inmates, or guards, especially not now.

There was always one damn thing or another on the line.

CHAPTER 11

S TARKS MADE A detour to the library, eager to find Paco so he could ask him to look after things until he got back. The memoir writer wasn't there, but Sam Carson was, seated at the desk in the back office.

Carson looked up when Starks got to the doorway. "Where the hell you been? I passed by and saw no one was watching the place. You want to keep this job or what?"

"Had to call my attorney. It was urgent. Then I . . . I got sick. I'm heading to the infirmary now. Can you cover for me until I get back?"

Carson studied Starks. "You are pale. Yeah, I'll cover for you. Sorry about snapping, but you know the library's not supposed to be left unattended for longer than a bathroom break."

"Thanks, Sam. I hope this doesn't take too long."

Carson waved him off. "Go on and take care of what you gotta take care of."

Starks made his way to the infirmary. The nurse practitioner sat at a desk, making notes in a file. His pen scratched against the paper for a few more moments, and then his hand lifted with a flourish after making a last punctuation mark. Still not looking at Starks, he said in a flat voice, "What do you want?" When no answer came, he glanced up. His eyes took in the tattoo, the shaved head, and brown eyes conveying displeasure. His pronounced Adam's apple bobbed when he swallowed. "How can I help you?"

"I passed out. Thought I should get checked."

"Take a seat." The nurse pointed at the chair next to his desk. He wrapped the blood pressure cuff around Starks left arm, stuck the stethoscope prongs in his ears, and began to increase the cuff pressure. "Were you out long?"

"Not long, but I hit my head."

"Does your head hurt?"

"Not now."

"Did it hurt when you woke?"

"Slight ache. It hurt worse before I went out."

Both men were quiet as the nurse did what was needed to get a reading.

"Your BP is 200 over 90. That's not good. Sit forward so I can listen to your chest." The nurse took several moments to do this. "Heart rate's a little fast, but that's to be expected. Lungs sound good. I'll get your file." He went to a long bank of gray filing cabinets.

"Don't you need my name?"

"I know it." The nurse practitioner pulled the file and said, "I'll be right back with the doctor."

Starks leaned forward in the chair, clasping and unclasping his hands. This was the worst time for anything to be going wrong, not that there was ever a good time. Every few seconds, he glanced at the door the nurse had entered and shut behind him, waiting for it to open.

After a few minutes, the nurse returned, followed by a thin, balding man with a comb-over, who was reading Starks's open file. The nurse resumed his seat at the desk.

The doctor went to an examination table, never once looking Starks's way. "Sit on the table." Still looking at the file, he told Starks, "Your blood pressure is elevated."

"I heard."

The doctor huffed, closed the file and dropped it next to Starks. One eyebrow went up when he saw the tattoo; no attempt was made to hide his disgust. He pulled a pen light from his lab coat pocket and began to examine Starks's eyes. "You said your head hurt before you fainted."

Starks flinched in response to the doctor's rancid breath. "It was a throbbing pain." He noted the name tag sewn on the doctor's lab coat read *Dr. Troy.*

"You usually have headaches?"

"Not usually, just sometimes. What could make me pass out?"

"Maybe your blood sugar dropped, or maybe for some reason your brain didn't get enough oxygen. Anything going on that might have caused that," he sneered, "like maybe someone had you in a chokehold at the time?"

"I'd just finished a phone call. I felt a sharp pain in my head that didn't stop, felt dizzy, and then it was lights out."

Troy got a tongue depressor from a nearby container. "Open." He used the pen light again. "No inflammation."

"Maybe you should run some tests."

The doctor ignored him.

"Maybe you should take my temperature."

Troy opened Starks's file again and ran his finger across a few lines of notes. "You suffered major head trauma a few months ago. Maybe it's related, maybe not. You have any unusual stress lately?"

"What kind of question is that?"

Troy stood erect with his chin jutted out and his lips stretched tight across his teeth. "Watch your attitude, mister. I'll schedule a CT. It'll take a few weeks to get the appointment set up."

"That's too long. I hope this isn't anything serious, but if it is, who knows what could happen during that time." Starks balled his hands into fists. "Do you know who I am?"

Troy's anemic complexion turned ruddy. "I don't give a rat's ass who you were outside. In here you're nothing. You're no better than the lowest animal we keep caged. Not that I owe you an explanation, but the CT has to be done at a hospital. That means a lot of damn paperwork to file, waiting for the appointment to be approved, and setting up secure transportation and guards. The process will go as fast as it goes."

"Do you have any recommendations while I wait? Isn't there a pill I should take to lower my pressure now?"

Troy glared at him for several seconds then said, "Refrain from strenuous activity and get—" The doctor's cell phone rang; the ringtone was the song "I'm Too Sexy."

Starks fought back the comment desperate to escape his lips and said, "Shouldn't that be turned off while treating patients?"

Troy ignored the question and reached into his pants pocket to silence the phone. "No strenuous activity and get some rest. Do that and your pressure should come down by itself."

"That's it?"

"Avoid salt." Troy snapped the file closed and returned to his office.

Starks picked up the folder and said loudly, "Hey, Doc, you forgot my file."

The nurse, face flushed, retrieved the file from Starks.

Starks glared at the doctor, who slammed his door, and shouted, "You know where you can stuff my file, staples and all." He slid from the examination table and walked toward the exit.

I'm not letting him get away with that crap, he thought. No pissant prison doctor is going to treat me like something he buries in kitty litter.

CHAPTER 12

STARKS STOMPED TO the phones. In line, his foot tapped and his expression alternated between dark and darker as he waited behind an inmate on a call. He was about to snap at the man and tell him to hurry the fuck up, until he heard him say, "Daddy loves his little girl. Never forget that. Daddy loves you, and he'll be with you again one day." Starks's impatience fell away, replaced by heartache for his own children.

The inmate's call ended. He turned and saw Starks standing behind him. Starks nodded and said, "I know how tough it is. When you go to prison, your family goes with you."

"Yeah. No matter how much this place sucks, knowing what you're missing with your kids sucks more." The man walked away.

Starks got the operator to place his call to Parker. "Sorry to call you twice in one day like this. After we hung up, I had an incident that requires medical attention . . . No, it was nothing like that. The infirmary doctor—last name Troy—said I need a scan but that paperwork et cetera is going to take weeks before I can get it. His attitude was disdainful. I realize we're all in here because of something we did, but that doesn't mean we don't deserve proper medical treatment."

"What would you like me to do?"

"See about getting the scan set up ASAP. And start an investigation into the healthcare practices by the infirmary here. Check infirmary staff's credentials and recommendations. Prison officials might be able to legally get away with feeding us garbage and some of the other demoralizing bullshit they do, but they shouldn't be allowed to fuck with our health. There are men in here, like me, who have families to go home to some day. We might go home undernourished, but we shouldn't be maltreated by the medical staff. We're human beings, damn it."

"I'll make some calls and get a team together. It may take them a few days to come up with a plan of action then get going on it."

"That works for me. Gotta go before the recording comes on. Thanks, Parker. I really appreciate it."

"Whatever's going on with your health, I hope it's nothing serious."

"You and me both. Unless something else comes up, we'll talk when I see you."

Starks put the receiver in place. What he saw when he turned around stunned him: About twenty inmates stood with their gazes fixed on him. Their hands raised and came together, their applause loud, their whoops genuine. After several seconds, Starks raised his hands to quiet them.

One inmate said, "We been complaining for years. Nothing's ever changed. This is the first time I've had any hope about that." Other inmates nodded and murmured their agreement. The inmate glanced at the men near him and said, "With the Dragon involved, maybe something will finally happen."

Starks scanned their faces. "I'll do what I can."

Hands patted him on the arms, back, and top of his head as he moved through the cluster. He heard word being spread as other inmates entered or passed through the area.

He'd been referred to—with respect—as the Dragon, an interesting and unexpected result he couldn't have planned better.

CHAPTER 13

SAM CARSON ASKED, "You gonna live?"

"I plan to. The doctor's ordering a test that'll have to be done at a hospital. Says it'll be some weeks before it can be done. I'm seeing if I can speed it up. He said to avoid strenuous activity and get some rest."

Carson arched back in the chair and linked his hands behind his head. "Library work ain't strenuous."

Starks smiled. "All things considered, I think I should rest today. I'll be back here for my afternoon shift tomorrow, unless something changes that. Are we square?"

"Get your butt to bed. See you tomorrow."

Inmates watched and whispered as Starks passed them on the way to his cell. They could be commenting about his passing out or the second call to Parker. Perhaps both. He knew which one he preferred their attention be on.

Jackson wasn't around and likely wouldn't be back for hours, as his dinner shift in the kitchen would start soon. Jackson often complained that they worked hours to prepare what inmates spent ten minutes or less eating. "But, who can blame them? Doesn't take long to poke a fork around in a pile of shit and realize nothing good's hidden in there."

Starks climbed into his upper bunk and lay back on the thin mattress. He was afraid, afraid he had a brain tumor or some other crazy affliction that would rob him of his health and possibly his life, that is, if some inmate didn't take advantage of his weakness and kill him before he could die.

The concept of dying brought his grandfather to mind. Growing up in his grandfather's house provided him with guidance he'd needed as a child and teen. Granted, some of it turned out not to be the wisest advice, but most of it was practical. Not only had his grandfather pushed him about a better-than-good education, he was big on taking care of the body. Old Ryan Lee Morgan had kept his physique by eating right, walking five miles a day, embracing hard work, and being sexually active with the several younger women he managed to maintain long-term relationships with. His grandfather had lived to be ninety-six, but didn't look a day over seventy-five in his casket.

Ryan's girlfriends had taken to each other at the wake. When they hadn't been weeping at their shared loss, they'd exchanged stories that caused them to weep harder, laugh, or cause eavesdroppers to blush. Keeping that many women happy simultaneously was a talent the old guy hadn't passed down to his grandson.

"Tomorrow's not promised to anyone, my boy. Acquire all you can, live a full life, have the fun you want to have, and always take care of your health so you have the energy to do it all. You don't want to die young and have another man take care of your family, do you? They're your responsibility."

No one can say Bret Simon is taking care of my family, Starks thought. But, the fucking freeloader *is* another man living in my house, with my children, and letting my money pay his way.

Ryan Morgan had lived long enough to witness the destruction—there was no other word for it—of his marriage and family, thanks to Kayla, but had died before Starks had helped it to implode even further. He was grateful every day his grandfather had been spared that.

Kayla was to blame, for what had happened then and for how he was feeling now. And Jeffrey, of course. It was remarkable that he hadn't had something go wrong with him before this, considering how they'd caused his stress to reach a new level, a level that seemed to now send his blood pressure to a dangerous number.

He'd have to deal with them, as soon as he knew what to do. The obstacles were clear. And serious. In the matter of Kayla, he needed to keep his children safe and their love for him intact, and her from stripping him of every last cent. As for Jeffrey, he had to not do anything that would destroy his business. Both situations had the potential to create ripples that became tsunamis.

Starks closed his eyes. He drifted into a hard sleep within a few minutes. He didn't dream.

Starks woke when Jackson called his name. He sat up and rubbed his face hard to wipe away the lethargy he felt. The time on his clock showed it was 7:30. Not only had he slept through the three and six o'clock counts, but he'd been allowed to.

"You okay?" Jackson asked. "I heard you passed out."

"Don't make it a big deal. I'm not."

Jackson sat in his chair. He stared up at Starks as he slipped off his shoes. "You went to the infirmary."

Starks shrugged. "Just a precaution."

"You're holding back on me."

"I'm not. The doc's ordering a scan, but I'm sure it's nothing. All right?"

Jackson slipped his yellow scrub shirt off, wadded it into a ball, and tossed it on the floor. "You looked ragged out. What'd'ya say we switch bunks."

"Don't you fucking dare treat me like an invalid. I'm fine."

Jackson held his hands up. "Okay, you're fine. Don't get your shorts up your ass."

Starks stared straight ahead.

"Something else I heard," Jackson said. "Heard you told your attorney to kick some prison butt about the crappy medical care."

A half-smile formed on Starks's lips. "Word spreads fast in this place."

"It doesn't just spread sideways, you know. Higher-ups will hear about it, if they haven't already. You can bet on it."

"Good. Maybe they'll take proper action and save me a shitload of legal fees."

"And maybe they'll throw your ass in the SHU."

"If they do they'd better kill me, because once I got out, they'd be a sorry bunch of motherfuckers."

"I think the ink from your tat is affecting your brain. You're turning into something of a wildcard."

The possibility that he might be on the brink of losing mental function terrified him, but he couldn't show it. "Sometimes playing it safe means taking a big risk. You play the cards in your hand and cheat if you need to so you win. As a former semi-professional magician, you know what I mean."

"Just don't get cocky and do something stupid."

"I don't do stupid."

"Hunh." Jackson faced his desk. After a few moments, he opened a book.

Starks's knew Jackson well enough to know he wasn't reading. "I know what I'm doing."

"Hunh."

CHAPTER 14

STARKS LINED UP for the 8:00 a.m. count. As usual, two guards took care of this task: One to check off inmates' names on a sheet on a clipboard, the other to hand out mail. More than half the inmates in his block were handed envelopes. Starks wasn't one of them. He still resented getting his divorce papers in the mail, and that the papers had been read by some prison official before he'd seen them. But he wasn't alone: all the envelopes and occasional packages handed out each day were already opened.

He decided to eat and read at his desk. An offensive odor came from below. He pulled the box of dirty clothes from underneath. Doing laundry wasn't strenuous, and he wasn't going to sit in the cell with that smell until his library shift started at one. It took only seconds to get everything together and he was on his way to the laundry room. Breakfast could wait.

The large rectangular space was vacant: No inmates employed to do laundry, no inmates hogging or waiting for machines. People had been there, though. The glass windows on the front-load machines against the wall to his left, with the exception of the first one, had clothes in them, even though the washing cycles had ended.

Starks noticed something else, something that shouldn't have been there. Red-tinted water inched its way across the floor, its origin from the corner where washers ended and the row of dryers positioned at a ninety-degree angle began. A groan came from the space created by that configuration. Starks no longer wondered what he would find there, but who. He slowed his steps, edging his way forward, and peered over the last washing machine.

Hot bile burned his throat and he felt light-headed. The grimy, lint-filled floor in that three-by-three space contained Skullars' crumpled body, whose legs were tucked under him. Blood leaked and oozed from multiple stab wounds. His clothes and hair were sopping wet.

"Aw, *damn* it. Skullars, it's Starks. I'm here, buddy."

Skullars coughed; blood cascaded over his swollen lips. He focused on Starks as best he could through puffed, bruised eyes. His mouth barely moved as he struggled to whisper, "Help me."

Starks rushed to the door and screamed for guards.

A guard not on his payroll turned into the corridor and shouted, "What's your problem?"

"Man down."

The guard sprinted forward, following Starks to the corner. "Goddammit." He pressed the button on his walkie-talkie to speak and got static. "Goddamn cheap shit they give us." He pointed at Starks. "Stay with him while I get help."

Starks grabbed his clothes and towels from the box. It was a meager pile, but he used every item to try to staunch blood flow. "Skullars, can you talk? Can you tell me who did this? C'mon, buddy."

The words were faint and delivered haltingly. "Dem batty boys . . . You know."

"Yeah, I know." Starks added gentle pressure to one of his towels placed against what he estimated was the worst wound. "I'm going to take care of those fuckers personally. I promise."

Skullars tried to smile. His body tensed then went completely limp.

Starks shook him. "Stay with me, buddy. Stay with me. Don't let those bastards win." No response came from Skullars.

Starks smashed a fist against the nearest dryer. He looked at Skullars' still form usually so full of vigor and life and felt a cold, silent rage swell inside him. "I swear to you they won't get away with this."

The first guard on the scene and four more rushed into the room, two of them pushing a gurney. One of them said, "Anyone checked him for a pulse?"

Another guard motioned for Starks to switch places. He climbed into the space and placed two fingers against Skullars' neck. "There's a pulse but not much of one."

Starks said, "Then there's a chance?"

"Maybe a slim one." The guard pointed at one of the others and said, "Let's get Bailey out of there. Maybe there's something the doc can do until the EMTs get here."

Two of them pulled the washer away from the wall as far as they could. It took the five guards and Starks to lift Skullars as carefully as possible out and onto the gurney. Three guards left with the injured man; the other two stayed to interview Starks. It took a half hour for him to convince them he'd found Skullars in the corner and the laundry room empty, and that the two of them were friends.

The guards finally left. Starks surveyed the space. The long table had stacks of folded clothes and clothes to be folded on it. The attack had been a brutal one, yet there was no blood splatter anywhere in the room. Nothing had been disturbed in a way to indicate a struggle had taken place. Skullars would have fought his attackers. They'd gotten to him in the shower room then dumped him in the laundry room. The showers were just around the corner, a relatively short distance to travel. Even so, this meant a number of inmates and guards had been involved in order to do what was done. And it had gone down not long before he'd arrived.

He grabbed his box but abandoned his blood-soaked laundry and headed for the door. He stormed to his cell, aware of but ignoring the dropped jaws and startled expressions as he passed inmates. Guards watched him as well, but they'd already gotten word about what had happened.

Jackson froze in place when Starks entered the cell. "Jesus, Starks. Is that your blood?"

"No." Starks pulled the knitting needle from his hem. "I need two more shanks. I know you have several hidden. Get them. Now, Jackson."

"What the hell's going on?"

"The guys Skullars refused to be a sex toy for got him. A fucking brutal attack. More than just the three of them. You can bet your ass some guards are complicit."

"And, what? You're going after them?"

"Get the damn shanks."

Jackson grabbed an empty envelope from his desk. He squatted near the base of the toilet, which he'd loosened bolts on. Using a shoulder, he pushed the toilet up a fraction of an inch and carefully slid the envelope into the narrow gap. Two six-inch blades slid out—kitchen knives minus handles. Jackson retrieved a roll of duct tape from under his shirt stack. "Keep watch."

Starks positioned himself at the entrance while Jackson wrapped the bottom two inches of each blade with tape. They switched places. Starks mixed a small batch of toxic paste and ran the two blades and his knitting needle through the mixture. He waved the three shanks to speed drying time.

"How do you know who did it?" Jackson asked.

"Skullars told me. It was all he could say before he lost consciousness."

"So he's alive?"

"Barely." Starks hid the needle in his hem. "I'll look for the bastards in the yard first. If they're not there, I'll hunt until I find them."

"You're going out like that?"

"Like what?"

"Your clothes are covered in blood."

"I want them to see me coming. I want them to know they picked the wrong fight with the right man."

"Give me the knives."

"No fucking way you're going to keep me from doing this."

"I'm not. I'm going with you. I'll hide them on me."

"I need the knives where I can get to them fast. Hand me the tape."

Starks slipped his shirt off. He tore a three-inch strip of tape from the roll and used it to secure the knife to the inside of his upper left arm. A one-inch strip was placed under the poisoned knife point. He did the same for the other knife on his other arm. Jackson had to help him put his shirt back on. The sleeves just covered the weapons.

"You got a plan, or you planning on winging it?" Jackson said.

"Maybe we can accomplish two things at once." Starks turned his chair around and motioned for Jackson to sit across from him. Their heads were inches apart as the two spent several minutes discussing strategies.

Starks said, "You clear about your part?"

"I'm clear."

"Follow my lead."

CHAPTER 15

ONCE IN THE yard, Starks halted to scan the area for three Caucasian men with fresh injuries, likely standing together, bragging as they recounted their "victory." The mid-morning light dimmed as dark clouds moved to cover the sun. A wind gust blew dust into the air. Starks, with Jackson behind him, edged his way north. The boisterous conversation in the yard grew subdued, but didn't stop completely. A few men muttered Skullars' name. Word was out about what had happened.

Starks spotted the three men standing with two other inmates in the northwest corner. One of the men facing the yard saw Starks and said something to the others, who turned to watch him. Their faces and arms, at least, were less bruised than he'd anticipated. Realization hit: their ambush had been as well planned as it had been executed; otherwise, Skullars would have injured them more severely.

What they'd done today was unforgivable. If they could do that to someone as large as Skullars, who had a better chance of defending himself—if the odds were fair, it wasn't difficult to imagine what they'd do to a smaller, weaker man. He didn't have to imagine, he knew.

Starks glanced at Jackson. Jackson was only an inch taller and about ten pounds heavier than he was; average-sized. Jackson knew what it was to be a target. Had several Los Hermanos not interrupted Big Bo and a few of his soldiers, Jackson would have been raped, as well as beaten.

Tough guys joined prison gangs. Weaker ones usually had no one to turn to, a consequence that resulted in their suffering at the hands of others. It was a fact of this life, one he intended to change. Today was as good a day as any to ramp up his intended power shift.

Starks faced Jackson, using the brief interval to draw the needle out and palm it in his right hand. Their gazes locked then Starks pivoted and approached the men.

One of the men puffed his chest and sneered. "What do you want, runt?"

"You left Skullars for dead. He was conscious long enough to tell me it was you. You danced, now it's time to pay."

"There's five of us and only two of you."

Jackson moved next to Starks and cleared his throat. Twice. His voice quavered as he said, "They're right, Starks. No one will blame you if you walk away."

Starks said, "Get out of here, Jackson." He glanced behind them and saw a small crowd had formed, with more inmates ambling in their direction.

Jackson tugged gently on the back of Starks's shirt. "C'mon, man. We're outnumbered."

Starks scowled at him. "Get out of here. I don't need anyone who's too chicken-shit to fight."

Jackson looked stricken. "Starks, be smart, man."

"Go play with your kitchen cronies, where it's safe. I don't need your fucking fake loyalty."

Jackson's expression turned to one of anger. "Your head's up your ass, Starks, and it's gonna get stuck there because of your inflated ego. Stupid motherfucker. Fine. You want to be a solo act, go to it. I don't need your shit." Head down, Jackson pushed his way through the men watching and waiting to see what was going to happen.

One of the five, a skinny blond, moved several inches forward. "Baldy here's mad 'cause he's gonna have to find himself another bitch." The other four laughed.

The largest of the five said, "Jackson's right about you, Starks. You are stupid. We're in Crazy D's crew. Maybe you heard about the Feared Brotherhood. You don't want to fuck with us."

Starks loosened the pressure his thumb had on the needle; he knew it was only a matter of moments before he'd have to use it. "Considering what you guys are into, it's not the right name for you. Maybe Degenerates Are Us."

The skinny blond looked at the other four. "You believe this fucking guy?" He moved up until his face was inches from Starks's. "I get it. You miss your dreadlocks bitch and wanna join him. We can make that happen, right here, right now."

Starks's thumb flipped the needle up between the middle and ring fingers of his right hand. The thrust of the needle into the man's solar plexus happened so fast, the man remained sneering for several seconds. Then the blond man's eyes opened wide in terror. Extraordinary pain caused by the poison dropped him into a fetal position on the ground and writhing in agony.

One of the other four said, "What the fuck? Starks barely touched him."

The largest man said, "Get the sonofabitch."

The four men rushed Starks, knocking him to the ground. He jumped to his feet, the needle no longer in his hand, but he couldn't take his eyes off the men to look for it.

The inmates came at him again. Under the crush of their bodies, Starks struggled to pull the knife away from his left arm, ignoring the sting of skin coming away with the tape. The shank was barely shoved into the abdomen of the man with black hair, who fell to the ground screaming. The largest man's fist connected with Starks's jaw, splattering blood onto the other two men who, in their confusion about what was happening, backed up a few inches.

Another blow was delivered to Starks's head. He went down. The three men sent a tornado of kicks to his face, head, and torso. Starks did the best he could to avoid as many blows as possible, but he was growing weaker. His biggest fear was that the other knife would puncture his skin; he pinned his right arm to his side and sheltered his face with his left.

Almost as suddenly as it started, the attack stopped. Starks raised his head a few inches to see what was happening. His attackers were gathered around the two on the ground. He heard the first man he'd downed scream, "He fucking stabbed me with something. It fucking hurts." The other man down was moaning but not talking.

The large man said, "We gotta get these guys outta here before the guards come."

Starks used this moment of distraction to get the last knife loose. Both shanks had enough poison on them to do more damage, if he was careful. It took all his strength to get to his feet. He stood in place for a moment trying and failing to calm his ragged breath. The image of Skullars gave him the small amount of strength he needed. He staggered forward and drove the shanks into the backs of the large man and the inmate next to him. They went down. Starks's eyes connected with the fifth man's stunned gaze; the man's face paled and he bolted.

Starks turned, swaying on his feet like a drunk. Around forty pairs of eyes watched him. His pain was tempered by the realization that the four inmates would be dead in forty-eight hours. The worst fucking two days of their lives. They deserved it.

Inmates milling about waited for him to say something. Starks took a few deeps breaths and stood as straight as he could manage and said in a loud voice, "This is what happens when someone fucks with me or anyone under my protection."

The thing to do now was walk away, to get back to his cell and get cleaned up. And, the knives had to be hidden. He glanced back at the ground for the needle, but couldn't see it. His right foot moved forward but his legs went numb. Starks crumpled to the ground. The attempt to get up was futile. It was also the last thing he needed after making his grand declaration. He used his right hand to prop himself up, felt the needle under his hand, and slid it back into the hem, taking two attempts to accomplish this.

Lightning streaked across the gray sky about a mile away; thunder rumbled. The storm was getting closer. Heavy footsteps moving fast came toward him. It took great effort to stuff the two knives into his socks, but he did it.

Starks collapsed onto his back. He lay there staring into the faces of two guards who didn't look happy to see him.

CHAPTER 16

S TARKS STARED UP at COs Luke Roberts and Brandon Simmons, two guards on his payroll, which meant less discussion or explanation required. He gave them a half-smile. They didn't smile back.

Roberts squatted and asked, "You okay, Starks?"

Simmons looked around at the observers. A number of them demonstrated their eagerness to disperse by backing up or starting to walk away, but a number of them didn't budge. He said loudly, "What the fuck happened here?"

Two guards joined them. One of them said, "Don't tell me: nobody knows nothing."

Roberts glanced at the four injured men several feet away. "I don't know what happened to them, but considering Starks here is the one wearing the most blood, I'd say they attacked him."

Between groans, the largest attacker shouted, "Starks fucking stabbed me."

An audible gasp came from several inmates. Starks stifled a smile. He almost wished he could get word out that anyone prepared to address this breach could save the energy; they'd only do his attacker a favor by ending his life sooner.

Roberts stood fixed in place, his expression one of obvious contemplation. He glanced down and asked Starks, "Did you stab him?"

"No. I was minding my own business."

Roberts told the other guards to get the four men to the infirmary.

"How're we supposed to do that?" one of them asked.

"Get some fucking gurneys or carry them on your backs or," he waved toward the inmates in the yard, "ask some of these guys to help you carry them. I don't care which, just get your asses moving."

Simmons took the lead. Facing inmates nearby he said, "I want eight of you guys to help carry those four to the infirmary. Move it."

The large attacker spoke up again. "He fucking stabbed us."

Roberts said, "One against four? That's some odds. Where's the knife?"

The inmate didn't answer. Instead, he screamed as the poison in his system forced his muscles to contract, drawing his knees painfully to his chest against his will.

Simmons said to the guards, "You gonna get these guys to the infirmary sometime today? And, why don't you practice a little crowd control while you're at it."

The extra guards kicked into gear, directing inmates, who grabbed arms and legs then started toward the main door, with several guards in tow. One guard yelled at inmates in the yard to mind their own business as he made his way back to his post.

Simmons radioed tower guards, telling them the situation was under control.

Starks glanced at one of the several towers. The barrel of a long rifle retreated into the small structure. As he sat up, he prayed tower guards hadn't seen enough to get him into real trouble. He pressed his hands into the dirt to keep himself propped up.

"Can you get up?" Roberts asked.

"Not without help."

Simmons and Roberts took his arms to raise him.

"Easy. I think a few of my ribs are broken or at least cracked."

Roberts said, "We need to take you to the infirmary."

"How in the hell," Simmons asked, "did you fight four guys?"

"Five guys. One of them ran away. As for how I fought them, it's amazing what you can do when your life or the life of someone you care about is threatened." Starks dropped to the dirt. "Roberts, if you check my socks, there are two items I need you to get rid of for me. You've got pockets; I don't."

Roberts squatted and pretended to check Starks's ankles. "Goddamnit," he muttered.

He was about to reach for the knives when Starks said, "Don't touch anything but the duct tape. Here," he removed the extra pieces of tape from his arms, "cover the tips and blades with these."

Simmons kept watch. "What the fuck are you up to, Starks?"

"Just trying to tip the scales in favor of the oppressed," he replied. "Justice isn't always fair. Take Skullars, for example. Only reason he was in here was because he went after the bastards who butchered his wife and only child. What he did may not be legal, but it was understandable. If I'd been Skullars, small pieces of those guys would have been scattered across three states. Skullars didn't bother anyone. He just didn't want to be anyone's bitch, and they—those guys—didn't like it. I'm here because I went after my wife's ex-lover when he pulled a knife on me, a knife conveniently never found. You guys have a tough job here; I respect that. But no fucking way can you protect every inmate. That means the responsibility falls to those of us with the balls to take it on."

"You know," Simmons said, "this shit's going to be investigated. You better pray everybody—and I mean everybody—keeps their mouth shut."

Roberts surreptitiously slid the knives points-down into one of his deeper pants pockets. He took one of Starks's arms and motioned for Simmons to do the same. "Why didn't you come to us first? You've probably put yourself in the crapper this time."

"C'mon, officers. It was five to one. I was down for the count. For all I know, other inmates did it to them while I was out of it. Maybe they stabbed each other in their frenzy."

Simmons said, "Providing extra protection is one thing, but we're not here to clean up every damn mess you intend to make."

Starks grimaced in pain with each step. "Anytime you want to back out and let someone take your place on the payroll, let me know."

Roberts intervened. "Look, let's not do or say anything any of us will regret. Of course we'll do what we can. But you need to realize we're going to have to deal with Spencer. Man's got a hard-on for you. He wants to nail you bad."

Starks spit blood on the ground and pushed at a loosened tooth with his tongue. "Tell him to take a number."

The first large drops of rain began to fall.

CHAPTER 17

STARKS SHIFTED HIS position in the hard plastic chair. Adrenaline had ceased charging through his system a while ago. Now, every part of his body ached or throbbed and exhaustion threatened to overwhelm him. Bed was what he needed, and soon, not sitting here in the infirmary waiting for—he checked the wall clock again—a full hour now. No one else was waiting to see the doctor, so what was the hold-up? The guys he'd stabbed were nowhere in sight, and he wasn't about to ask if they were still at Sands or had been transferred to Grace Hospital. He needed to be considered a victim of their attack.

The nurse had checked his cuts and abrasions when he'd first arrived, treating any that needed cleaning and ointment. But he needed his ribs X-rayed and something mild for pain, two things that only the doctor could address. What the hell was the man doing?

As he had, several times since the wait had started, Starks replayed the fight in his mind. Perspiration beaded on his forehead: Jackson was right. He was tempting fate by acting reckless. Those five men could have killed him. If more of Crazy D's gang had been there, he'd be on his way to the morgue right now.

According to Jeffrey, Mason's powders were effective for approximately six months. Thank God he'd received them in June and not at the start of his incarceration mid-January. The powders should remain full-strength until October, but that was a best-guess. The word *approximately* made him anxious. It might be wise to order more, sooner than later.

Only a small amount of Mason's deadly concoctions had been provided, as only a minute amount was needed for a single potent attack. Still, he'd have to be careful how much he used and when. Granted, a little went a long way, but running out of them before he could get more was not a scenario he cared to create. If things were different, he'd call Jeffrey the moment he left the infirmary and word his request in a way no one listening in could decipher. But he couldn't call Jeffrey. Not anymore. An ache of a different kind thrummed in his chest.

Footsteps interrupted Starks's thoughts. Dr. Troy, with his futile comb-over, headed his way.

Troy said, "Back so soon?" He took in Starks's appearance. "Maybe you should avoid fights for a while."

"I didn't have a choice in the matter."

"I doubt that."

Troy used his penlight to check Starks's eyes then prodded Starks's swollen jaw.

Starks flinched. "What the fuck, Doc?"

Troy's face burned red. "Don't use that language with me." He jotted a few notes onto Starks's file then said, "Get some rest, apply ice, and stay out of fights."

"You need to X-ray my ribs. A few are either cracked or maybe broken."

"Wasting taxpayers' money on you isn't my idea of the right thing to do. You want to get yourself beat up on a regular basis, go ahead. But don't come running to me to put you back together every time."

"What kind of a doctor are you? You're a fucking sadist. Where's the other doctor who works here? If he's not here today, I'll come back tomorrow so I can get proper care."

"You're out of luck, Starks. I replaced Wilson. Now get the hell out of my infirmary."

"What about something for pain?"

"You lowlifes are all the same, you always want drugs. Think you deserve to numb your time here. Here's what you do. Go to the commissary and buy some aspirin. Just don't swallow a bunch of them and expect me to send you to the hospital for another little holiday." The doctor marched back to his office, slamming his door after him.

Starks turned to the open-mouthed nurse and said, "Sooner or later, that bastard's going to be sorry. I only hope it's sooner." He stopped at the door. "How's Skullars Bailey? I haven't heard anything about his condition."

The nurse hesitated then said, "Still unconscious at Grace."

Maybe Skullars had a chance.

Starks left, carrying several levels of rage with him. He was almost to his cell when Jackson caught up with him.

"Heard you survived."

"Nice of you to sound so relieved."

"You're not moving too good."

"Sonofabitch doctor refused proper medical care. No X-rays, nothing for pain. 'Take a couple aspirin and don't ever call me again.' Bastard needs his license taken away, or shoved up his ass. Either one works for me. I did, however, find out that Skullars is still alive. That alone was worth the price of admission."

Starks entered the cell first and headed straight for his bed. His attempt to climb up to his bunk made him groan in agony.

"Shit, man," Jackson said. "You're in no condition for that. My offer to switch bunks is still on the table."

"This time I'm going to take you up on it. I need to recover as fast as I can. Climbing up and down won't get me there." Starks lowered himself carefully into his chair. "I need you to swap the stuff around."

Jackson nodded and got busy. After a few moments, he said, "You know you were crazy to try to take on five guys by yourself." When Starks didn't answer, he added, "You were kind of harsh with me out there."

"Yeah, well . . ." Starks winced and rubbed his ribcage.

Jackson sighed. "You need to be careful, man. Don't go out of control. You could've gotten killed."

"Same thought occurred to me."

"You went after some of Crazy D's men. He's not called crazy for nothing."

"Everybody's called something."

"You can bet he's going to come after you."

"I'm ready."

"Yeah, right. In the condition you're in, only thing you're ready for is a fucking tea party, if that. We're seriously outnumbered, man. Did you happen to pay attention to that? Yeah, you've got some guards on the pay, but you need more inmates standing up for you."

Starks dragged out a sigh. "By the way, I had to get rid of the extra shanks. Couldn't risk it."

"Not good news, but there are more knives where those came from." Jackson made up the bottom bunk. "Lie down before you fall down."

Starks lifted himself from the chair and slowly positioned himself on top of the thin mattress.

Jackson began to pace. "We ought to recruit the three guys I introduced you to last month. We gotta start somewhere."

"I told you that loyalty is important to me. Those three were members of Bo's gang and they betrayed him. What makes you think they won't do that to me?"

"And I told you: They hated Bo. Look, fact is you've started another battle. If we're gonna win, we need soldiers."

Starks draped an arm over his eyes. "Do what you want, Jackson."

A baton rattled across the cell bars. Starks and Jackson glanced at each other, sharing a similar thought stemming from prior experience: Starks was getting called before the council then thrown into the SHU.

Starks sat up. "Officer Jakes. Haven't seen you for a while. You dropped by for a particular reason?"

"You have a visitor."

"I've been expecting my attorney. Glad he finally made it."

"It's not your attorney. It's a guy named Jeffrey Davis."

Starks's pupils darkened. "Tell him to go fuck himself." He saw the CO's eyebrows raise and the surprise on Jackson's face.

"You sure that's what you want me to tell him?"

"Positive."

Jakes made a pseudo-salute with his baton then started back down the corridor.

Jackson said, "That's some kind of message for your best friend."

"Leave it alone."

"He supplies the powders, man."

"He was the courier, and not the only one I can use."

"Quoting Alice while she partied in Wonderland, 'Curiouser and curiouser.'"

"I said leave it."

"If I leave it, we're fucked."

The numerals glowing on Starks's digital clock showed it was a few minutes after five in the morning. The portion of the long, narrow window centered on the back wall let in a strip of illumination from the halogen lights positioned strategically, and in large numbers, around the grounds. Starks used a foot to push his twisted blanket into a crumpled pile at the end of his bed. Movement came from the upper bunk.

Jackson hung his head over the edge to look down at him. "Starks, you've got the most fucked-up sleep patterns."

"We should talk."

"About?"

"Things you said yesterday."

Jackson leapt down. He pulled his chair close to the lower bunk. "I'm listening."

CHAPTER 18

ONE MINUTE TO four that afternoon, Starks ended his library shift and started in the direction that would take him to the yard. He hated how wary he felt: confidence had been second nature for him most of his life; although, Kayla would have said it was cockiness based on a sense of entitlement.

One of the Hermanos called out a greeting to him, snapping Starks back into the moment. He derided himself for allowing his focus to slip. Even with the prepped needle in his shirt hem, it was a huge risk to traverse prison corridors while daydreaming. Too easy to be ambushed.

Jackson had better be on time.

Starks stepped into the yard. A small dust devil lifted up then dissipated just as fast on a grassless patch to his right. He scanned faces of the inmates milling around. Looked for enemies. Looked for Jackson. Found him standing with four African-American inmates. Jackson saw him and nodded.

Starks started toward the fence directly across from him, using his peripheral vision to watch for anyone who might approach him. It seemed to take forever, rather than less than a minute, to make it to the meeting spot. He was too damn jumpy on the inside. At least experience had taught him how to hide it.

Jackson said, "You remember Pete, Tommy, and Stinky."

Starks met each man's eyes then nodded once, grateful that Stinky was standing upwind. He understood the man's reason for not showering more often—if it kept horny inmates away, more power to him—but he couldn't stand to smell him.

Jackson gestured toward the fourth man, who was tall, with a bulk that was a combination of solid and pudgy. "This is Tank, for obvious reasons."

Tank looked directly into Starks's eyes. "Yo."

Starks said, "You all know why you're here?"

"We're here," Stinky said, "'cause you need us."

Pete stepped forward. "I told you last time we talked I'm in. I'm ready."

Tommy added, "Me too. I heard how you took on five of the Brotherhood, alone. And why. You got balls, man. People be talking about that."

"What anyone who joins me needs to always keep in mind," Starks told them, "is that I'm all about loyalty. Loyalty gets rewarded. You each need to earn your stripes to prove that loyalty."

Pete formed his hands into fists at his sides. "I earned some of those stripes for you the day you took out Big Bo."

"I'll keep that in mind," Starks replied.

"What we gotta do to earn those stripes?" Pete asked.

"I'll let you know."

Pete kept eye-contact with Starks. "We gotta get a dragon tat?"

"That's a thought. It'll show who you're aligned with. However, if you do, make it just the head. Tatman knows not to ever use mine again."

"We gotta pay for it?" Pete asked.

"I'll pay."

Tank nodded and said, "What about the rewards? Jackson says you're generous."

Starks held Tank's gaze for a moment. "When I say I'm going to take care of someone, I do it. That's all you need to concern yourself with. However, if the only reason you're joining is for what you can get out of it, and not who you can be because of it, don't bother. Believe me. I'll know what your motivation is." The men went still. "Jackson will let you know when and where we'll meet again. However, it wouldn't hurt if we eat together, walk together, and watch each others' backs as much as possible. Got it?"

The men nodded.

Jackson's eyes were aimed at something behind Starks. Using his chin as a pointer, he said, "I think someone wants to talk to you."

Starks turned to find CO Roberts a couple yards back and moving in fast.

"Starks, council wants to see you."

"Now?"

"Sooner."

CHAPTER 19

STARKS SAT ON his bunk and counted his blessings, at least the one foremost on his mind. Fortune had smiled on him and saved him from a month or more in the SHU. The months he'd spent in the Segregated Housing Unit earlier in the year, followed by more time in monitored isolation after his suicide attempt, had nearly driven him out of his mind.

Testimonies given to the council by correctional officers Roberts and Simmons the prior afternoon contributed to this save. He knew he could count on them. It was the tower guards who had concerned him more. Only one tower guard, positioned nearest where the fight had taken place, said he'd seen the confrontation from start to finish, and swore the men attacked Starks, who'd attempted to defend himself. Starks kept it to himself that the guard must have been dozing or looking elsewhere when the altercation began. In one way it was reckless to go one against five, but in another way, it had been smart. Even Spencer said he could not fathom that Starks would be so stupid as to stack the odds against himself in that manner. But there was the matter of stab wounds. When asked, Starks shrugged and said he was too busy getting his ass kicked to notice what else his attackers were doing. Roberts and Simmons stated no weapons had been found.

It was obvious to everyone in the council room during the hour that had dragged on and on, that Tony Spencer was livid about not being able to nail Starks regarding the fight. Spencer said that sooner or later, Starks's luck would run out and he'd find himself unable to avoid the consequences of his actions.

But, today is a new day, he told himself.

After spending several minutes debating what to do with his Saturday, Starks decided to stay in his cell, at least for a while. He needed time alone to think. One thing in particular worried him: Crazy D hadn't said or done anything yet regarding retaliation. It was only a matter of time.

Starks shook his head at the nature of things at Sands. Jackson had told him Crazy D's given name was Darren Williams. Whether the inmate had come up with that moniker himself or it had been provided by another prisoner didn't matter. The fact was it would be difficult to create fear in anyone by telling them *Darren* was coming after them. *Crazy D*, however, was a bone worth chewing on.

Now he was about to join those men who'd earned nicknames in here. So far, he'd been referred to as the Dragon and the Dragon Lord. He smiled. *Not a bad start.* However, he reminded himself, a good start doesn't always guarantee a good finish.

His life with Kayla had had a good start. He pounded his forehead with a fist. *Stop fucking lying to yourself.*

For almost twenty years, he'd allowed her to fool him with her pretense of being shy, modest, virginal. When she'd affirmed repeatedly that he was the only man she'd ever been with and that their union was sacred, he'd chosen to believe her. He could practically hear Matthew Demory ask him if his own need for other women was more about abandonment issues regarding his father than getting physical desires satisfied. His answer, if he and Demory were still having weekly sessions, would be the same as every prior time when Demory came up with such counseling babble: *Bullshit.*

It seemed longer than only a few years ago that his charmed reality was fractured by Richard and Jenny Hayes. The former best friend of his wife had confided in her husband, and he in turn informed Starks about what Kayla was really up to, and had been up to since college. So many, many men—in hotels, cars, behind closed doors at her workplace, and God only knew where else she'd spread her legs—all of this leading up to her three-year affair with Ozy Hessinger. He'd ignored the signs that appeared over time, especially during their last six years together: the hemlines that climbed higher, the necklines that dropped lower, and how often she went out with "the girls" and didn't come home until late, usually staggering-drunk.

The facts had crushed him. But the fact that had done him in was the one he'd only recently learned from Parker about Jeffrey. That Jeffrey had screwed Kayla while Starks was at a university class was egregious. That they'd done it in his grandfather's basement added insult to injury, as his grandfather would have said. What he didn't know for sure was whether or not they'd continued to betray him during all the years that had followed.

The manure pile his life had become kept getting deeper.

CHAPTER 20

"WHAT'S THE MATTER, Jackson?" Starks closed his library book, sat up in his bunk, and gave full attention to his cellmate, who looked in at him from the threshold of their cell. Jackson stared at him with lips compressed into a hard line. Starks sighed and said, "Do I need to say please?"

Jackson plodded to his chair and sunk into it. "Just heard . . . Sorry, man. Skullars died."

It took a moment for the news to register. Starks's head dropped into his hands. "This fucking place! These fucking people!" He threw the book against the wall.

"I hear you," Jackson said. "Not that it makes up for it, but the four guys are dead."

Starks pointed toward the ceiling. "For you, buddy. For you, your wife, and your son."

Silence lingered a few moments then Jackson spoke. "Word going round is Crazy D's coming after you. Soon."

"About damn time."

"I'm not feeling the same excitement about that you seem to be."

"It's one thing to face an enemy. It's another to sit around worrying about it." Starks walked to the cell door and stared toward the first cell on the left of the corridor. "I wonder who they're going to put in Skullars' cell. I wonder if Skullars had any family left to mourn him. I never asked."

Starks checked the clock. "Ten thirty. Next count's in half an hour. You should have time to get word to our recruits between now and then. Tell them we're having our first meeting in the laundry room at noon sharp."

"They won't be happy about missing lunch, no matter how much it sucks."

"We don't need to meet for long, but tell them they won't go hungry. I'll take them to the commissary afterwards. My treat."

"I'm on it." Jackson bustled from the cell.

Starks picked up the book from the floor and carefully straightened the bent pages. His chest and limbs felt weighted with loss. For a little over a decade, his life had been about profits and gains. Back then, the only losses he suffered were the occasional business contract and the huge rewards that would have resulted. He'd turned the word "loss" into a verb that motivated him to find a way to win even bigger.

Then everything flipped. Unanticipated, devastating losses started to come into his life like storm waves on a shore, and didn't appear to be letting up any time soon. The losses were like multiple exorbitant overdraft fees, as though he'd taken more from life than he was supposed to, and now he had to pay and pay, when he was already so close to running on empty.

He walked to the small mirror above the lavatory-toilet combo and looked into his reflected eyes. After a few moments he said, "You'd better dump that fucked-up philosophy, right now."

CHAPTER 21

THE LAUNDRY ROOM had one person in it when Starks arrived. Nick was at the long table in the middle of the room, folding inmates' clothes. He looked up and nodded. "Need your laundry done, Starks? Where's your box?"

"Not today, Nick. I need you to disappear for twenty or so minutes. I'll comp you with an equal amount of commissary."

Nick grinned. "Sure thing. It can take longer, if you like."

"That should be enough time. Don't want to get you in trouble for being off the job."

"Man's gotta eat and visit the john sometime." Nick took a load of clothes from a washer, tossed them into a dryer, got it going then left.

Jackson arrived with the four recruits. Starks directed them to follow him; he stopped in front of a dryer spinning clothes. "I don't know if you heard, but Skullars Bailey died. So did the four guys I got in the yard. I know for certain three of them were the ones who killed Skullars. The other two may have just gotten in the way, not that that bothers me. I don't know if any of you knew Skullars, but—"

Tommy said, "I seen him around. Big Jamaican buck."

Starks narrowed his eyes and said, "He *was* a big man, in more ways than one, and" he shifted his gaze back to the others, "he was going to be an important asset for us. A couple months ago I saw him deal with the three bastards by himself, with nothing but his hands and his wits. This time they went after him armed, with more of them and guards willing to look the other way. Only way they could've taken him out."

Tank stood erect. "I'm big."

"Yeah," Tommy said, "but he was bigger."

"Not by much," Tank replied.

"We're wasting time," Starks said. "If people in here are going to gang up in order to take out someone Skullars' size, someone who didn't bother anyone, then no one is safe, not that anyone in here ever is. The only way to improve our chances is to join forces. But we need to get organized. Now. Another problem is betrayal." He glanced at Pete.

Pete said, "Big Bo was a bastard. Spell that in capital letters. You hear me? He didn't look after the men who looked after him. Didn't ever treat us like men. Treated us like something he had to wash off his shoe. I heard you're different. Hell, I seen it for myself. You big on loyalty? I say, man gives loyalty, he gets loyalty back."

Starks focused on Pete for a moment then faced the others. "I always take care of the people who take care of me. I couldn't have succeeded the way I did before I came here if I hadn't done that. If any of you betray any member of this gang or the gang as a whole, you need to know now that the penalty will be an extremely unpleasant death."

All the men but Jackson shuffled in place.

"From this moment on," Starks said, "anyone fucks with one of us fucks with all of us."

Tommy crossed his arms. "What do we get out of this, other than protection?"

Starks smiled and said, "Benefits and profits. Starting now. Soon as we're done here, we're going to the commissary, as I'm sure Jackson told you. Get whatever you want—on me. After that, if you need anything or have a problem, I'll do what I can to get what you need or make whatever or whoever leave you alone or leave permanently. In exchange, you do what I need you to do. Any questions?"

Pete asked, "What's next?"

"Crazy D is going to come after me, soon, which means he needs to have to face all of you as well. I don't know when, how, or how many of his people will be involved. Pay attention to what's going on around you at all times. Get any information you hear about Crazy D's plans to Jackson or to me. We may have to be spontaneous, but I'd rather have a strategy in place, as much as that's possible, and based on solid information. For now, stay sharp, and try not to be anywhere where you can be cornered, especially not alone. Be suspicious of anyone who isn't standing here now. Unless any of you have questions or something to say, let's go to the commissary."

Tank said, "You not shittin' us about getting whatever we want?"

Starks nodded once. "No limit."

Pete jutted his chin forward and said, "There's a lot I want."

Starks smiled and placed a hand on Pete's shoulder. "And I believe you should get everything you want and deserve."

CHAPTER 22

STARKS AND HIS crew sat on the heavy wooden bleachers hot from the unflinching midday sun. His four recruits had been like kids turned loose at Christmas in the commissary. He still didn't trust Pete as completely as he'd like. As soon as he had that thought, the inmate's gaze met his. Pete grinned as he shoved the last bite of sweet roll into his mouth.

He'd asked them to put themselves in harm's way, for his sake. Bullshit, he thought: it's as much for their sakes. But now, he was responsible for them, for their lives.

Tommy shifted forward, his eyes aimed straight ahead. "Trouble's coming."

The others faced the direction Tommy was looking.

Pete said. "Crazy D."

"Is he the one in the middle?" Starks asked.

Pete nodded. "That's him. And there's three more of them than us."

Starks studied his opponent. "How many in his gang?"

"No idea."

This wasn't at all what Starks had imagined someone called Crazy D would look like. But since when did crazy have a specific appearance? His adversary was slender and more than a head taller than the tallest of the several men walking with him—he stood out like a hen with its chicks. Lank black hair hung to the man's collarbone. The black swastika on the right side of his neck all but shouted its presence against pale skin. Crazy

D was a pretty-boy; there was no other word for it. Perhaps comments, ribbing, and taunts he was sure to have heard all his life drove him over the edge a long time ago. If there was one thing Starks understood, it was just how easy it was to be driven there.

Starks wanted to believe, in part, that his opponent's appearance meant he could let his guard down a bit, but that would be foolish. The men with Crazy D were obviously tough.

Starks glanced around the yard. Four guards patrolled the northern end of the space to his right; five more were spread out on the southern end. COs Simmons and Roberts were in the latter group; CO Jakes was in the former. They were watching him. His hope was that they continued to pay attention the way they were supposed to. He got to his feet, moving a yard in front of the bleachers. His men followed suit.

Crazy D waited until he was about two yards away then stopped. "Starks."

"*Darren.*"

Starks's crew snickered. Anger flared on Crazy D's face then dissipated just as quickly.

Starks noted the self-control demonstrated by his adversary. Perhaps it wasn't wise to trigger the man, but he wanted to make it clear from the start that a name wouldn't intimidate him.

Crazy D proffered a smile that didn't reach his eyes. "Word's out that you're starting your own gang. That's fine, Starks; smart, even. But let me give you a lesson in etiquette. If you have a problem with a leader's people, you arrange a conversation." He moved forward, until he was inches away. He tilted his head sharply toward his left shoulder. The *pop* in his neck was loud. Crazy D tilted his head down until his nose and Starks's nearly touched. "What you *don't* do, little man, is go around killing people who are protected by the man you need to speak with. Are we clear?"

"What's clear to me, Darren, is that you should get the fuck out of my face."

Crazy D arched his left eyebrow. "Obviously, courtesy is wasted on you."

"What's obvious," Starks said, "is that your guys couldn't get Skullars to wax their prongs, so they killed him. Seems to me, you should be teaching etiquette to them. Or maybe you gave the order because you wanted Skullars and he didn't want you."

Crazy D's fist landed dead center of Starks's chest.

Starks propelled backwards into Pete, who righted him.

Tank charged forward like an over-sized bowling ball, knocking Crazy D and the two men nearest him to the ground.

Conversation's over, Starks thought.

Fists, knees, and feet flew. Expletives littered the air. Inmates rushed to swarm around the fight. Their shouts and cheers were interrupted by whistles blown as guards, intent on reaching the brawlers, used nightsticks on onlookers. Pepper spray was shot directly into faces; some of it carried on the steamy breeze, back onto several of the guards and other inmates who hadn't moved away quickly enough.

Amid the coughs and curses, CO Simmons shouted at the observers, "Back off, you sonsofbitches."

CO Roberts shook his head. "Cuff 'em."

One of the other guards asked, "Cuff who?"

"Anyone with a bruised face or scraped knuckles, dimwit." Roberts looked at Starks. "You and the ones who were sitting with you stay here. Everyone else, get the hell inside. Now!"

Starks men clustered around him.

Roberts said to the extra guards, "Get those guys inside. We three will take these." He gestured toward Starks and his crew.

Crazy D strained against his handcuffs. "This isn't over, Starks. You're fucking dead. You hear me? Dead!"

"Take a number, *Darren*." Starks watched the man struggle against his restraints as guards shoved and dragged him and his followers inside. He turned to Roberts and said in a lowered voice, "Let the others walk ahead of us so I can tell you what you, Jakes, and Simmons are going to report to the council."

CHAPTER 23

INMATES FROM BOTH gangs were confined to their cells the remainder of the weekend, with the exception of mealtimes, which they were escorted to and from by guards, unless they chose to eat from whatever food stash they had in their cells. In the case of Starks's small fledgling group, this meant all of them ate well, or at least had better eats than they would have been served in the chow hall. Starks's timing for the visit to the commissary couldn't have been better planned, which he was certain put him in good favor with his recruits. Something he had no control over was that all privileges had been suspended—phone calls, visits, showers, and time outside—until the council could deal with all of them on Monday.

Ten thirty Monday morning, Starks, Jackson, and the other four crew members stood outside the council room for a somber half hour.

"No one's asked," Jackson said, "but I will. What are we waiting for?"

Roberts answered, "The council decided to deal with Crazy D and his guys first."

"So, they're in there now?" Starks asked.

Roberts replied, "They finished with the others earlier. It's just Williams in there."

Five minutes later the door opened. Crazy D's eyes and expression matched his name when he saw Starks. "Thirty days in the fucking SHU because of you. Keep in mind what I said, Starks. It's more than a promise; it's a guarantee."

One of the guards said, "Shut up. You'd think you lived on a fucking podium, the way you go on and on. Love to hear yourself talk. Well, I don't." He whacked Crazy D with his nightstick. "Move it."

Crazy D wrenched his head around as the guard dragged him forward. "I'm coming for you, Starks."

Correctional officers Simmons, Jakes, and Roberts did well at their turn in front of the council. Roberts reported, and the other two confirmed, that they'd observed Darren Williams and his bunch approach Starks and the guys with him, who had been minding their own business on the bleachers. That Williams had provoked the fight by striking Starks. That it was a matter of self-defense for Starks and the inmates with him. And that Williams had made a death threat to Starks, which Roberts pointed out, had just been repeated within earshot of the council.

Tony Spencer pushed his glasses back into place and glared at Starks. "Five days in the SHU."

Starks stepped forward. "For what? You heard what happened. You heard him threaten me again when he left, if you bothered to listen."

"I heard. But one thing I'm sure of is you're guilty of something."

"What about them?" Starks nodded toward Jackson and the others. "They were in the wrong place at the wrong time; although, had they not been there, I'd be dead instead of standing here."

Spencer stacked the folders in front of him. "For them, all privileges suspended for a week."

The men groaned and complained, but when Starks glanced their way, each man subtly indicated his appreciation. They got off easy, Starks thought, and know I'm the one to thank for it. That I, as the saying goes, am taking one for the team.

Spencer removed his glasses, huffed air on the lenses and wiped them with his tie. "And, Starks, as your time in isolation is to be brief, your hour-a-day out is suspended."

"What about shower time?" Starks asked.

Spencer checked his lenses then slid his glasses back on. "Get him out of my sight."

Simmons and Jakes escorted the men back to their cells. Roberts took Starks in the other direction.

"Technically," Roberts said, "I'm supposed to deliver you to the SHU in shackles."

"Do what you have to do."

Roberts led Starks to a guard room and apologized at low volume as cuffs and heavy chains, connected to the heavier chain wrapped around his waist, restricted his hands and feet. The CO kept his pace slow as Starks shuffled alongside him to the restricted unit.

Once inside the unit, Starks glanced at the round clock on the wall behind the main security desk. The black hands on the white face showed the time as three twenty-one, same as his previous stay in the SHU. Twice a day the stuck clock showed the right time; though, an inmate in windowless isolation never knew when that was. Track of time was lost. When released, some things were the same, some were not. If the stay in isolation was extended, many inmates were never the same. Personal experience had taught him this.

They halted in front of a solid steel door with a five-inch square window a few feet above a slot for meal trays, and waited as a guard assigned to the unit unlocked the door. The guard stayed to watch as Roberts removed the restraints.

"See you in five days, Starks."

Starks nodded once. "Officer Roberts." The metal door clanged shut behind him.

The surroundings were all too familiar to him—the six by eight concrete rectangle, a concrete slab for a bed with no mattress or pillow. The blanket provided was bunched on the floor. Like the last time, the thin, scratchy fabric had holes and unidentified but highly suspect stains. Using two fingers, he picked the covering up by a corner. Its rancid odor reached him from arm's length, and he wondered if they ever cleaned the damn things. Starks resisted the urge to fold the blanket and instead threw it toward a corner near the door.

Spencer's need for some level of revenge didn't stop with just the five days in isolation. Sometime around noon the slot on the door opened and a tray with a brick of nutraloaf was pushed through. One flavorless pound of shredded cabbage, carrots, pinto beans, mystery meat, fake eggs, and bread mixed together and baked. Inedible. Worthy of being banned by law as cruel and unusual punishment. If this was all he was served during his time in the Hole, he was in trouble. Eventually, he'd have to eat some of it to keep his strength up. Leaving here weakened, when an attack was imminent, wasn't an option. The question of where Crazy D's cell was entered his mind, but he dismissed it. Even if they'd been placed next to each other, there was nothing he could do about it.

By Starks's calculations, he had around 119 hours left in solitary to think—about what Crazy D had planned, about his children and how long it had been since he'd seen them, especially Kaitlin, whom he hadn't seen since the day before he'd come to Sands. He hoped Kayla was making sure their children were being properly cared for by their nanny. Even pregnant, Kayla still put herself and her need to party with her boyfriend first. Or was it boyfriends—plural?

In an attempt to quell such thoughts and the emotions they dredged up, Starks did every exercise he could think to do, often needing to rest and gulp air until the pain from the not-so-very-old stab wounds, as well as new injuries, subsided.

Margaret Hessinger's lie had put him in here. He was certain she'd found the butcher knife Ozy meant to use on him. And he wondered if she ever regretted lying for the husband who'd cheated on her nearly as egregiously as Kayla had cheated on him.

And he wondered about the Hessinger children. Had they recovered from the trauma of watching him beat and bloody their father until he was unconscious? Had their nightmares stopped?

His hadn't.

CHAPTER 24

THE NEXT FIVE days were anything but quiet. He'd learned through previous experience that some inmates in the Hole usually carried on day and night. This time was no different. Finally, the cell door was unlocked and shoved open to reveal CO Simmons on the other side, along with the guard who'd been there when Starks had come to the SHU.

"Time's up, Starks," Simmons said. He told the other guard, "I'll take it from here."

The guard frowned and said, "I'm not leaving until I see your backs walking away. He thrust the shackles at Simmons.

"Those aren't needed," Simmons told him.

"You got a problem with the rules, Officer?"

Simmons hesitated then grinned. "Good thing you SHU guys are hard-asses. That's what these numb-nuts need."

"It's what they fucking deserve," the guard replied.

Once Simmons and Starks were far enough away, the shackles were removed.

"First thing I need," Starks said, "is a shower. Had to wash up with cold water that came out in a trickle."

"That's the least of your worries, Starks."

"What do you mean?"

"We ain't getting paid like we're supposed to. You told Roberts you'd take care of it. We been patient. We shouldn't have to be patient."

Starks faced Simmons. "Rest assured all of you will be paid. I'm going to take care of it as quickly as I can."

"As I said, heard that before."

Starks felt his face grow hot and looked away to keep Simmons from seeing this. What the hell was he thinking? He'd flat-out forgotten about the matter.

They continued toward Starks's cell block. He didn't want to believe Jeffrey was deliberately doing this to him, but it was a possibility he couldn't afford to ignore. That left Parker. Parker could meet with Jim. The private investigator was supposed to have set everything up, and obviously had, because the guards had received some payments, just not recently. Maybe something had slipped up with the man Jim assigned to deliver the payoffs. If the guy was keeping the money for himself, no way Jim would know this, unless word got back to him.

Starks and Simmons turned into the corridor that led to his cell. Simmons came to an abrupt halt. "There's something else."

Starks controlled the deep sigh that wanted to escape. "Let's hear it."

"Me and the others been talking. You're too fucking reckless. You keep getting into shit you expect us to get you out of."

"How long have you worked here, Simmons?"

"Seven years. Why?"

"Then you should understand what it takes to survive in this hellhole. If you don't, try to imagine it." Starks fixed his gaze firmly on the guard. "You go home every day. I have to live twenty-four/seven with murderers and rapists. I've come close—too close—to being killed already. Someone's after me again. So don't you dare lecture me about what I have to do to survive. I pay you guys a hefty fee to keep me protected. It hasn't worked out for me, has it? *Has it?*"

The CO stayed quiet.

"*That's* something you and your buddies should discuss."

Simmons' cheeks colored. "We'll do better, Starks. I swear. But try to see our side. It's just . . . it's just that if what's been happening continues, sooner or later, people are gonna ask questions, including the wrong people. You know? We'll all land in the shit if that happens. We don't want things to get worse than they are."

"I hear you. But I have to do what I need to. I can't guarantee that matters won't get worse; they may do just that. I'll do what I can to keep things simpler for all of you, but you do what you're all goddamned paid to do. Anything else you want to say?"

"Nah."

"I'll walk the rest of the way myself. Just stay and watch my back."

"Ten-four."

Something had to be done, and fast, before everything fell apart before it even took hold. It was so much easier outside these walls, to be the man at the top and in control of everything and everyone. Sharing that position in here wasn't a pill that would ever go down without difficulty. No, that wasn't a concept, much less an outcome, easy to swallow at all. It didn't suit him.

Maybe he should have accepted the proverbial olive branch Crazy D had extended to him. Maybe like in Mafia movies, they could have talked and resolved the issue between them. This isn't the movies, he reminded himself. He had no idea whether or not Crazy D was someone whose word was any good. No honor among thieves, he heard Jackson whisper in his mind. He wasn't about to trust anyone with his life.

Maybe it would have been better had Parker never told him about Jeffrey screwing Kayla. Or had at least waited until he was out of prison to tell him. It would have been so much simpler to remain ignorant until he was far away from here. Now, knowing there was a glitch with guards' payments, he couldn't rely on his best friend to handle fixing this for him.

Jeffrey had come here to see him, and he'd not only refused the visit, but sent a clear and nasty message back. What if Jeffrey had bad news to tell him? Maybe something had happened to one of his children. No, his mother would have gotten word to him. Or Parker. Someone. No one had left an urgent message for him to call. No one had shown up here.

Then it struck him: he had all these people in his life, and yet he felt completely alone.

He could hear Demory ask, "Whose fault is that?" And he'd readily provide a list to the counselor. And Demory would go after him for that as well; would ask him when he was going to take responsibility for his choices. He'd have to ask Demory if there was anything in this dark existence that *wasn't* his fucking responsibility; that all he'd seemed to have, for as long as he could remember, was a shit-pile of nothing but responsibilities. He was doing the best he could. Didn't anybody in his life get that?

Of course not. They were all comfortable in their lives, comfort he was directly responsible for.

Especially Jeffrey's luxurious life.

What had Jeffrey thought when he'd refused to see him? No way to know if the guard repeated his message verbatim, unless he asked. If the guard had done that, was Jeffrey shocked, confused? Or did he know exactly why his friend had turned on him?

Was Jeffrey, at his core, as frightened about the future as he was?

CHAPTER 25

HIS PROTECTION PROVIDED by guards was in jeopardy. This reality clanged in Starks's mind like a bell, one tolling ominous inevitabilities. He sat on the bottom bunk, his head lowered, eyes fixed on the concrete floor, yet seeing only the potential violent scenes his imagination insisted he consider.

Jackson sauntered in. "Hey, man, you're back!" His smile faded. "What's up?"

"I've got more problems at the moment than I have solutions."

Jackson pulled the chair out from under his desk and plopped into it. "Here's something that should make you feel better: The guys can't stop going on about what you did for them. They're saying you showed them what a real leader should be about."

Starks nodded and blew out a breath. "That's good, but it was close. They wouldn't have been as happy with me if they'd had time in the SHU as well, and were fed nothing but nutraloaf."

"Fucking Spencer."

"Any word on the Crazy D situation?"

Jackson's plastic chair creaked when he leaned back. "It's pretty quiet, for now, at least. He's still in isolation, of course. I don't know if anything's planned to go down before he gets out, but you can bet your ass that something will happen when he does."

"We need to watch our backs. And we need to recruit more guys."

Jackson's mouth stretched into a broad grin. "I'm ahead of you there.

I didn't sit around with my thumb up my ass while you were in SHUville. We have four new guys with us. I'll set up a meeting so you can check them out."

"Don't bother." Starks lay back on his bed, with his fingers linked behind his head. "You know what kind of people we need and how to motivate them. I trust you to handle it."

Jackson was silent for a moment then said, "A part of me likes that you're delegating. Another part is trying not to freak out that you're letting go of some control rather than hogging it. What's up with you, man?"

Starks shrugged. He punched his pillow and shifted position several times.

"Can't get comfy?" Jackson asked.

"There's a hard bump that wasn't here before."

Jackson's grin widened. "Thought you'd seek and find by now. It's a cell phone. Get up."

Jackson lifted the mattress and pulled the slender device from a slit in the cover and foam. He pressed the power button. The phone came to life.

Starks held his hand out. Jackson gave him the phone, which Starks shut off.

"There are rules to follow," Jackson said. "Always keep it on silent mode. Always dial out using sixty-seven. Always have a lookout so you don't get caught. There's a big fucking penalty if you're caught."

"Where'd you get it?"

"One of Sanchez's guys works in the kitchen. He cut me in on their racket. Inmates pay by the minute to use the few phones available."

Starks's business radar pinged. In an over-populated place like this . . . "Who controls this cell phone business?"

"Sanchez, Crazy D, and Seth."

"I don't know Seth, but the Crazy D part is problematic. How much is their cut?"

"No idea."

"Where do they get the phones?"

"Couple guards bring prepaid phones in. They get their cut of what inmates pay."

"I want in."

Jackson slapped Starks on the back. "Now you're talking." He grew somber. "It's all or nothing, you know."

"What do you mean?"

"It's like a cartel they have going—phones, booze, drugs."

"I won't handle drugs. As a father, I can't do that. And I don't want to deal with alcohol, but I'll handle phones." Starks turned the phone over in his hand. "How many inmates know about this set-up?"

"Not as many as you'd think. They only got it started latter part of last year. Had to find the right guards."

"Tell Sanchez I want to meet with him about this."

"Consider it done."

"Who are the guards involved?"

"Don't know."

"Find out. And, so you know, I'm hanging onto this one."

Jackson grinned. "That one's yours. I asked for an extra. Figured it'd be an incentive for you."

"This is one time I don't object to you playing mentalist in my regard." Starks locked his gaze with Jackson's. "Let's see how well you can use your talent on Sanchez."

"What are you up to?"

"Profit and gain."

CHAPTER 26

S TARKS'S SHIFT IN the library on Mondays usually started at eight thirty, but his time in the SHU had altered his schedule for the current week. He wasn't due to start his shift until noon, which he found out when he showed up after the eight o'clock count. Sam Carson looked relieved when he saw him and asked if it was at all possible, could he keep his ass out of the SHU, because the library wasn't the same without him. Starks laughed. Then an idea came to him. He knew the library stock better than anyone. He made sure no one was looking, especially Carson, and removed a large, ratty book from a shelf, one no one ever read.

Jackson had taken off to start his shift in the kitchen. Alone in the cell, Starks opened the 600-page book, wet some of the pages at the sink then returned to his desk. He used the knitting needle to remove paper segments he flushed down the toilet. The phone fit perfectly into the inch-deep hole. He chose to disregard one of the rules and turned the phone on. The solution to at least a few of his problems was a phone call away.

He grabbed the book and sat on his bed, with his back to the wall and the blanket pulled over his crossed legs. The open book was placed on his lap at a sharp angle. Sixty-seven was dialed then Michael Parker's cell phone number. When Parker uttered a tentative hello, he said, "It's Starks."

"I almost didn't answer. Curiosity won, since I'm very particular about who has this number. Where are you calling from? Usually the operator—"

"I don't have a lot of time, Parker."

"What can I do for you?"

"What's going on with the prison doctor matter and my CT appointment?"

"First, I'm coming to see you later today. We have a lot to discuss about the divorce, and it's better if we do that in person."

"That was my second question."

"Regarding the doctor, I've filed a complaint. Dr. Troy may find himself leaving his position there quite soon. I made it plain that if prison officials don't meet my demands, I'll take it further. I'm certain Sands doesn't want the negative publicity I promised. Your CT scan is scheduled for Friday. I was able to pull some strings."

"You're definitely effective. Even if we hadn't been friends more than a decade, you'd be the guy."

"Happy to help. You're in an untenable situation. When I imagine myself in your shoes, it makes me shudder."

"I appreciate your understanding. One more thing. You know my private investigator?"

"Jim Rogers."

"I need his number."

"Hold on while I get it." Parker repeated the number twice. "You have it?"

"Got it. Thanks. I'll see you this afternoon."

"Starks . . . take care of yourself."

"I'll do my best. By the way, I may be on my shift in the library when you arrive. Tell that to whomever so they know where to find me. See you then."

Starks ended the call and dialed the number he'd memorized. The call went to voicemail. He immediately re-dialed. This time, the person answered but stayed silent.

"Jim, it's Starks."

"Starks, man, how the hell are you?"

"If I said I can't complain, you'd know I was lying."

"You calling from a burner?"

"You got it. Jim, the matter Jeffrey set up with you—"

"Yeah. That's some shit, huh?"

"I'm not sure what you mean, but I've heard some payments have been missed. That's put me in a dangerous position."

"Jeffrey was supposed to go there and explain."

Shit. "I haven't spoken with him. What's up?"

"The designated person got murdered. Had a hard time finding someone I could trust to take his place, but everything's back on schedule starting this Friday, including back pay."

Starks's sigh was audible. "Thank God."

"Sorry about any problems that caused. I'm surprised at Jeffrey. He knew it was important to get word to you so you could cover your ass."

"Shit happens, and messages don't get delivered."

"Hope it's going to be okay. I hate to think I had a part in anything happening to you because of this."

"It'll be okay now. Appreciate all you're doing, buddy."

"You need anything at all that I can take care of, you let me know."

"Again, thanks."

Starks hid the phone in the book and put the book at the bottom of the stack. At least now he knew what was going on, and that it had been resolved. He'd get word out as soon as he could.

He was tempted to chide himself for not seeing Jeffrey when he'd come. At least part of his life would have been less stressful had he known what was going on. Hindsight was a waste of energy.

And certain people were a waste of space.

CHAPTER 27

APPREHENSION FLUTTERED IN Starks's stomach. Parker would arrive in a matter of hours to discuss the divorce. There was no going back. Ever. He'd always care about Kayla, as she was the mother of his children, but any love he'd felt for her had been destroyed. Even the rage he'd felt had diminished to occasional bouts of anger. There were more pressing matters that required his focus and energy.

Another realization came to him: He hadn't thought about Emma in weeks. The time they'd had together before prison had been almost magical. She was the opposite of Kayla and the other women he'd been with, and she didn't deserve to be put through this turbulence.

Emma had supported him in such a loving way when his grandfather had died. They'd stood together on the steps of the church, her hand in his, as they'd waited for the funeral service to begin.

"He was the only real father I ever had," he'd said.

Emma placed her arm around his waist. "I know. And he was so proud of you. His eyes always brightened whenever he saw you."

"I wish life had worked out differently. That I'd met and married you instead of Kayla."

She placed her head against his shoulder. "Everything happens for a reason, baby. You appreciate me more because of her. And, you wouldn't have your children, had it gone any other way."

"You're right. You know, she didn't even bother to call my mother to offer condolences. Didn't send flowers, either. After everything my mother and grandfather did for us while we were in college, including the funds they provided every month to help us pay bills. And they paid every penny of the expensive wedding Kayla and her mother insisted they had to have. All that, and Kayla shows my family no respect at this time."

"I know, baby, but how she is shouldn't surprise you. You said it: She's a viper. If it's not about or for her, she's not interested. Her type conveniently forgets where they came from and who helped them along the way. Don't let her steal your attention. Your family needs you now. Focus on them. Your grandfather would want that."

Emma had been right, of course. Kayla had been under his skin since the first time he'd seen her in high school. Her ability to take up that space was finally starting to fade.

He'd fooled himself into believing what his grandfather and uncles told him when he turned fourteen. It was their version of the birds-and-bees conversation. They emphasized the importance of a wife being a virgin. They discussed the difference between a wife and a side-woman. His grandfather had several women on the side his entire life. The men of his family told him a wife had to be a proper woman, reserved to some degree, but side-women needed to do everything the wife wouldn't or shouldn't. "Treat the other women as though you respect them, even though you don't." His uncles had laughed at his grandfather's statement and nodded in agreement.

He'd followed their advice. He claimed Kayla's virginity when they were teenagers, and had been good to all the women he slept with while he and Kayla were married. The difference was generational. Women in his family of his grandfather's generation put up with extramarital affairs and kept silent. Most women his age were more independent. Some might put up with affairs, if a man paid their way. Some wouldn't.

Emma was divorced, a single mother, and had dated on occasion after she had a legal right to do so. Nothing promiscuous, unlike Kayla. No sexual encounters in odd places, and not with married men. And certainly not with more than one man at a time, as Kayla had done. With Emma, what you saw was what was there. Kayla had deceived him with more skill than he'd ever imagined she possessed.

He'd told Emma when she'd surprised him with a visit at Sands, to stay away, at least for a while. Now he was sorry he'd done that. Or maybe he wasn't. How would a woman as good and kind as Emma react when she saw how he looked now, with no hair to run her fingers through, like when they made love? His groin ached in response to the memory.

Starks closed his mind to thoughts that taunted him. He closed his eyes and didn't open them again until the announcement for the eleven o'clock count blared over the speakers. He chided himself for being stupid. It was dangerous to fall asleep in his cell during the day, where anyone could get to him.

After the count, he ate from his food supply, shaved his head, and washed up. He prepped the small knitting needle with fresh toxic paste, hid it in the hem of the clean shirt he put on, and tucked the fake thumbs into his pants pockets.

At eleven forty, Starks decided to go to the library early. He wanted to give Sam a heads-up about Parker so the library manager could arrange to have someone fill in for him, in case it was needed. Unless Sam decided to fill that role.

He was almost to his destination when he met up with CO Roberts, who was on corridor patrol. "I've got news you and the others want to hear," Starks said. "The problem was with the payments conveyor, but that's been resolved. Starting this Friday everything's back on schedule with a new guy. Back payments will be caught up, along with the current payment."

Roberts smiled. "You're right. That's good news."

Starks made sure they couldn't be overheard. "You know about a cell phone operation in here?"

Roberts hesitated then said, "Maybe."

"I expect a direct response when I ask a question. Let me put it another way. Would you like to make extra money?"

"I'm listening."

"Keep this between us. Let whoever supplies the phones know I'll pay them twenty percent more than they're getting now. And, I'll increase your pay by ten percent if you handle this the way I want you to."

"I'll take care of it."

"You're the best of the bunch, Roberts. Not a word to the others about this, unless I say otherwise."

Starks left Roberts and made his way to the library. He needed this scheme to work, for a number of reasons. And he needed the guards' confidence in him back where it had been at the start.

Now all he had to do was get to the library, meet with Parker, and do whatever it took to divorce Kayla and keep her from taking everything, including his balls.

And stay alive another day.

CHAPTER 28

CO SIMMONS CALLED out from the library entrance, "Starks, your attorney's here. Let's go."

Starks went to the back office where Sam Carson worked at the desk. "My attorney's here."

"I heard. Everyone heard. Tell that CO this is a fucking library, so keep his volume down."

"Like I can tell any CO what to do."

Carson arched his eyebrows. "If I placed a bet about that, would I win?" He chuckled and said, "Be on time tomorrow."

"Yes, boss."

"Boss, my ass."

Starks and Simmons started toward the conference room. The first few minutes of their trek were silent. Then Simmons said, "Roberts told me the good news. I was kinda worried for a while."

"We certainly don't want that. What we do want from now on is mutual trust, and for good reason. Right?"

"Right." Simmons halted. "This is it."

Starks entered the conference room and closed the door behind him. So focused on how the meeting might go, he was momentarily puzzled about Parker's shocked expression. He rubbed his shaved head with his right hand, making it look as though the dragon was attacking him.

"Sorry, Parker. Unless I see myself in a mirror, or someone comments, I forget about my appearance." He crossed the small space and shook hands with his attorney. "How are things at Parker, Birnhaum, Bailey, and Todd?"

"Everyone's fine." Parker gestured in a halfhearted manner at Starks's arm and head. "Why?"

"Jeffrey and Kayla's betrayal pushed me to an edge. I went over." Starks dropped into the chair across from Parker.

"This 'new you' is so vastly different from the professional man I've known for years."

"I'm still the man you know."

Parker drew his glasses from his shirt pocket and perched them on his nose. He looked over them at Starks and said, "I hope to God that's true. Understandably, being here will change some aspects of who you are. That can't be helped. But, Starks, please make every effort to not lose yourself. It's a somewhat lengthy, but temporary situation. You'll get out of here one day and will want and need to return to society."

"You're preaching to the choir. But this is one of those 'walk in my shoes' matters."

Parker pushed his glasses firmly in place and leaned forward, forearms on the table. "I can give you some good news. We're getting Dr. Troy removed."

"That's a fact?"

"It is. I verified that the proper agencies read my complaints, and I spoke with the warden. Fortunately, my name and reputation carry clout, even with those people. In fact, the warden called me on my way here, to make us an offer. He's willing to make the changes he can and push for appropriate changes he can't make without approval, as long as we sign an agreement to keep everything related to this matter out of public awareness."

Starks nodded. "Whatever it takes, but there are a few things I want to make sure happen. Dr. Troy is out of here, ASAP. I want better medical staff, upgraded equipment, and guaranteed quality care for every inmate."

"All reasonable requests and doable up to a point. However, Troy will likely be here until they hire a replacement. If he bails, they'll have to hire a rent-a-doctor, which could be just as bad. He may be a recalcitrant physician, but for the time being, he's the only one they have. Plus, he needs to sign off on the referral for your CT scan before Friday. Not to worry, though; he'll cooperate. I'll make sure of it. As to your other requests, the warden knows it's in his best interest to do what he can to fulfill them, but he isn't the sole decision-maker. However, he knows I'm not going to let this go until substantial improvements take place."

"I respect people who make things happen."

"Glad I could help. Now, about Kayla. I received papers from her attorney. She wants half your business and half of all assets acquired throughout the marriage."

Anger heated Starks's face. He slammed a fist against the table. "That whore isn't going to get it. Sure, she had a job, for a while. But it was me who worked my ass off seven days a week to provide a life of luxury for her and our kids. She repaid me by . . . No need to tell you what you know. She gets fifteen thousand a month for the children. She's getting the house, all the bills paid, her Ferrari. I'm being more than generous."

Parked held up a hand and said, "I know. And I told her lawyer to shove her demand up both their asses. It's not going to happen. This is a formality, anyway. The negotiation process has to start somewhere. Even if they want to ignore ethics, there are laws in the state of Massachusetts. For one thing, you're no longer an owner of your business, so she can't touch that. She's dreaming." Parker cast his eyes downward. "Also, Kayla changed her no-fault petition for divorce to fault, citing adultery and abusive treatment."

"Fucking bitch."

"I know this is hard to hear, Starks, but let me continue before you get too wound up. State law allows the petitioner and respondent to submit a property division agreement. We'll attempt an agreement, but let's prepare ourselves for that not happening as easily as we'd like, just in case. She's going to get something, one way or another. If an agreement can't be reached, the Court will decide for you."

Starks flung himself back in the chair and crossed his arms. "And they'll screw me over big-time."

"Not necessarily. The Court takes a lot of things into consideration in order to make an equitable property division, and the law here states that this does not mean an *equal* division."

"What considerations?"

"Length of marriage, health of both parties, how much each spouse contributed to the marriage, their ages, station, earning abilities, sources of income and so forth. Even their conduct while married."

"Then I am screwed."

"Not necessarily. Your criminal trial was publicized. The recorded testimonies are available to the Court, and I'll insist they review them. Kayla admitted to adultery with Hessinger but was accused by a reliable witness of long-term sexual behavior with many others. You were accused of adultery, but no proof was given."

"Kayla knew about Michelle. She had me end the relationship over the phone, while she listened."

"I see. That could be a problem, if she mentions it. But the Court may see your one proven infidelity as nothing compared to Kayla's numerous ones. However, if they spend the funds to dig, they could likely find proof of more; though, I doubt they'll do that. Whether Kayla digs or not is another matter. Additionally, you're in a maximum security prison. That fact may work to your advantage or disadvantage. My question is, What specifically do you want me to do?"

"I'd like to hear your thoughts first."

Parker rested back in the chair. "You and Jeffrey legally transferred your interest in the business to your mother, who's now a silent partner, and you've been removed from the board. And, you're in prison. You're not obligated to pay anything to Kayla at the moment."

Starks shook his head. "My kids and their well-being are a priority. I'm not cutting off funds for that."

"Of course not. But, technically, you aren't earning income at this time or for the remainder of your sentence."

Starks's shoulders sagged. "Only fourteen and a half years left to go."

"And because of this particular situation, custody isn't currently an issue. I say that now. It could be, if the Court sees Kayla as unfit. Right now, she seems to be involved solely with Bret, and behaving, for her, that is. Sorry to bring custody up. I felt it important to mention, but you don't need to concern yourself with that."

"I'm not worried. They'd live with my mother, if they had to. You asked what I want to happen." Starks tapped a forefinger on the tabletop as he made each point. "I want Jeffrey to stop all payments made directly to Kayla. He's to make them to my mother. Anything Kayla needs for the children will have to be approved and paid for by my mother. I don't want Kayla to get another fucking cent directly from company-related funds."

"We'll go with that, until the Court intervenes." Parker jotted a quick note onto a tablet. "There's the matter of assets. Kayla wants to liquidate the home, stocks, mutual funds, and so on."

Starks chuckled. "We purchased the house when the market was high. What we paid three million for is now worth less than two. Make her keep it for now. Tell her to refinance it and take my name off the loan. Let her and her loser lover worry about the payments. We'll see how long that lasts."

"What about the three condos?"

"The one in Hawaii was bought for my mother and is in her name. Kayla can't touch it. The other two were bought for half a mil each. They're valued at half that now. Sell them and give the bitch her share. My share goes to my mother to put into an account in her name, with me listed as beneficiary."

Parker kept up with his note-taking. "Bank accounts?"

"There was around four hundred thousand in the main one when I came here. She can have half of what's in that one and the few smaller ones. They're joint accounts. For all I know, she moved every damn cent into one or more accounts in her name. Better check that. However that turns out, considering her spending habits, she'll go through that money in less than a year, if she hasn't already." Starks shifted forward. "Also, update my will. I want twenty-five percent of any funds I have to go to Emma. Fifty percent is to be divided among my children. The remaining twenty-five is to be divided among any of my surviving maternal family members. Make sure that maternal part is clearly stated. My father's side of the family has no rights. He abandoned me and my mother, and so did they. And put it down somewhere that Kayla isn't to show her face at my funeral. My kids can go with my mother."

Parker stopped writing, removed his glasses, and looked straight at Starks. "I'll take care of this, of course, and we'll have more to discuss as we move forward, but this adjustment to your will . . . Should I be more concerned about you than I already am?"

Starks's eyes met Parker's gaze. "Anything can happen at any time in here, or anywhere. Best to take care of these matters as quickly as possible."

"Starks—"

"Parker, if I have anything to say or do about it, nothing will happen to me for a very long time."

CHAPTER 29

STARKS ITCHED FOR a fight, but one he could win without breaking a sweat or skin or bones. He needed a win. Before prison, it was all about the win. It still was, only wins were much harder to come by these days.

He turned left out of the conference room and made his way to the infirmary.

The nurse practitioner looked up when Starks shoved open the door. His face was ashen when he asked, "Can I help you?"

"I want to see Troy."

"I'll tell him."

The nurse hurried to the private office, shutting the door behind him when he entered.

Starks heard raised voices, but couldn't make out what was being said. About two minutes later, Troy and the nurse entered the waiting area.

A blast of air from the cooling vent lifted Troy's sparse comb-over like a tattered sail. He slapped it back into place and barked, "Here to gloat after whining because the bad doctor didn't give you a lollipop?"

Starks's smile stopped at his lips. "You took an oath to help others. That didn't exclude anyone from getting proper care and right treatment from you."

"You're all so arrogant. You commit crimes and end up in prison. Then you holler about your rights. None of you considered the rights of your victims. Hypocrites, the whole goddamned bunch of you."

"You're out of here, Troy."

"That's Dr. Troy. And let me remind you, you smug sonofabitch, as a doctor, I'll always have a job. You're lecturing me? That's a laugh. Look at yourself in the mirror. Literally and figuratively. You may have been a somebody before, but now you're just disgusting. The whole damn bunch of you is a waste of taxpayer dollars."

"Don't feel so secure about always having a job. Word has a way of getting out on the Internet these days. The media's always looking for someone to aim their laser at."

Troy worked his jaw for a few seconds. "That would violate the privacy agreement. Yeah, the warden told me." He jabbed Starks's chest. "You blab, and your 'arrangements' will go down the toilet. You'll screw up everything. On second thought, go ahead and talk. I can work in any country anywhere that needs doctors. But you'll be stuck here with inmates who'll kick your ass, or bury it. Now, get the hell out of my infirmary."

"I'm going, but there's one last matter. Sign off on the referral for the CT scan my attorney set up. Take care of it immediately, or risk finding out what happens if you don't. Now," Starks smoothed down the lapels of Troy's lab coat, "after you take care of that, enjoy packing your shit. And don't worry about another job. You're right. A good-looking, charming guy like you won't have any problems getting a paycheck. As for getting women?" Starks shrugged. "That's another matter. Better stick to sheep."

Starks left the trembling, red-faced doctor. His pace was slow along the corridor; he wasn't sure where he wanted to go next. It felt good to deliver revenge that was deserved. Perhaps he'd be able to stick it to Kayla in a similar manner. He'd never hurt her physically; that was a rule he honored with regard to women, but she deserved to feel some of the same measure of pain she'd caused and still wanted to cause him.

Maybe she *had* felt that way when she found out about his affair-turned-to-love with Michelle. Maybe everything she'd done since then, and now, was her way of taking revenge.

If she ever found out about Cathy and Kyle . . .

Lost in thought, he turned into an unfamiliar corridor and halted his steps. The muted sound of metal banging on metal was one he hadn't heard at Sands before. He followed the hammering to a door marked *Authorized Personnel Only*. The door was ajar.

He stepped across the threshold.

CHAPTER 30

THE L-SHAPED ROOM was cluttered with metal, wood, tools, and bits of furniture in need of minor and major repair. Their material scents mingled with that of strong glue and soldering. Starks edged his way through the items littered around the concrete floor, following the banging sound. He turned the corner and stopped. Pounding a piece of metal was an older man, bearded, with thinning white hair plastered to his sweaty scalp.

The man wiped his face on a shirtsleeve and saw he wasn't alone. His eyes raked over Starks. He laughed silently and leaned against the work table, hammer in hand. "Frederick Starks. Been meaning to meet, but you were either in the Hole or the hospital whenever I felt like making the effort."

"Who the hell are you?"

"Gabriele Bianchi."

Starks's surprise was obvious, and he didn't miss the fluid Italian pronunciation. "Mr. Bianchi—"

"Gabe."

"I didn't realize you were here."

"There's a lot you don't realize."

Starks stiffened his posture. "What's that supposed to mean?" Gabe laughed. "I amuse you, old man?"

Gabe pointed the hammer at Starks. "Your name does. Now my name means God-given strength. Nothing else to say about that. But Frederick?

Means peaceful ruler. You're anything but. You're like one of those scrappy yapping dogs that could fit into a Christmas stocking."

"I *was* peaceful before I came here."

Gabe shook his head. "You lie to yourself. Most people do. If you want to see who and what a man really is, put him in a difficult situation." He made a fist. "Put the squeeze on him. You'll see soon enough what's inside."

"I've been in plenty difficult situations and proven myself."

"They weren't difficult enough. Not until the one that got you sent here. And when you got here," Gabe shrugged, "you took to violence the way a fly takes to manure. You may know who I am, but I know about you. We've got a lot in common."

"I'm nothing like you. For one thing, I'm against organized crime."

Gabe guffawed. "You've done nothing but organize it since you got here."

"You're full of shit." Starks turned to leave.

"And you're a driven man, Starks."

"Damn right."

"Driven by emotions. You wear 'em on your sleeve," Gabe grinned, "and on your head and arm. No shaved head or tattoo is gonna prove who you are, to others or yourself. Only your choices can do that."

"You're not so smart, Mr. Mafioso. You're here, just as I am. For longer, if I recall correctly. Didn't your law degree teach you how to avoid that?"

"Law degrees don't make a difference when you're set up."

"You're saying you didn't kill your wife's lovers or that other guy?"

"Like I said, we got things in common. I can see that makes you uncomfortable. The truth does that. You're as hasty with your judgment as you are with your temper. You're one of those ready, fire, aim types when you get angry. That's a good way to get into trouble. You'd think you'd've figured that out by now. But you keep doing the same thing, thinking the result'll be different."

"A philosopher. Just what this place needs."

"Sometimes philosophy is all you got."

Starks glanced around. "What is this place? Looks like a repair shop."

"In-house. My grandfather taught me how to fix things. They let me fix whatever needs it."

"I'm amazed they trust you with tools and sharp objects. Lots of weapons available. Anybody can get in here."

"Only reason that door was open is because it needs a repair. Was fixing the piece when you came in. Now you're gonna leave and I'm gonna fix the door so it stays locked like it should."

"I've been kicked out of better places."

"That's one difference between us. Nobody ever kicked me out of any place."

"Not if they wanted to live."

Gabe laughed. "You're safe. From me, at least."

"Small comfort."

"You gotta learn to take it when and where you can get it."

*

The next several days were as uneventful as a day in prison can be. Starks was relieved in one way—everyone needs downtime, he told himself. But the energy inside the prison and in the summer-sweltering yard crackled like the proverbial calm before the storm.

He considered visiting Gabe. He didn't like the old man's comments about them having things in common, but the fact was that Gabe was the only man at Sands who could relate to a wife's infidelity in such a publically humiliating way, betrayals of others, and the loss of wealth and luxuries. No one else understood that at the same level.

Gabe also reminded him of his grandfather in some ways. The age and white hair, of course, but also the straight-talk. Ryan Morgan may not have always been right with his advice, but he'd always been as honest as he could be with Starks. Gabe would probably be as honest as he dared to be, if the old guy ever let him in the room again, that is.

It bothered him that he wanted to trust Gabe Bianchi, to confide in him as he would have his grandfather. That was foolish, and Gabe would probably say the same thing. Both of them understood that loyalty was more often than not a matter of dollar signs or a what's-in-it-for-me mentality. The aging Mafia don knew that as well as he did.

Still, he believed he could learn from him. All he had to do was not piss the guy off.

CHAPTER 31

S TARKS COULDN'T MOVE. Gabe had him strapped to a table in the workroom. The old guy talked to himself, sometimes laughed aloud, as he prepared a piece of metal then soldered it over Starks's mouth, muffling his screams of terror and pain. Starks, eyes squeezed tightly shut, writhed against the constraints, but he was trapped. His nearly silent screams stopped when he heard his name shouted over and over. He opened his eyes. Instead of Gabe, he saw a wide-eyed Jackson leaning over him.

"Shit, Starks. Everyone in the whole damn block has their heads poking out to see what the fuck's going on in here. I thought your nightmares had eased up."

Panting hard, Starks swiped sweat from his forehead. "So had I."

"Maybe you need to see the counselor. You think the guys in here, especially the bad-asses, are gonna want to follow a leader who screams in his sleep?"

"I don't need a counselor. I'm fine. Besides, I'm not the only man in here who screams, sleeping or not."

Jackson plunked into his chair and shoved his feet into his shoes. "Yeah, you're just peachy."

Starks sat up. "Change the subject or get the fuck out of here. You're annoying me."

Jackson waved his hands in the air. "*Ooh*, I angered the dragon. I'm so scared."

Starks scowled and said, "Jackson."

"Count's in two minutes. Get yourself organized. I'd appreciate it if His Nibs would sit with me at breakfast so I can talk with you before my shift starts."

"What about?"

"Always so impatient. I'll tell you at breakfast."

"Whatever."

Starks's last shoe went on as the count was called over the loudspeaker.

Starks and Jackson walked to the chow hall, as well as got their trays in silence. They rapped on the table and took seats across from each other.

"All right, Jackson, you have my attention."

"I've recruited a few more people. They and the others want to know when the meeting you talked about is gonna happen."

"Soon."

"Not what they were hoping to hear, but I'll let them know." Jackson stabbed fake scrambled eggs onto his fork. "That nightmare you had was worse than usual. What's up with that?"

Starks spooned oatmeal into his mouth, grimaced and swallowed. "Ever heard of Gabe Bianchi?"

Jackson tensed. "Why're you asking about him?"

"I met him yesterday."

"Stay away from him. He's bad news."

Starks put his spoon down. "He's well-spoken, educated. A little too philosophical for my tastes," he shrugged, "but each to his own. And, he reminds me of my grandfather."

"Don't let that fool you. The boss of the Bianchi family isn't someone to mess with."

"Former boss."

"Don't believe that for a second."

"He's someone who can get why I did what I did."

Jackson pointed his loaded fork at Starks. "We all get it. The difference is he intended to murder his wife's lovers, you didn't."

"Even though Ozy didn't die, the result was the same: we're both behind bars."

"Don't think you'll be best buds, because you have something in common. Even though he's been locked up for a while, people don't like to mention him. They believe he's still dangerous, even in here."

"Maybe he is, maybe he isn't. I don't like to believe everything I hear. You shouldn't, either."

"You gotta watch you don't have a side-view mirror perspective, especially about that old man."

"Enough about Gabe. I'm taking a couple-hour trip out of here today."

"How'd you manage that?"

"I'm going for the scan Parker set up."

"Dr. Troy's a quack. Something ought to be done about him."

"He's on his way out. I saw to that."

Jackson laughed. "Score one for the dragon. Let's hope his replacement is better."

"If he isn't, I'll deal with him as well."

A nightstick came down hard on the table. Starks and Jackson looked at the guard glaring at them.

"You girls have gabbed long enough. You're a minute over the ten allowed. Follow the rules and get outta here or lose some privileges."

"Not a problem," Starks said.

"I've got to start my shift, anyway," Jackson replied.

The two inmates rapped on the table and carried their trays to the dump-'n-stack area.

"Good luck with the scan."

Starks lowered his voice. "Keep it to yourself, Jackson. I told you for good reason. I didn't want you asking where I was, and I don't want everyone knowing what's going on. Anyone asks, say you don't know."

"Got it."

Jackson made his way to the kitchen; Starks turned right. Despite Jackson's admonitions, he wanted to see if Gabe was in the workroom. Then he'd go to the gym, hit the showers, and be back in his cell for the eleven o'clock count. His shift in the library started at one. Then it would be time to head out for his appointment. He wondered which guards would be assigned to escort him.

And he wondered if the scan results would render his plans moot.

CHAPTER 32

STARKS GRABBED WHAT he'd need for a shower and some clean clothes. Jackson had been adamant that Gabe was dangerous, but he didn't anticipate any trouble. Anyone who could be as calm and composed as Gabe was in this place had to be considered wise, or he had a real good reason not to be afraid. Plus, the former—or current—crime boss had garnered significant respect from Sands inmates; he was left alone, not that it was difficult to imagine why.

He wended his way through the few corridors to the L-shaped room, grabbed the handle of the heavy door and twisted. The door was locked. Starks knocked hard, but got no response. Ear pressed firmly against the door, he heard metal against metal. Starks pounded on the door and yelled, "Gabe, it's Starks." Still no answer. Either Gabe couldn't hear him or didn't want to be bothered.

Starks leaned against the door. He'd wanted to see Gabe more than he'd realized. Disappointment wasn't something he found easy to take. Like the time his grandfather promised a new bicycle for Christmas and didn't deliver. When he was older, his grandfather explained that he'd done it on purpose, because Starks needed to learn that life wasn't fair.

"There will be times you won't get what you want, son, at least not when you want it."

"But you promised."

"Had to. Wasn't easy, but it was the best way to teach you not to believe everything people tell you, especially if they say they're going to give you what you want. You have to watch people. You have to learn to trust your gut. Let that be the voice that's louder than your desires, especially ones others say they're going to fulfill. Something seems off, it is. Plain and simple. You got that bike eventually, didn't you?"

"You made me work for it."

"That's one of the best lessons I could give you. Real success that has any meaning has to be earned. You keep these lessons in mind. You'll be stronger for it."

His grandfather's lessons were often harsh, but they put calluses on him in a way no softer life could have. Even though the money-strapped years of college, the low-paying jobs that followed, and starting his first business caused him to pace the floors at night wondering how, when, and if he'd ever get out of that poverty, he'd been tempered to disappointment and persistence, unless giving up and moving on to something else was more profitable for him.

Starks faced the door. He pounded several more times and counted to sixty. He listened again. No sound came from inside.

He hit the door with his fist once and shouted, "I'll be back. You're going to talk to me."

Starks got the usual nods of respect from Los Hermanos members. He watched them as he put the weights back in order before starting his set. One of the gang, Felipe, led a practice session that Starks took to be impressive, fast-paced wrestling moves. Starks abandoned his workout and instead stood nearby, watching. Each time a man joined Felipe on the mat, he had his opponents submitting to chokeholds in less than a minute.

Felipe announced the workout was over. Starks approached him. "That was some fancy wrestling moves you were demonstrating."

"That's not wrestling, man; that's Brazilian Jiu-Jitsu."

"You're from Brazil?"

Felipe laughed. "Puerto Rico. I'm a Jiu-Jitsu champion, or was. Won several medals. Some of my competitions are on YouTube."

"I'm impressed. Would you teach me some of those moves?"

Felipe grabbed his towel from the mat and wiped sweat from his head and arms. He avoided looking at Starks. The other members of the gang gathered their towels and things, but it was apparent they were listening.

"I'll pay you," Starks said.

"It's not that. Need Sanchez's permission. I'm supposed to teach only the amigos."

"Is it best if you ask him or that I do?"

"You. Pay the man the respect he requires." Felipe chuckled. "I hope he says yes. I'd get a special tattoo just for that, right here." He pointed to his upper right arm. "Dragon Trainer." The other Hermanos laughed. Felipe picked up his gear and made for the door, trailed by the others in the gang. He turned, pointed to his right arm, laughed out loud then left the gym.

I'll see what I can do to get you that tattoo, Starks said to himself.

CHAPTER 33

S TARKS RETRIEVED JACKSON'S roll of duct tape, tore off two strips, which he pressed flat on his abdomen. He tucked the cell phone into his underwear and headed out for his library shift. Once in the office, he taped the phone under the desk, in a place no one would discover without deliberate effort.

At 3:35 three guards came for him. None of them were on his payroll or familiar to him. The room went silent. Paco and six other inmates sat motionless as one guard put shackles on Starks.

One of the guards said to them, "This isn't your business."

The inmates pretended to go back to what they'd been doing, occasionally casting furtive glances at Starks.

A guard said, "Let's go."

Paco wore an expression that was clearly quizzical. Starks smiled and winked. Paco shook his head.

Two of the guards secured Starks in the back of the van; one of them opened a small panel in the roof to let air in. The three guards climbed into the air-conditioned cab, one guard acting as driver. He cranked the engine and jolted the van into motion.

The twenty-minute ride was bumpy and sweltering for Starks, but he ignored this as much as he could—he was leaving Sands for a while again, this time conscious. The hazy summer sky was a solid wash of milky blue. Trees and shrubs were flush with every shade of green. Wildflowers carpeted the fields they passed. Starks closed his eyes, raised his face toward the vent and inhaled. It wasn't the fresh-air scent he'd hoped for, but memory let him recall summer days when he was a free man.

The van slowed and turned right into the medical facility. People walked out of their way to avoid Starks and his escorts. Most of the staff made an effort not to stare. After signing in, the first stop was at the lab for blood to be drawn. Then Starks and the guards went to the waiting area in the radiology department, where every chair was filled with anxious patients and family, made even more so by the new arrivals. Starks was certain the reason he was called in next was to get him in and out as fast as possible.

The four men followed a nurse to a small office, where a white-coated man behind the desk, his profile to them, typed on a keyboard. He didn't look up when they entered or when the nurse placed Starks's folder on the desk.

Starks saw the name plate. "Dr. Garrett Hall. I'll be damned."

Garrett focused on the man in shackles across from him, initial confusion evident in his expression. "Starks! I recognized the voice before the . . . uh . . ." He gestured with a hand that he then dropped self-consciously to his desktop.

"I look different."

"That's one way to put it."

"It's good to see you, Garrett. Long time. I'd shake, but . . ." He held up his shackled hands.

Garrett said, "The restraints have to come off."

"No can do, Doc," one of the guards replied.

"He can't go into the machine with them on."

"We can take them off before he goes in, but not before."

Garrett came around his desk. "Follow me." He picked up Starks's folder and read as he walked.

They entered another small office. Garrett said, "Okay, the restraints need to come off here, before I take him into the next room."

"Where he goes, we go," a guard said.

Starks laughed. "It's not like I'm going to escape. There's only one way out of here and you're blocking it."

The same guard said, "We'll take them off at the scanner."

"No," Garrett said, "you take them off here. The only two people going into the next room are doctor and patient. We have rules we have to follow as well." He pointed behind him. "That's a big window. You can watch him from in here. But doctor-patient confidentiality starts as soon as Starks and I cross that threshold."

Shackle-free, Starks went ahead of Garrett into the anteroom to where the scanner was positioned. Garrett closed the door behind them. Starks stretched and said, "Those things are heavy. All that aside, how the heck are you? Looks like you've done well for yourself."

"You helped it happen. I would never have been able to afford top-notch lawyers like the ones you set up for me to help with that . . . *little* issue."

"That's what friends do."

"Have a seat. There's something I need to discuss before we start the scan."

Starks sat on the edge of the chair. "You look worried."

Garrett opened the folder, exposing the top sheet. Got the results of your blood work."

"That was fast. Uncommon, even."

Garrett blushed. "Not for prisoners."

"Let's hear it."

"Your CBC is abnormal, and your hemoglobin levels are dangerously low."

"That's way too technical for me. What does it mean?"

"It can mean a number of things such as severe anemia, maybe from a bleeding ulcer. It could also mean colon cancer or kidney problems. We'll get this scan done and see what's what head-wise. But I'm amazed the prison doctor didn't catch this."

"The man doesn't care. Parker's doing what he can to get him replaced as soon as possible."

Garrett nodded. "A blood transfusion may be needed. Who in your family could donate?"

"Kayla and I are both Type O, not that she'd give me any blood; she only takes it. I know that two Type Os can only have Type O children. One of my three could donate."

"Who's the oldest?"

"Blake. He's thirteen."

Garrett frowned. "Legally, he'd need to be seventeen. We can't use him."

"Can't I sign a consent form or something?"

"You could if he was sixteen. We can get blood from another donor, if Kayla won't do it. What about your mother?"

"Type A. I want my son to do it. Let me talk to Parker and see if there's anything he can do."

Garrett scratched his ear. "Actually, in special situations where there's medical value for a family member, someone under that age can donate. Further tests may prove that need."

"Let's do them."

"First," Garrett turned to a computer terminal and began clicking through icons, "let's get you to sign a form so I can get your son's health records." He turned a small piece of equipment toward Starks. "It's all electronic these days. Just use the pen attached and fill in the information you know. There's a place for your signature and one at the bottom for you to list yourself as his father."

It took about two minutes for Starks to fill in the form. "Now what?"

"Now we do the scan, a different blood test, and then I admit you for an overnight stay."

Starks glanced at the guards. "They're not going to like it."

"Not my concern. You are. Unfortunately, we're required to place you in the—"

"Secured mental ward. Been there, done that."

"Yes. Sorry. It's in the file."

"At least the food here will be better than what I usually get."

"Must be really bad where you are. The food, I mean."

Starks exhaled. "It's not a place where you find much that's good."

CHAPTER 34

STARKS SLEPT AS well as could be expected, considering all that was on his mind and the occasional night screams from patients in the mental ward. He forced himself to linger over, rather than gulp, a breakfast of pancakes with syrup, bacon, real scrambled eggs, toast with real butter and jelly, orange juice with pulp, and coffee—brewed, not instant.

There was no TV in the room, just a small barred window on the side wall. No telephone was provided. He ignored the tiny window on the door; there was nothing in the ward he wanted to look at.

Starks pushed the tray table aside then double-checked that his clothing, folded by him so the knitting needle wasn't detected, was still untouched in the built-in closet. He went to the window. It was overcast; a light drizzle speckled the glass. He guessed it was around nine; breakfast had been delivered at 8:29—he'd asked.

Someone unlocked the door. Starks smiled when Garrett came in.

"How're you feeling this morning, Starks? Were you able to sleep?"

"At the moment, I'm feeling pretty good." Starks patted his stomach and nodded at the food tray. "I slept well enough. The noise level here is slightly less than at Sands."

"I have some good news for you. No neurological problems showed up on the scan."

"That's a relief. So, what do you think caused the headaches and me to faint?"

"The abnormal CBC could be a factor. It's also possible the headaches are stress-induced." Garrett sat on the edge of the bed. He ran a hand back and forth across his mouth and kept his eyes aimed at the floor.

"Garrett, you're stalling about something. What is it?"

"This isn't easy."

"Talk."

Garrett looked straight at Starks. "Blake is Type A."

"That's not possible."

Garrett blew out a breath but stayed silent.

Starks's voice was a whisper. "Are you telling me Blake isn't my son?"

"One of his parents would have to be Type A."

Starks shook his head violently. He paced for several moments then slammed his fist into the wall. "That fucking whore."

"I'm truly sorry, Starks."

Starks faced him. "No." He shook his head. "A mistake was made in the typing somewhere along the line. Some half-asleep technician mixed things up. We have to be absolutely sure about this. How do we prove this one way or . . ." Starks slid down the wall. He dropped his face into his hands and sobbed. "It can't be. It just can't be."

"It's in his medical records." After a moment he added, "The only way to remove any doubt is with a DNA test. Kayla would have to approve it, of course."

Starks used the hospital gown to wipe his face and eyes. "No." He nodded once firmly. "That's not how we're going to do this."

"I don't understand."

"I need your help. Not in any way that'll get you into trouble. But this has to be done differently."

"I owe you. How can I help?"

"Did the prison post a guard outside my room?"

"They tried but I wouldn't allow it. Told them no way was I going to disrupt the patients in this ward."

"Do whatever you have to, to keep me here for several days, probably at least four more days. Find a reason. And get me a burner phone with a couple hours on it. Get it to me by this evening. For now, give me your phone and step out of the room. What you don't know can't bite you later."

"I'm only asking in case I get paged, but how long will—"

"Not long. I'll knock on the door when I'm done."

Garrett handed Starks his phone then left the room. It took four tries to key in the number.

CHAPTER 35

THE PHONE RANG three times before Jim Rogers answered and said, "Garrett Hall? Do I know you?"

"It's Starks."

"How'd you get this phone?"

"Borrowed it. I'll be calling you from a burner starting tonight. There's something urgent I need you to do. There's a huge bonus for you, and I need you to act fast and not get caught."

"Aw crap. Let's hear it."

"I need you to get DNA samples of my three children . . . and Jeffrey's."

"What the fuck, Starks?"

"Get the samples as soon as you can. The big question is this: can you get the samples to a lab that will test the DNA immediately *and* keep quiet?"

"I know a guy. He'll do it, for a price. Rush is extra."

"Pay him. I'll check in with you tonight, once I have the new phone. If you need me to advance funds, I'll call Parker."

"I should be able to cover any upfront costs."

"Good. Any questions?"

"No."

"Not even why I'm doing this?"

"Pretty damn obvious. Damn, Starks. Jeffrey? Does the shit ever stop with that woman?"

"Probably not until she's dead. But right now, I feel like I'm suffocating under a pile of it."

"I hear you. One thing: I need your DNA."

"Get some from my house. Do it in a way that Emma never knows you were there."

"This may take a few days."

"Make it faster. Time's squeezing in on me. I know what I'm asking, but I also know what you're capable of."

Jim let out a sigh. "I'm on it."

Starks disengaged the call and dragged himself to the door. He knocked and handed the phone to Garrett. "Except for meals, if I can even eat, and when you bring me the phone, I'd like to be left alone as much as possible, at least for a while."

"I understand."

"I don't."

Starks closed the door and returned to the window, where he stood staring at the gray void of sky.

Emotions competed for his attention. Devastation was one of them. What if Blake wasn't his son? He'd cherished the boy since he was in the womb. Was it possible to cut off all love for a child if you discovered he wasn't yours? And if it was true, what would this do to Blake? It crushed him to think about it. The fact that he was concerned about this had to be a clear indication of his love for the boy. Didn't it? After all, people adopted babies and loved them as their own.

But they knew the truth.

If Blake turned out not to be his, whose was he?

Starks strained to recall every feature of Blake's face to search for any similarity to Jeffrey, as well as to himself or anyone in his family. But his mind was in too much turmoil. He couldn't trust it to be accurate.

Are any of the children I've loved and cared for mine?

He rushed to the toilet and vomited. He rinsed his mouth and splashed cold water on his face then lay curled up on the bed. Tremors wracked his body.

"Damn you, Kayla." Tears streamed from his eyes. "How much more are you going to take from me, you selfish bitch?"

Maybe this was his punishment for living his life the way he had, the way his grandfather and uncles had told him was his right as a man.

What if his only natural child had been Kyle?

Starks buried his face in the pillow and wept.

CHAPTER 36

HE COULDN'T TOUCH his lunch. When Starks's dinner tray was delivered just after five, he forced himself to eat every bite, reminding himself that keeping his strength up was vital.

He got out of bed and stood at the window. He paced, washed his face, paced some more, returned to the window, noting the sun now caused long shadows on the ground seven stories below.

Garrett knocked as he opened the door. He reached into his pants pocket and handed a cell phone to Starks. "I put twenty hours on it. Think that'll be enough?"

"More than enough. Thanks."

"How're you doing?"

"I've had some rough moments. Appreciate you keeping the interruptions down."

"It was okay for those several hours, especially after a shock, but that has to change. I need your vitals checked and so forth."

"Do what you have to."

"I'm concerned about how this is affecting you. Any problem with a headache or any other symptom?"

"Surprisingly, no. At least not yet. But that may be because I lost my breakfast. Maybe that got some of the poison out of my system."

"Maybe. But if a headache starts, buzz for a nurse. I'll leave instructions about what to give you for it. I've got to get going. One last thing: I know it sounds trite to say this, all things considered, but try to keep the stress down."

Starks laughed without humor. "I'll see what I can do."

"Maybe a mild sedative would—"

"No. Thanks. I want to stay sharp."

"I'll see you tomorrow, then. Try to get some rest. I'll leave instructions about something to help you sleep, in case you change your mind."

"Again, thanks. For everything."

As soon as the door closed, Starks called Jim Rogers. "Just got the phone. Please answer as quickly as possible whenever I call."

"Aren't you being reckless having a phone in prison?"

"I'm at Grace for tests. I'll be here a few days."

"You okay?"

"I'm fine. Any progress?"

"So far I got samples of your DNA and the kids'. I'm pretty sure I can get Jeffrey's later this evening. For whatever reason, he's been home all day."

"How're you doing this?"

"You really need details?"

"Just curious."

"Let's just say I'm grateful for rubber gloves."

Starks sat on the edge of the bed and was silent.

"Starks? You still there?"

"Still here."

"I hope this turns out well for you, buddy."

"How well it turns out is relative at this point."

"Literally."

"Once you have Jeffrey's sample, how long before you can get everything to your guy?"

"He's on call. Because it's more than two samples, he needs to do it after hours. But he's ready. He's got a new girlfriend he's trying to impress. The extra money is already burning a hole in his pocket."

"Poor bastard. All right. I'll check in with you tomorrow morning."

"Yep."

Starks dropped the phone onto the bed and his head into his hands. He'd have an answer soon.

The thought terrified him.

CHAPTER 37

S EVERAL TIMES, STARKS came close to asking for something to help him sleep, but resisted. He regretted his decision in the morning.

He dragged himself to the shower hoping cold water would help him stay awake. Breakfast was as good as before, but Starks was on automatic as he ate.

Jim should have gotten the samples to his lab guy the night before. Eager for an update, Starks pulled the phone from under his mattress. The door clicked open. He slid the phone back into its hiding place.

Garrett Hall came in. "Those twisted sheets and the way you look tell me you didn't sleep well, if at all. You should have asked for something." Garrett listened to Starks's heart and took his pulse. He checked Starks's nails and lower eyelids.

"I'll sleep later. What are you doing?"

"Confirming my decision to give you a blood transfusion today."

Starks stood up. "That wasn't the plan."

"You need one sooner than later. The results of the second blood test, your heart rate, the pale color of your nails, et cetera, are all signs telling me to move quicker. I know I said stress can cause headaches, but anemia, which you have, can cause them, as well as insomnia, dizziness, anxiety—symptoms you also have, plus a host of other symptoms you don't want, including hair loss; though, yours," he grinned as he glanced at Starks's head, "was obviously deliberate."

Starks didn't respond to the humor. "I'd rather wait."

"I know. But I need to take care of this anemia situation now so it doesn't get any worse and create more serious problems for you. As for the blood to use," Garrett's cheeks reddened, "when I saw the test results this morning, I took the liberty of having them check for a donor match from what we have stored."

"When?"

"I'm waiting for someone to come for you now. I'm going with you so I can check how you're doing during and after. It'll take an hour or more for the transfusion, probably two. Afterwards, I want you to rest and not exert yourself for forty-eight hours, even though you should start feeling better within twenty-four. If you don't, I'll know to do more extensive tests."

Two burly male nurses entered with a wheelchair. They scowled at Starks and adjusted their postures into no-nonsense stances.

"Shift your attitudes," Garrett told them. "Your assumption about this man is wrong. He's a longtime friend of mine." At the surprised expressions they wore, he added, "Despite how he's altered his appearance, and what misinformed people decided, he's not a criminal. Plus, I'm tagging along. You're safe."

Everything happened so fast, it wasn't until the sting from the I.V. port inserted into his left arm that Starks remembered he was waiting for information he was both anxious to get and dreaded.

CHAPTER 38

HIS BEDDING HAD been changed in his absence. Starks raced to the side where he'd hidden the phone, felt under the mattress and couldn't find it. He flipped the mattress onto the floor. Perspiration beaded on his forehead. He grabbed the buzzer to have Garrett paged and noticed the drawer on the small dresser next to his bed was open a quarter inch. Relief flooded through his body. Because the phone was there rather than removed. Because his possession of it hadn't been reported. So far.

Heart pumping hard, he dialed Jim's number.

Jim answered after one ring. "Starks. Finally."

"I couldn't call until now. What's the status?"

"Had to wait on Jeffrey until the early hours. Seems he's got insomnia or something."

"Must be going around."

"I got everything to my guy around seven thirty this morning. He'll hang back after everyone leaves and get started. Takes about ten hours to run one profile, but they have enough equipment for him to do all of them tonight. We're meeting over breakfast at six to go over the results."

Starks stood in the ray of sun streaming through the window. "Appreciate it, Jim."

"Sorry all this shit's landing on you, buddy."

"You've seen the bumper sticker about that."

"Just seems you're getting an unfair share of it."

"I'll contact you in the morning."

Starks ended the call and stayed standing where he was. In less than twenty-four hours he'd know something about how much of what he'd believed about his family and life was a lie.

First Kayla. Then Jeffrey. Now Blake and God knew who else. When it came to Kayla, anything was possible. His hatred of her had started to wane. That was over now. Rage overwhelmed him. Rage that had no moral, legal, or ethical outlet he could live with. The woman was a vampire. If given the chance, she'd drain him, chew on his bones, and look for more ways to take his soul piece by piece.

He picked at his dinner, tossed and turned in bed, unable to settle down. At nine o'clock, he decided inner turmoil wasn't the way to go so soon after the transfusion. He wouldn't learn anything from Jim until morning. A sleeping pill was delivered ten minutes after his request. One night of peace wasn't too much to ask. After all, he didn't know when such an opportunity would happen again.

It was twelve after ten when he checked the time on his phone before slipping it back under the pillow. He was asleep in moments.

CHAPTER 39

A SHAFT OF EARLY morning light filtered into the room. Starks stretched and yawned. He lay unmoving, too relaxed to open his eyes, and thought about what he'd ask Emma to prepare for his breakfast. He was famished. But he'd wait until the aroma of coffee lured him from bed; it felt too good where he was to move yet. Maybe he'd ask her to have breakfast in bed with him. Then he'd show her how deep his appreciation could go. He smiled wide at that thought and opened his eyes. Reality spiraled back to him, like water down a drain when the plug is pulled.

Two sensations competed inside him: More energy from the transfusion *and* a high level of anxiety. All he had to do was get past this latest battle heading his way and then he'd figure out a way to live with what was and still win. His grandfather had told him if he wanted to pay others back for the harm they did to him, win and win big. "Don't just survive, son— thrive! It'll piss them off, but they'll kowtow to you. They won't be able to help themselves." However, he couldn't picture Queen-in-her-own-mind Kayla going down that path.

He pulled the phone from under his pillow to check the time. Six thirty-three. At this moment, if all had gone according to plan, Jim and the lab guy were discussing one of the most crucial aspects of his life.

Starks took the phone with him into the bathroom. The hot shower felt good but didn't calm the emotions tugging at him. By six forty he was seated on his bed, watching the outside light change and wondering when he should call. Repeatedly, he checked the time on the phone. At five after seven, he dialed Jim's number. It was time to get this over with.

"I don't know how much you know or don't know, Starks, which means I don't know how much the results might shock you."

"Just tell me."

"Blake's not yours."

Starks drew in a deep breath, held it then let it go. "What about Nathan and Kaitlin?"

"Yours."

Starks cradled his head in his left hand. "Thank God."

"I take it you suspected this about Blake."

"What about Jeffrey? Did his DNA match . . . is he Blake's father?"

"I gotta say I'm stunned you thought he might be, but no."

"So, we don't know who Blake's father is."

"I do."

Starks leaped up. "What do you mean?"

"You're his father, the only one he's ever had. Look, I can understand you might be feeling a lot about this. It's the shit, far as I'm concerned." When Starks stayed silent, Jim asked, "What are you going to do about it?"

"I haven't gotten that far. I'd hoped it was a mistake."

"Any suspicions about who the sperm donor may have been?"

"Who the hell knows how many guys she was screwing then. She probably doesn't know, either. In fact, it was pretty fucking charitable of her to let two of the kids be mine. That or it was insurance. She does stupid things, but she's not actually stupid."

"Again, Starks, sorry."

"Put the results in your safe and keep them for me."

"Consider it done. Anything else?"

"No."

"Reach me if you need me."

Starks lay back on the bed, his gaze fixed on the ceiling. What was he going to do about Blake? What could he do? He hated the idea of Kayla believing she got away with it, that is, if she even knew, herself. That was a question only she could answer, and he didn't want to hear her lies, even though he had proof. If she didn't know, the truth would stick it to her in a profound way. If he told her or anyone in his family, even if they didn't mean it to happen, the news could too easily get back to Blake.

Jim had called Blake's biological father the sperm donor, removing anything personal and familial from the equation. Was he right?

When he'd first heard he was going to be a father, he'd been nervous and thrilled and proud. He'd watched Kayla's belly swell with the child he thought was his. It was easy to recall how he felt when Blake took his first breath and made his displeasure loud and clear about being squeezed out of his warm *cocoon*. The first time he held the boy in his arms and said, "Hello, Blake. I'm your daddy." The first time that remarkably tiny hand wrapped around one of his fingers and wouldn't let go. The first smile. How the boy's eyes lit up and his whole body was animated with excitement when Starks came into the room. The moment "Da-da" was spoken for the first time, more like a beam of bright light than a sound. Each of these moments, and so many more, had shattered him in profoundly joyful ways then glued him back together again, stronger than he'd been before.

How would he feel the next time he saw Blake? Could he look at the boy in the same way, feel him with the same heart? He imagined Blake looking back at him, talking to him—"Dad, Dad! Wait till I tell you—"

It wasn't just about the financial responsibility a person incurred for a child, or that they shared the same address and used the same last name. It was the moments that couldn't be purchased, only exchanged with the currency of love. Blake was his son in every way but blood.

He decided it would take a medical emergency to force the truth from him.

If Kayla thought she'd put something over on him, that couldn't matter. Sure, there would probably be times when the fact angered him, but he could and would put Blake first.

What if she was waiting for the right moment, in her self-absorbed way, to tell this fact to him so she could crush him even more? His foremost thought was to protect Blake. Kayla could go fuck herself and anyone else she wanted to.

He would never have to see Kayla's face or hear her voice again once all his children were adults. They'd be old enough to understand, and to make their own choices regarding their relationship with their mother.

As he mused about this, the breakfast tray arrived. Starks ate slowly, imagining the day of his release from Sands. He'd buy a huge house on several acres so his children, and someday their children, could visit, or live there, if they wanted to. If Emma was still part of his life then, her family could do the same. He'd be polite when his children or grandchildren mentioned Kayla, maybe even ask occasionally about how she was doing. He'd be the gracious, wise head of the family, surrounded and adored by his loved ones.

Better stick with reality, schmuck.

Starks fell asleep faster than he had in months. He barely woke when a technician came in to draw blood.

Nor did he want to.

CHAPTER 40

ABOUT AN HOUR after the lunch tray was delivered and the plates practically licked clean, Garrett Hall entered Starks's room. "Your vitals are looking good. How are you feeling today?"

Starks, who'd been dozing, sat up in bed. "Better than I have since before my life got flushed."

Garrett's smile faltered. "I'm pleased with the improvement."

"Then why the face?"

"If it were up to me, I'd keep you here as long as possible. But it's not. They wanted me to discharge you today but I fought for tomorrow. Told them observation after a transfusion should be forty-eight hours. If you continue doing as well as you are—and I insisted on personally checking you tomorrow morning—I have to discharge you."

"It was going to happen eventually."

"But was it enough time for whatever you were doing?"

"Yes. You helped me in a number of significant ways. I won't forget it."

"Can you take the phone back with you?"

Starks shook his head. "I'll give it to you tomorrow. Wish I *could* take it, with all those unused minutes, but even if I could hide it up my ass, they'd find it."

Garrett grimaced. "Full search? Even after you've been here?"

"If I had a cavity in a tooth, they'd look inside it."

"You're made of tougher stuff than I am."

"You either get tough or go crazy. Or become every asshole's victim or bitch."

Garrett looked away and said, "If you can, get more rest. Real sleep is better. I'll see you in the morning, but if you need me, buzz and they'll page me."

Starks extended his right hand. "You're a good man, Dr. Hall."

Garrett clasped Starks's hand. "So are you. Even if some people in your life forgot to remember that. Just promise me that *you* won't forget it."

"I don't like to make promises I'm not certain I can keep."

CHAPTER 41

A FEW MINUTES AFTER eight o'clock Tuesday morning, Starks lingered in what he believed might be the last hot shower he'd take alone for fourteen years and five months, unless some other medical matter or emergency sent him back to a hospital.

Still in the bathroom, he pulled the rubber thumbs from his scrub pants pockets, mixed the poisonous powders with a small amount of water, applied the paste to the knitting needle then tucked the needle into the shirt hem.

No longer able to rely on Jeffrey to get the powders from Lewis Mason, he'd get Jim to take care of this from now on. He'd have to get word to Mason about this arrangement and add Jim's name to his visitors list. No way would Jim be as excited about being in on this secret as Jeffrey had been. Jeffrey had practiced a magician's trick in order to transfer the thumbs to Starks, was proud of himself when it went smoothly. Jim was smooth, but it would never be the same.

If things were the same, he'd have called Jeffrey and confided in him about Blake, Jeffrey being the only person he would have trusted, other than Jim and Parker, with the truth. What was he going to do about Jeffrey?

It seemed that lately the question of what to do about someone was taking up a lot of his time. The people in his life were becoming like bowling pins: it was anyone's guess as to who would be left standing in the end.

He slipped on his scrub pants and shoes. His back was still damp, so he carried his scrub shirt with him into the room. Garrett Hall was seated on the bed, checking messages on his phone.

"Be right with you, Starks. Just need to . . . done." Garrett looked up. His face paled and his eyes widened. "Jesus, Starks. Reading about injuries in your file was one thing, but seeing them is—"

"Unless they pull or ache, I don't give them much thought."

"As a doctor, I'm used to seeing anything and everything. As your friend, I'm furious."

"Maybe one day I'll get them tattooed so they look deliberate. It'll make it easier to go to the beach. I'll get looks no matter what. Might as well choose why."

Garrett shook his head. "It was always like you to make a positive out of a negative. Okay, let's get this exam done."

Several minutes later, Starks asked, "What's the diagnosis?"

"The anemia is taken care of, for now. I'm sending you back with a prescription for iron tablets. Take one a day."

"How long?"

"I'd say until you're out of prison and can get decent food. If at all possible, try to keep the stress down, or find a way to deal with it."

Starks decided not to state the obvious.

They shook hands. Garrett took the burner phone from Starks and slipped it into one of his pants pockets. "Time to sign a discharge order I don't want to sign."

Starks slipped his scrub shirt on and waited.

As though fate was screwing with him yet again, the lunch tray arrived moments before the three Sands guards from before did. One guard leaned against the door to keep it open.

Another guard said, "Aw, ain't that too bad, Starks." He lifted the cover from the plate. "Looks good, smells good. Too bad you're in such a hurry to get back to your cell. Otherwise, we'd let you stay and eat every bite of this delicious food. Now, get your ass off the bed and take the stance."

The third guard secured the chains on Starks's wrists, waist, and ankles.

The first guard chuckled. "Time to do the Sands Shuffle."

They reached the locked ward door. One guard knocked on the glass. A nurse buzzed them through. She frowned and said, "All patients have to leave in a wheelchair. It's the rule."

The guard propped his thumbs on his belt weighted with a walkie-talkie, Taser, nightstick, and holstered gun. "We got our own rules, and they say he walks his ass outta here." He turned away and said, "Let's go."

The ride back to Sands was as expected: blistering from the August sun that pelted the metal van roof, jostling, and punctuated with occasional rude comments from the guards.

Starks's arrival at Sands was the same process as before of wait and wait some more, in order to eventually get to every prisoner's least favorite room.

"Welcome back, Starks," a different guard said. "You know how it goes: strip, shower, and smile for me when you bend over."

"One of these days, you might buy me dinner first."

CHAPTER 42

THE CHOW HALL was still serving lunch, but the last thing Starks wanted to do was field questions. He checked Jackson's work schedule taped to the wall. His cellmate's kitchen shift should have ended at eleven thirty. No telling where Jackson was at the moment, but he'd have to come to the cell for the three o'clock count. His own schedule showed he'd normally have worked today, getting off at four. He did want to get his phone, but that could wait.

The proper thing to do would be to go to the library and see if Sam needed him. But doing the proper thing wasn't what he wanted to do. Sure, Sam would probably get word he was back, but the manager might believe his assistant was resting. He had no desire to rest; in fact, he had no desire to do anything, especially deal with emotions that had their teeth sunk in deep and wouldn't let go.

He thought he'd dealt with the matter of the DNA results; that he'd never let it bother him again. He was wrong. Nothing he told himself quieted the voices wrestling inside him. How long would it take, if ever, for him to get past or over this newly discovered betrayal on Kayla's part, or to land in one place about how to feel about Blake?

Despite his mental state, Starks's stomach growled. He could go to the commissary for a sandwich, but he didn't feel like moving. An unopened packet of cinnamon rolls was all that was left of his stash. The simple matter that nothing of his had been taken while he was gone was an indication he had clout. Trucking someone's commissary, even when they were around, was an all-too-common practice. No one had ever done it to him. So far.

He dropped into the chair at his desk. Chemical additives had kept the rolls from going stale, not that he cared how they tasted. It was just filler, empty of real substance.

Like so much of my life.

Starks still sat in the same place, staring with a deadened expression at the wall, when Jackson came in.

"Man, I thought you were supposed to be back the same day. I asked, but no one would tell me anything. What happened? What'd the scan show?"

"It didn't show anything wrong."

"Then why they'd keep you?"

Starks shrugged.

"Something's up. For one, you, Mr. Clean, left that wrapper on the desk instead of sanitizing it before you threw it away. I'm surprised the world didn't stop spinning."

Starks leapt up and flung his chair toward the cell door. "Fuck people. They're nothing but a bunch of parasites."

Jackson picked up the chair from just outside the entrance and returned it to its original place. "Jesus, Starks. What's going on?"

"It's nothing you can help me with. I need to talk to Gabe."

Jackson pointed a finger at Starks. "I warned you about—"

"When I want your opinion, I'll ask for it. Right now, keep your thoughts to yourself."

"But—"

Starks held his hand up in protest then exited the cell saying, "Save it, Jackson. I need to talk to someone who'll empathize, and that's not you."

CHAPTER 43

S TARKS TURNED RIGHT out of his cell block and hurried forward. CO Roberts was coming from the other direction and flagged him down.

"Hey, Starks. Went looking for you Saturday and heard you were out. You okay?"

"I'm fine. What did you need?"

Roberts lowered his voice. "Still working on the cell phones."

"Don't take too long."

"I'll give the guy a push. It's just . . . he's not someone you can push too hard. His influence is one you don't want to fuck with."

"I'm counting on you." Starks continued on at a quick pace until he reached the workroom door. It was locked. Two hard knocks went unanswered. His fist was halfway up, ready to pound the metal, when the door opened.

Starks lowered his hand. "You have a few minutes?"

Gabe motioned for Starks to enter then bolted the door. "Heard you were in the hospital again. Not from a fight you lost, for a change."

"I came to talk to you, not get my balls busted. Enough people are doing that already."

"Count yourself fortunate."

"In what way?"

"One thing going for you is you got balls. Your problem is, like I told you last time, you let your emotions run you."

"From what I hear, I'm not the only one with a temper."

"My temper doesn't drive me. Logic and strategy does. Unlike you."

"What gives you the right to think you know me?"

"A degree in psychology."

"I didn't know that's covered in a law degree."

"I got two degrees. One to learn legal loopholes, the other to understand what makes people tick. Only way to know how to manipulate people is to know what motivates them."

"I've always found money to be the great motivator."

"That's why I'm smarter than you. For example, I listen. You're always running your mouth."

"Forget you, old man. I'm out of here." Starks started for the door.

"You're too sensitive for your own good. Starks."

Starks stopped but didn't look back.

Gabe pulled out one of the two chairs at a small table. "Sit down. You got something on your mind. I said I listen. I'll listen."

Starks hesitated then took a seat.

Gabe sat across from him. "Whenever you're ready."

Starks expelled a breath. "Any chance I can swear you to secrecy and it sticks?"

"In my world, talking can get you killed or invite a hostile takeover. But, it's up to you."

"I had a blood transfusion at the hospital. In the process, I discovered my first child, a son, isn't mine."

Gabe released a slow whistle. "Did she trick you into marrying her because she was pregnant?"

"No. We were married a while before Blake . . . She had fibroid tumors. The doctor told her she could get pregnant but it might be difficult. We were thrilled when we found out we . . ." Starks massaged his temples.

"If my wife had done that to me, she'd've had an accident. So would the fucker who'd knocked her up."

"This is thirteen-years-and-two-more-children-who-*are*-mine later. What would you do in my situation? That's a rhetorical question, by the way. I'm aware of the situation regarding your own wife's activities and what you did to her lovers."

"They had to be put down."

"That's not what I intended to do to Ozy. I'm not like you."

Gabe shrugged. "We each handle things our own way, and our ways weren't so far apart. You'd see that if you dropped the judgment. The question is, What are you gonna do?"

"For Blake's sake, I'm going to keep my mouth shut, unless I don't have a choice."

"She doesn't just bust your balls, she wrings them."

Starks nodded. "The thing is, I'm not sure whether she does or doesn't know he's not mine. Not sure I want to find out." Starks stared at his clasped hands resting on the table. "She knows I screwed around. Not as much as her, but a good bit." He continued to talk, uninterrupted by Gabe, about Kayla's infidelities and his, about his successes and failures in business, about Jeffrey's betrayal.

Gabe leaned back and studied Starks. "Shit happens, but you gotta find a way to climb out of that hole, and in a way that doesn't shove you back in by someone's hands or your own. Fact is, you and I didn't manage ourselves and our lives in a way that worked as well as we'd've liked. Sometimes life becomes a tempest. That happens, you gotta walk through it with the intention of coming out alive. These things going on now aren't easy, but they're happening on the outside. Here," he waved a hand, "is where your focus needs to be. You've pissed off a few people. And if I read you right, you intend to piss off a few more before you're done."

Starks gave him a half-smile. "That's a possibility."

"A probability. You have an agenda, but do you have a plan? Are you thinking ten steps ahead of where you are now, or are you gonna keep winging it the way you have been?"

"I'm not winging it. Why is everybody so damn eager to get on my case?"

Gabe pointed a finger at Starks. "You're more reactive than strategic. That's ignorant and dangerous. You're smarter than that. Another thing, you spend too much time feeling sorry for yourself."

"Wait a damn minute. I thought we were getting along."

"We are getting along. And this is me getting along so well that I'm telling you to get your head out of your ass or you're gonna get mangled." Gabe glanced at the clock on the wall. "Quarter to three. Get going so you don't miss the count."

Starks got up abruptly. "What are you, bi-polar or something?"

"I'm intolerant of self-pitying whiners. Now, get outta here. And don't wait too long to come back. We're not done talking."

"You can forget my coming back."

"You will."

"You're too arrogant for your own good."

"Pot and kettle."

CHAPTER 44

AFTER THE COUNT, Starks went to the commissary to stock up on sandwiches and anything else he'd run short of or wanted for the sake of having it. He stood in the center of the space and turned in a slow circle. His shoulders slumped and he shook his head. Extravagant shopping had been a pleasurable experience. The true measure of his success and power was the day he realized he no longer needed to care about cost. He'd busted his butt to reach that point. Giving gifts that wowed recipients was now reduced to occasionally treating inmates to the low-end basics in stock or that had to be ordered. The power of the purchase, he muttered.

Starks returned to his cell. He tossed a sandwich to Jackson, who reclined on his bunk. "Jackson, I know you're itching to ask questions or give me reports about whatever, but I don't want to hear anything or talk about anything. If that's too difficult, tough. I want to be quiet with my thoughts."

"Sure thing, Starks. Wallow away. Thanks for the sandwich. And the warm camaraderie."

"We'll talk later."

"My day is now complete."

"Go fuck yourself."

"If I could do that, I'd stay in this cell all day."

The next morning, after the eight o'clock count, Starks and Jackson met up with some of their crew who waited for them in the yard. Several of the faces were new and not ones Starks had noticed before. He nodded at each one as Jackson introduced him as the leader, but his mind was still too preoccupied with his own disturbances to remember their names; he'd leave that up to Jackson for now. All he had to do was memorize their faces.

Tank, Pete, and Stinky approached him, grinning as they showed off small dragon heads tattooed on their right hands.

Tank said, "We figured we'd earned them in the fight with Crazy D's bunch. Tat Man said you paid him to never use yours again. You weren't around to ask, but we convinced him it was okay to give us small versions that didn't exactly match yours. Hope you're not pissed we got them without talking to you first."

"It's fine."

"Hey," Pete said, "look over there." He pointed to the opposite side of the yard where three inmates surrounded another inmate who looked too young to even shave. "Those sharks are circling a guppy."

"We should go over there," Starks told them.

"Maybe we shouldn't," Jackson said. "Not our business. Enough fights find us. We don't need to go looking for them."

Several of the recruits looked back and forth at Starks and Jackson. Starks's expression made it clear he wasn't pleased. Jackson held up his hands in surrender. They followed Starks's lead and moved toward the confrontation with casual gaits and postures, stopping within hearing distance.

The tallest of the three in the confrontation said, "I'm gonna teach you a lesson today, you little prick."

The young man raised his hands. "I'm not looking for a fight. Besides, I don't think it would be a fair one." He glanced at the other two inmates glaring at him. "Your girlfriends might decide to jump in."

Other inmates in the yard who'd gathered around laughed.

The tall man grabbed the young man's shirt with his left hand. He clenched his right hand and drew it back, ready to connect. "Lookit, fellas, we got us a goddamn comedian here." He moved his face to within inches of the young man's. "I don't like comedians."

The young inmate waved a hand in front of his face. "Damn. Ever heard of a toothbrush? Or a Tic Tac? Your breath kicks like Bruce Lee."

More inmates laughed, including Starks and his crew.

One of three men grabbed the young man and put him into a head-lock. The tall man delivered blows to the young man's face and abdomen. The third man kicked the young man in the chest.

Starks moved forward and said, "That's enough. Fight one-on-one or drop it."

The tall man turned to face Starks. "Fuck off, unless you want some of this."

One of the other two said, "He's just joking, Starks. He don't mean it." He said to the tall man, "Let the kid go." Turning back to Starks he added, "We was just training this new fish. You know, teaching him some respect."

The tall man's expression reflected equal parts of rage and confusion. He shoved the young man to the dusty ground, and the three inmates started to walk away. Starks heard the tall one ask what the hell was going on and the other inmate say he'd explain once they were inside.

Starks put his hand out to help the young man up. "What's your name, son?"

"Trevor."

"Got a last name?"

"Morgan."

"I've got a group coming together." He gestured toward the men standing around him. "We're still in the early stages of organizing, but we watch each others' backs. You're welcome to join us so you don't have to worry about this kind of thing happening again, or at least, not so easily." He pointed to Jackson. "This is Jackson, my go-to guy. You have a problem, talk to him. We'll see what we can do to make your problem go away."

"I can handle myself."

Starks arched an eyebrow. "That's not what it looked like to me."

"No way I'm joining a gang. I want to get out early, for good behavior."

"Off to a good start, I see. Fact is it doesn't always work out that way. We're not like the gangs here that go looking for trouble or creating it. We're more like a club or . . ." He glanced at Jackson.

Jackson smiled and said, "Fellowship."

Starks nodded. "We step in to protect those who need it and each other." He gestured toward the bleachers and said, "Sit with us a little while."

Starks, Trevor, and Jackson sat in the center of the entourage; names and nods were exchanged.

Trevor wiped his palms on his pants and blew out a breath. "Look, I'm letting you know right off I'm not available for sex."

A few seconds of silence were followed by laughter.

Starks said, "We don't roll like that." He looked at the new recruits. "And anyone who does will wish he hadn't." He turned back to Trevor. "I just said we're into protecting others. Look, Trevor, you're obviously a prison virgin. I was one myself not too long ago. As much as you intend good behavior, one or more assholes in here are going to fuck that up for you. What you don't want is for them to fuck you up." Starks lifted his shirt.

Trevor's eyes opened wide, fear and repulsion obvious in his expression. But he wasn't alone in his reaction.

"Attractive, aren't they?" Starks said. "Trying to go it alone or with the wrong people can get you into shit you never dreamed of. Someone I liked and respected was murdered in here not too long ago. Skullars Bailey was a good person who didn't belong here, and was bigger than Tank. I saw him take out three guys like they were twigs, not that they didn't make him bleed first. He wasn't looking for a fight; he didn't want to get into trouble, either. They wanted him to be their sex toy. He refused and fought back. I saw what they did to him in retaliation. Feel as cocky as you like, but play it smart and keep your jibes to yourself." Starks smoothed his shirt back into place.

Trevor's gaze drifted to Starks's face. "Okay if I get back to you?"

"Don't take too long. In here, seconds can mean the difference between life and death."

CHAPTER 45

I T WAS GENUINE relief Starks felt when he saw Trevor standing behind Jackson in line for their breakfast trays. It was satisfying to see the other recruits, as well. Half the crew sat across from the other half, with only minor shifting of places so they weren't squeezed together. Starks made certain he sat next to Trevor.

Tank was positioned across from Trevor, and the only one of them who shoveled food into his mouth.

Trevor said, "You'd think you were eating prime rib the way you're going after this slop."

Tank swallowed and said, "I don't play around when it comes to eating. Had too many days with no food when I was growing up. Tastes good, tastes like shit—don't matter to me; it's going in my belly."

Trevor said, "Looks like you made up for lost time."

"Now I'm *doing* time." Tank laughed and added, "Three squares and a bed. This is a fucking luxury hotel compared to what I had before."

Starks cleared his throat. "I'm calling a meeting in a few days. Everyone sitting here now needs to be there. I'll pick a time that should work for everyone. We'll meet in the laundry room."

Jackson asked, "Wouldn't the yard be better?"

Starks shook his head. "Too easy to get into some kind of altercation. Just make sure you bring clothes and whatever, even if you don't wash them."

A few minutes later, Tank rapped on the table. The others did the same, causing more than a few heads to turn their way at the racket.

Jackson caught up to Starks on his way out of the chow hall. Keeping pace he said, "Sanchez told me to tell you he'll meet with you in the library at two o'clock today."

"Tell him I look forward to it."

"He wants me to be there."

"Is that a problem for you?"

"Not exactly."

"Sanchez likes you, Jackson, if like is the right word for it. So why are you acting anxious?"

"His expression made me think he's not happy about something."

Starks smiled. "I wouldn't worry about it."

"Anybody who doesn't worry about The Razor needs his head examined." Jackson trailed Starks into their cell.

"Relax. We're going to talk a little business, is all."

"I hate it when you're closed-mouthed. You keep calling me your go-to guy. I need to know what's what."

"Anyone asks you for information you don't have . . . you're a self-proclaimed mentalist: fake it."

"When are you going to get that I'm on your side?"

Starks grabbed a book and plopped onto his bunk. "I'll see you at two."

He'd learned the hard way that everyone was first and foremost on their own side, no matter what they said. Their mantra was always, "What's in it for me?" Just as in business, you had to give them enough to keep them hanging around in hope of getting more. There was a time he'd believed in absolute loyalty, before his stupidity or naivety was shattered by reality. Sure, the family he grew up with was loyal to each other, but that kind of devotion stopped there. And even then, there was more often than not a personal agenda attached. As far as people who didn't share your blood went, you could forget it. Loyalty was a word bandied about with the same indifference as the word love. Empty syllables that sounded good.

He wondered how loyal Jackson would feel after he learned what the real plan was.

CHAPTER 46

S TARKS RETRIEVED HIS phone from under the desk and tucked it away. A few minutes after two, Jackson entered the library followed by Sanchez and two of his soldiers. Starks indicated with a nod of his head for them to follow him into the office. Inmates glanced up, saw who was there, and went quickly back to what they were doing.

Once the office door was closed, Starks extended his hand to Sanchez, which the Hermanos leader shook.

Gesturing to each of his men, Sanchez said, "This is Miguel. And this one is Antonio."

Starks shook their hands then focused on Sanchez. "I'll get straight to the point: I want in on your cell phone business."

Sanchez looked at his men and chuckled, "What cell phone business?"

Jackson cleared his throat.

"C'mon, Sanchez." Starks grinned. "No games, okay?"

"The business is doing okay without you. Why would I want to split my profit even more?"

"Do you know what I did on the outside?"

Miguel stepped forward. "This is prison, amigo. What you did out there don't mean shit in here."

Sanchez frowned and said, "*Callate la boca.*"

Miguel drew back. "*Con respeto.*"

Sanchez cracked his knuckles then studied the ragged nails of one hand. "You and me, we have what we call mutual respect, but I really don't know you to do business with you."

"What if I told you I can increase your profit by thirty percent? That's after the split."

Miguel and Antonio glanced at Sanchez, who stared at the ceiling. "I'll give you a chance to prove yourself." He aimed his dark eyes at Starks. "But I warn you: I'm not someone you want to fuck with."

"Wouldn't think of it," Starks replied.

"I have a question," Jackson said. "What about the others involved?"

Starks looked at Jackson then at Sanchez. "I'm not doing business with anybody but you. You're the only one I trust."

"My partners don't like you, but money talks. If you can make us more, they'll allow you in *and* leave you alone. I'll make sure of it."

"Even Crazy D?"

"Let me worry about him."

"Then that's settled."

"That business is, but there's something I want from you."

Starks fought back the self-satisfied smile. Here it was: The agenda. "I'm listening."

"I want a two-year supply of the powders. I'll pay. Or, you can take it out of my profit."

Starks shook his head.

Sanchez narrowed his eyes and flexed his hands. Jackson glanced toward the door.

"Let me explain," Starks said. "It doesn't work that way. Each batch's effectiveness lasts only so long. Plus, it took a while to whip up the small amount he prepared for me. I'll need time to work on this."

Sanchez's grin stretched wide. "I like you, amigo. You're very . . . accommodating."

"Tell you what. I'll arrange the powders, of course, but I'll pay for the first batch, if you'll let Felipe train me and my crew to fight."

"You call it a crew?" Sanchez shook his head and grinned. "I tell *you* what, amigo," he moved closer to Starks, "you pay for these powders, and I give you a discount on the training for four men. The rest of them you pay full-price. Business is business, si?"

A brief discussion ensued about how payment would be handled, commissary always the winner. They shook on it. Sanchez swaggered out of the office with his two men trailing him.

Jackson asked, "You're seriously going to get him the powders? You realize how that would mess everything up?"

"He's not getting a fucking thing."

"Shit, Starks. The man's going to slice and dice you and sell the bits as mementos to inmates."

"I'll tell him something he'll believe, as I just did."

"You're too damn reckless. Maybe he'll be forgiving when you increase his profits, but I doubt it. He wants the power of the powders, man."

"I don't plan on splitting anything." In response to the expression on Jackson's face, Starks added, "Don't worry, you'll get your cut."

"I'm more worried about the cut The Razor will give us. What the hell, Starks? You on a fucking suicide mission?"

"I'm on a mission to take over."

A stunned moment of silence was followed by, "You're going to get us both killed."

"You know what your problem is, Jackson? You only look at the next move in front of you. You have to look ahead. Ten steps ahead."

"Sure. But when I see a cliff ten steps ahead, I don't keep going."

CHAPTER 47

THE NEXT MORNING, on his way out of the chow hall, Starks saw the man he wanted to see and quickened his pace to catch up to him.

"Felipe, I have something to discuss with you."

"Sanchez told me. When do you want training to start?"

"We'll arrange that however it works for you, but I'd like my lessons to be private. And I want a head start on the others."

Felipe stared at Starks a moment then nodded. "You don't want to be seen as less in front of your men."

"Something like that."

"I can train you at noon. If you can't make it then . . ." Felipe shrugged.

"I'll be there."

"We start today."

Starks tried to read in his cell but was too restless to sit still. He scoured and polished everything in the cell he could. He reorganized his meager possessions, and Jackson's, not caring what his cellmate might say about his things being handled. Then he repeated some of his morning exercise routine to warm up his muscles.

When the clock read a quarter to noon, Starks grabbed what he'd need for a shower after training and made his way to the gym.

Felipe was doing stretches on his usual mat. He rotated his shoulders to loosen them and said, "All right, Starks. We'll start with the basics."

Starks put his towel, clean clothes, and toiletries down. "I'm ready."

The session lasted forty minutes. Starks, drenched in sweat, was sore but satisfied.

Felipe said, "You've got some skills, but we need to work on refinement, once you've learned more. I saw you wince and rub your abdomen a few times."

"Just the scars. They'll loosen up."

"You have to tell me if anything we do is too much. Last thing you want to do is reopen wounds."

"I seem to excel at that. Not these," Starks patted his abdomen. "The ones you can't see." He pointed to his heart.

Felipe nodded. "When do you want me to start training the others?

"In a couple weeks. I'll set it up with you first."

Felipe smiled. "When you want something, you expect to get it."

"I'm just like everybody else in that respect."

"Maybe, amigo. But I think not." Felipe's attention went to the door. "My people are here."

Starks turned to look as he wiped his face and head with his towel. "Do they have a problem with you training me and my men?"

"They know better than to argue with Sanchez. Besides," Felipe grinned, "they know how much I want the tattoo."

Starks grabbed his items and headed for the door, nodding as he passed the five Hermanos soldiers. He needed to get trained and good at it soon. Same for his men. There was only so long he could stall Sanchez about the powders and the phone profits. Timing was everything. Eventually, as the saying went, the shit would hit the fan.

He and his men had to be ready.

CHAPTER 48

S TARKS RUSHED THROUGH his shower then speed-walked back to his cell. He stuffed the cell phone into his underwear then hurried to the library.

Sam Carson was seated at the desk in the office. "Your expression says you're either going to tell me why you can't be here or ask me to get the hell out so you can do whatever."

Starks grinned. "A little of both this time. I have something I have to do every day at noon. We need to arrange my morning shifts so I can be there on time."

"Always up to something." Carson rubbed his face with both hands. "Anyone else, I'd say no way or tell him to find another job. What the hell. Whatever."

"You're a good man, Sam. You can go now."

"I can—? You got some balls on you, you know that?"

"That's what women tell me."

Carson slapped his hands on the desk and pressed against it to raise himself. "Maybe one day you'll tell me what the hell you're cooking up." He reached the door and said with fake deference, "Would you like me to close the door, sir?"

"If you don't mind."

"Fuck you."

Starks laughed and sat in the chair. He retrieved the phone and punched in Jim's number. "What do you know about Gabe Bianchi?"

"Shit, man. What are you getting yourself into?"

"I'm just curious. Do you know anything or not?"

"Basic stuff. Bianchi took over when his father, Marco, kicked it."

"I know. I'm looking for more."

"He's got two degrees. One in—"

"I know about them. What else?"

"His only son planned to follow in his father's footsteps but was murdered. Rumor was one of Bianchi's soldiers did it. The guy ended up with his body in the Hudson River and his head at Fresh Kills landfill on Staten Island. I don't know if Bianchi did the deed or ordered it, but however that went down, he was convicted."

"So he might be innocent."

"I wouldn't go that far."

"What else?"

"You getting involved with this guy?"

"We've had a few conversations, but I'm not involved with him as such."

"Watch yourself. The guy's no slouch when it comes to intelligence, in every sense of the word. He's hardcore. His way of thinking and acting is in his bones."

"No worries."

"Yeah, right." Jim hesitated. "I know it's not my business, but is everything okay between you and Jeffrey?"

Starks gripped the phone. "We're fine."

"If you say so."

Starks tucked the phone away and leaned back in the chair. His chest heaved as a sigh escaped him. There was only so long he could avoid the Jeffrey matter. Sooner or later he'd have to talk to his former friend, especially as he hadn't yet figured out how to disentangle himself from the man, and it looked like it would have to be sooner. The main issue was whether to use him or abuse him in the meantime.

CHAPTER 49

STARKS'S SHIFT ENDED at four. He was still pissed at Gabe, but found his feet aimed for the workroom. The thing to do was turn around and forget that metal door even existed. It took several knocks before Gabe opened it; his expression made clear his lack of surprise.

Gabe sat at the small table and gestured to the chair opposite him.

Once seated, Starks said, "Why is it that I never see you outside this room? Not in the yard, chow hall, or even walking around."

"I go where I want to go."

"Where's your cell? When do you shower? Where do you eat?"

"Why so nosey about my business?"

"Do you get special privileges? Is that why you're allowed to isolate yourself?"

"Only privileges I get are the ones I pay for." Gabe grinned. "That's another thing we have in common." He waited for Starks to speak. When nothing was said, he asked, "What can I do for you?"

"You were insulting the last time. So was I. I'm big enough to apologize."

"For me to feel insulted, I'd have to believe you were right. Since you felt insulted . . ." He waved a hand.

"I can't catch a break with you." Starks hesitated then said, "You're right that I sometimes make decisions and act based on how I feel. Not all the time. I'm usually more methodical."

"Maybe that's how you were before your world got inverted. That's not how you've behaved in here. What I want you to get is that high-strung people may be feared, but they're not respected. They're like some bird that squawks too much and too often and needs to be silenced. Emotions have their place, but not when they cloud judgment." Gabe leaned forward and pointed a finger at Starks. "You don't walk around like a man in charge. You walk around like a man always on the defensive. Nobody's gonna respect that. It's weak. Maybe they'll go along short-term—people are attracted to flashy things—but they won't go the distance." He rested back. "Weak people make others feel afraid. People who're afraid tend to strike out because they want the feeling to go away."

"Isn't it smarter to have people fear you? Don't *you* want that, especially in here?"

"Depends on who it is and the situation. Most of the time, I prefer to work it so that loyalty or at least respect exists instead. Easier to get people to do what you want them to. Fear makes them reckless. It makes everyone reckless."

"So you scare them into respecting you."

Gabe shook his head. "You can't force someone to respect you. You want respect, you gotta demonstrate how well you can handle yourself. That way, you don't have to work so hard for it. They may not like you. They may not be loyal to you, but respect can go a long way. You," he pointed again, "keep demonstrating a serious lack of self-control."

Starks flung his arms up. "Here we go. All right, let's hear it."

"You wouldn't be in here if you'd handled the matter of your wife's boy-toy smarter."

"To use your words, pot and kettle, old man."

"I'm here 'cause I was framed."

"Me too."

Gabe's laugh reflected genuine amusement. He sobered and said, "Your lack of self-control cost you. It's still costing you." He held up a hand. "We're not talking about me. You destroyed your life. And what's he doing? He's walking around. Probably still banging somebody's wife, if not yours."

"I doubt he's banging Kayla. She's pregnant with her boyfriend's kid."

Gabe blew out a puff of air. "She's a ball wringer, all right. Back to my point. You could've handled it differently."

"I thought if anyone understood, you would."

"I do. All those men, and you targeted him, for whatever reason. Okay, so he was the guy you zeroed in on. You could've had a P.I. follow them and take photos. The photos could've been sent to the man's wife and to the wives of all those other guys your girl was boffing at the office. You gotta pick your revenge and be smart about it. You follow?"

"There are a couple people in my life who deserve revenge."

"Your friend, for one, right? Let me tell you something about that. The way things are set up, he's your primary lifeline. You still need him. A smart man uses his enemies until he no longer needs them."

"They're all a bunch of fucking liars."

"*Everybody* lies. We'd've eliminated our species long ago if we all told the truth all the time. You think I'd've ever told my nana her minestrone was too salty? Break her heart? No. I ate two big bowls and washed it down with a lot of Chianti." He jabbed the table with a finger. "We decide which lies we have to tell. We decide which lies told to us we'll let slide and which we won't or can't. The trickiest lies—the most dangerous—are the ones we tell ourselves. No one's responsible for that but us. You should think about that."

"You think I'm lying to myself?"

"I know you are. It's up to you to figure out what about and why. Some lies are okay to believe. Others can get you killed."

"Everything used to be simpler."

"Reality isn't what it used to be."

Starks scraped his chair back and stood.

Gabe said, "You're leaving already?"

"The lies we tell ourselves. It's something to ponder." When Starks reached the door, he paused and faced around. "I'm sorry about your son."

Gabe's face contorted. He turned away. "No parent should ever have to . . ." He cleared his throat.

"I know."

Gabe focused moist eyes on Starks and studied him. "Something else we have in common?"

That night, Starks lay in his bunk. Gabe had a point. But it wasn't always easy to recognize self-inflicted lies for what they were, at least not right away. Nor was it as simple a matter as the old man's comment might lead a person to believe. Maybe believing *that* was a lie as well.

Every lie he'd ever told was to protect himself—and others, especially when he believed that whatever he'd done or was going to do was either right or was his right. Was that an example of lying to himself? He'd had a right to keep Kyle's existence a secret in order to protect himself and his family. He was sure of it. It would have ruined everything to admit he had a son with another woman. Of course, others would have said if he hadn't done what he shouldn't have, there would be nothing to lie about. It boiled down to a philosophical difference. Didn't it?

Gabe said the most dangerous lies are the ones we tell ourselves.

What am I lying to myself about that Gabe seems to be aware of and I'm not?

Gabe Bianchi's life and success were a result of knowing how to lie, when, and to whom. His incarceration—a failure—was the result of someone being a better liar than him.

Fuck it. The old guy was messing with him.

Starks doubled his pillow to fit under his neck. He lay in the semi-darkness, listening to Jackson snore.

CHAPTER 50

STARKS AND JACKSON stood at attention immediately outside their cell door for the first count of the day. The guards started on their side of the corridor, ticking off names and handing out envelopes to a fortunate few.

"I never get any mail," Jackson said.

"In my experience," Starks replied, "it's overrated."

When the guards paused in front of Starks, one of them said, "Visitor's waiting for you. Must've wanted to get the worm."

"Any idea who it is?"

"Guess it'll have to be a surprise. Wait until count's over." The guards ambled to the next cell.

Jackson said, "I hope it's not your attorney. Seems whenever he sees you, it's bad news, and that's followed by one of your bad moods."

"It can't be him. They would have taken me to a private room. I always worry that whoever it is might bring bad news about my kids."

The comment had been made so easily, the words and the sentiment so familiar, and he wondered whether he should mentally segregate Blake from Nathan and Kaitlin, since they were his blood.

The count ended about fifteen minutes later. Starks tossed a sandwich to Jackson. He peeled the wrapper from his own, took a bite and said, "Might as well get this over with. See who wants to dump the latest pile of poop on my head."

"It could be good news, you know."

"I suppose anything's possible. Later."

Starks paced himself on his way to the visitation room. A little past the halfway point, he tossed the unfinished sandwich into a trash can. Once at the entrance, he hesitated then stepped forward. It was early enough in the morning that only a few inmates had visitors, making it easy to spot Jeffrey seated in one of the beige plastic chairs at the round vinyl table they'd sat at before, when their friendship was solid. That friendship was a façade, he reminded himself, because Jeffrey was a deceiver.

He wanted to tell that to the women visitors trying not to pay attention to his former friend. Taller, more muscular, café-au-lait-skinned, better looking Jeffrey, who had always turned heads and attracted women. He'd never resented how Jeffrey looked until now, and felt the contrast of his new "inmate" appearance down to his bones.

As though a mental message traveled between them, Jeffrey looked up eagerly, saw Starks standing in the doorway, but then quickly looked away; he hadn't recognized him.

Starks's heart pounded, his tongue felt thick. He scrambled to recall any bits of wisdom from his conversation with Gabe. His mind was blank. He wended his way around the tables.

Jeffrey noticed and looked straight at him, realized who he was and stood up. He held out his hand. "Bro, good to see you, but damn. I thought some whack-job was heading for me. What the fuck's happened to you? And, you want to tell me what's going on?"

"Which question would you like answered first?"

Starks pulled out a chair across the table from Jeffrey. Jeffrey's ignored hand dropped to his side. He lowered himself into the chair. "Your choice."

"I'm happy to see the look is effective. That was intentional. What happened to me was Kayla and how she's fucked everything up. As for what's going on, not much. What's going on with you?"

"Last time I came here, a guard said you told me to go fuck myself. I'm wondering what that's about. I'm wondering why you haven't called me since then to explain."

Starks shook his head. "Some of these guards are incompetent. Nobody told me you were here."

Jeffrey's shoulders relaxed. "I tried telling him it was a mistake." He chuckled. "That's a relief. I didn't know what the hell was happening. So everything's okay with you?"

"It's fine. I'm fine."

"Why haven't you called?"

"A lot's been going on. It's easy to lose track of time."

"Jim said he told you about the issue with the payments, which is one of the things I'd intended to explain. But forget all that. I have current stuff to tell you."

Starks's voice was even. "Are my . . . are the children okay?"

"They're fine. Although, you need to know I'm pretty sure Kayla's been using their child support for lavish weekends away, spa days, and redecorating the house. And we're not talking cheap. She also bought a Jaguar. Bret's driving her Ferrari."

"Wish I could see Kayla's face when she gets the shock."

"Want to tell me what you mean?"

He was surprised Jeffrey didn't already know, but kept this to himself. He trusted Parker to handle the matter the right way. "Later. What else?"

"Get this: Margaret Hessinger wants to talk to you. Seems Ozy isn't taking her divorcing him well. She thinks she can maybe learn something from you she didn't hear during your trial. I can't imagine what, though."

"Tell the lying bitch to hold her breath. If she expects any help from me, she's out of her fucking mind. What else?" Starks rested his forearms on the table. He linked his fingers and squeezed them together hard. His feet jiggled up and down under the table. He avoided looking at Jeffrey.

Jeffrey cracked his knuckles. "Kayla lost the baby."

Starks's expression went flat and his body still. He stared at his hands.

Jeffrey continued. "It happened a little over a week ago. The nanny told me things aren't going well between Kayla and Bret since it happened."

"Not my business, unless it affects the kids."

"I'm surprised you don't have more to say about that. Aren't you relieved, or something?"

Starks's face turned a deep shade of red. "Stop the act, Jeffrey."

"What?"

Jeffrey's confusion was almost convincing, which enraged Starks even more. "I can't do this any longer."

"Do what? What's got into you?"

"You. And Kayla. You still plug her when she's pregnant, or do you take a break?"

"Have you gone fucking crazy?" Jeffrey studied Starks for a second then asked, "Are you on any new meds?"

"Did it start during college, or were you sticking it in her during high school? Did you do it anywhere other than in the basement of my grandfather's house?"

Jeffrey sat fixed in place, his eyes and mouth opened wide.

"Thought I didn't know about it. Thought you'd covered your ass well enough; that I'd never find out." Starks leaped up. His chair flew into the chairs behind him. He rushed around the table, launching himself at Jeffrey. "I'll fucking kill you, you fucking snake. All this time you've been lying to me."

Two guards rushed forward. One of them pinned Starks's arms behind his back while the other one radioed for backup. Starks kicked the table over.

Jeffrey's chair crashed to the floor as he jumped back. "You've got it wrong, Starks. I swear to God I never . . . It was Phil Wright."

"Fucking liar."

"I know about the basement. But it was Phil, not me. I swear to God. I'd never do such a thing to you."

Starks struggled against the guard restraining him, ignored the shouted order to shut up and calm down. "Parker told me your college buddies said it was you."

"They're a bunch of pricks. They got irritated at how much you bragged about Kayla saving herself for you and only you. They were jealous twits who could barely get dates, much less laid. Phil told me what he'd done. I beat the crap out of him, but I didn't tell you, because I didn't think you could handle it. I figured you'd get rid of me before you'd ever get rid of Kayla."

"Liar!"

"Those guys said they were going to tell you that you were in love with a slut and didn't know it. I threatened to do to them what I did to Phil, or worse, if they ever said anything to anyone, especially you. Or if they ever so much as looked at Kayla again."

"You didn't tell me, because it was you. Sure, maybe Phil had a go at her. Maybe they all did. But you took your share of her. In my house. In the same bed where I made love to her. I trusted you, you traitorous sonofabitch."

Three guards rushed in, one of them with shackles. Starks struggled and tried to avoid them. Two guards took his arms, two took his legs. They attempted to drag him from the room. Tables were pushed aside, chairs toppled. Inmates and visitors scattered to the far walls and stayed there.

Starks yelled, "Fucking liar. It was you."

Tears welled in Jeffrey's eyes. "For God's sake, Starks, you have to believe me. Call Phil. I'll get his number for you. Please, Starks. Call him."

Starks watched Jeffrey collapse against the wall, his body wracked with sobs, his face etched in anguish.

He could imagine Gabe shaking his head at how easily he'd lost control. And barring him from ever visiting the workroom again because he was a simple-minded lost cause. The old guy was right: He was like a quiver of arrows shot without aim. If he didn't learn how to handle his emotions, especially his temper, he was going to fuck everything up to hell and back. Especially his chance to survive. But how much was he supposed to take from people who betrayed him?

Jeffrey's screams for guards not to hurt him was the last thing Starks heard before the voltage of two Tasers knocked him twitching and drooling to the concrete floor.

CHAPTER 51

ONE OF THE guards radioed the infirmary, ordering Dr. Troy to the SHU. Starks would have protested had he been able to speak. As it was, his breaths came hard and fast as he fought muscle contractions.

The steel door of the cell thudded against the wall when it was flung open. The guards put Starks face-down on the mattress-less concrete slab.

Dr. Troy was a minute behind them. "What's the problem?" he asked. "Whoa. It took two Tasers for this guy?" He barked a laugh. "Look who it is. Well, Starks, isn't this fortuitous: I'm still here. And," he leaned over and whispered to Starks, "I'm going to enjoy this." He grasped the two barbed probes in Starks's back.

A guard said, "What about anesthetic?"

"He's a tough guy," Troy replied. "It would insult him if I deadened the pain. I wouldn't want to do *that*." Troy twisted the barbed electrodes and yanked them out then did the same for the probes in the back of Starks's left thigh. Blood pooled around the holes in the shirt and pants leg. Troy opened his medical bag and handed the guard nearest him a small stack of gauze squares and a roll of tape.

The guard took them and said, "You're supposed to treat him."

"I just did. I treated him with the contempt he deserves." Troy snapped his bag shut and left whistling.

The guard sent one of the others for the first-aid kit. He cleaned and bandaged Starks's wounds then said, "You must've done something pretty shitty to that guy for him to act like that." He checked his watch. "Been about ten minutes now. If you're not feeling the effects wearing off yet, you will soon."

Alone and locked in, Starks stayed face-down, the pain in his back and leg diminished by the sensation that overshadowed it: He couldn't get Jeffrey's reaction out of his mind. The agony in Jeffrey's eyes had been genuine. He was sure of it. Despite what he'd said and done to his friend, Jeffrey had pleaded for the guards not to harm him. Starks's chest constricted, not as an effect of being Tasered, but in contrition. He wanted to believe what Jeffrey had told him. As soon as he could, he'd have the matter investigated. It would drive him crazy not to.

His muscles began to relax. Starks sat up carefully, keeping his leg and back away from the coarse surface beneath and behind him. He rested in that position for a moment, giving his body time to recover fully.

A seldom practiced feeling overwhelmed him: Remorse. Remorse for going after his friend without further verifying the information, for doubting their friendship and Jeffrey's loyalty. Remorse at the thought of what Gabe would say when he heard what had happened, if he'd even still talk to him, and it was certain the old guy would hear about it. Why would Gabe even consider spending another ounce of energy on someone so hot-tempered, on someone who didn't heed advice given to him by a person he insisted on bothering for—what? What was it that he really wanted from Gabe? He'd already disregarded everything the man had told him.

Maybe he was hoping for something similar to happen with Gabe as it had with him and Trevor. He'd felt compelled to take the young inmate under his protection, to guide him. Some guide, he thought. Trevor's hope was for good behavior to get him paroled. And here he was, big protector, in the SHU yet again, because he wasn't able to control his temper. He'd already screwed up his own chances of early parole a number of times. If he didn't wise up, he'd give Sands officials a reason to keep him for life, if someone didn't quash that option by killing him.

A knock on the door startled him. The hip-high cuff opened there was a knock on the door. The hip-high cuff opened. No tray was pushed through; instead, a familiar voice said, "It's Roberts. Come to the door so I can talk."

Starks made his way to the door. His back and leg throbbed painfully with each movement. "What is it?"

"Christ, Starks, it just doesn't stop with you, does it? You expect us to do our job then put booby traps down for us to fall into. We appreciate the money, but damn."

"You don't understand."

"I understand that I had to bribe some guys out of my own pocket so I could file a report saying your visitor attacked you and you had to defend yourself. The council may investigate, or they may chalk it up to typical behavior from you. If they check with this Davis guy, he may not corroborate the story. Same for the others in the visitors' room who saw what went down. You better pray Spencer doesn't check, for your sake and mine. They find out I lied for you, I'm fired and fined. Then they'll investigate every guard in this place."

"Okay, Roberts. You've said your piece. Any idea how long I'll be in here?"

"Spencer's talking it over with the others. He wants sixty days. The others are saying it was a misdemeanor infraction. Even they can see he'd like to stick it to you if you so much as burp in the chow hall. Starks, man, you need to get your head on straight."

"I appreciate what you're saying and why, but the last thing I need right now is a lecture. I would like to know if Crazy D is in this same corridor."

"One over."

"That's something, at least. I'm going to give you a phone number for a guy. Name's Jim. Soon as you can, meaning immediately, call him. Here's what I want you to say." Starks gave Roberts the number and details. "Tell him where I am, for now. Tell him the first thing I want him to do is tell Jeffrey I'm sorry and ask him to agree to say he provoked me, if anyone asks. And I want him to get a number for Philip Wright. One more thing. Get a cell phone to me."

"You get caught with a cell phone and Spencer will make sure you spend the rest of this year right where you are."

"That's not a request, Roberts. Ask Jackson to give you mine."

"Shit, Starks."

"Just do it."

"You trust Jackson?"

"Why do you ask?"

"He's pretty tight with Hector Sanchez."

"How tight?"

"Can't-slip-a-hair-between-them tight."

"I'll look into it, soon as I'm out of here. I appreciate your help."

"I'll get on this. Someone's coming. Gotta go."

Roberts closed the cuff. The only slightly muted cacophony of shouts and wails of other isolated inmates engulfed Starks the way darkness bears down on a frightened child at night. He was surrounded by others, yet once again in the place he dreaded most: alone with his thoughts.

CHAPTER 52

THE NIGHT WAS one of missed sleep, partly from a mind Starks couldn't quiet and partly from being unable to find a comfortable position. He'd shifted around and cursed through the long hours in the dimly lit cell, especially at the option of either putting his weight on his wounds or having his face pressed to the grimy blanket. He chose pain over pungency. Worn out, his eyelids lowered.

Just as sleep was finally coming, the cuff squeaked open and Roberts called his name in a loud whisper. Two gloved hands waggled a clean set of scrubs through the opening. Starks ignored stiffness and pain to hurry to the door.

"Cell phone's between the shirt and pants. I talked to that Jim guy. He got Wright's number and I keyed it in for you."

"Good job, Roberts. What time is it?"

"Almost five. For God's sake, don't get caught with that thing."

"Thanks. Now get out of here."

Guilt about how likely it was that he'd screwed up with his friend ate at him. There was a possibility Jeffrey had told the truth. There was a possibility that Jeffrey had conspired with Phil about what to say if Starks called. There was a possibility that Jeffrey didn't believe he would call Wright. Only one thing was certain: mistrust was exhausting.

He debated about when to place the call. Waking someone before sun-up on a Sunday morning was probably best. It would be difficult to fabricate a story and stay consistent with one or more lies if a person was half asleep, as well as caught off guard.

After three rings a sluggish voice said, "Who the hell is this?"

"A blast from the past, Phil. Frederick Starks."

"Starks? Shit. I mean, I thought you were in prison."

"They let me out for good behavior."

"That's great. But why are you calling me?"

"I'm sure you know from media coverage what I learned about Kayla's many indiscretions all those years." Wright didn't answer. Starks heard him breathing a little faster, could practically hear him try to clear the fog from his mind. "Look, Phil, if anyone understands, I do. Kayla used people for her own purposes. Still does. I'd really appreciate it if you'd confirm that she used you too. That's all."

"I need to change rooms."

After a half-minute of silence, Starks, keeping his tone calm said, "You know how dirty she played me."

"Yeah, but my involvement with her was years ago. No reason to bring it up now."

"Thanks for admitting it. But I heard you told someone it was Jeffrey, not you. What was that about?"

Wright chuckled. "Guess I was still holding a grudge." He yawned. "Sonofabitch put me out of commission for a couple days for banging Kayla and bragging about it. I'd tried to convince him to do her; told him he wouldn't be sorry for tapping that. That's when he beat the crap out of me. You know what she was like, Starks, or you do now. Always in heat."

"You're saying she approached you?"

"Whispered in my ear what she wanted to do to me and what she wanted me to do to her, all the while rubbing against me. What else could I do?" Wright laughed. "She told me how to sneak into the basement of your house. I told her she was fucking crazy; that it was too risky. Told her I knew better places. She said it was there or nowhere. I know you know what I'm talking about. You were married to her and still never let a beautiful piece get away."

"You're right, I do know. I know she meant nothing to you. I know you were a dumb fuck who thought he could do what he wanted with another man's woman. Could lie about a guy's best friend, thinking you wouldn't get caught, wouldn't suffer any consequences. What *you* need to know is that I'm not going to let you get away with it."

"C'mon, Starks. We were kids."

"You weren't a kid when you lied about Jeffrey."

"Yeah, but—"

"I believe in payback, Phil. Or maybe you'd like to act on your desire to relocate far away."

"I don't have a desire to . . . C'mon, Starks." His laugh was empty of everything but tension. "You're yanking my chain, right?" When Starks didn't answer, he said, "You do anything to me, you sick fuck, and you'll find your ass back in prison for good. So, don't you dare threaten me. In fact, I'm going to report you as soon as I hang up. Anyone needs to relocate, and fast, it's you."

"You report anything to anyone, and you'll regret it. Believe me, I'll know, and my people will act faster than you can take your next breath."

"Fucking psycho." Wright disengaged the call.

Starks had no intention of doing anything to Wright. He'd intended to scare the piss out of him and had. It was a stupid and childish thing to do, and the satisfaction he'd anticipated didn't happen as expected. Still, he'd have felt less of a man if he'd done nothing.

The next call was going to be hard but it had to be done. His hands trembled and perspiration coated his forehead. He punched in the number then began to pace the four steps the cell dimensions allowed. When he heard "Hello," he swallowed hard and forced the words out.

"Jeffrey, it's me, calling to ask if you can ever forgive me. I have no excuse other than that this place and everything that's gone on the last few years has affected me. I feel like a train hurdling along the tracks and the bridge up ahead is out. I've been betrayed and lied to so many times that I never stopped to realize you'd never do that to me. God, Jeffrey, the things I said to you. I attacked you. If you never want to have anything more to do with me, I'll understand. But I hope it doesn't go that way."

A few seconds of silence passed then Jeffrey said, "Can I talk now?"

"Say whatever you need or want to." Starks slowed his pacing and waited for the warranted verbal onslaught.

"As to whether or not we remain friends, it depends."

Starks stopped moving. He took in a ragged breath. "Name it."

"Are you going to grow your hair back?"

Starks laughed then choked back a sob. "You're saying if I grow my hair back, we can be friends again?"

"What's this 'again' business? Always. Bald, short hair, long hair, bad toupee—you're my bro."

"I don't deserve you."

"None of us are perfect, but you didn't deserve any of this."

They avoided talking about anything serious until the lights were raised to full wattage.

Soon, guards would open the window flaps to check on inmates. Then breakfast trays would be delivered. At some point he'd be taken for a supervised shower, which meant he'd have to be deft at keeping the phone in his underwear when he stripped. Another thought came to mind. He grabbed the shirt from the set Roberts had brought. A sigh of relief came when he saw it was one of his own; the hem was already prepped for him to hide the small knitting needle. He changed into the clean scrub set and transferred the needle and rubber thumbs into their respective hiding places.

He picked up the used bar of soap in the puddle of scummy water on the rim of the lavatory and made a mark on the wall, wondering if he'd have enough soap to mark the number of days Spencer kept him in the Hole.

CHAPTER 53

ACCORDING TO THE soap marks, it was Tuesday, day four, and still no word about how long he'd be in isolation. Breakfast had been unsalted liquid fake eggs and unsalted watery oatmeal, neither of which he could stomach. It almost made a nutraloaf brick seem appealing. Almost.

The cuff opened and the aroma of roasted turkey wafted through to Starks. A voice called out that it was lunchtime. His stomach growled in response as he walked to the door to verify he wasn't dreaming. On the tray held by gloved hands was a plate heaped with servings of real turkey and mashed potatoes, both in pools of gravy.

It took about two seconds to recall what happened the last time someone in isolation received an unexpected treat, one he'd arranged. "What the hell is this?" he asked. His stomach sounded its desire loud and clear. "Who are you?"

"You have friends with pull in here, Starks. You know what they say about a gift-horse. I'm not going to stand here all frigging day. You want this or not?"

"Tell whoever I said thanks."

Starks used both hands to grab the tray on the sides; the last thing he wanted to do was drop it. Something silver streaked through the opening. Starks jerked back, but not fast enough to prevent the sharp blade from making a diagonal slash across his right wrist. Blood spurted across the tray, his clean scrubs, and every nearby surface. He thrust the tray through the opening, hopeful the crash that reverberated in the corridor drew attention. A single set of footsteps raced to the left. His original bloodied shirt was on the floor a few feet from him; he used it to press hard over the three-inch slice in his skin. The wound wasn't deep, but it needed medical attention; his attacker had hit a vein. Over and over, Starks shouted for help. He felt faint so moved a few feet away and slid down the wall to the floor. And waited. Other inmates took up the call and shouted as well.

It seemed too long a time until Starks heard a curse come from the other side of the door; heard the person kick the tray aside so he could look through the small window. Starks held up the blood-soaked garment. He heard the guard radio for assistance. The lock disengaged. Three guards entered the cell; the last one in carried shackles.

"What the hell's going on, Starks?" the first guard said.

"I was lured to the door with the promise of a decent lunch and was attacked."

"Lunch isn't for another two hours."

"No way for me to know that, is there? All I knew was that I was hungry. We're wasting time and blood talking about it." He moved the shirt to show them his wrist.

"We gotta get him to the infirmary. Can't cuff him. Okay, Starks, you keep pressure on the wound. We're gonna hold onto you. One wrong move, and the doc's gonna be pulling more barbs out of you. You got that?"

"Fine. Can we go?"

Two guards held onto his arms. The third one stayed within Taser distance behind him as they sprinted, half-dragging him at times, to the infirmary.

Something new was at the entrance to the medical space: A metal detector. It blared when the guards rushed him through. He pretended to faint, which wasn't far from how he felt from shock at being attacked and panic about being caught with illegal items.

The guards hoisted him onto an exam table. One of them shut off the alarm and said, "How do they expect us to walk through there with all our gear and not set the damn thing off?"

One of the other guards answered, "It's annoying, but we don't want inmates walking out with weapons. So, get used to it."

This was an unanticipated dilemma. But at least one thing was going his way: Dr. Troy wasn't there. Instead, a different doctor—Marc Stewart, according to his ID badge—was on duty.

Once informed of who his patient was, Stewart instructed the nurse practitioner, also new, to clean the wound while he glanced at Starks's file. He frowned as he read for a few minutes then took over when it was time to add stitches.

"You're lucky, Starks," Stewart said. "Your attacker just missed an artery."

"I moved back when I saw something shiny come at me."

"That reflex kept the wound shallow. Nicked a vein, but that's shallow as well. Just messy. The other cut near it that's healed—does it have a matching one on the other wrist?"

Starks flipped his left arm over to expose the wrist and the several-months-old scar on it.

"What did you use to make the cuts?"

"Plastic fork."

Stewart sighed and turned to the nurse practitioner. "Prep a bed for Mr. Starks. I'm keeping him overnight."

The guard who'd first seen Starks said, "No way. He's in isolation. You said it's not serious. Give him a couple stitches. He can heal in the SHU."

"Mr. Starks very recently received a blood transfusion. Based on his recent tests and results, I need to keep him under observation overnight, and I need to give him something for pain. End of discussion." He turned to Starks and said, "If you even think of giving me a problem, forget it. I'm a former Marine medic with access to tranquilizers."

The guard huffed and said, "We'll inform everyone who needs to know."

Stewart studied Starks. "When was the last time you ate anything substantial?"

"Several days ago."

"That's unacceptable. What about your iron tablets?"

"Every day, except since I was put in isolation on Saturday."

Stewart faced the guards. "I've been here two days, and some of what I've witnessed is unconscionable. I want a hot meal delivered here within thirty minutes. And when Mr. Starks returns to isolation, he'd better damn well be fed and get his iron tablet every day, or there'll be hell to pay."

Starks slid off the exam table and was escorted to the secure patient section. The guards left grumbling.

"They're not happy," Starks said.

Stewart shrugged. "Not my problem."

"You're a huge improvement over the last doctor. Although, I'm being gracious by calling him that. He's a sadist with a license to practice on prisoners. Speaking of him, you might need to check the wounds on my back and on the back of my left thigh. Dr. Pain removed Taser hooks with no anesthetic and his bare hands."

"That guy deserves a Code Red. But he's out of here for good. Let's get your clothes off—they're ruined, anyway—and let me take a look."

"I'll need some of my own clothes from my regular cell. And, before we do this, I need the toilet."

Stewart pointed. "Bathroom's there. And," he pulled something white and folded from a nearby cabinet, "here's a hospital gown. Put your clothes in the receptacle marked as hazardous waste. While you're at it, wash off the blood. Everything you need's in there."

Starks closed the bathroom door and leaned against it. Too many trips through airports around the world had taught him that cell phones and even aluminum foil gum wrappers set off sensitive metal detectors. There was no way he could take the phone and needle with him when he left without setting off the one at the entrance. Nor could he dispose of the items with his scrubs. The alarm would trigger when the hazardous waste bag was removed, and he'd be linked to the illegal items or at least be the number-one suspect. It wouldn't be difficult to replace the items, just inconvenient. Jackson or Roberts could get another phone, and knitting needles came in pairs: he knew where Jackson kept the brother to his needle hidden.

A quick glance revealed the only place to hide them was in the small air vent on the back wall. The two screws had slight rust on them. He tested one screw with a thumbnail; it moved. He turned the water on then removed the screws and cover. After wiping prints off both items, he hid them as far back as he could inside the vent. It would be a bitch to lose them, but a bigger bitch to be caught with them. He wanted to get out of the SHU sooner than later.

The fake thumbs in his pockets were put on top the small stack of folded towels. Once he was clean and in the gown, he slid the thumbs on, rubbing the edges until they blended with his skin. There had never been a reason to sleep with them on. There was a first time for everything.

I don't need all these fucking complications, he thought.

CHAPTER 54

STARKS DRAGGED HIS eyelids open as the nurse practitioner positioned the tray table, with breakfast on it, in front of him. He sat up and remembered the thumbs, feeling for them with his fingers. One was missing. He thanked the nurse and waited until he left, then hunted for the rubber appendage, glancing at the large window occasionally to make sure his somewhat frantic search wasn't observed. The thumb was under the covers. Starks smoothed it into place. As soon as his heart slowed its racing, he began to eat. Despite what the doctor had said, it was possible they'd lie to Stewart about what they fed him once he was back in isolation. This might be the last so-called decent meal for who knew how long.

Stewart entered the secure space and dropped clean clothes on the end of the bed. "Those are from your cell. You should feel rested this morning. I gave you something to make sure you slept."

"It worked."

"Your vitals are good and your color is better. No reason to keep you here." He kept his gaze on Starks and said, "I checked your prison file; I was curious about why you're in isolation. Not your first time there. Maybe you should give some thought to making it your last."

"If it were solely up to me, it would be. If you try to stay out of trouble here, there's always someone eager to force you back in."

Stewart looked like he wanted to say something then changed his mind. "Get dressed. The guards will be here soon."

"I appreciate everything you did for me. And I'm relieved you're a real doctor, not a psycho quack. Just so you know, there are some decent people in here."

"And I'll probably have to sew them up at some point as well. Come by in two days so I can check how everything's healing and change the bandage. If anything bothers you before that, come in right away."

Stewart left. Starks took his clothes to the bathroom. He washed his face and ran a hand over the stubble on his head, smiling at the memory of what Jeffrey had said. His smile faltered when he opened the bathroom door and found two guards waiting for him. "I'm ready," he told them. He nodded at Stewart on his way out and congratulated himself for his decision when the guards made him walk through the metal detector alone. Satisfied that he wasn't leaving with anything he shouldn't, they put the shackles on his ankles, waist, and left wrist and escorted him back to the SHU.

The lock clanged firmly into place when they left him alone in the cell. He sat on the concrete bed, his back against the wall, knees bent, and thought about his attacker, who could have acted on behalf of any one of the people he'd antagonized. But it was more likely someone acting on instruction from Crazy D. Any real leader in here had guards on the payroll. And, he realized, it was possible that one or more guards could be double-teaming him. It was a disquieting thought. Was there a way he could identify every crooked guard at Sands and get them on his payroll, to mitigate that possible problem? He laughed at himself. Such a task would be not only involved, but would take too much money. *One problem at a time, Starks.*

He'd have to deal with Crazy D at some point, but he wanted to find out who, in fact—not rumor or supposition—was responsible for this latest, albeit feeble, attack. And it had been feeble. The most anyone could have done from the other side of the door was a moderate injury, unless they poisoned the food. Another unsettling thought.

This wasn't a murder attempt, it was a warning: *I can get to you if I really want to.* Now, it was a matter of confirming who'd sent the message. And paying them back in kind.

CHAPTER 55

A FEW HOURS LATER, the cell door opened and CO Roberts stepped in. "Heard about the attack, Starks."

Starks held up his bandaged right wrist. "My question is, Who set it up, who gave the order? I'm banking on Crazy D. Since he's still in solitary, he had to involve a guard. How else could someone legitimately get by the video cameras?"

"Spencer reduced Crazy D's confinement time; he got out Monday afternoon."

"Why'd Spencer do that?"

"No idea. Every guard in the SHU is under scrutiny now. But we're all being more cautious. Warden's talking about making us wear body cameras with audio. Lucky for us it's not in the budget and can't make it in there for another year."

"That would certainly screw us," Starks replied. "Why are you here?"

Roberts smiled. "Taking you to your cell. Doc Stewart chewed Spencer's ass about you being attacked with more than one Taser for a relatively minor infraction, then abused by his predecessor, and then knifed by someone while in what's supposed to be a highly secured area. His words, almost verbatim."

"Stewart's not one to take crap from anyone, and he's a conscientious doctor. I owe him one for getting me out of here." Starks extended his arms.

"Sorry about the shackles, Starks. I'll put them everywhere but your injured wrist. And, considering the atmosphere, it's probably best if we do this transfer with no talking."

Inside Starks's cell in D-Block, and once the restraints were removed, Roberts faced Starks, his discomfort obvious. "You said if you were ever injured, you'd cut our pay in half. Considering all what's happened lately, that gonna happen?"

Starks made Roberts wait then said, "No. But if you guys don't run better interference, it will."

Roberts expressed appreciation and left.

Starks stood alone in the center of his cell. He longed for a hot shower but decided that wasn't smart. An attack could happen just about any-where, anytime, but going to the showers alone and injured would be ask-ing for it. He'd been a bit too stupid a bit too often lately. Jackson's word played across his mind: Reckless. Gabe had also used that word.

As it was, there were more immediate tasks to take care of.

Jackson's extra knitting needle was where it was supposed to be. Starks prepped it and tucked it into his shirt hem. He was pleasantly surprised to see his cell phone still inside the book. Roberts had played it safe and got-ten the phone from outside, on his own time and dime. On my dime, he told himself. He recalled Roberts' comments about how trustworthy Jack-son really was and smiled. Roberts had decided involving Jackson was too big a risk.

It was five after noon. Some of his men would be in the chow hall. He could get a few of them to agree to protect him while he got the shower he needed and craved.

The chow hall was crowded, but the number of men waiting in line for trays had whittled down to four. That wouldn't last. The next wave would arrive soon. Starks made his way to the line. A number of inmates he didn't know made a point of telling him hello. He surveyed the tables, looking for members of his crew and picked out Hector Sanchez first, who gave him a thumbs-up. He nodded and wondered what that was about. Two tables over had Crazy D and several of his gang at it; some of them glow-ered at him, some snickered. Darren's expression should have scared him, but it didn't. It did amplify his desire to deal with the man in the only way he'd understand, or as his grandfather used to say, *Some people need to be talked to by hand.*

Starks got his tray and made his way to the table where Tank and several of his crew sat. His crew greeted him with smiles and atta-boy praises. Inmates at other tables waved.

He took a seat across from Tank and said, "*What* is going on?"

Tank grinned. "You said you were going to do something about Troy and his lackey, and you did. Some of those guys had a reason to go to the infirmary. Said it was the first time they felt like human beings since they been here. Word got around."

"I'm glad it worked out, for my sake, as well as theirs." Starks looked at Trevor, who sat one man over from Tank. "Nice to see you're still with us. You made a wise decision."

"Seemed logical to me. I always try to use logic when—" Trevor's focus shifted to behind Starks. He scowled and said, "Assholes. There's a guy slightly newer than me over there. Some guys are harassing him. We should rescue him."

For a few moments, Starks watched the inmates torment the short, slender young man. Trevor was right, of course. But he'd only just been released from solitary and was in no hurry to return. "Not our business," he said.

Trevor's eyes opened wide. "Not our business? The poor guy doesn't stand a chance. You helped me. Why won't you help him?"

"I helped you because you amuse me."

"Big thanks. But I'm not here for entertainment purposes. Besides, maybe he's even more amusing than I am."

"I said no."

"That's fucked up, Starks. I'm going over there and inviting him to join us." Trevor started to rise.

Starks hissed, "Sit your ass down."

Trevor ignored him. He was halfway up when Tank's arm reached around Pete, gripped Trevor's shoulder hard enough to make him wince, and then shoved him back into his seat.

Tank pushed his face in front of Pete's. "When Starks talks, minnow, you listen. We look for trouble if Starks tells us to look. If he says yes or no, he's got a good reason. You like to be *lo-gi-cal*, well, logic this: The man just got outta the fucking SHU. Your sorry ass gonna put him back in there the same day he got out? You want to spend time in there, yourself? Put all of us in there?"

Trevor's cheeks flamed. "They shouldn't be allowed to get away with that."

Starks said, "There's a lot in this world that isn't right, kid." He wanted to know what was going on behind him but didn't want to watch if he wasn't going to act. He said to Tank, "Tell me what they're doing."

Tank nodded. "One of 'em just dumped the fish's full plate upside down on the table and hit the guy in the head with the plate. Not hard enough to hurt him bad, but it didn't feel good."

Starks didn't have to look to know the eyes of his men were focused on him, waiting to hear what he had to say. "Have they stopped?"

"The guy's getting up. He forgot to rap on the table. Guard's chewing him out, making him pick up the mess. Here he comes."

Starks and his men watched the young man walk, head down, to dump his tray. Someone threw a bread roll at him; it hit the back of his head then fell to the floor. The young man picked up the roll and bit into it as he made his way to the exit. The four inmates who'd harassed him and several at their table laughed; others grimaced.

The slight-framed inmate stopped in the doorway. He turned around slowly, pointed at the four men and spoke, struggling through his stutter to get out the words "You'll regret this."

The four men laughed even harder at the staccato pronouncement, and stopped only when a guard told them to settle down.

Tank shook his head and turned to Starks. "I'd spell that t-r-o-u-b-l-e. And I wouldn't be surprised if it pays us a visit sometime in the future."

"No reason it should," Starks said.

"No disrespect, but you're like a magnet for trouble. Like ants to honey."

"Frankly," Starks said, "I'm tired of getting stung by venomous creatures and having to suffer and heal."

Pete stopped chewing and said, "What's that mean?"

Starks felt weariness press in on him. "I'm not sure yet."

CHAPTER 56

STARKS ABANDONED THE idea of a shower. He couldn't shake the confusion about what he was feeling and didn't want to have to carry on a conversation with anyone. He made one quick stop to replace the two damaged scrubs sets then headed for his cell.

Jackson showed up about fifteen minutes later. "Heard you were back, and that you got knifed. Through the damn cuff. How's the injury?"

Starks was stretched out on his bunk. He glanced at his bandaged wrist and shrugged.

Jackson pulled his chair from under his desk and sat. "You PMS-ing on me, again?"

"I've got a lot on my mind."

"If you talk about it, some of that mental clutter can empty out."

"I don't think it would make any sense. It doesn't make sense to me. Not yet, at least."

"Try me."

Starks sat up. He rubbed his hands back and forth on his pants legs. "I feel like I'm unraveling, and I don't know whether I want to stop it or wait and see what happens."

Jackson whistled and leaned back. "What cranked that engine?"

"I don't know if it was any particular thing or if it's everything. I think I'm going in one direction and then find myself off course."

"Man, that's called life. You zigging along, and then life zags you. You gotta roll with it. You know?"

"I used to wake up every morning knowing who I was, what I could expect from myself and my life. Then I discovered some of my reality was a big fucking lie. I'd been strutting around, all the while being a fool and the only one who didn't know it."

"Your ego got sucker-punched by the truth."

Starks glanced up at Jackson then lowered his head again. "Yeah. And the punches keep coming. I've got scars inside and out. Like I'm being shredded strip by strip. I keep thinking I've done what was needed to stop it, and then . . ."

Jackson nodded. "Either someone takes a piece out of you or you set yourself up for it to happen."

"Something like that."

A guard called out from the door. "Starks."

Starks and Jackson jumped. At the same time, Jackson said, "Make a noise or something," and Starks asked, "What is it?"

"You have an appointment with the counselor at two. Be on time."

"I'm not talking with any counselor but Matthew Demory. When he's back, I'll go."

"He's back."

"When did he return?"

"What's it matter?" The *clack* of the guard's nightstick against cell bars diminished as he continued to the end of the corridor.

Jackson said, "How do you feel about talking with Demory again?"

"I have to remember to tell him he's got good timing."

CHAPTER 57

I T HAD BEEN a few months since he and Demory had seen each other. The first time he'd met the counselor two guards had taken him to his appointment in shackles, which were left on during the session. His attack on Boen Jones and other disruptive behaviors had resulted in an extended stay in the SHU, which led to his failed attempt to end his life. Prison officials foisted weekly counseling sessions on him. He'd resented Demory initially then had come to find time with him useful, if for no other reason than to vent about Kayla. In the several months they met for sessions, a lot occurred, to both of them. They shared a history. It was limited in some ways, and deep in others.

Starks paused outside the office and peered through the double-paned security glass on the top half of the door. Demory was in his brown leather chair at his desk, scribbling on a tablet, as usual. He paused, holding his pen about a half inch off the paper. More silver mixed with brown at the temples of Demory's thinning hair. The counselor had dropped a few pounds; the buttons on his shirt still strained against the fabric but no longer seemed moments away from popping off.

The office looked the same: Pale blue walls with aqua lines curved like waves on the ocean, faux Oriental rug under the maple desk. Several drawers of the maple filing cabinet were open, with folders raised askew and papers sticking out. The urge to put the small mess in order was replaced with a smile.

Starks knocked and waited. Demory looked up, grinned, and waved him in.

"Starks! I was told you look different." He pointed to the tattoo. "Added a little color to your life. Good to see you again." Demory went around his desk, his hand extended. They shook then Demory returned to his chair.

Starks positioned the extra chair two feet in front of the desk and centered so that he faced the counselor straight on. "I wondered if you were ever going to come back to this stimulating institution."

"I was gone a little longer than anticipated. Had some family matters to attend to. I'd ask how you are but I read the updates in your file, and," he gestured toward the bandage, "I can see some of it. I'd hoped you'd changed your mind about talking to my substitute while I was out."

"I made it clear that no way was I going to start from scratch with someone keeping your chair warm."

"I wish I hadn't had to be away. You've been a little too busy in my absence, none of it the direction I'd hoped you'd go in while I was out."

Starks shrugged. "I aim for the right direction and someone diverts me."

"We've talked about this before. If you believe that, you're letting others control your life."

"They're doing a damn good job of fucking with it." Starks slouched back in the chair. "Pretty easy to be judgmental when you can leave for the day or get out of here for an extended time. And not because you're unconscious."

"I'm not judging you. I'm asking you to claim responsibility for your decisions."

Starks stood up. "I'm sick of everybody thinking I'm always wrong, of being judged." He raised his shirt and pointed to his scars. "See these?" He ripped the bandage from his wrist. "And now I've acquired a new one. If this crap keeps happening, I'm going to have to change my name to Lionel, for all the tracks people are putting on me. You wouldn't last a day in here, Demory. All your reasoning wouldn't make a damn bit of difference. There are some people in here you can't reason with; you can only react to them. You can only do your best to stay alive and intact. It's like treading water while the sharks circle. Just when you think you're okay, one or more of them sneaks up from below and bites a chunk out of you."

"I didn't mean to upset you, Starks. And I'm not judging you. I want to help. That's all. And you know very well there are people everywhere you can't reason with. Their unreasonableness is their problem; how you respond is yours. Now, why don't you sit down and tell me what's bothering you the most. Something is. Don't deny it."

Starks's shoulders sagged. He stayed where he was for a few seconds then returned to the chair. "I thought Kayla screwing all those men was the worst kind of betrayal. I was wrong." He dropped his head into his hands and rubbed his face hard. "I have DNA proof that Blake isn't mine."

"A counselor isn't supposed to say this, but Jesus. I imagine you have more feelings about that than you know what to do with. And, on top of everything else."

"You're lucky you only have to imagine them. I've loved and taken care of that boy for thirteen years. Thirteen years based on a lie. You see this?" Starks jabbed a finger at the center of his chest. "I feel like my fucking heart's been ripped out. I don't know what the hell to feel anymore. If I'm angry, people tell me I'm wrong. If I'm upset, people tell me I'm wrong. I'm getting damn tired of it.

"I did everything for so many people and instead of seeing me as kind and generous, they saw me as weak and gullible. They used me, took advantage of me. Sure, Kayla more than anyone, but that level of deceit is something I have to contend with every day in here. Any choice I make in here is driven by that. Everyone sees the crap I get into, but I'm doing some good, as well. But, who's paying attention to that?"

Demory's cell phone buzzed. He slid it from his pocket, silenced it, and placed it to his right on the desk. "Sorry about that. Please keep going."

"I have to be on alert every second of the day. I walk around wondering who's going to stab me in the back, literally and figuratively. That gets to you after a while. As for my so-said gang activities, it's a protective measure. The purpose is defense, not offense."

"I do see your reasoning, and we need to discuss it. But I want to discuss the matters of Kayla and Blake first. That's too huge to skip over. I know you feel crushed because of what you've learned, but one of the things I've been trying to get you to do is look at this from more than just your perspective."

Demory put his pen down. "Kayla cheated on you; you cheated on her. She had another man's child while married to you. You had a child with another woman while married to her. Whether Kayla knows about that child or not doesn't change the fact that each of you did pretty much the same things to each other. Maybe she cheated on you first, but—"

"She did."

"You didn't know that. Your cheating wasn't tit-for-tat. Your infidelity was yours alone, with no care, seemingly, about how it would affect her and your relationship."

"Sounds like you're siding with her. Again."

"I'm not taking anyone's side. Never have. I'm here to try to help you see the facts, rather than just your interpretation of them. Both of you wronged the other. Repeatedly. You can see that what Kayla did was wrong, but until you see that what you did was wrong, you're going to keep stumbling through life like a man newly blind."

Starks didn't respond.

"Look, Starks, when you accept your contribution to what happened then, and is happening now, your overall perspective will shift. When you have a different perspective, you'll make different choices. Better choices. We've covered this before. If you wait for Kayla or anyone else to change first, before you alter your thoughts and behaviors, you may wait forever. How long do you really want to keep suffering in this way? Pain happens, but it's our choice to suffer or not. You were a big man out there. You need to be a bigger man than Kayla or anyone in here who wants to drag you down with them. Is any of this registering?"

Starks exhaled hard and stayed silent. He focused on the small window behind Demory. A pigeon landed on the sill and looked in at him. It bobbed its head and seemed to study him before it flew away.

Demory picked up his cell phone. "My phone was running slow. I found out it had a virus. Someone told me to do a hard reset. They forgot to tell me to back up my information. I lost everything on there. Took me a while to put most everything back, but the phone's running better than ever now."

"What's that have to do with me?"

"Sometimes in life you need a hard reset. You'll lose some people and things you care about, but gain others. Coming to Sands was punishment for something you did, but it's also an opportunity for a hard reset. Things happen in our life for a reason; it's up to us to figure out what that is. Do a hard reset, Starks. Start fresh. Put the past where it belongs." Demory put his phone down. "Now, I'd like to talk about how you feel about Blake."

Starks got up. He kept his tone moderate. "I'm surrounded by lunatics, assholes, and pseudo philosophers. I thought I could talk to you; that you'd get what I'm going through. You're too busy telling me I need to fix myself, like your damn phone. As though it's that simple. If you can't understand where I'm coming from, with everything you know about me and my life—and you don't know everything—you won't understand anything I have to say about Blake or anything else that's happened since you left, much less how I feel.

"Don't ask to see me again. Don't insist on sessions. If you do I'll sit here and contemplate my navel while you pop out platitudes. This session is over. We're over. The only thing I have to say is fuck everyone. The only way anything or anyone in here or out there is going to change is if I make them do it."

"I'm sorry to hear that's how you feel. If you change your mind, I'm here for you."

Starks got to the door. He turned the knob then looked back at Demory. "Get a clue. Then do your own fucking hard reset."

CHAPTER 58

S TARKS SAT ON his bunk with his back against the wall. The book with the cell phone hidden inside was open and propped on his bent knees. The call was necessary, but he also knew it might be unpleasant, at least in part.

"Hi, Mom."

"*Hmph*. If you're calling me, you must want something. What's wrong now?"

He knew her well enough to visualize her posture: Her right arm pressed against her stomach as her hand supported her left elbow, the phone cradled in her left hand and pressed hard against her ear, her lips nearly a straight line. "How are you? How's the family?"

"Other than feeling unimportant to you, we're all fine." Lynn Starks was quiet a moment then asked with a softened tone, "What about you, son?"

"I'm doing as well as I can."

"I hate every bitch and bastard who put you there."

"I know."

"Did you call because you missed your mother, or is there something else?"

"I do miss you, but you're right about the something else. It's about the children."

"She hardly lets me see them. Says their schedules are full is why there's no time for me. That's bullshit. Are they all right? Did their bitch of a mother do something to them? Has she abandoned them?" Her voice became higher and thinner. "Did that sonofabitch boyfriend do something to my grandchildren?"

"Calm down. It's nothing like that. They're okay. I need you to take over the financial aspect of their care. Parker should be contacting you soon."

"Kayla will never allow it."

"She'll have to. Parker told me that since I'm in prison and not earning, I'm not obligated to pay anything. However, the kids aren't going to suffer. I instructed him to do what's needed to get payments for the kids sent directly to you." Starks explained how the new arrangement would work.

Lynn said, "I heard what the slut was doing with the money meant for my grandchildren. I also saw her get into her flashy new car the other day. She had to move the seat back when her pregnant belly was cramped by the steering wheel."

"I guess you haven't heard. Kayla lost the baby."

Lynn Starks cackled loudly. "Serves the slut right. Guess she'll have to go to an exclusive spa to get pampered now. She's done that a few times since you've been in prison. I guess your sentence is too hard on *her*."

"Check in with Parker to see what his progress is. Ask Jeffrey to be the go-between, if you need or want one."

"The less I have to deal with that tramp the better. You should have listened to me all those years ago. I knew what I was talking about. But no, you let your lust—"

"I have to go. People are waiting for the phone."

"Let them wait. I have something important to tell you. There's someone I want you to meet."

"Who?"

"You won't be in prison forever. And, I heard that with good behavior you can get out early. You'll start over, and that'll be easier if you have a proper wife."

"Where's this going?"

"I ran into Samuel Boseman. You remember Samuel and his daughter Jamila. She's unmarried but wants to be. She'll even wait for you. You know theirs is a good family."

Starks went still, wondering if his mother had lost her mind. "You know I'm with Emma. She's waiting for me. When I get out, we're getting married."

"And you'll make yet another mistake. She's not for you, son. She doesn't cook or clean. And she doesn't want any more children. You can't be happy like that."

"First of all, I can hire a maid; my wife doesn't need to be one. Second, between us, we have enough children. I don't want anymore. I'm almost forty now. If I do have to serve my full term, I damn sure don't want to get out and start another family. Third, Emma makes me happy. She's a far better person than Kayla could ever hope to be. She's intelligent, financially independent, beautiful, and kind-hearted. Fourth, Emma does cook; I just don't expect her to do it for every meal. She cooks for her child all the time."

"She may be better than Kayla, but she still wants a life of luxury. You need a woman who'll give, not just take."

"Emma's very giving."

"Jamila is right for you. She's old-fashioned, like me. We've spent hours on the phone and talking over coffee. She can't wait to meet you. You listen to me; she'll make a good wife."

"Just not for me. I'm not interested. My time really is up. I have to go."

Lynn sighed. "I'm not going to discourage Jamila. Emma's not going to wait for you. Do you hear me?"

"And if Jamila does wait—a woman who doesn't really know me but knows I'm in prison, what does that say about her?"

"Why don't you ever listen?"

"I'm hanging up before I get into trouble."

"Emma has a child. Do you really want to raise a child who isn't yours?"

Her words pierced him, and he wondered if she'd feel the same if she knew the truth about her "first" grandchild. For a fleeting moment, he saw reflected through his mother, his own question about the quality of love and his confusion as to how to feel about Blake.

"Say hello to the family for me."

Starks turned the phone off. His chest was tight. He didn't want to think about the Blake matter right now. He hadn't given much thought to Emma for a while; too many other things had occupied his mind. He hoped she was strong enough to wait for him, but his mother might be right about that. Was it even fair to hope Emma would still be there throughout his entire sentence and when he got out?

One more bitter pill life might expect him to swallow.

CHAPTER 59

HE NEEDED AIR. Starks put the phone back into the book and returned the book to the bottom of the stack. The digital numbers on the clock showed it was five minutes to three. After the count, he'd check out the yard, see who was outside.

The idea of losing Emma nagged him. Maybe he should marry her now. That would mean they'd be allowed conjugal visits. And although he'd told his mother he didn't want any more children, if he got Emma pregnant, she'd never leave him. He checked his reflection in the mirror. If he decided to propose, it wouldn't be until his hair grew out and he looked more like the man Emma loved to ride or wrap her legs around. He'd have to take his chances about the tattoo. He could always tell her that inmates held him down and forced him to get it. He could lie about his hair as well. In for a penny, in for a pound, as his grandfather used to say. She'd believe him, feel sympathy for him. She'd marry him to make him feel better.

He glanced at his stitched wrist and thought of all the scars his body now bore. Emma had often made it a point to tell him his body was perfect. How would she feel about it now? If he had this many scars after just several months, what was he going to look like when he got out? Bile rose in his throat. Starks turned the tap on and slurped water from his hand. It almost helped.

Inmates hurried to their cells as the count was called. Afterwards, Starks made his way through the two corridors, to the door that opened to the yard.

The heat encaged him as soon as he walked into the enclosure. It hadn't rained for days. Patches of brown covered more area than anything green, not that there was ever much of anything green.

He scanned the area. A few members of his crew had a modified basketball game going with several of Hector Sanchez's gang. He went to where they were playing; declined the request to join them, saying he preferred to watch. The last thing he was in the mood for was games. Any kind of games, he told himself. Nor could he play with his wrist, which he needed to get re-bandaged.

Demory was playing the game of counselor, not realizing that what he was really doing was playing the position of those who see themselves as righteous. So easy to condemn others when you don't have to live their life.

His mother was playing the game of matchmaker, a woman who'd been divorced twice and gave up on intimate relationships. Kayla was a game master. Once again, Jeffrey was the one who was true.

Jeffrey had said that Margaret Hessinger wanted to talk to him. Why would he talk to a woman who'd lied in court and caused him to end up here?

Maybe he should talk to her. He could tell her specifics about Kayla and Ozy not revealed during the trial. Maybe even make some stuff up. Really drive the stake in and twist it. But, maybe he didn't need to make anything up. Kayla's former best friend, Jenny Hayes, knew even more than she'd been allowed to say during the trial, more than she'd been willing to tell him.

The prospect of such a conversation energized him. He'd talk to Margaret. But first he needed to talk to Jenny.

He heard the shout of "Head's up" a second too late. The basketball struck him in the torso. Apologies flew from both teams. He waved them off like gnats, tossed the ball back, and made a mental list. The first thing he'd do was add three names to his visitor and call lists: Margaret, Jenny, and her husband, Richard, just in case. Then he'd call Jeffrey to set up a visit from the Hayes.

Then he'd see Margaret. He hoped his original decline of a conversation hadn't ruined his chances. Maybe Jeffrey hadn't gotten back to Margaret yet.

He turned to head for the entrance and was stopped by one of his newest crew members, who ran up to him panting hard. "Starks. I was looking for you."

"What is it?"

"Trevor. Fool got into a fight with Tank. Doesn't know when to stop or listen."

"I've forgotten your name."

"Mike."

"Catch your breath and tell me what happened."

The inmate bent over, hands on his knees, inhaling and exhaling a few times. "Trevor was cracking jokes on Tank. Tank told him to stop. He didn't. Things got out of hand. I'm telling you, man, Trevor's mouth is gonna get him damaged."

Starks frowned. "Where are they now?"

Mike looked toward the entrance. "They just walked out."

Starks blanked his expression as he watched them approach. He looked both men over. Neither man had any obvious injuries. "What the hell's going on with you two?" The several curious crew members stopped playing and joined them. Sanchez's soldiers respected the privacy a leader might need with his men.

Trevor answered, "Nothing. Some people can't take a joke, is all." His smile was quick and just as quickly gone. He toed the dirt.

Tank shrugged when Starks looked at him. "Kid needs a muzzle."

Trevor looked up. "You're too sensitive. Like a girl. And, Starks said I'm here because I'm amusing."

"I ain't amused, Trev," Tank said. His expression was unreadable when he turned his gaze on Mike.

Starks noticed. The code was clear about snitching to an official, but this was among them. Still, he didn't think Tank appreciated Mike being a tattler. For that matter, he wasn't sure how he felt about it, either. "Let me make this plain: No fighting can happen among us. We stick together. Anyone has a problem with a member of the crew, talk to me. If there's anything to settle, I'll do it. And, Trevor, respect the men who have your back."

Tank said, "Pups sometimes need a swipe when they get too frisky. Nothing to worry about."

Starks shook his head. There was never nothing to worry about.

He left them in the yard. The first stop was to add the three names to his lists. The second stop was to the commissary for a couple of sandwiches. Back in his cell, he checked to make sure it was safe then called Jeffrey and asked him to set up a visit with Richard and Jenny Hayes and to tell Margaret Hessinger he would speak with her soon, but, he added, not until he met with the Hayes. He also told Jeffrey that his mother would need his help dealing with Kayla, and why.

Starks ate a sandwich, unaware of how it tasted, surprised when he noticed the crumpled wrapper in his hand clinched into a fist. There really was always something to worry about. Kayla was going to shit gold bricks when she learned about the new payment plan for the kids' expenses. She'd lost the baby, and because of that loss and the loss of easy funds, she was probably going to lose Bret, if he hadn't already left her. Would Kayla, to anesthetize her feelings, subject the children to more men? He needed someone to keep a watchful eye on the situation so the children could be protected. His mother, Jeffrey, Parker. Maybe even Jim. A nanny could be expected to do only so much.

His mother. She was searching the dregs for a wife for him, nurturing a union that was never going to happen. But he wasn't giving Emma the attention she deserved or needed if he wanted her to stay with him. He prayed his mother didn't have a conversation with Emma as well.

His still-healing wrist needed another bandage, but he was supposed to see Dr. Stewart tomorrow anyway. He'd also have to find out when Stewart would release him to resume his training with Felipe. Last thing he wanted to do was reinjure the wrist so badly that it permanently affected how well he could defend himself. Neither did he want to remain untrained longer than necessary.

Trevor and Tank had scuffled, and Mike had told on them. Was the man protecting the interests of the crew by telling, or was he an even bigger problem?

Then there was Hector Sanchez and Crazy D. He could put Sanchez off only so long about the powders he'd never get. Of course, he could continue to lie. But there was an expiration date on that as well. And whether it was Crazy D or someone else who'd ordered the attack on him while in the SHU, old Darren was going to come after him sooner or later. When Sanchez and the others involved got stiffed for the cell phone business . . .

Why don't you just dig a grave now and get it over with, Starks mumbled to himself.

CHAPTER 60

IT WAS FOUR thirty. Starks bounced between antsy and bored. Maybe the guys still had a game going in the yard. Watching them might take his mind off all the threads that needed to be woven into something he could use to his advantage.

The light outside grayed as a dark cloud wafted in front of the sun. His crew members and Sanchez's men dripped sweat; the basketball slipped from their hands as often as it didn't. Droplets sprayed off the ball with each dribble. Starks joined his non-playing crew members cheering and shouting from the bleachers.

Pete said, "Hey, Starks. Where's Jackson these days? He's been kind of MIA lately."

"He's around," Starks said. "His shift in the kitchen keeps him busy."

Pete pointed to the right. "There's that weird motherfucker from the chow hall."

Starks and the others watched as the unkempt, gangly young man walked in small circles, his gaze fixed skyward. He stopped suddenly and looked at them.

Trevor said, "Don't make eye-contact with him."

One of Tank's eyebrows went up. "Hunh. One minute you want to be his bodyguard and the next you want to ignore him. What's up with you?"

"He's weirder than I thought," Trevor answered.

The stuttering inmate laughed, as though he'd heard what was said, and then started his circling again, occasionally looking their way, all the while muttering to himself. Starks wondered if the guy could read lips.

Two inmates approached the stuttering inmate. One pushed him to the ground, the other spit on him. The young man rolled to the side before a kick from the second inmate could land.

"Weird or not," Stinky said, "we gonna let that happen?" He looked directly at Starks.

Starks didn't respond.

Stinky leaned forward. "What'd'ya say, Starks? We gonna help him or not?"

Starks felt the eyes of his men focused on him. "No."

Trevor kicked the riser. "I thought we were about protecting the weak. Looks like we're selective."

"That's right," Starks said. "And I do the selecting. If we try to save everyone in here who needs it, we'll be fighting around the clock. That is, when we're not buried in the Hole. I have my reasons for who I get involved with and when. Either you trust me or you don't."

He could see and feel the tension in his men, their bodies ready to fight on his order, the order that didn't come. Something else had Starks's attention. Another young man, obviously new, stood by himself across the yard; his fingers gripped the chain-link fence and he faced the white wall and barbed coils on top of it, just as Starks had done when he'd first arrived. Even if Starks couldn't see the young man's expression, he felt certain he knew what the new inmate was feeling: A level of shock about actually being here, fear for his safety, fear about holding onto hope in such a hopeless place. The inmate glanced to his right, showing half his face to Starks. He appeared to be even younger than Trevor.

Something inside Starks pushed him to his feet, made him walk over to the young man. He watched the young inmate's eyes widen as he went toward him, and then remembered how he must appear. He held up his hands in the universal sign that conveys no harm intended.

"Don't be scared, son." The young man's eyes fixed on his were the same shade of brown as Nathan's. He hoped to God none of his children ever had a reason to reflect the same terror in their eyes as he was seeing now.

The inmate inched away. "I don't want any trouble."

"And I'm not going to give you any." Starks held up a hand. "I swear. Relax. Before you hyperventilate. When did you get here?"

"This morning."

"That's some induction process, isn't it?"

"I feel violated."

"That's a fact. How old are you?"

"Nineteen."

"You don't even look that old. I'm Starks. What's your name?"

Wearing a stunned expression, the young man answered, "Kane Sandler."

"I knew a senator named Sandler. He your father?"

"No father. Just my mother."

Starks studied Kane's pale face etched with fear. He reminded himself that the kid was here because he'd done something that warranted it. Or maybe not, Starks also reminded himself. Then again, with a face that all but had the word *innocence* stamped on it, maybe the kid had always gotten into trouble and always gotten out of it. Because of that face. That might have worked outside these barriers, but it wouldn't work inside them. Sands perverts would see that innocence, façade or fact, as a temptation they couldn't and wouldn't resist.

"Son, you're all but flashing a sign that says 'Victim here' to some of these guys."

Kane's gaze skittered around the yard then returned to Starks. He chewed on his bottom lip and stayed silent.

"I know how I must look to you." Starks ran a hand over his head. "I did the tat and hair for effect. It works for the most part. I'm letting my hair grow back."

"It's effective, all right."

Starks stifled a chuckle. "There are gangs in here. If you're unprotected, they're going to go after you every chance they have or can fabricate. Despite how I look, I intend to protect those they'd prey on, as best I can." He pointed to his wrist. "I was on the other side of a secured steel door and still got this." He raised his shirt then lowered it when the boy gasped. "Those happened not long after I got here, because I was unprotected. I'm not saying protection is a guarantee nothing will happen to you—I'm certainly proof of that, but you're a hell of a lot better off if people know someone has your back. I have what I call a crew. We look out for each other. We're even doing special defensive training. If you're smart, and I think you are, you'll join us so you're not doing your time on your own."

"I don't want to do anything that'll mess up my chance of early parole for good behavior."

"I should put that on a T-shirt and sell it. Look, I had the same intention. Others in here don't always respect or honor our good intentions."

Kane chewed on a cuticle and looked everywhere but at Starks. "I can't do ten years in here."

"It's no real comfort, kid, but ten's better than life. What are you in for?"

"Being in the wrong place at the wrong time with the wrong people. In a stolen car containing concealed drugs and weapons. One of the weapons was used in a robbery where someone got hurt. Asshole roommate." In a sing-song voice he said, *'C'mon, Kane. You gotta drive my friend's car to the repair shop. I'd do it but I have a class then, and he's got the flu'.*" Kane's face was crimson. "Total asshole. At least my sentence was reduced because it was a first offense. My roommate disappeared right after I called and told him I'd been arrested, so no way to prove I was used."

"That sucks, kid. Word of advice: It's probably best not to proclaim your innocence. Inmates will think better of you if they believe you're guilty. And, you don't want anyone to start a rumor that you're an infiltrator here to spy on them."

Kane chewed his bottom lip then said, "What are you in for, Mr. Starks?"

"Just Starks." He grinned. "I was in the wrong place at the wrong time with the wrong people. Now, show me you can be smart. Come meet some of the guys who'll have your back."

Kane hesitated. Starks nodded his head to the left and waited. The young man let out a breath he'd been holding and walked alongside Starks to the bleachers.

Starks glanced at the young man. Nineteen; not even old enough to drink, and marking his crossing into manhood here. At least Kane would still be young when he got out. If he lived long enough. Starks inhaled, felt his posture straighten. He'd do whatever it took to make sure this kid got out of here alive. All he had to do was survive as well.

CHAPTER 61

SEVEN THIRTY-SIX. TIME to start his morning routine and be done by the eight o'clock count. Starks passed Jackson in silence, who sat at his desk reading. At the small mirror above the combination toilet and lavatory, he studied his reflection. His hair had grown a quarter-inch. He smoothed shaving cream onto his face and dragged the razor across his skin. When done, he wiped down the sink.

Jackson said, "Only you would rinse a razor you're gonna toss. What about your head? You haven't put a blade to it in days."

"I'm done with the scalped look." Starks tossed the disposable razor into the trash. "By the way, I picked up a new recruit."

Jackson grinned. "Can't have too many of those. He muscle, like Tank? A tough mother?"

"Not exactly."

"Exactly how not exactly?"

"He's about my size. An inch shorter. Says he's nineteen; looks sixteen. I bet he's the youngest inmate here."

"Man, we need recruits who can pull their weight, not mascots or pets. Or children who need their noses wiped."

Starks shook his head. "The kid needs protection. No one else in here's going to do that, not without making him their bitch. Besides, he makes me think of my boys. God forbid they ever end up incarcerated, but I'd hope someone would care enough to look after them." He realized what he'd said: My boys. A statement made out of habit. That, and out of history, he told himself. Maybe family wasn't solely about blood. Maybe it was as much about shared history. Blood didn't always result in family, as his own absent father proved. One example that immediately came to mind, one he couldn't deny, was that he'd always felt Jeffrey was as much a brother as if his mother had given birth to both of them.

"Are you listening to me?" Jackson said.

"Are you saying anything worth hearing?"

"I said we can't rescue everybody."

"I know. We have to be discerning. I chose this kid."

"Dragon has a soft spot. Who knew? On another subject, what about the Sanchez situation?"

"What about it? Are you feeling guilty about how I'm treating your buddy?"

Jackson slammed the book closed. "I don't know if people like Sanchez have buddies. But you know he literally saved my ass several times. I'd probably still be unable to sit if Sanchez and his guys hadn't fucked up Bo's plans to assault my back door. And I think you're forgetting Sanchez is called The Razor for a reason."

"I'm not forgetting anything, Jackson. You're a worrier. And a nag."

"Maybe I'll stop worrying if you tell me the plan."

"I'll let you know just as soon as I have a firm one in mind."

Jackson was about to comment when the announcement for the count blared out.

The two inmates stood next to each other in silence just outside the entrance to their cell. When the count was over, Starks said, "I'm heading to the chow hall. I told Kane—that's the new recruit—to make sure he was there so he can meet the crew members he didn't meet yesterday. You joining us?"

"Can't. Have stuff to take care of in the kitchen. I'll have to meet your hatchling later."

"If you're ready now, I'll walk with you."

Jackson clasped his hands and drew them to his chest. "Oh, yes, please. Your mere presence will keep me safe."

Starks sighed. "My own personal court jester."

Jackson bowed and swept an arm toward the corridor. "After you, your majesty."

Starks's laugh was hollow to his ears. The truth was that he wanted to be king or emperor or whatever in here, but it was taking much more effort than he'd planned on. There were too many inmates vying for the position of kingpin at Sands. Out in the world, he knew exactly how to move those people out of the way and keep them on his side, or at least doing what he wanted them to. The same tactics didn't apply now.

Nothing and no one was a given anymore.

CHAPTER 62

EVERY MEMBER OF Starks's crew but Jackson was at their usual table in the chow hall. Kane and Trevor sat next to each other chattering away like new college dorm buddies. Starks asked Pete, who sat across from them, to move over. He'd have to watch the two youngest crew members carefully. Had to make sure some of Trevor's flaws didn't transfer to Kane. Had to discover Kane's flaws. That lesson had been learned as soon as he'd started hiring staff all those years ago: Discovering their weaknesses early, as well as their strengths, saved time, energy, and money. He was already behind the curve on that one with his growing crew. No option but to trust Jackson's choices.

"Morning, everyone," Starks said as he sat. His attention was drawn to three tables directly ahead of him: The inmate who stuttered was being bullied by the two men who'd accosted him in the yard. The young man's cheeks were flush and his lips pressed tight.

Trevor turned to see what Starks was focused on. He faced back around. "I hate to say it, but the poor guy practically asks for trouble with the way he behaves. I think he has some kind of mental thing going on."

Starks said, "Maybe. But no matter what's going on with a person, a fine line exists between standing up for yourself and trying to be invisible so you're left alone. In this place especially, you risk losing, whichever one you choose."

"Yeah," Stinky said. "With some of these guys, it doesn't matter what you do. They wanna go after you, almost nothing stops them. Sorry to say it, but I think Stutter Man is as good as dead, and sooner than later."

"Don't call him that," Starks said.

"Huh?"

Starks faced Stinky. "It's an affliction, not a lifestyle choice." He glanced at the faces watching him. "Anyone in this crew makes fun of someone because of an obvious physical or mental abnormality is out. Understood?" Several of the men wore surprised expressions, but heads nodded in response.

The inmate being picked on shouted, "L-l-leave m-m-me a-l-l-lone."

The two inmates heckling him laughed. One of them said, "Or w-w-w-what?"

Inmates at that table and near the young man rapped and got up with their trays. Conversations began to die out as inmates realized something was going on. One guard on duty meandered in the direction of the potential altercation.

The two bullies took seats together at the table behind the stuttering inmate, with their backs to him. Starks kept his gaze fixed on the young man. Anger fluttered in his gut about what some people believed they were entitled to do to those weaker than or just different enough from themselves.

The guard, satisfied, walked on. Conversation volume picked up. Starks watched as the picked-on inmate put a hand under the table and scratched his leg. Saw the flicker of a smile on the young man's face that vanished as quickly as it had appeared. The young man kept his composure as he glanced around the room, unobtrusively marking where the guards were. Then he rapped lightly on the table. In one fluid motion, he swung around on the bench and used both hands to jab something into the backs of the two men. He picked up his tray. Whatever he'd used was hidden, one in each hand, and positioned under the tray, out of sight.

Both inmates who'd been attacked had done nothing more than reach a hand around to rub the area before continuing their conversation, as though bitten by an insect and choosing to ignore it after the initial sting. Neither of them noticed their mirrored gestures. There was no shouting, screaming, moaning, or writhing going on. No attention had been drawn to the impressive silent attack.

The young man emptied his tray and added it to the stack. He glanced back at the table; his shoulders shook in silent laughter. Then, as though becoming aware he was being watched, he ran his gaze around the room, until it landed on Starks.

Starks's nod was slight, so that only the young man saw it. He fashioned his expression into one that he hoped conveyed the message intended: *Good for you.* What was the trauma that had caused the young man to stutter, and how young he had been when it happened? Maybe the guy was slow-witted, or maybe he was cagey as hell. Maybe some of each. Whatever was going on, Starks wanted to know for sure. He never liked to bet on anything without knowing something about the odds.

The young man had done something to the two inmates who were intent on tormenting him. It was akin to and far less incident-provoking than his retribution had been on Big Bo Jones.

Starks kept what he'd observed to himself.

CHAPTER 63

S TARKS FIRST STOP was at the infirmary. He stayed silent as Dr. Stewart cleaned and re-bandaged the wound on his wrist while chewing him out for not coming in sooner. His next stop was to tell Felipe that Stewart had put an, at most, three-pound limit on what he could lift, along with no repetitive or strenuous motions. Felipe stated flatly there would be no training until Starks was given clearance by the doctor.

There was one thing more he needed to do: find out where he stood with Gabe.

It took three hard knocks with his left hand before the door opened. Gabe's eyes locked with Starks's then traveled to the bandaged wrist. He shook his head and motioned for Starks to enter.

Starks didn't wait for an invitation to sit.

Gabe took the chair across from him. Silence for several moments was followed by, "Why should I waste my breath on you?"

"I know. I—"

"You act like you don't know dick. Is anything I've been saying making a dent anywhere in your rock head?"

"I'm sorry."

"Sorry doesn't cut cheese."

"Maybe I should leave." Starks started to get up.

"Keep your ass in that chair." Gabe rubbed his face hard, until his scowl was gone. "Only a schmuck goes on the attack in front of guards and witnesses. Took two fucking Taser hits to get you to stop." His expression shifted. "What's it like . . . getting Tasered? I've only been on the trigger end."

"I don't recommend it."

Gabe laughed and slapped his thigh. "I like you, Starks, but you're a buffoon."

"At least you're still talking to me. I wasn't sure you would."

Gabe shrugged. "How's the wrist?"

"Healing. Frustrating. I'm limited for a while. I don't like how that puts me at risk."

"That's why you should think ahead. You did this to yourself."

"How's it my goddamned fault?" When Gabe glared at him and didn't answer, he said, "I shouldn't have been in the Hole in the first place."

Gabe pointed at him. "Exactly. At least, not for the reason you were." He rested back in the chair. "Is your friend Jeffrey out of the picture now?"

"It was a mistake. He was set up. I confirmed it with the guy who lied. Then I apologized to Jeffrey. He was the friend he's always been about the matter." Starks smiled. "Said there was no problem between us as long as I let my hair grow out."

"I'm with him about that." Gabe ran a hand over his thinning hair. "If you got it, wear it." He gestured at Starks's wrist. "Speaking of set-ups, who do you think sent you the warning? You do realize that's what it was."

Starks nodded. "I put it on Crazy D. He was in isolation because of me."

"It was his fault he was in there, not yours. He's busting your balls. Make no mistake: he's gonna bust more than that."

Starks nodded. "I need to deal with him sooner than later."

"Unless he forces your hand, don't do anything until you come up with as infallible a plan as possible. You hear me?"

"Loud and clear. Speaking of ball-busting, I did a bit of that with Matthew Demory the other day. The counselor?" Gabe nodded. "I went to see him in good faith—I was ordered to, but it's like he's got a one-track mind about how I'm at fault and need to forgive and forget. I used different words, but basically told him to stick it."

"Until he sits on this side of the bars, there's only so much he can understand."

Starks rested his forearms on the table. He linked his fingers and stared at them, debating whether or not to say what he was tempted to. "I'm more comfortable talking with you. We do have certain things in common, so you get me and what it's like better than anyone here."

"Don't make me your shrink, your priest, or your mommy. Demory's the guy if you want to whine about your life, not me."

"I don't whine."

"That's one of those lies you tell yourself."

"Do you take pleasure in going after me?"

Gabe pointed a finger at him. "You're whining now. You want someone to talk straight to you, come here. Look, Starks, we all have habits we're unaware of. Whining happens to be one of yours. It pisses me off. Maybe you never did that before the shit came down on you, but you need to take a good look at how you've been since. I'm not saying any of it's easy. I'm saying how you handle yourself when a fucking hurricane is blowing through your life matters. It counts. It shows others who you really are. If you've got any sense, you look at yourself, as well as others, and learn from it."

"You treat me like a four-year-old."

"Then stop acting like one. You've got your own personal war about to break out in here. Don't look so shocked. I track the heartbeat of this place. I look ahead and imagine potential scenarios. If I hadn't learned to do that, and fast, I'd've been taken out a long time ago. You need to get your head out of your ass—how many times will I have to tell you that?—and pay attention."

"I am paying attention."

"Okay. Sure. You're on it." Gabe held up his hands. "I guess I'm talking to hear myself, here."

"You could help me with strategy."

"What's the point? I talk, you nod, and then you blow it. I can guide you to the water trough, but what you do after that is up to you. Just do us both a favor and stop trying to drown yourself. Stop acting like you're stuck on stupid."

"Anything else?"

"Yeah. Keep an eye on that Trevor kid."

"If you know something, tell me."

"He's got authority issues and a big mouth."

"I can manage him."

"You can't manage anybody until you manage yourself. You believe anything different then your head really is—"

"I get it, all right?"

"For your sake, I hope you do."

CHAPTER 64

STARKS PACED IN his cell. He couldn't train, couldn't work out with weights, couldn't yet devise a plan about Crazy D that kept him safe and unsuspected of the crime he needed to commit. He was contemplating doing laundry when CO Roberts showed up.

Roberts nodded toward Starks's wrist. "Hope you're healing all right. No word yet about who and how, but that's not why I'm here. You've got visitors."

"Visitors—plural. Who?"

"Just was told to tell you. By the way, I finally convinced the lead guy to talk to you about the cell phones. He wants to hear what you have to say."

"Set up a meeting."

"I'll take care of it. Want me to walk you to the visitation room?"

Starks thought for a moment. "Stay about five yards back."

"You got it."

Starks left the cell first, pondering who waited to see him. After going down the miniscule list of possibilities, one with zero appeal pushed forward in his mind: Maybe it was his mother with—God help him—the wife she'd chosen for him. If it turned out to be true, he'd turn around and get a guard to tell them he wasn't seeing anyone today. Then he'd call her and ream her.

Just outside the door, he paused and took several deep breaths. The last thing he wanted to do was enter the space looking ready for a fight, no matter who was on the other side waiting for him. The guard nearest the entrance glared at him and rested his hand on his Taser, making clear what would happen if he was tempted to give a repeat performance.

He spotted Jeffrey at their usual table. Jeffrey waved. Two children sprinted across the room, shouting, "Dad. Daddy."

Tears welled in Starks's eyes as he wrapped his arms around them. Both children clung to him.

A guard approached and barked, "Limited contact."

Kaitlin looked at the guard with her soulful brown eyes. Through quivering lips she said, "But he's my daddy. I haven't *seen* him in *forever.*"

The guard cleared his throat and walked away.

Starks held the children at arm's length. "Let me look at you. Blake, you've grown maybe two inches since I saw you last. And Kaitlin, my beautiful little girl, you've grown as well. It's so good to see you. Come on, we need to sit."

The three crossed the room. Kaitlin held tight to Starks's hand.

"Bro." Jeffrey raised his fists in a pretend fight stance. Starks rolled his eyes.

Blake said, "Dad, can we get sodas and snacks from the vending machines?"

Starks's right hand automatically reached for the wallet that wasn't there. His cheeks colored. "Sorry, kids, I don't have any cash on me at the moment."

Jeffrey pulled six one-dollar bills from his pocket. "Let me." The children raced to the machines.

"Thanks for that, Jeffrey. The treats and for bringing them to see me."

"Happy to do it. Kaitlin was miserable. Said it was unfair her brothers got to see you and she didn't. The boys were going to toss to see which one came, but Blake said since he was her *big* brother, he was the one to come along to keep her safe on her first visit. The three-person limit is a pain. At least your hair's grown out a bit. Not as scary for the kiddies." Jeffrey cracked his knuckles.

"When you do that, you're anxious. What is it?"

"Don't want to upset you, bro, but Blake told me Kaitlin's been calling for you in her sleep. The setting's not ideal, but I think you need to make it a point to see her as often as you can. I'm happy to bring her and one of the boys anytime."

Starks pressed his fingers to his eyelids and cleared his throat. Blake and Kaitlin returned to the table, each taking a seat on either side of Starks.

Blake said, "Cool tattoo, Dad."

"It's nothing. Just something to do." Starks turned to Kaitlin and stroked her hair. "How are you, sweetie?"

"I'm okay." She wrinkled her nose. "But I don't like that." She pointed at Starks's dragon. With a gentle touch, she rested the pointing finger on the edge of the bandage. "You got hurt. What happened, Daddy?"

"Just a careless accident. Wasn't watching what I was doing. It's fine."

Kaitlin leaned over and placed a light kiss on the gauze wrapping.

Starks's breath caught at the gesture. "Now I know it'll heal perfectly."

Kaitlin beamed. Then her expression became serious. "Can you come home with us when we leave? Please. Please. Please."

"Not today. But one day I will."

Then reality settled on him. Starks looked at Blake. The reminder that this boy wasn't his son clanged in his head. Not mine, but only by blood, he told himself.

Blake turned his gaze toward Starks. "Why are you looking at me like that, Dad?"

Starks swallowed hard. "It's just that you're becoming such a young man now."

Blake sat upright. "I want to be as tall as you."

Starks's chest tightened. "For all we know, you may be taller."

A quarter hour passed quickly as Kaitlin held her father's attention with stories of what was happening in school and with her brothers. Blake sat in silence, so unusual for the boy who was always the most vocal of the three children.

"You're being very quiet." It took several seconds for the word "son" to follow. Blake shrugged. "You're not going to go teenager on me, are you? Tell me what's going on with you. With school."

"School's okay."

"Something's bothering you."

Blake shifted in his chair. "I have a girlfriend. Sara's really pretty. Mom doesn't like her." He turned the soda can in circles and swung one leg back and forth, kicking the chair leg under him.

Starks snorted then pretended to muffle a sneeze. "Did your mom give a reason?"

"She got all upset when I said I love Sara and that I'm going to marry her as soon as we're both old enough."

"You're only thirteen, Blake. You're too young to be thinking like that, much less understand what love or marriage really means. Enjoy Sara's company, but put your attention on your studies so you can be successful. Be a success, and I promise you you'll have more girls to choose from than you can dream of."

Blake's jaw jutted forward. He half-shouted, "I don't care what you or Mom say. I love Sara and I'm going to marry her."

"Lower your voice, boy, and watch your tone." Starks leaned in. "Listen, Blake, I'm speaking from experience. In five years this girl won't be the same as she is now, maybe not even in five months. Neither will you be. You're too young to even think about this kind of decision. I don't want you to miss out on the experiences you can have, or to get hurt. I promise you, boy, it's just hormones kicking in."

"It's not hormones. Look, Dad, I know you're talking about you and Mom. But that's never going to happen to me."

Starks started to grab Blake by the arm then stopped himself. The last thing he wanted to do was ruin Kaitlin's visit or get Tasered in front of the children. As it was, she was watching them with wide eyes and chewing on her bottom lip. Starks took a few breaths then said, "As long as you live in our house, you'll do as you're told."

Blake slumped in the chair. "It's not *your* house anymore. You don't live there. You live . . ." A red flush covered the boy's neck and face. He dropped his chin to his chest and stayed still, except for the swinging leg.

Starks glanced at Kaitlin. Tears threatened to spill from her eyes. He winked at his daughter then forced a smile as he looked at Blake. "I know my being here is hard on all of you. This is a topic that can be discussed— calmly—another time. Who knows? Maybe you'll still feel the same about Sara after college. Just know that as true as that may turn out to be, it's also true that things change. People change, and life has a way of changing people. That's all I'm saying.

"Jeffrey," Starks said, "these two look like they could go for another snack. Would you mind?"

Jeffrey said, "How about it, kids? Want something else?" At their nods, he handed each of them two dollars. The children hurried to the other side of the room.

"Okay, Starks, it won't take but a minute or so before they're back."

"Did you get Richard and Jenny to agree to see me?"

"They'll be visiting you soon." Jeffrey looked past Starks. "The kids are heading this way. Anything else personal you need to discuss?"

Starks shook his head.

His visitors stayed another half hour. Blake was polite with his answers, but moody. Yet, when it was time to leave, his hug around Starks's neck was solid. He said in a low voice, so only Starks could hear, "I miss you so much, Dad."

"I miss you, too. Son."

Starks had reacted to Blake's adamant statements like any good father would. But he couldn't blame the boy. When his family met Kayla and disapproved, he'd had an immoveable disposition on the matter. He'd been far more rude to his mother, grandfather, and other relatives whenever the topic of Kayla came up not in her favor.

Whatever conflict he felt about Blake being another man's biological child, it was impossible to stop acting like the boy's father, as he had done, as he had believed, for more than a decade. Long-held feelings were not so easily shut off.

The truth of that thought and what all it might encompass made his gut roil.

CHAPTER 65

STARKS WAS ON his way to the laundry room when a guard stopped him and said, "Visitor's waiting."

"Communications must have gotten crossed. I just had visitors."

"Guess it's your lucky day. You got another one."

"One? Any idea who?"

"What do you care who?"

"Would it really be too much to find out and tell us?"

"Be happy anyone comes here." The guard mumbled to himself as he walked away.

Starks hurried to his cell to drop off the box of laundry before returning to the room he'd left only a half hour before.

Emma Guyson stood out like a bright platinum-blonde star in a low-cut red dress. She bounced up when she saw Starks, revealing shapely tanned legs made longer in stiletto heels. He reminded her that their hug had to be quick.

They sat next to each other at the table where she'd waited. "You look so different," she said. "Your beautiful hair, an enormous tattoo, and you're injured."

"You, on the other hand, are even more beautiful. I didn't think that was possible."

Her smile in response altered to an expression of concern. "What's happening, Starks?"

Starks forced a chuckle. "It's nothing." When Emma didn't relax, he said, "Look, I cut my hair because summer's a scorcher here. No trees or shade anywhere. I got the tattoo on a dare and because I was bored. The wrist thing was a result of my being clumsy. But I don't want to talk about me. I want to hear about you and how you're doing?"

"That's not what I meant."

Starks took hold of her hand. "Then you need to tell me."

"Last time I saw you, you told me to stay away."

"You know why. I want to protect you from this environment."

"And I told you it doesn't matter. This is the only way I can be with you. But I agreed because I didn't want to complicate your situation, and then you never called. You never call. You don't include me in your life. That's why I had to come here. To see what's going on. I'm beginning to wonder if you ever really loved me."

Starks raised her hand to his lips and kissed her palm. "You have no idea how much I'd like to show you how I feel."

"Don't make this about sex." Emma tried to pull her hand away.

Starks tightened his hold. "I don't mean to exclude you. I swear to you that it isn't intentional. Thoughts of you keep me sane. This life is hard, baby. I'm still adjusting. Sometimes I wonder if I ever will."

Emma brushed her shoulder-length hair back. "We promised that we'd never have secrets, especially after what Kayla put you through. I get the feeling you're keeping things from me."

"I swear to you I'm not."

"Then tell me about your life."

"There's nothing to tell. It's the same thing day after day. That's why I'm eager to hear about you."

Emma sat with controlled stillness. "Kayla really did a number on you. It's altered your ability to trust. Even me. I get it. It was all about firsts with her—first love, first child, first house, and so on. You shared some of the most significant experiences of your lives. I feel like I'm competing with that and will always have to."

Anger flashed across Starks's face. "Everything you say about firsts is true, but you don't have anything to worry about. You surpass that selfish slut in every way." He squeezed Emma's hand. She winced and he loosened his grip. "I count myself fortunate to have you in my life. You're stunning, intelligent, and you understand how important loyalty is to me. Look, I'm doing what I can to get released early. Then you and I are going to get married. We're going to create and share extraordinary experiences."

Emma stroked the back of his hand with her manicured nails. "When we first started seeing each other, a few people told me not to take your interest in me seriously. They hammered the fact that it's never smart to get involved with a man who isn't yet divorced."

"I'm glad you didn't listen. But why are you telling me this?"

"Because I'm afraid I'm a rebound relationship."

"You're not."

"You aren't over Kayla yet. Not completely. Maybe not even close." Kayla shook her head when Starks started to protest. "Let me finish. Look how angry you still get when she's mentioned, the passion expressed when you berate her. It makes me think you're not nearly ready for a true relationship with anyone else. There's no space for that. You're still too filled with her."

Starks crossed his arms at his chest. "I see what's going on. It's you who doesn't love me. If you did, you wouldn't be talking this way. Maybe you feel your loyalty is misplaced. If you came here to end it, get it over with."

"I don't mean to hurt you. I only want to be honest with you about how I feel. I do love you. I am loyal to you. I told you I'd be waiting for you when you got released, and I mean it. It's just that if your feelings have changed, I'd like you to be honest about that so I don't play the fool. I did that before with my ex-husband. You know from your own experience how that feels."

Starks nodded. "I'm sorry. I realize this is hard on you. Yes, I'm still healing from the wounds Kayla inflicted, but I swear to you that you have me heart, mind, and soul. I'm yours. As long as you want me, which I hope is forever." Starks pressed her hand to his chest. "Hard as it's been, if Kayla hadn't done what she did, you and I wouldn't be together. That's something I'm thankful to her for. Will you forgive me?"

Emma's eyes watered. "I will if you will."

Starks kept hold of her hand. "Now, baby, tell me what's been going on with you." He listened more carefully to her words than ever before.

Emma's kiss was still warm on Starks's lips as he speed-walked to his cell. Once again he felt as though everyone wanted something from him, as though he was a well that never ran dry.

Didn't he have a right to hold back information from Emma? Wasn't it his job to protect her? There was nothing she could do about his problems, so it was senseless to burden her with them. But he couldn't tell her that; she'd take it as an offense. He was certain that if she knew how dire his circumstances were, she'd run and never look back.

Emma had made it clear she didn't feel protected, she felt abandoned. He'd have to do better about that. And, maybe she hadn't followed her friends' advice about him, but it was obvious she believed it or was beginning to. He'd already gone through similar nonsense with Kayla, who chose to ignore him and listen to friends instead, friends who advised her to cheat on him or leave him. Emma was wrong about Kayla's hold on him. Just because his temper flared whenever he spoke about his soon-to-be ex-wife didn't mean anything. It was ridiculous for Emma to believe any differently.

She hadn't been as nurturing or effusive with her affections as the last time she'd visited. It seemed to him she was projecting onto him, as Demory might say, what she was feeling. It wasn't his love and loyalty in question, it was hers.

Emma spoke of not wanting to be made a fool of. Well, neither was he going to allow that to happen to him again. He positioned the book with the phone on his lap and pressed the digits of Jim Rogers' number.

"Good to hear from you, Starks. How's it going?"

"I want you or someone reliable to follow Emma. I want her phone calls and e-mails monitored."

"Right. The girlfriend. How long?"

"Long enough to see if she's changed her mind about me."

"Looks like you don't trust her."

"Trust, especially when it comes to women, is no longer a word in my vocabulary."

"I'll set something up ASAP."

Starks returned the book to his desk. He faced the slender window and watched clouds gather in the sky. Maybe it would rain and bring relief from the dry heat. He'd pay good money to be relieved of all that weighed on him.

Emma had reminded him of an important lesson his grandfather had taught him: tell women whatever they want to hear, but never trust them.

He'd ignored the last half of that message with Kayla. He wasn't going to repeat that mistake.

CHAPTER 66

PEWTER CLOUDS HUNG over the yard, yet indicated no real threat—or promise—of rain. An errant breeze kicked up dust that landed on sweat-coated inmates who'd decided outside was better than in, but did nothing to cool skin or tempers.

Starks joined several of his crew who sat on their usual segment of bleachers. He was getting a report about their initial training with Felipe when Stinky interrupted him.

Stinky used his chin to point. "There's the guy that stutters."

Starks, as did the others, turned his gaze in that direction. Other inmates in the yard watched the young man, as well. Their laughter solidified Starks's decision. He said, "Wait here," and then approached the young man.

"My name's Starks. What's yours?"

The inmate stuttered out, "Ethan."

"Looks like you're a magnet for bullies. You join my crew," Starks motioned toward the bleachers, "and we'll look out for you."

Ethan squinted at Starks then glanced over at the crew. "Can't."

"Why not?"

"They look away when I look at them."

"That's because they don't know you."

"You don't know me."

"Only one way to change that."

Ethan pointed at Starks's tattoo. "Can I get one of those?"

"If you earn it, you can get a dragon head on the back of your right hand. No one but me has this tattoo."

"Because you're the Big Cheese?"

Starks grinned. "Something like that. Let's go meet the guys."

They started toward the bleachers. Four inmates blocked their way. One of them said to Ethan, "Hey, retard, you think you're gonna get away with what you did?"

Starks said, "Leave him alone. He's with me now."

"I don't know who the fuck you are, but I'm not talking to you. I'm talking to him." The inmate jabbed a finger against Ethan's chest. "Hey, retard, you this retard's little bitch?"

Starks's men rose from the bleachers and sauntered toward the action. One of the four inmates backed off and left.

The outspoken inmate said, "I got no problem with you. But him, I do. If you don't get outta my face, that'll change."

Nearby inmates moved close enough to listen.

Starks replied, "You don't know who you're talking to."

"I don't give a fuck who you *think* you are. You and your little stuttering bitch are dead meat."

Gasps came from the small crowd that had gathered. Starks's men assumed postures that made it clear they were ready. The inmate noticed; he shifted on his feet. A flash of concern crossed his expression then he scowled. He curled his fists and arms, ready to strike.

Starks said, "Sorry, boys. This isn't the time to play. I've got business to take care of. I'll catch up with you later." He said to Ethan and his crew, "Let's go." Still within earshot, he heard someone explain to his would-be attacker why he should leave Starks and his soldiers alone.

Once back on the bleachers, Starks introduced Ethan. His men remained silent, though their questions hung thick in the oppressive heat: Why was he including Ethan? Why had he walked away from the brewing conflict? These were questions they didn't have the balls to ask him. Not yet, at least. And, perhaps, one more, like was he growing weak?

"I have my reasons for what just happened. We need a meeting. Get word to crew members who aren't here. Laundry room. Tomorrow morning, after the eleven o'clock count."

It was time to take care of some housekeeping.

CHAPTER 67

A T BREAKFAST THE next day, the crew crowded around the chow hall table, minus Jackson who was on kitchen duty. Ethan sat between Tank and Stinky, looking as excited as a three-year-old with a shiny balloon.

Starks took a seat and surveyed the faces of his crew. "Where's Kane this morning?"

Tank answered. "Tried to get him to leave his cell but he wouldn't. He's got that look I've seen before, like he wants out."

"We all want out," Starks replied. He poked at a reddish-brown scoop of what he presumed was meant to be hash.

"I mean as in eternal-rest out."

Starks put his fork down. "You're serious?"

Tank nodded. "Looks like a trapped animal ready to chew its own foot off."

"Where's his cell?

"A-Block, third on the right."

Starks rapped on the table, dumped his untouched food, and hastened to the exit. He got to the cell as quickly as he could. Kane was in the lower bunk, curled into the fetal position and facing the back wall.

"Kane. It's Starks." He sat in the chair next to the bunk. "Tell me what's going on." One sniffle was followed by another but the young man didn't move. "I'm not leaving until you talk to me."

After several moments Kane said, "I'm a coward."

"Every man in here is afraid, even if he doesn't show it."

"You don't understand."

"I'm pretty sure I do. Besides, you've got us, buddy."

"I've got no one."

"That's not true. For better or worse, I and my crew are your family in here. Maybe not one you would have asked Santa for, but we're here for you. Believe me. I understand how you feel."

Kane shook his head. "You can't. You just don't know."

Starks rubbed the back of his neck. He'd never had this kind of conversation before and wanted to get it right. "I was terrified when I got here. Every man in here is scared shitless every day. Don't let their, or even my, posturing make you think any different. I'm going to tell you something I never talk about to anyone, and I'd like it if you never mention it." His statement got Kane's attention. "I wasn't here long before I got myself thrown into isolation for a month. Damn near lost my mind. Did something really stupid: Tried to kill myself. And that stupid act got me even more time in isolation, with a video camera watching me twenty-four/seven."

Kane's head turned slightly. "You tried to kill yourself?"

"I'm glad now that I failed. I'm glad that the second time I was going to attempt it, I stopped myself."

Kane swiped tears from his face and rolled over. "You tried twice?"

"One and a half. The second time, I had the shank against my jugular, ready to go. I'd been betrayed and publicly humiliated by the person I loved most. People had lied at my trial, causing me to land here. I was brutally attacked—I showed you my scars. So, yeah, I wanted to end my misery. But that second attempt? My heart never pounded so hard in my chest. It didn't want to stop beating. Not yet. Made me realize just how much I wanted to live and get the hell out of here. Stuck in the SHU, I had a lot of time alone to think. Suicide will get you out of here, but that's not the way. The way is to survive. The way to survive is to have protection, and you've got it. My protection. I know ten years is a long time, especially at your age. But you'll be twenty-nine when you get out; younger if you get out earlier. Hell, son, there are young men out there who don't even know what they're going to do with their lives until they're thirty. Sometimes not even then."

Kane sat up but he resisted looking directly at Starks. "When I got sentenced, my mother told me she disowned me. She said she no longer had a son."

Starks nodded. "Sounds a bit like my mother. They can be real hardasses at times. What about your father?"

"I told you. He wasn't there."

"Mine abandoned my mother and me when I was three."

"I didn't know that. At least you had him for awhile. My mother forbade me to have any contact with my father. She was too proud to have him in our lives." He glanced up at Starks and sniffed.

"No disrespect to your mother, but she shouldn't have done that. I know firsthand that pride can create or worsen problems." How many times had Demory pressed him about how he let pride spin him out of control? How many times had he told the counselor to go fuck himself when he said it?

Starks grinned. "You remind me of my boy Blake. He's just become a teenager. I don't like to think what those years will be like without me there every day to guide him. I don't even know if he'll let me put my two-cents in. Young men like to think they know enough to muddle through or to take risks they don't begin to grasp the possible consequences of. And the older they get the more they believe that. Right?" Starks grinned and nudged Kane's arm.

"Tell you what, Kane. I have some connections in here. I'd like to make sure you're okay and stay that way. What do you think about becoming my cellmate? Nothing kinky about that invitation." He raised a hand. "I swear on my children."

Kane wiped his nose on his sleeve. "What'll Jackson say?"

Starks grabbed a wad of stiff toilet paper and handed it to Kane. "I'll persuade him to say yes. How about it?"

Kane nodded and laughed. "I'm moving into the dragon cave."

Starks stood and said, "Hope you like the top bunk, kid."

"I'd sleep on the floor, if I had to."

"I'll get to work on it. We have a meeting in the laundry room after the eleven o'clock count. Be there."

Kane perched on the edge of his bunk. "Absolutely. And, Starks . . . thanks."

Starks left feeling like he'd accomplished something spectacular. He hadn't felt that way in a long time. His successes in here were valid but empty of meaning beyond preserving his own life. And today, just now, he'd saved one. He'd given a young man hope. It felt good. And confusing.

CHAPTER 68

"JACKSON, YOU WERE up with the worms this morning. Even missed the count."

"I checked in. There was something I had to take care of."

"Such as?"

Jackson shrugged. "Something personal. Not a big deal."

Starks watched Jackson, whose expression stayed unreadable. "If you say so. The crew's meeting after the count at eleven. I checked your schedule. You're free. If you're not, you need to be."

"Where?"

"Laundry room."

"It's gonna look suspicious if we keep meeting there."

"Let me worry about that. Just show up."

"Sure thing, boss man."

Starks ignored the barb. "Had to talk to Kane this morning. The kid hit a pocket of depression, the kind that leads to inmates hanging themselves or drinking drain cleaner. I think I convinced him that wasn't the way. I hope I did."

Jackson shook his head. "I said it. Instead of soldiers you're bringing in toddlers who need to be potty trained. Or on meds."

"I don't want any shit about Ethan. As for Kane, he does remind me of my boys. He's got that same innocence in his face and demeanor."

Jackson unspooled a length of dental floss and began running it between his teeth. "So you feel responsible for him."

"Something like that. I got too close to that *ledge* a few times. I know what it's like." Starks hesitated then said, "I want him to move in here."

Jackson dragged the string slowly between his teeth. "He gonna bunk with you?"

"Don't be an ass. I'd like you to switch cells with someone in this block. I want to keep it easy for us to talk. I told Kane I'd arrange it."

"You had no right, man. You wanna bunk with the kid, you move."

"All the commissary you want for a month. On me."

Jackson turned the tap on high, prepped his toothbrush and ran it around in his mouth for a minute. He rinsed and spit. "Two months. And you better make damn sure my cellmate isn't any crazy mother."

"I will."

"You about to piss off some guy who wants to move about as much as I do."

"They move people around all the time."

"When's this supposed to happen?"

"As soon as I can set it up."

"Who you gonna get to do that?"

"I'll figure it out."

"Two months of commissary?"

"Make it three."

Jackson stuck out his lower lip. "You love him more than me."

Starks threw a towel at him. "I wouldn't do this if I didn't feel it was a matter of life or death."

"What can I say? It was good while it lasted."

CHAPTER 69

MOST OF STARKS'S crew was in the laundry room when he and Jackson arrived. The last few trailed in within minutes. Tank was one of them. Grinning, he fake-boxed Jackson's arm playfully and said, "Where you been? Thought maybe you joined a different gang."

"I've been working and minding my fucking business."

Tank put his hands up. "Somebody's got a thorn branch up his ass this morning. No offense meant, man."

Starks said, "At least three of you get washing machines going so we cover our voices."

Pete said, "What if others come in?"

"I took care of that." Starks waited until the machines began to fill with water. "Move in close enough to hear me. New members, the first thing I want to do is emphasize loyalty. Any of you—new or not—feel you can't be loyal to the crew, this is your chance to leave. Stay and betray," he looked at the men, "and the consequences won't be pleasant."

The men glanced at each other. Pete said, "We're with you."

Starks nodded. "Second thing is income for you. I'm working on getting burner phones. Inmates will pay to use them. Once we're in business, use common sense about who, what, when, how, and where you tell. Let new users know the first hour is on me. After that, it's a dollar for every half hour or increment. Whether they talk five minutes or thirty, it's a dollar. Explain the consequences of getting caught with a phone; although, most of them should already know this. Anybody gets caught, it's on them. Anyone caught who snitches," Starks dragged his index finger across his neck. "Got it?"

One of the new members asked, "What's in it for us?"

"You'll each be in charge of your phone. You'll get all the fees for the first month for people you line up. Those of you standing here now use the phones for no charge. Within limits. You tie up the phones with your calls, there won't be any fees to collect or too little to matter." Starks pointed at the group. "And you keep that arrangement to yourselves. We get any new crew members, they'll get phones as well, and they'll get the same bonus but they'll pay fifty cents a half hour for calls, same increment plan as for users. You're all on the honor system. Give me a reason to believe you're cheating, and you're out of business and the crew. Don't get greedy and blow the whole thing up. Or land some or all of us in the SHU. Any questions?"

Pete said, "Just asking, Starks, but what happened in the yard yesterday? How come we didn't stand up to those guys?"

Starks looked at Pete a few moments then directed his gaze around the small crowd of men waiting for his answer. "In here, especially, you have to decide when to fight and when to wait. Fight every time, and you'll find yourself in isolation more than out. That's no way to live or even exist. Not only that, if you always engage," a slight smile formed on his lips, "you lose the element of surprise later on. If you show your hand every time, you've got nothing to go on, no way to win. As far as those guys in the yard go, don't worry about it. I'm taking care of that particular matter. The person we need to be concerned most about right now is Crazy D." He held up his bandaged wrist. "You know I was attacked while in the SHU. The most likely one behind it is him, even if he wasn't holding the knife. Whether it was or wasn't him behind the attack, he still has it out for me, which means he considers you guys targets as well. We need to act before he does."

"Now you're talking," Pete said.

Ethan stepped forward several inches and stuttered, "Let me take care of him, Starks."

After a moment, all the crew members but Starks laughed. Starks's scowl silenced them. He was quiet for several moments then said, "Okay, Ethan. You handle it.

"Meeting's over. Do laundry if you need to or leave. I know that some of you have other things to take care of." Several men nodded at Starks and left. Some of the men whispered among themselves as they cast wary glances at Ethan.

Jackson sidled up to Starks. "Are you serious? Or crazy? Why are you letting that nutcase handle something this important?"

"His name's Ethan. I'm not yet certain whether his behaviors are real or faked. What I do know is what I saw with my own eyes." Starks recounted what he'd witnessed in the chow hall. "No one saw what he did but me, and that's only because I paid attention. It was a slight of hand—two hands—a former stage magician like you should appreciate."

Jackson nodded and cast his eyes to Ethan. "Wish I'd seen that."

"You're the only person I've told. I'd like to keep it that way."

"No problem."

Jackson and Starks watched Ethan, who stood in front of a dryer, grinning as he watched clothes flopping around, moving his head in a circle to match the spin.

"Let's hope," Jackson said, "he's as clever with this task, and doesn't get skewered."

"He's faster and smoother than he looks."

"And maybe the most expendable?"

It was almost a quarter to six that evening when Mike caught up with Starks on the way to his block. With a lowered voice, he told Starks, "Just heard the three guys that faced off with you and Ethan in the yard were found under the bleachers, moaning and not too eager to get up. You said you'd taken care of them. Was it our guys?"

"If a few of our crew show up with dragon head tats, maybe it was." He winked. "Almost time for the count. Get going so you're not late."

"When do I get my tat?"

"When you've earned it."

"When's that going to happen?"

"I'll let you know."

Starks headed to his cell. Why would his crew consider getting the tattoo as important as his boys had scout badges? He'd gotten the dragon partially as an act of rebellion and as a talisman to keep him strong as he forged ahead with his plan. His crew's motivation was nothing like that.

He glanced at inmates as he continued to D-Block. Some of the men laughed and kidded around. Their smiles tried but failed to hide other feelings always apparent in their eyes. He stopped outside his cell and looked back.

Then he knew: No matter the number of men here, each one of them felt alone. They wanted to belong, to matter, to count to and for something. And to someone. The tattoo was a symbol of belonging. It meant they were included. Chosen. Accepted just as they are.

The effect of his plan was taking on new texture, one beyond his original goal.

He didn't know how he felt about that.

CHAPTER 70

FISTS ON HIPS, Starks glared at Tank. "I asked you to spot me. Are you going to do it or just stand there scratching your balls?"

Tank glanced at Stinky, who was a few feet to their left, prepping to do shoulder presses. Stinky shrugged. Tank said, "You shouldn't be pressing weights till the doc says you can."

"Lower your voice." Starks looked around to see if anyone was listening. If anyone was, it wasn't obvious. "It's my wrist, and I say it's healed enough. It's been over a week. Now, spot me."

"Whatever you say."

Starks positioned himself on the bench. It was a struggle to lift the heavy weight from his chest, but he did. There was a slight twinge in his wrist after the fifth rep, but he made it to the fifteenth. He sat up and said, "That was my max weight. So far."

"That was a good set. Some heavy pressing for a guy your size. Wrist okay?"

"It's fine."

Starks watched several of his crew work out. Three of them sported fresh tattoos. In business, he'd had influence over his employees, who were loyal out of respect for his massive success and business acumen, and how he took care of those under him. Here, it wasn't a matter of influence, but of control. He had control over his crew, but he wasn't certain yet about their loyalty. How much loyalty do some drowning men feel about saving others going under near them?

Still, they seemed willing to obey his commands. For now. Some might view this as power. It was, in a way, but it came with responsibility he wasn't accustomed to: Life or death. His crew members, so eager to fight, hadn't realized this about his role as leader. Not yet. For them, fighting or not fighting was all about reputation. It was about making a statement that said you weren't an easy target. Every inmate at Sands felt—knew—he walked around with an invisible bull's-eye on his back. If an inmate was edgy, he had cause. But it was imperative to figure out when to stay on the edge and when to go over.

He turned his attention to Ethan, who was doing a half-assed job of curls with a five-pound dumbbell. The young man stopped the curls and started to wave the weight in a circular motion above his head. Starks narrowed his eyes and wondered, again, if Ethan was not in his right mind or was deliberate about crafting a dog-and-pony show.

Stinky completed his sets of shoulder presses then stood next to Starks. "Not that I doubt you or your decision, but are you sure about that guy? I don't feel as confident as you do about him handling Crazy D."

"I know why you doubt him, but is there another reason you're asking?"

"It's been days since he volunteered. So far, all he's done is ask questions about Crazy D."

"Sounds like he's getting intel."

"Some intel. He's asking about weird shit like what kind of food Crazy D likes, how fast he eats, how often he uses the toilet. Sounds more like a bizarre fetish."

Starks nodded. "Seems like an odd direction, but I'm sure he has a plan, or will."

"His questions are gonna draw Crazy D's attention to him."

"But they're so innocuous people will think they're part of his mental affliction. Even if Crazy D hears about it, and he will, he won't take it seriously."

"Yeah, but it's obvious Ethan's with you. You don't think that'll make Crazy D suspicious?"

"It might. But Crazy D is arrogant. He won't see Ethan as a threat. He might even try to get Ethan to switch teams, just to stick it to me. There's a lot about Ethan I'm not sure of, but I believe he's loyal to me. I took him in when no one wanted anything to do with him, unless it was to hassle him."

"I don't know." Stinky looked left. "Dave's heading our way."

"I really need to get the new crew members' names down."

Dave stopped in front of Starks and Stinky. "I got some new recruits lined up. Told them you gotta approve first. Some of the other guys did the same. We're also getting some," he glanced around, "potential customers as well. Those inmates are damn excited about getting more time to talk with their families. And others. Unmonitored. Know what this means for some of these guys?"

Starks nodded. "I do." He kept to himself that certain gang leaders weren't going to be pleased at all. That was a bridge he hadn't yet reached.

But he was getting closer.

CHAPTER 71

HALF THE TABLES in the visitation room had people at them. Still, it was easy to spot Jenny and Richard. They sat as near the exit as possible and looked as tense as most first-timers waiting for an inmate to arrive. Jenny saw him first. She nudged Richard with her elbow and waved. Starks smiled and waved back.

Richard stood, Jenny stayed seated. Starks extended his hand, which Richard shook, and then he gave Jenny a light kiss on the cheek.

Jenny waited until Starks sat then said, "Jeffrey told us you look different. I just didn't expect . . ." She blushed and ran her fingers through her short auburn hair.

"Everything's probably a shock for you: this place, me."

Richard cleared his throat. "I'm guessing you're trying to look like you fit in, right? I mean, this isn't the new you or anything. Is it?"

"You got it," Starks replied. "Just playing the part so people leave me alone as much as possible."

Jenny asked, "So how are you, really?"

"I'm hanging in there. Everything okay with you two, with your kids?"

"We're all fine," Richard replied. "It's you we're concerned about. We know you've had a rough time since you got here. More than rough."

Starks shrugged and smiled. "You know me; I bounce back. I find or create a way through obstacles."

"Always admired that about you, Starks. Anyway, Jeffrey said you wanted to see us. What can we do for you? Name it. If we can do it, we will."

Starks looked directly at Jenny. "Everything you said about Kayla and Ozy during my trial was what you told me before this fiasco ever happened. Is there anything else you know but perhaps forgot or hesitated to tell me? Or didn't think it was important enough to mention? Anything at all may help me."

Jenny focused on her hands folded in her lap. "Kayla told me a lot."

"Too damn much," Richard said. "I should never have allowed you to resume your friendship with that slut."

Jenny kept her eyes aimed down. "I didn't know she was like that."

"You knew soon enough. And you still kept going out with her."

"I thought I could be a positive influence."

Richard snorted. "Backfired, didn't it? Damn near cost us our marriage." He faced Starks. "I still can't believe that after how hard you worked for twenty years to buy the selfish bitch everything she wanted, she cheated on you. And how she could fall in love with that bastard, Ozy, a married man for God's sake, is still something I can't figure out."

Jenny placed her hand on Richard's arm. "You always get distraught when you talk about her. We're here for Starks."

Richard took a deep breath and let it out. "Sorry. It's just that I hate the woman." He stared at his wife's hand on his arm.

Starks expected Richard to take Jenny's hand in his, but he didn't. He glanced from one to the other. "I'm sorry if my bringing this up is upsetting."

Jenny cast a quick look at Richard then back down. She removed her hand from her husband's arm. "It's not always easy, but sometimes you have to practice forgiveness."

Richard turned in his chair to face his wife. "If you mean I should forgive Kayla, you can forget it. If you mean I should forgive you for what you did and almost did while going to clubs with her, I'm doing the best I can."

"People make mistakes," Jenny muttered. "Kayla once said that most men aren't as forgiving as women are." She looked at Starks. "I see Kayla in church fairly often. Not every Sunday, but—"

"Seriously, woman?" Richard said. "She was going to church when we met her. She wasn't pious then and she isn't now. It's all for show. Believe me, everyone knows the truth. She's not fooling anyone but herself. She's still the whore she always was."

"Richard, honey, you need to calm down. Guards are looking this way. We're here because Starks needs our help. My help." She looked at Starks. "If I have any to offer."

Richard rubbed his face. "Again, I'm sorry, Starks."

"It's okay. I still get enraged sometimes. It can sneak up on you." Starks directed his focus at Jenny. "Is there anything else you can tell me about Kayla and Ozy's time together?"

Jenny chewed her bottom lip as she thought. "She used to meet Ozy at his house, whenever his wife was out of town with the kids."

Starks arched his eyebrows. "I bet Margaret doesn't know that. She's the kind of woman who would've dragged the bed outside and burned it."

"It wasn't just the bed," Jenny said. "The sofa, dining table, Jacuzzi, against the walls, the patio table—"

Richard shook his head. "Disgusting. What kind of man fouls the sanctity of his home, where his wife and children sleep? I agree with you, Starks. Margaret got an earful during the trial—the poor woman was shocked and humiliated over and over. But if she'd heard that, forget the bed. I think she would have burned the house down." He eased forward. "I have wondered if she ever told the wives of Ozy's co-workers how they all screwed Kayla?"

Jenny's face turned florid. "It wasn't just Kayla. Kayla said there were other women in the firm who were involved."

"Don't you dare defend her." Richard raised his fist to slam against the tabletop.

Starks stopped him. "Easy, Richard."

"I just can't believe all these married women were doing this to their husbands."

"What about the married men?" Jenny said.

Richard glared at her then shrugged. "Men will always be men. Women are supposed to tend to their men. That includes behaving as they should. With propriety. And gratitude."

"Are you one of those men?" Jenny asked. She stared at her husband and waited for an answer. When one didn't readily come, she said, "Practically every day of my life, you go on and on about what happened and didn't. And all the time you may be doing the same or . . . or . . . even worse." She focused on Starks. "The same goes for you." She waved a hand in the air. "It's the end of the world when a woman does it, but a man gets approval when he does the same thing. And, he expects it."

Richard said, "It's not the same. Never has been. Never will be."

"Excuse me, *husband*, but it is exactly the same thing. Worse. Because men think it's their right to screw around. They're considered gods in the fraternity of men when they do. But they're just as much sluts as women are, if you insist on labeling women that way."

"Now just a damn minute, Jenny."

Starks ran a hand back and forth over his head. "I started this. It's not what I intended."

"No," Jenny said. "You didn't start this. Richard did."

Richard sat erect. "I said just a damn minute."

"I'll give you 'just a minute'. You talk about everything Starks bought for Kayla. Money doesn't buy love and loyalty; love and loyalty given earn the same back. Or should. Some men make promises to love and cherish their wives then break those promises. And they wonder why they lose their wife's affections."

Richard jabbed a finger against the table. "I don't know where this is coming from, Jenny, but you'd better settle down. Right now."

"Richard . . . just shut up." Jenny slouched back and folded her arms across her chest.

"Did you just tell me to shut up? What do you want, equality? Fine. Next time there's a noise at night you get up and see what or who it is. You shovel the snow off the long driveway. And while we're at it, why don't you get a job and work like a dog to pay the mortgage and all the other bills. See how you like that instead of staying home and being taken care of."

"When you're away on business, I am the one who gets up to check a noise. You use a snow blower, and you refuse to let me work because, quote, 'a wife's home and family are her job'. What you don't understand about relationships, Richard, is more than I can explain to you. That is, if you'd even bother to try to understand."

Starks was stunned. Jenny had always been so timid, so accommodating to whatever Richard wanted. It was the very comparison he'd pointed out to Kayla repeatedly. He'd never heard Jenny speak like this to anyone, especially not her husband. "Listen, you two, again, I'm sorry for stirring anything up. You don't know how sorry."

Jenny harrumphed and looked away. "Maybe you stirred it, but it was already stewing in the pot."

"I feel responsible," Starks said. "If it wasn't for Kayla, and me, this discord between you wouldn't be happening."

"Don't be so sure," Jenny replied.

Starks heard her mumbling to herself. The only word he heard clearly was "doormat."

The three were silent for several moments then Jenny spoke. "Kayla did say there were some things she did that she'll never tell; that they'll go to the grave with her."

Starks believed he knew one of them, but he was surprised to hear there was more than one item on that list.

Richard turned his gaze from his wife to Starks. "At least you're clearing Kayla out of your life. Good riddance, I say. Emma's much better for you."

"It's not always that simple," Jenny said. "Kayla probably still cares about Starks and Starks probably still cares about her. Do you, Starks?"

Richard stared at his wife. "I don't know who you are anymore. She didn't care about him before. She sure as hell doesn't care about him now. You almost sound like you think they should get back together. After all the shit she's done to him."

"And he's done to her, Richard. But they built a life together. They had children together. As for Emma, she comes across nice enough. But there's something about her I don't like. I can't name it; I just know it. Sorry if that offends you, Starks."

Richard shook his head. "Emma's quality and from a good family. She makes her own money, enough to support herself and her child."

"Kayla worked," Jenny said.

Richard sighed. "Again, you sound like you're defending her. Sure, she worked. She went to the office five days a week and worked her mouth and her twat. Emma's not like that. Plus, she's smart enough to know a good thing, which she has with Starks. And I'm not talking about just the money."

Starks said, "That's how I feel about Emma."

Richard nodded at Starks. "Just don't make the same mistakes with her. Emma's a diamond that could use some polishing, but she has a good heart. Speaking of Emma, has she been here to see you?"

"She's visited a few times." Starks glanced at the clock on the wall. "I've got to get going. Jenny, is there anything else you can think of?"

"Not at the moment."

"If you do, tell Jeffrey. He can tell me during his next visit. Easier for him to come here than I'm sure it is for you guys."

Starks's chair scraped against the floor when he stood. "Thanks for coming all this way to see me. I really appreciate it. And I hope you guys can get back on track. You're a good, solid couple. A family. You don't know what it's like to lose that. And to know you'll never get it back."

A few more awkward words people tended to say at the end of a visit were exchanged. Starks turned to wave at them before leaving the room.

Jenny hadn't had as much new information as he'd hoped, but what she said about Ozy and Kayla using Margaret's house for some of their liaisons might be enough. Depending on what it was that Margaret actually wanted with him, and he'd only know that when she told him.

One thing was clear: His friends' marriage wasn't as stable as it used to be. Or as it had *appeared* to be. That was the fault of Kayla and her destructive power over others. There wasn't much he could do about that.

All he could do was wonder what Margaret Hessinger wanted to see him about. When, or if, she did come to see him, he'd have to keep his temper under control.

How was he going to sit across from the woman who could have saved him from prison, and not lose it?

There was a possibility he'd find out.

CHAPTER 72

SAM CARSON HAD been surprised when Starks asked to take over a shift on a weekend, stating he wanted quiet time to think. Carson's reply was that he could only imagine what Starks was conspiring about now. The library was all but empty for a Saturday afternoon. Paco sat at his preferred computer. Starks was in the office, cataloging the latest shipment of magazines.

He looked up when he heard Paco say louder than necessary, "*Buenas tardes.*" He had to give it to the old man for acting like a dog that barks when people approach the front door.

CO Roberts saw Starks watching through the window, nodded at him, and started toward the office. He was followed by a guard Starks recognized and wasn't happy to see.

"Officer Roberts, how can I assist you?"

Roberts waited until they were fully inside the office then closed the door. "Starks, this is the CO I told you about." Roberts gestured to the other guard and said, "Red Brunson, this is Starks."

Brunson chortled and said, "You might say we're familiar." He plunked into the extra chair.

Starks took a seat behind the desk. "Your buddy's being funny, Roberts. Although we weren't introduced, the CO's finger certainly got to know me in a more intimate fashion than I might have liked."

Brunson replied, "Believe me. You guys get the better end of the deal.

Pun intended. According to Roberts, you're a kind of environmentalist here at Sands."

"I don't follow."

"You're into spreading the green."

Starks barely smiled. "You could say that. Roberts says you're the top guy."

"Inmates think gang leaders get away with shit, but they don't do anything unless they do it through me, especially form gangs. I have the pull in this place. With guards *and* officials, those on the take, that is. I know who's who better than anyone here. Don't think I'm not onto you forming your own gang. I was waiting to see how it went before I let you know how things really work in here."

"Sounds like you're a man to have on my team."

"I'm not on anyone's team but mine. I'll let you in on one of my secrets. The only Sands guards not on the take in some way are the ones new on the job. You got any idea how many new guards are here?"

"How many?" Starks said.

"None." Brunson laughed.

Starks strained to keep his feelings from showing. "I know some of them were involved in the murder of Skullars Bailey. Indirectly, I'm sure. Only way his attack could've happened was for one or more guards to look the other way."

"What can I say? Shit happens in this place."

Starks fought hard to control his anger. "Kind of like, 'If you can't beat them . . .'"

"Something like that. Roberts, here, says you pay well. That's good to hear, because you're going to need to. I got three COs I work closely with. They get paid or no deal."

Starks rested back in his chair and studied the man. "I respect that you look after your guys. Here's my offer regarding cell phones and protection. You and—"

"Unless your offer is what you give Roberts or better," he poked Roberts in the arm, "keep it."

Starks focused on Roberts, who said, "I had to tell him or there was no deal."

"You okay with that arrangement?" Starks asked.

"Absolutely. With Brunson in on it, you not only ramp up your protection, you can start or expand any enterprise and have a better chance of it going well."

Brunson cracked his knuckles. "That's right. You do well, we do well." He extended his arms. "*Everybody's* happy."

Starks said, "I don't know about happy. But, profit is always a good thing."

The CO rested his hands on the desk and leaned in until his face was no more than a foot from Starks's. "So's control. I believe we're fishing in the same pond about that."

Starks nodded. "We have a deal. I'll get everything set up so payments start no later than a week from today. Same arrangement, though: Roberts is the go-between."

"I trust him. Just make sure I can trust you."

Roberts stepped forward. "I told you he's okay, Red."

Brunson stood and stretched. "I'm mostly up in front, but my three guys walk the beat inside and in the yard. They'll talk to you sooner or later. Just know other eyes will be watching. My guys will keep their distance, unless they have to interfere. Try not to give them a reason to interfere, and definitely not one that brings the council in on anything. You follow me?"

"I'm right with you." Starks rose and extended his hand. "So we're good?"

Brunson took Starks's hand and squeezed harder than necessary. "As long as you handle your end the right way, we are." He let go and hooked his thumbs on his belt.

Starks glanced toward the window, saw Paco watching, saw Paco shake his head and turn back to his computer. "I have two immediate requests, Brunson."

"You don't waste time, do you?"

"Not when it's important. I want you to transfer Kane Sandler to my cell. My current cellmate is Ronald Jackson. I've discussed this with both men and they've agreed. I'd like Jackson to stay on my block, though. And I'd like this to happen sooner than later."

Brunson scowled. "Didn't take you for a backdoor type."

"It's nothing like that. Kane's no more than a kid. A scared kid. If he's with me, maybe he'll do better."

"If you want to play nanny," Brunson shrugged, "who am I to stop you? I'll take care of it."

"And, I need burner phones as fast as you can get them to me. Let's start with twelve."

"You got cash to pay for 'em?"

"Take care of it. I'll add it to your first payment."

"It'll take a few days for the phones. Can't walk into a place and buy that many without looking suspicious."

"Smart guy like you will figure it out. I need all twelve by Monday."

"Consider it done. But a word of advice: ditch the attitude."

The COs left. Starks waited a few seconds then walked up to Paco.

The old man turned in the chair to face Starks. "What you into, amigo?"

Starks replied, "Self-preservation."

Paco nodded. "It takes what it takes."

"Will you play monitor again? Just for about fifteen or so minutes."

Paco waved a hand. "Sure, sure. Go do whatever. I'll be here when you get back. Unless *el buen Señor* takes me."

Starks hurried to his cell as fast as wouldn't draw attention. Brunson had said nothing happened that he didn't know about. Was that one hundred percent true? Probably eighty to ninety percent was more like it. He'd have to feel his way through that potential landmine. Nothing and no one would be allowed to intrude on his goal to eventually occupy the position at the top. And he had no intention of sharing that place.

What he was paying out was adding up fast. Jeffrey might not say anything about these expenses continuing to escalate, but he'd have thoughts about it. Starks also knew that whether or not Jeffrey spoke up, he'd take care of it.

He got the cell phone and dialed his friend's number.

And wondered if he'd just dug a deeper hole.

He shook off the feeling by reminding himself that when a hole is dug, there's a mountain of dirt on the side.

It was up to him to climb it.

CHAPTER 73

FIVE AFTER FOUR that afternoon, Starks exited the library. When he was two yards from his cell, he heard noises coming from inside, as though the space was being tossed. He slowed his steps, positioned himself against the wall, and edged forward. At the entrance he peeked around and let out the breath he'd been holding. "What are you doing?"

Jackson frowned and shoved a towel into a half full plastic bag. "What do you think? You might have told me."

"I didn't realize the move would happen this fast. I made the request only a little over three hours ago. I intended to tell you the next time I saw you that it was being arranged."

"Someone saved you the trouble."

"You're pissed."

"I'm inconvenienced."

"Where'd they transfer you?"

Jackson pointed to the cell to the left of theirs. "Next door."

"Even better than I'd hoped." Starks turned his chair around, sat, and rested his forearms on the back.

Jackson sniffed a pair of socks, shrugged, and tossed them into the bag. "The guy they moved wasn't as glad, until he heard it was at your request. *Happy* to do it." He shook his head. "All I have to say is—" Jackson's attention shifted to the entrance. "Your new cellmate's here."

Kane held a plastic bag with all his possessions in it, blushing as he shifted from one foot to the other.

Jackson moved his chair to the opposite wall and pointed at it. "C'mon in, Kane. I'm almost done here."

Kane dropped his bag next to the chair and lowered himself into it. "Sorry to be a bother, Mr. Jackson. I hope you don't mind, you know, moving and all."

"You hear that, Starks? Called me mister. Kid, you just earned a few points. But drop the mister or you'll make me feel old." He tucked his bag under one arm and scooped up his blanket and pillow with the other. "That's that, then. Time to make the long trek to my new home."

Kane hopped up. "I can help you carry some of that, especially if you have to go a ways."

Starks said, "Jackson's kidding. He's going into the next cell."

Kane laughed, but it sounded forced.

Jackson reached the cell door and said, "I hope you two will be very happy together."

Starks threw an ink pen at Jackson and missed him deliberately.

"Top bunk's yours, Kane. Go ahead and get settled in."

"Yes, sir."

"I told you before, it's just Starks. I'm not your father or your commanding officer."

Kane's face burned red; he aimed his eyes at his feet. "Yes, sir. Starks."

It was easy to see that Kane was anxious and eager to please. Starks opened a book and pretended to read. Best not to cause the kid to feel watched. Maybe the act of unpacking would help him settle down.

Starks returned his focus to the book, but didn't read. Instead, he wondered what he'd taken on. And why. Sure, he understood what Kane felt about being in prison, and wanted to help. But the weight of the burden created knots in Starks's shoulders and stomach.

He hadn't felt this particular pressure of responsibility since Blake had been born. But Blake wasn't his. Not one inmate he now hauled behind him was ultimately his responsibility.

So why did he feel so damn responsible?

CHAPTER 74

SUNDAY MORNINGS AT his former home with Kayla had tended to be sedate. Even Starks's children had reflected the calmer, slower energy. Until the five of them headed out to the pool in the spacious backyard of their Weston home. Then all bets were off as the children burned energy stored overnight. He and Kayla would recline on the chaise longues and sip Bloody Marys while the housekeeper prepared a brunch that catered to everyone's preferences. Those days were now relegated to his memories-only file.

The fact, he admitted to himself, was that those more pleasant days had disappeared long before he was incarcerated. That had been the Sunday morning routine until the last two years he and Kayla lived together, before he moved out for the second and final time. During their last few months together, Kayla's Sunday mornings involved taming a hangover from too much partying, not that she limited going out until all hours to Saturday nights only. Plus, there were their fights about what time she'd come home and who she'd been out with. His own partying with other women was done on weeknights, but never overnight, unless he lied to Kayla about a business trip. And he never partied in a way that would infringe on weekend family time. Once their fights started happening frequently, there was no more family time outside or anywhere. The children stayed upstairs unless the crash of objects thrown or police showing up brought them in a thumping rush down the stairs to see how much of their world had shattered along with glass.

Children had a right to feel secure, protected. That his children hadn't felt this was a different kind of scar he carried.

That slower Sunday effect had influence at Sands as well. Inmates, typically, were less rowdy. Some went to religious services and bible study. Some kept mostly to their cells, catching up on sleep. The worst of the bunch scouted for easy marks among inmates; their dysfunctional way of proving to themselves they were still alive, still had power, even if only over those weaker than themselves. Most visitors preferred Saturday over Sunday as the day to make the trip to and from the prison to see their loved ones or friends.

The first night with Kane had gone well enough. Almost too quiet. Kane deferred to Starks in every way, even waited to be spoken to. The kid needed to get a backbone. And, nearly every time he looked at the young man, he found those wide brown eyes aimed at him. Like the cocker spaniel he and Kayla had over twenty years ago, only Kane's hair was dark instead of caramel. Starks half expected the kid to trip on his paws or wag his tail when he was given any attention.

At breakfast, where all but Jackson and Ethan were at the table, Kane announced he and Starks were now cellmates. Faces turned toward Starks, faces with a variety of expressions that weren't difficult to read. No one said anything. For too long. Only Trevor made his thoughts known when he snorted. Then they got back to the business of trying to eat the unpalatable offerings and talking among themselves.

Tank sat on the other side of Starks. At a volume only Starks could hear he said, "What's up with that? You have any idea how that looks to these men?"

"Anybody has a problem with anything I do or don't do, tell them to take it up with me." Starks broke a piece off the hard roll and popped it into his mouth. "Do you have a problem with this new arrangement?"

"Nah, man. I know you're straight. I figure Kane's maybe like a substitute for your kids or something."

"My speech about loyalty wasn't me blowing smoke."

"You can count on me. Anyone complains it's 'cause they don't know a good thing. They wouldn't get the same treatment from any other leader in here. Any of them doubt that, all they have to do is watch and learn."

"I don't like my decisions to be questioned. Any decision."

"I'll make sure they understand."

Starks said to his crew members, "When I'm done here, I'm heading to the yard. Any or all of you are welcome to join me."

Trevor smirked and said, "We know Kane will. Hey, we should take bets on how *brown* his nose gets and how fast."

Starks lowered his fork and put his full attention on Trevor. "Another crack from you," he looked up and down the table, "from any of you, and you're out. Did you all get that or do I need to repeat myself?"

Tank glared at Trevor. "You gonna be the rotten mother in the bunch?"

Color spread across Trevor's cheeks. "I was just joking around."

Starks rapped on the table and stood. "Join me or not. If you want out altogether, do it now, before I entrust you with anything you're too immature or too stupid to handle."

Kane rapped and got up. Two-thirds of the crew followed Starks to the yard. They sat on the bleachers, some with their eyes closed against the sunlight; others watched what was going on around them.

One of the newer inmates glanced at Kane several times, until he closed the few feet that separated them. "If I get a couple gloves and a ball, wanna toss a few back and forth?"

"Sure." Kane looked at Starks, who nodded, and then bounded from the bleachers.

Tank said, "He really is a kid."

"He's going to have to grow up fast. There's only so much coddling I can or will do. The rest is up to him. By the way, what's that inmate's name?"

"Willie."

Kane and Willie stood about ten yards apart. Starks watched the ball pass easily back and forth between them. Like the way he and Jeffrey used to play as kids, or how he'd played catch with Blake and Nathan. With Kaitlin, play was usually a tea party with her favorite dolls and stuffed animals, all named, of course. She used to roll her eyes at him when he got one of their names wrong or forgot altogether. She was eight going on nine. Maybe the tea parties had stopped. Starks felt his throat tighten with longing and grief at what he was missing. The losses were too great to measure without cracking even more inside.

Willie and Kane added another couple yards between them. Willie's pitch overshot. Kane ran to retrieve the ball, which bounced and hit the back of an inmate's thigh. The inmate, nearly as bulky as Tank, grabbed Kane by the throat and lifted him off the ground.

CHAPTER 75

STARKS ROCKETED FROM the bleachers. His feet churned up dust as he ran at speed. He skidded to a stop and said, "Put him down."

The man sneered. "Sure. I'll put the little cocksucker down. Permanently."

Starks's left hand grazed the knitting needle in his hem. To draw it out and use it, as exposed as he was, would be a devastating move. "You know what I mean. Release him. Now."

"Or what?" The expression on the man's face altered when he glanced past Starks. The crew approached and formed a circle around them. The inmate moved his feet several more inches apart to secure his balance.

Tank cracked his knuckles. "You heard the man. Put. The boy. Down. Or we gonna put you down."

Kane gasped as his face turned darker. His struggle against the man's grip diminished as each second ticked by.

It was taking too long. Starks retreated and went behind his crew members, until he was in back of the man. Kane's bulging eyes shifted to him; pleaded for help. Panic and rage competed inside Starks. He swung his right leg back hard then forward and kicked up. The man let go of Kane and crumpled to the ground, cradling the injured genitals between his legs.

Starks dashed to Kane, who gasped and sputtered for air. The attacker's handprint showed red on the boy's neck. Kane would never forget this moment, and would have the bruise that drove it home for about a week. "Let the breaths come slow and easy, kid. You're okay."

He stood and scanned the yard for the guards. It wasn't that he wanted to involve them, it was that he didn't. A few COs on his payroll were watching; the shake of Starks's head was subtle. The guards turned away and pretended not to notice what was going on. Starks faced his men who waited for orders. "Some of you take that trash to his cell and explain to him why what he did isn't to ever happen again. Nothing too severe, just enough to make an impression. We don't want any of us put into isolation. The rest of you get the crowd we attracted to go back to what they were doing."

Five of his crew half dragged, half carried the inmate away; Tank was one of them. The others did as told. Inmates in the yard moved away slowly.

One inmate lingered and said to Starks, "You do that for everyone in your gang or just him?"

Starks glared at the man for a moment then said, "I protect my people."

The inmate nodded, said, "Good to know," and then departed.

Starks squatted next to Kane. "How you doing, kid?"

Kane answered in a hoarse whisper, "I'm okay."

"Can you stand?"

Kane nodded. Starks helped him to his feet. "We'll sit on the bleachers while you recover."

He looked away as Kane swiped tears from his face. Pretended not to hear the sniffles. Listened to the kid's ragged breath, half from being choked, half from terror. Felt the body next to him quake—the familiar aftermath of a narrow escape. Or not escaping at all but managing to survive. Sweat streamed down Starks's face. But it wasn't from heat or exertion. It was because a realization punched him in the gut: He'd come close to killing the guy to protect Kane. Had wanted to kill him. Felt frustration when he faced how dangerous it would be to use the needle with so many watching.

How grotesquely satisfying it would have been to use it.

To protect Kane.

He cared too much. It wasn't smart. Protective of his men was one thing. This was another. It defied reason.

He needed to get control of his emotions. Like Gabe kept telling him to.

What the hell is wrong with me?

CHAPTER 76

KANE, TANK, AND six other members of Starks's crew were engaged in various activities in the gym when he joined them. Kane did that puppy thing as soon as he saw Starks. *At least he won't pee on the floor.*

The kid's response to him was flattering. And annoying. He needed to say something to Kane about this before the behavior created and fed tension in crew members. It was time to tell the kid to tone it down. To act like a man.

Starks told Tank to spot him and got into position. He was on his sixth rep when Ethan raced in, moving in fast circles around the bench. Starks sat up and said, "Stop moving. Now."

Ethan came to an abrupt halt in front of Starks, but he was unable to stay still. "G-gotta t-t-talk to you, Starks."

"Talk."

He pointed to a corner. "Over there."

Starks followed Ethan; practiced patience while the young man stammered his message.

"Until it's okay, Starks, stay where people can see you. Don't be alone. Ever."

"What's going on?"

Ethan grinned, winked, and sped off. Starks went back to the bench.

Tank asked, "What was that about?"

"My guess is it's part of his plan for Crazy D."

"You think he can carry it off, whatever *it* is?"

"I don't know. But it seems that part of the plan is to keep me out of it so I can't be blamed. Not that others wouldn't hold me responsible since they know he's with me."

"If I was you, I'd be worried."

"I should make him tell me what he's going to do."

"Maybe better you don't know. If he's caught, and Spencer looks to blame you, you won't know anything. Besides, everyone knows Ethan ain't quite right."

"Safety in insanity." Starks's attention switched to the entrance. "Trevor. Looking more arrogant than usual. I think he's going to be a problem."

Trevor swaggered to the area where the crew members clustered.

"Glad you decided to join us," Starks said.

"Was in the library checking stuff on the Internet. About you."

Crew members' conversations dwindled then ceased. Starks stood and said, "If you want to know something about me, ask."

"Didn't think it was the kind of thing you'd appreciate being asked." Trevor glanced at Kane then back at Starks. "Thought you might have a thing for boys. Didn't find anything about that anywhere. That's a relief. Unless you paid big bucks to hide it. But, man, that wife of yours . . . she was getting it on. Total babe. I'd have gotten in line for that."

Starks leaned forward. "You don't want to go there, Trevor."

"Which 'there' do you mean?" He laughed.

"You should stop. Now."

Trevor strutted slowly up and down in front of the crew. "His wife's a prime piece." He faced Starks. "So what happened with her? I bet you weren't hard enough or long enough to give her a good tickle. Is that why she field-tested so many dicks?" He dropped the grin and faced the crew. "If a man can't control his woman, he shouldn't have the right to tell us what to do."

Tank bolted around the bench. "You on bad ground, boy. Better make your apology and back off."

The thumping sound of blood rushing in Starks's ears was amplified by the silence in the gym. Everyone's attention was fixed on him.

"I want an answer to my question," Trevor said, "because what I've seen so far is someone who's inconsistent about how to operate. Fight, don't fight. Recruit, don't recruit. And, then he does something I really don't understand: He moves Jackson out of his cell and Kane in. I know I'm not the only one wondering about that. I mean, look at the boy," he pointed at Kane, whose face had lost color. "He's so anxious to please Starks, I bet he'd do anything—and I mean anything—Starks asks."

Kane said, "Shut up! You don't know what you're saying."

"Stay out of this, Kane," Starks said. "Trevor's issue is with me."

Trevor laughed. "You put a big fucking cartoon dragon on your arm to look scary. Was that to make up for a tiny dick?"

Starks fisted his hands. "What's your agenda, Trevor?"

"I don't think I lined myself up with the right man." He motioned toward the crew members. "None of us did."

"The boy's a fool," Tank said.

Starks moved forward, until he was less than two feet from Trevor. "You're out of the crew."

"You're the one that needs to be out."

Starks's fist landed in the middle of Trevor's face. Blood spurted from the young man's broken nose. He tackled Trevor, had him on the ground, and his hands around the inmate's throat.

Tank wrapped his arms around Starks and pulled him off. "He ain't worth it, man."

"Let me go. I'm not done with him."

"He's nothing but shit on your shoe. Scrape him off." Tank let go of Starks and grabbed Trevor by the front of his shirt. "I've seen stupid before, but not like you. Get outta here. You see us walking, you go the other way. You talk about our business, and those'll be the last words ever leave your smart-ass mouth." He released Trevor, who sauntered to the door, where he turned and gave Starks the finger.

Starks looked at his men then at the other inmates, who stared back for a few seconds then turned away. He balled his trembling, bloodied hands into fists. The dragon on his arm now seemed gauche, a source of humiliation.

What inmates had heard would spread around his area of the prison. To inmates. To guards. No way to stop it. Everything he'd done recently might now be translated as nothing more than posturing. Having no substance. That without a crew to back him up, he was nothing—just a man with a lot of money who bought people.

He found himself entrenched in a miasma where truths and lies converge, where the strands of each entangle and become impossible to follow, much less separate. He was disintegrating, like New England fog that burned off in sunlight to reveal what was in the shadows.

The damage, which took only minutes to achieve, was done. It was severe. Possibly irreparable. Unless he killed Trevor. Any other gang leader would have done the job then and there. Retaliation would be expected of him. Despite the fact that he'd killed before, whether by his hand or because he'd arranged it, if he didn't take care of this, there would be no reputation to recover. He'd be a victim, yet again. But the idea of ending the life of some arrogant, loud-mouthed young prick didn't feel right either.

Starks heard someone behind him and turned. Kane watched him through eyes filmed with tears barely held back, his expression one of misery, which Starks found perplexing.

If he killed Trevor, what would Kane think?

Why should he even care?

Bile, and a scream he had to suppress, surged upward.

CHAPTER 77

TANK SPOKE IN a voice that carried. "That fool's looking to get himself killed. Any leader takes him in is gonna do it just to find out what Starks has going on. Then he's gonna end him. Damn fool can't be trusted. Man, y'all just got an education about what not to do. Hope y'all learn from it."

Starks glanced at the faces of his men and other inmates in the area. Tank's words seemed to be sinking in. He prayed they took root.

Felipe entered the gym. His steps slowed as he looked around. He spotted Starks and approached him. "Tension's thick. What's going on?"

"I just cancelled someone's membership in my crew. He challenged me."

"The guy with blood all over him."

Starks nodded. "That's the one."

"He's lucky he's still alive to bleed. Or is that temporary?"

"Haven't decided yet," Starks replied. "Change of subject: I started working with weights again. Didn't bother my wrist. No reason we can't resume our lessons."

Felipe looked at him. "Want to try again, amigo?"

"Okay, it bothers it a little, but—"

"We'll wait until next week. Don't overdo the weights thing. Only what's comfortable then stop."

"I guess there's no point arguing with you. Okay, I'll leave you to it. Going to pick back up where I was when that idiot interrupted me."

Starks's crew had returned to their activities, as though nothing had happened. None walked out. Maybe he'd be okay. He called to Tank then went to the bench.

"Thanks for what you said. Anybody making noise about what happened?"

"I think they're okay. If they're not, they're not talking about it. Not with me."

"Could be because you stood up for me."

"Could be because you fixing to put money in their pockets."

"Keep me informed about any static. If I need to talk to them, I will. In the meantime, spot me."

Starks completed ten reps then did some ab work. During one of his sit-ups, he noticed Felipe stood, shoulders slumped and dumbbells in hand, not moving. He finished his set then joined Felipe. "I know downcast when I see it. Anything I can do?"

"Nothing anyone can do. My papa's dying."

"I'm sorry. That's the last thing you want to hear at any time, but especially when you can't be with him."

"Like I'm being fucking ripped in half."

"He's being taken care of, right?"

"I thought they were okay. They didn't want to tell me how bad it is. I found out this morning that Mama quit her cashier's job to look after him. Papa's on hospice, but that doesn't take care of everything else. My brothers and sisters are too young to work or too young to earn much, when someone does hire them for small jobs. The rent's behind three months; they just got the eviction notice. There isn't enough food, unless a neighbor brings something to them." Felipe threw the dumbbells to the floor. "I've let them down. They suffer, and there's nothing I can do to help them."

Starks gestured to the bench. "Let's talk."

Starks reached the corridor that led to his cell block. Jackson turned into the corridor from the opposite direction.

"Starks, I gotta to talk to you."

"Not now, Jackson. I need to make a call."

"The call can wait. Sanchez wants to know when he can expect the powders. He's getting impatient."

"I told him it would take a while."

"A lie I recall well."

Starks slowed his steps. "Tell him I want to meet with him."

"I'll do that, but what are you going to tell him?"

"Exactly what I want him to hear." They stopped at Starks's cell. "I won't be long. Wait for me in your cell. We'll talk then."

CHAPTER 78

THE EIGHT O'CLOCK count went as usual, including no mail for Starks. None for Kane either, he noticed. They started toward the chow hall when CO Brunson, carrying a paper bag, stopped them halfway out of their corridor.

"Need to see you, Starks. Alone," Brunson said.

"Kane, wait here for me. I shouldn't be long."

Brunson scraped Kane's chair across the floor and plopped into it. Starks turned his own chair around and faced the CO.

"Got fourteen phones instead of twelve. I put a thousand minutes on each phone. When minutes get down to about three hundred, let me know. Phones, minutes, my time and gas—fifteen hundred. Make sure it's added to my payment next week."

Starks took the bag from Brunson. "No problem. Good thinking about the extras. Anything else?"

"Just make sure payments are on time. My wife says I'm no fun when I get cranky."

"I'll keep that in mind. And, thanks for the cellmate swap. It was fast and smooth."

"That's what my wife says about my dick."

"Sounds like your wife has a lot to say about you."

Brunson chuckled, hoisted himself from the chair, and exited without another word. Starks turned in a slow circle, contemplating where to hide the phones.

Kane cleared his throat. "You in trouble, Starks?"

"Just the opposite. Right now, I've got to hide these phones until I can give them to the crew. Keep watch at the door without looking suspicious. Tell me if anyone's coming, but don't yell." It seemed ridiculous to have to provide such details to the kid, but so far, he hadn't demonstrated a great deal of common sense.

Kane took his post. Starks placed each phone flat under his mattress, as close to the back wall as possible, along with the paper bag. "Let's get some breakfast."

As they walked the corridors in silence, Starks wondered if he still had a crew. He felt fairly certain Tank would stay with him, but the others? His sigh of relief was genuine when he saw the members seated at their usual table. Jackson was working the breakfast shift in the kitchen; Trevor was nowhere to be seen. Starks and Kane got their trays and joined the others.

Keeping his voice low, Starks said, "I got phones ready to go into service today. After we eat, meet me in the laundry room. I want to get this taken care of so we can start bringing in some cash. Stagger who gets up and when from the table."

Once half the group left, Starks and Kane followed protocol then returned to their cell. The phones went back into the paper bag and under Starks's few dirty clothes in the cardboard box, with Kane's added on top.

Nick and another inmate assigned to laundry duty were the only people in the rectangular room. Starks arranged to comp each man with commissary and told them to leave for about fifteen minutes. They didn't hesitate. Two minutes later, his crew was in place, with Jackson the only one absent.

Starks handed phones to nine members, including Kane, but not Ethan. "Each of you is responsible for your phone. Someone steals your phone, report it to me. You lose or destroy it, replacement cost of the phone and minutes comes out of your earnings.

"Each phone has a thousand minutes. When you get down to three-fifty, let me know. Every Friday afternoon take turns meeting me in the library or meet me in my cell. Bring the phone and the money collected. I'll confirm everything's in order and you'll get paid. If for some reason I'm not available, Tank takes over for me." He glanced at Tank, who puffed his chest and nodded. It was a strategic move as much as a tribute, and they all knew it.

Starks turned to Ethan and said, "You've already got something going on. If you need a phone, I'll let you use one. Better if you don't get caught carrying."

"N-n-n-no one to c-call."

He rested a hand on Ethan's shoulder, smiled and said, "Maybe not now, but that could change, right?" He turned back to the men clustered around him. "Keep in mind what I said: Don't cheat. You don't need to. Any of you have some unusual circumstance that comes up and you need extra cash, see me. I don't want any of you to go without something you really need. That includes your families. Everyone clear?" Heads nodded in response; several inmates' expressions revealed their surprise at his generosity. "Any questions?"

Mike said, "Do we have to do laundry now?"

Starks grinned. "Up to you. Remember to be careful who you tell, and don't get caught. If you get caught, say you found the phone in the yard, or anywhere plausible, and were on the way to turn it in or were turning it in at the next count."

Starks dropped the extra phones, including Kane's under the clothes in his box. "Let's go back to the cell."

"Stand watch, Kane." Starks removed his cell phone from the book and deepened the hole cut into the pages. He dropped the extras into the slot, handed a phone to Kane, and then used his phone to call Jeffrey's number. The call went to voicemail. He left a message about Brunson's additional payment and hid the phone.

"What do we do now, Starks?"

"Let's go to the yard. I want to see if business is kicking into gear like I expected."

"You gave me a phone, but I don't know anyone but the guys. Plus, truth is, I'm scared to approach anyone."

"I know, but it would've looked odd not to give you one. When I think you're ready, you can start your own operation. For now, your phone can be another spare, if we need one. As for the money side, you're not going to be left out. I'll give you a percentage of my take, for keeping your phone safe."

"But I won't be contributing anything. I shouldn't get anything for doing nothing."

"That's my business. Hide your phone and let's go."

"Where should I hide it?"

Starks shook his head and sighed. "For now, stick it in your underwear. Later, we'll make a slit in your pillow or mattress."

Starks watched his crew move around the yard like they were at a networking event, yet they were careful, inconspicuous. And they were smiling. He smiled as well.

The door to the yard swung open. Jackson looked around, spotted Starks and started toward the bleachers.

"We're now in the phone business, Jackson. I've got an extra one for you. We can go to my cell now, if you've got the time. Need to be there for the next count, anyway."

Jackson nodded. "Sanchez wants to see you this afternoon. One thirty, out here."

Starks searched the yard for Tank, found him and said, "I'll be right back."

Tank noticed Starks heading his way and went to meet him. Grinning, he said, "I think we gonna be needing extra minutes before mid-week."

"Good to hear. Get word—quietly—to the crew to meet me here in the yard at one twenty. Sharp."

"What's up?"

"It's what's may be going down."

"We need shanks?"

"Carry, just in case."

"What's this about?"

"Strategic business maneuvers."

On his way back to join Jackson and Kane, Starks smiled at how fortune had been on his side. He'd swapped Saturday in the library for today, without realizing how that would work in his favor.

It was almost like old times. Almost.

CHAPTER 79

NO REWARD WITHOUT *risk*. Starks had printed, framed, and hung those words behind his desk at his office, as a reminder to him and his staff every morning. He was now minutes away from putting the phrase into practice and himself to the test in very different circumstances.

Starks patted the freshly prepped needle secured in place. "Time to go, Kane."

"What's this meeting about?"

"You'll see. However, if it goes south, get yourself out of there."

"Now I'm really scared."

"There's something you have to learn and learn now: You need to adapt to feeling scared and taking action anyway. No way to escape either in here. You can't allow fear to paralyze you, kid. That's no way to live, and it's a sure way to die. Even while you're still alive."

Jackson stood with the crew; his expression was tight, and Starks didn't like seeing that. Ethan, however, bounced on his toes, his demeanor eager, or just damned pleased to be included. Starks wasn't sure which.

The last thing he wanted was to draw attention to the meeting, if he could help it. He scanned the yard. Only about four dozen inmates were scattered around the enclosure. Six guards alternated between observing prisoners and carrying on their conversations with each other.

"Okay, men. Hector Sanchez will be here soon, and I'm sure he won't come alone."

Stinky said, "The Razor?" Mumbles erupted in the group.

Starks held up his hands to quiet them. He pointed at Stinky. "How's the start of your phone business going so far?"

Stinky laughed. "Cha-ching." Others nodded and stated similar success.

Starks raised his hands again. The men settled down. "And I'm sure you not only want to protect this enterprise but see it boom. Right?" Affirmations and nods came from the group. "That's what this meeting's about. My intention—my commitment to each of you—is for you to succeed big. For that to happen, certain measures have to be taken." Starks's focus shifted to the door to the yard. "And that's going to happen now. Sanchez and three of his men are heading our way."

Sanchez's expression went from complacent to a scowl. He said something to Felipe, whose smile faltered and was quickly replaced with concern. The other two Hermanos' postures stiffened.

Sanchez stopped, keeping a distance of two yards between him and Starks. "Amigo, why so many men?"

"Training. It's good for them to learn about negotiations and deals."

"There's no negotiation, no deal. Only the promise you made to me. I think you're stalling. This makes me question your intentions. And your respect."

"I can see why you'd think that. And it's time I address it. You're not getting the product. I'd be a fool to provide it to anyone else, and you know it." In his peripheral vision, Starks saw Felipe flinch. "And I'm taking over the cell phone business. You and your people can continue to operate, but I get forty percent. The other sixty can be split among you. I think that's generous on my part."

Sanchez's dark eyes were flat, cold. "You a loco motherfucker. I think a little worm has crawled into your brain and needs to be cut out."

"I'm not loco, I'm determined."

"No." Sanchez moved forward and jabbed Starks in the chest. "What you are, amigo, is *muerto*. When I tell Crazy D and Seth about you, no one's going to be able to find all the pieces."

"Crazy D doesn't scare me. As for Seth, I don't know who the fuck he is, but he doesn't scare me, either. The fact is this: Align with me, and you, your partners, and your men will profit. I'll see to it. And, you'll keep your rep." Starks smiled. "Hell, it'll probably improve."

Sanchez snarled and said, "You fucked up, *hombre*. I'm going to give you to Crazy D; you deserve it. Me? I like to take care of things fast." He grinned. "Maybe not so clean, but fast. And, Seth? You may not know him now, but you will. Seth does what Crazy D tells him. Crazy D likes to play with his victims. They gonna start with your soldiers and play with you last." He pointed to Kane. "Maybe they do your pet first. Maybe they make you watch."

"They, or you, touch any of my men or me, and—"

Sanchez laughed. "What? We'll regret it?" He put his face inches from Starks's. "I was fair with you. I did deeds for you. Now you fuck with me?" He backed up and looked at Starks's crew. "If you want to keep living, join me. Me and my *hombres* know who you are. We know where you sleep. I give you until tomorrow to decide." He looked at Jackson, who shrugged and shook his head once. Sanchez, glaring, pointed a finger at Starks then sauntered toward the prison door.

Stinky kicked at the dirt. "What the hell kind of negotiation training was that?"

Starks hoped his smile camouflaged his concern. "The kind that gives you a feel for your opponents."

Stinky shook his head. "You can bet your ass I'm feeling them now. They're gonna slice and dice us."

"I don't think that's going to happen."

"But you can't be sure."

Starks glanced at Ethan, who stopped twitching and winked. "Pretty sure." He faced forward. "We're all safe until tomorrow, but stay in groups as much as you can. Stay armed, but don't get caught. And I'm asking you to stay loyal. No reward without risk."

"It's a damn big risk you're asking us to take," Stinky said.

"One I'm taking myself. One I'm taking for all of us. Think about what you have to gain with me driving the bus." Starks faced his crew. "I swear that if you leave me, there will be no penalty other than handing back your phone and forfeiting any payment. I also swear that if you stay with me, you won't regret it. Sleep on it. I'll be on the bleachers after breakfast tomorrow. If you join me, I'll know you're in."

Starks tracked where Jackson was, which was almost to the door. He told Kane to follow him to the bleachers, where he sat and watched Tank talk to the crew. Watched what seemed to be a debate flair then settle a few times. Tank strolled to the bleachers and sat facing the yard.

"I think it's gonna be okay, Starks. Told them Sanchez ain't gonna let them live if they switch teams. They might as well stay where terms are more than fair. Told 'em you're climbing the ladder in this shithole and willing to take them up with you. Asked them to think of it like a mowing machine: why push when they can ride."

"What a ride," Starks replied.

CHAPTER 80

J ACKSON WASN'T AT the three o'clock count, where he should have been. Starks wanted an explanation about the silent exchange between his former cellmate and Sanchez.

He abandoned the idea of going to the gym and then to the showers. It was best not to be too readily available to Sanchez, Crazy D, the yet-to-be-identified Seth, or any of their soldiers. He dropped to the floor and repeated his morning routine, pushing himself to the point of dripping sweat, stopping before he tipped into exhaustion. Stripped down to his underwear, he did an abbreviated bath at the lavatory. Starks didn't look at Kane, but he felt the young man's eyes watching every move.

"How do you do it, Starks?"

"Do what?"

"How do you face off with those kinds of people, especially after . . . after what's been done to you?"

Starks shifted his stance in front of the small mirror so he could see Kane reflected in it. The kid's eyes were fixated on his scars. "They don't exactly give me a choice, do they?"

"I don't mean to be disrespectful, but did you break a promise with that guy?"

"Not exactly. He ordered me to do something I didn't want to do, had no intention of doing, and for good reason. He was right that I stalled him. It was necessary. I had to set some things up before I gave him the news."

"Seems like you're daring him."

Starks smoothed shaving cream onto his face. He was quiet during the first few strokes of the razor. "I never was any good at being a follower. Maybe it was one of the stories my grandfather told me. When he was a boy, he worked a summer on his grandfather's farm. Used a plow pulled by a mule. Said after the first five minutes of following the mule, he realized he didn't care for the view. That's what it's like for me if I'm not in the lead."

"Is that your plan, to be the leader in here?"

Starks positioned the razor and dragged it down his cheek. "My original plan was to mind my own business, be as invisible as possible, and get out early for good behavior. That lasted about a week. Boen Jones decided I was his target. He was twice my size. And he made it clear he wasn't ever going to let up. I had a choice: Be tormented by him every damn day, which would give other inmates permission to do the same, or stand up for myself, even if it meant dying. I've done things—had to—that I never imagined myself doing. I've discovered what I'm capable of, when I'm forced into a corner."

Kane nodded. "Since you got here."

"Since before." Starks rinsed the razor and his face. "Might as well face the fact that while you're here, you may discover what you're capable of, as well." He caught Kane's odd expression reflected in the mirror before the boy turned away.

What the hell is that about?

They stayed in the cell, reading in silence. Dinner was a couple of sandwiches and sweet rolls from Starks's commissary stock.

Book in hand, Starks moved from his desk to his bunk and back, unable to settle in one place. Wherever he sat, he positioned himself to watch the corridor, to watch for Jackson so he could ask him the questions that beat against his skull. But Jackson didn't return, not until a minute before it was time for the electronic doors to slam shut and lock them in for the night. And when he did pass Starks's cell, it was a brief, cursory glance he aimed his way. As though concern about whether his crew would diminish or disappear wasn't enough, there was also this matter to worry about.

Starks resolved to catch Jackson first thing in the morning and learn why he was avoiding him.

CHAPTER 81

SUNLIGHT SQUEEZED THROUGH the narrow window. Starks watched the thin strip of illumination edge its way across his blanket. Like my life, he thought, reduced to a sliver of what it used to be and should be.

He got up from his bunk, stretched, and started his morning routine. One thing was on his mind: pin Jackson in place so he could find out what was going on.

Kane yawned and sat up. He peered out the window and said, "Clouding up again. I wonder if it's ever going to rain." After a moment he added, "Ever noticed how waiting for rain has a feeling to it? It's like a kind of tension you hope is going to end soon so you can feel normal again."

The overhead lights flickered then went to full illumination. Starks said, "Like something hanging over your head."

Kane swung his legs over the edge of the bunk and grinned. "Like waiting for the other shoe to drop."

"When the apple is ripe, it'll fall."

"Make hay while the sun shines."

They laughed. Starks grew somber and said, "When the iron is hot, strike."

Starks tossed two packages of sweet rolls to Kane and opened one for himself. "I need to stock up soon."

"Especially since you're sharing with me."

"No problem."

The sound of cell locks being released echoed through the block; the doors squealed open. A familiar voice announced the count. Starks and Kane took their positions outside the cell. Starks looked left. Jackson was there, staring straight ahead.

Starks whispered to Jackson, "I want to talk to you."

Still not looking at Starks, Jackson said, "Later." He sped off as soon as the count was done.

Starks said, "Let's go shopping, kid."

They left the commissary carrying a bag crammed with foods and toiletries for their use, as well as two more full bags. Rather than returning to the cell, they went into the yard. COs Roberts and Simmons were two of the guards on patrol duty; they and Starks acknowledged each other.

Starks sat with Kane on the bottom riser. His crew milled about in the yard, talking, nodding, and, he was sure, lining up phone customers. He waved at Tank, pointed to the members, and indicated they were to join him.

Tank rounded up the crew. He made it to Starks first and said, "They're all in."

"Good work, Tank."

"Didn't have to work for it. They get it."

The crew lined up in front of Starks. He thought about making a small speech, thanking them for their loyalty. Instead he said, "The stuff in the bags next to Kane is for you guys. A treat for my crew."

The inmates rummaged through the items, grabbing what they needed or wanted. Wrappers and bags were ripped open and contents consumed. At least for now, his crew was content.

Guards' radios crackled loudly. The COs listened and responded, each of their expressions grave.

"Something's wrong," Starks said. His crew grew quiet. Each of them scanned the yard to see what was going on.

An announcement ordering lockdown blared from the speakers, ordered inmates to return to their cells immediately and in silence. Starks stood on the next riser up and searched for Roberts in the crowd of complaining inmates swarming toward the door. Roberts, as were the other guards, shouted for inmates to be quiet and get inside.

Tank said, "Don't look good."

"No, it doesn't," Starks replied. "Everyone get to their cells. Watch your back in the crowd."

Starks and Kane turned the corner into D-Block. Guards yelled, "All the way into your cells. Move it and shut it."

Starks put the bag from the commissary on his bunk and sat next to it. "Sit down, Kane."

Kane perched on the edge of his chair. "What's going on?"

"We'll know soon enough."

Silence pervaded the block, broken only by footsteps thumping down the corridor. Two COs not on Starks payroll stopped at the cell. Starks sighed.

"Starks, Spencer wants to see you."

"What's the problem?"

"Call me CO, Officer, or sir." He motioned for the other guard holding the shackles to move up. "Assume the position."

"What does Spencer want with me? And, what's with the shackles? Officer."

"Spencer will tell you. Shackles were his orders."

Starks held out his wrists and said to Kane, whose face had drained of color, "I'll be back. Wait for me here."

The CO said, "Don't count on it."

CHAPTER 82

INVESTIGATIVE OFFICERS BENTLEY and Kratz stared at Starks from behind the table in the council room. Spencer glowered. The guards hustled Starks toward the table, yanking him to a stop two yards from its edge.

"You're in the shit now, Starks," Spencer said.

Starks remained silent, wondering which of his ventures he was being busted for and how it had happened. Trevor came to mind. Or Sanchez. Or maybe Jackson's ambitions had finally pushed him to cross the line. Sweat started to pool in his armpits.

Spencer pointed his pen at Starks. "Darren Williams."

"What about him?" Maybe this was round one of Crazy D's revenge.

"You've had problems with him."

"No more than anyone else; he's that kind of guy. You're going to call every inmate in here he's pissed off? You won't sleep for months. So, what exactly is the problem?"

Spencer sneered. "Listen to him. Calls it a 'problem.' Why don't you tell me how you managed to separate Williams' head from his body. And why the hell you put his head in a dryer and gave it a spin. You've ruined an expensive piece of equipment."

Starks's mouth dropped open.

"Don't pretend you're shocked, Starks, unless it's because you've been caught."

"I'm not pretending. Nor do I know anything about this. Why are you trying to pin this on me?"

"A suspicious, brutal death of an inmate you've had run-ins with and who, in front of us, promised to get you. Should I keep going?"

"You can keep going until you run out of air. It wasn't me. I have to assume it happened sometime this morning. I can account for my whereabouts. Every second. I was in my cell until after the count. Then I went to the commissary—which you can check easily enough—then into the yard where COs saw me, including Officers Roberts and Simmons. At no time was I in or near the laundry room. And I certainly didn't have time to decapitate anyone then clean up. Look at me. See any indication of a fight? You think Crazy D would've gone down without one?"

Kratz cleared his throat and leaned in. The three men at the table conferred in voices too low for Starks to hear what was being said. Spencer's complexion grew florid. He sat erect, and his chest heaved with each breath. "Get him the hell out of my sight."

One guard grabbed Starks roughly, shoved him forward, while the other CO held the door open.

"Are you going to remove these restraints?" Starks asked.

"Not until your cell."

Starks shuffled along the corridors, aware of nothing he saw, but playing a film on the screen in his mind of Ethan matching the rotation of his head with the clothes spinning in a dryer.

Then he recalled there was another person at Sands whose victim's head had been found at a landfill.

CHAPTER 83

THEY TURNED INTO Starks's cell block. Left and right, inmates paid attention. Several of them nodded at Starks, making it obvious they believed he'd taken out Crazy D, which meant, somehow, word had spread. Their supposition about his involvement could prove to be partially accurate, one way or another. The truth was something he had to find out as soon as he could.

One of the guards unlocked Starks's cell door. The other said, "Assume the position."

Kane was on his bunk, huddled in the corner, head down on his arms that wrapped around his knees pulled close to his chest. Starks found it remarkable then got angry that the young man stayed like that despite what was going on. *As though that position would block an attack.* He called out.

Kane raised his head. His mouth opened then shut when Starks subtly shook his head. Once the door was relocked, with Starks inside, the guards left.

"Relax, Kane. I'm not in any trouble." Starks ran the cold water tap, splashing his face and the back of his neck.

Kane cleared his throat. His voice quivered when he said, "Everyone's heard what happened. And we know who—"

"Don't!" Starks marched to the bunks. "No one knows anything about this. Do you understand me?" Kane nodded. "You don't talk about it ever, with anyone. Are we clear?"

Kane inched back and said, "Sure. I didn't mean to upset you."

"I'm trying to protect you. You're so fucking naïve, it boggles me."

"Geez, I'm sorry." Kane chewed a cuticle. "How long do you think we'll be in lockdown?"

"No idea."

Inmates began to shout. A guard yelled for them to shut the fuck up. Starks positioned himself at the entrance to see what was going on. Guards went cell-to-cell and ordered inmates to approach the barred door one at a time. Each man removed his shirt and pants and rotated in a slow circle. Kane was flustered when it was his turn, but managed not to lose it. The request wasn't made of Starks. When the inspection was completed and guards exited the corridor, voices broke out at full volume.

Four hours later the cell doors opened again.

Starks said, "Let's see if any of the guys went to the yard." Instead of turning right, Starks turned left. Jackson wasn't in his cell.

*

Absent from the crew waiting on the bleachers were Jackson and Ethan. Tank saw Starks and said something to the crew. All heads turned in his direction. He was a yard away when they all began to talk at once.

"Was it Ethan?"

"Couldn't be. Right, Starks?"

"That re—guy's not smart enough to do that."

Tank said, "What about it, Starks? Think it was Ethan who chopped Crazy D?"

It was understandable that they were uneasy. The attack had been beyond what even he had anticipated. "I think you can relax. It would take someone far larger and more powerful than Ethan to do what was done. It would take several people, in fact."

Some of the men laughed in relief. Comments were made about how ridiculous it was to consider scrawny Ethan as the culprit.

Starks needed to find him. "Where is Ethan? Anyone see him after we were let out?" No one had. "Where's his cell?"

Tank answered, "B-Block."

"Unless any of you have a reason to leave, wait for me here."

Alone in his cell, Ethan sat cross-legged on his lower bunk, doodling on the window glass with his finger. Starks made his presence known.

Ethan turned around slowly, grinning as though lost in a world no one but he could see. Starks pulled up a chair and sat. Neither of them said anything for several moments.

Starks spoke first, keeping his voice at a level only the two of them could hear. "Looks like Crazy D won't be a threat anymore."

Ethan's grin stretched wider. "The sonofabitch was so easy."

Stunned at the smooth delivery of that sentence, Starks stayed still and speechless.

Ethan chuckled and continued. "I convinced him I was desperate to give him a blowjob. That I believed the nectar of his loins would give me super powers; though, I used different words, of course." He laughed. "You were right about his arrogance.

"I'd reconned enough to know that no one ever goes to the laundry room until about nine thirty. Crazy D showed up minutes after the count, eager to humiliate me. Had me beg. I stripped and stuffed my clothes and shoes into the same dryer where I'd hidden the knife I'd procured from . . . but that would be telling. I left the dryer door open and wagged my penis and ass at him, pleading in full stammer, even called him my master.

"The bastard doubled over with the hilarity of it all. That's when I severed his revolting swastika in half. It's not that simple to do, you know. Then I clean myself with bleach and soap powder at the sink—I'm going to itch and burn for a week." To emphasize this, he scratched various parts of his body with a ferociousness that left marks on his arms, neck, and face.

Starks released the breath he'd been holding. "What did you do with the knife?"

Using animated gestures, Ethan said, "I taped it to my calf, got dressed, and went to the chow hall for a breakfast of pig slop. When I was done, I pretended to scratch my leg—though, as you see, it's no pretense. The tray was put into position so I could hide the knife, which I deposited into the food scraps. I stuck my hand in, pretending to rummage around, making sure the knife descended farther and farther down. I retrieved a half-eaten roll, which I ate to the disgust of inmates and guards."

Several silent moments passed then Starks said, "That was a clear, concise, stutter-free report."

"Ethan Greene, at your service."

"I was right to reserve my assessment of you."

Ethan's posture went rigid. "What do you mean?"

"I wasn't entirely convinced you were as affected as you made out to be. Especially not after your clever demonstration in the chow hall."

"It was practically harmless. Those two had blood in their urine for a week and a backache. They recovered easily enough with bed rest and antibiotics."

"It was slick. I'll give you that. You're proficient in your—is disguise the right word?"

"Drama training. However, I'd appreciate it if we kept my charade a secret between us, say, in payment for a favor performed with finesse."

"The only way anyone will learn the truth is if you tell them. I persuaded the crew it was impossible for you to have done it; that all they had to do was consider your size to see *how* improbable."

"Good thinking, Starks."

"I'm relieved you're on our side."

"Make no mistake, I'm on my side. But you didn't judge me. Even though you had doubts, you showed compassion in a wasteland, and you entrusted me with an important task. Now, I have a favor to ask."

The words didn't come easy, but Starks was obligated to say them. "Name it."

"Whenever you need a similar performance, do think of me. An actor needs practice to keep in good form."

"I'll keep that in mind."

Starks stood and extended his hand, which Ethan shook. Ethan returned to his bunk and resumed scrawling nothing on the glass. Starks headed back to the yard. He wanted to get Kane and return to their cell.

There was something he was certain of: Ethan was talented.

Useful.

Insane.

CHAPTER 84

THE EVENTS OF the morning delayed lunch by a couple of hours. Starks and his crew crowed around the chow hall table for sandwiches of stale bread and one thin slice of bologna with dried edges paired with plain, unsalted boiled macaroni. The lack of conversation in the room had its own electrical current. Brutality was common in maximum security prisons, especially because inhabitants had done something brutal to get there. But what had happened to Crazy D seemed to rattle even the hardcore prisoners. Particularly because no one, aside from two inmates and the victim, knew with absolute certainty who was responsible.

Starks glanced around the room for Sanchez, but neither he nor any of his men that Starks knew were there. He wondered if they were being questioned by the council. Wondered if the atrocity would cause Sanchez to break code and point a finger at him, without realizing his alibi was sound. No. If Sanchez suspected Starks, he'd deal with the matter personally. Starks looked over at Ethan, who continued his performance complete with jerky movements; he winked at Starks.

Starks rapped on the table, stood and said, "Kane, go with the crew to the yard. I'll catch up with all of you later." He didn't wait for a reply. Tray emptied and stacked, he headed for Gabe's workroom.

The door opened after the second knock. Gabe said, "Had a feeling you'd show up." He gestured to the small table and chairs.

Once seated, Starks picked up a pencil and turned it end over end, each time touching the tips to the table.

Gabe said, "Want to tell me about Crazy D?"

"I don't know anything about it, other than it happened."

"Right. Spencer hauled you in to amuse himself."

Starks tossed the pencil down. "I wasn't involved. I had proof."

"So, someone did you a favor."

"What do you mean?"

"Someone took care of him and now you don't have to."

"I hadn't thought of it like that."

"Hadn't you?" Gabe shrugged. "First time I don't know who did what. We don't have to talk about that. What's done is done. There's something else I want to say to you."

"I'm listening." Starks picked up the pencil then put it down.

"Heard you defended Kane. And how. That was good thinking. You could've taken it further, but didn't. Guards would've stood up for you, since you were saving another man's life."

"It always amazes me how well informed you are."

Gabe smiled. "It pays."

"I'm sure."

"Heard about Trevor, too. I warned you about him."

"He blindsided me. Humiliated me in front of my guys and others. I thought maybe everything I'd built up had been demolished. Thankfully, it hasn't been. And even though I didn't kill Crazy D, people are giving me credit. I can see it in their eyes. My rep's still good, if not better."

"If you say so. What are you going to do about Trevor?"

"I haven't decided."

"One decision has the power to change everything."

"I know that."

"Life-changing decisions aren't always easy to make, Starks. In here, you're forced to make them more often than out there. Being in here is like being in an ongoing war. Between inmates, inmates and guards, between what was and what is. These wars are fought in stark surroundings, vacant of the good things you once enjoyed or strived for. Bleak so you're reminded every day that a decision you made got you locked up."

"What's your point?"

"You got a lot of battles going at once. Let me give you something to think about. The biggest battle is fought inside us, between the part that wants to remain human and the part that questions whether that can happen. Especially when everyone else is engaged in the same inner battle. Some believe the only way to end it is to strike out at others. Like a pressure cooker that needs an outlet for the steam that builds inside. If there's no release, the pressure blows the lid off and you're cleaning the kitchen, floor to ceiling."

"Again, what's your point?"

"Sometimes we're given only one option: Them or us. Sometimes we have options, like with the guy who went after Kane. You've got options about what to do about Trevor. You just have to decide which part of you will do the choosing, the part that wants to remain human or the other one."

"I guess that means you're not going to tell me what to do about him."

"Not my decision."

Starks pressed his fingers against his eyelids. "And your point is that I should consider my options."

"*Your* options, Starks. What you want to do. Not what others expect you to do."

Starks nodded and stood. "Here's me, going to consider my options."

"Sometimes it feels like our life has turned to ashes."

"So I've learned."

Gabe nodded and pointed a finger at Starks. "Be like the phoenix and rise from those ashes. It's your choice. That's if you want to climb out of the hole you've fallen or been pushed into. Or dug for yourself."

Outside the workroom, Starks leaned against the wall. Ashes. He felt covered head to toe with the stuff. The decision to kill Boen Jones and Mike Lawson had been ones he'd had to make. They'd tried to kill him. Only some twisted luck had caused them to fail. Crazy D had to go because there was no doubt about his intentions. Those deaths happened as a result of his calculated decisions based on facts, not because someone insisted he take action.

As for Trevor, he seriously doubted the guy would personally attempt a physical attack; though, he could probably get someone on board to do it. What the hell was the kid's beef with him? The only thing he'd ever done was correct him about his attitude. Surely he hadn't been that offended or embarrassed, and he wasn't the only one corrected about how Ethan was to be treated.

Ethan.

Did Ethan know what Trevor had done? He must. It was almost a given that at least some of the crew had talked about it in front of him, if not other inmates who'd witnessed the confrontation.

The question was, Would Ethan take the initiative to go after Trevor, or was he waiting eagerly for permission?

That was only one question. There was one more.

What am I going to do about this?

CHAPTER 85

STARKS'S CREW EXPECTED him to join them in the yard. It was the last thing he wanted to do. He needed time to himself, without another person's thoughts occupying the same space as his own, without hearing another person's movements or breaths.

Footsteps came up fast behind him. Starks gripped the hem of his shirt, bent into strike position, and swiveled around.

Mike, red-faced and puffing, skidded to a stop. He clutched a folded towel, with toiletries poking out the end, to his chest. "I been looking everywhere for you. Got cautioned three times for running."

"What's up?"

"I was going for a shower." Mike shook his head and took a few deep breaths. "Got stopped in my tracks at the entrance. Sanchez was in there. Heard him say you gotta be taken out and soon because you took out Crazy D, and because you broke faith with him. Sanchez told someone to set up a meeting in a place where he won't be interrupted when he executes you—that's the word he used."

"Lucky you were there."

"That's not the worst."

"What is?"

"I heard who said he'd take care of arranging it and getting you there."

"Who was it?"

"Jackson."

CHAPTER 86

"LET'S PUT YOUR stuff in my cell. Last thing we want is for Sanchez to know he was overheard and that it was you."

They were in and out of Starks's cell in seconds. Starks pushed the door to the yard open and strolled toward the bleachers, with Mike at his side. "Stop looking around like a twitchy mouse." After a moment he added, "And don't mention Jackson."

"But, Starks—"

"Leave him to me."

All but Jackson congregated on the bleachers. Ethan stopped circling his arms overhead and studied Starks, who thought maybe the young man-slash-actor had radar.

Tank said, "We're sweating like pigs waiting here for you."

Starks motioned for Mike to sit, but remained standing. "Listen up. Sanchez is ready to act and fast. He's got someone," he flashed a look at Mike, "setting up a meeting somewhere isolated enough so he can kill me." No one spoke, but all eyes were aimed at him. "I don't think Sanchez will bring more than a couple soldiers with him. More men than that would draw too much attention. Plus, I'm sure he believes he can take me by himself, and wants to. I'll bring a few men with me, for the same reason. I want Tank and—" Ethan, seated alone behind the crew, tapped his chest once. "And Ethan."

The men were silent a few seconds then the protests erupted.

"Settle down," Starks said. "The reason I picked Ethan is my own. For one thing, he's good at creating a diversion. Any of you tried what he gets away with, it would be suspicious."

Stinky eyed Ethan. "Yeah, but a diversion ain't gonna make The Razor forget why he's there."

Ethan yowled, dropped his pants, and mooned Stinky. Stinky jumped to the next riser, ready to fight.

Starks said loudly, "Enough."

Tank frowned and said, "Any idea when we gonna get the word?"

"I'm sure it'll be soon."

"Shouldn't we be doing something?"

"We are," Starks replied. "We're waiting for someone to approach us."

Kane jumped up. "I'm going with you." Other crew members voiced the same intention with equal insistence.

"No. And I don't want to hear anymore about it."

Starks listened to the heated discussion going on around him. Boisterous voices drew his attention to the left. Sanchez and four of his gang had entered the yard. Sanchez sneered at Starks for several seconds then turned away.

A minute later, Jackson came through the door and started toward the bleachers. He stopped a few yards away and motioned for Starks, who got up and joined him.

"Sanchez wants a meeting."

"When and where?"

"Four fifteen. In the showers." Jackson turned to leave.

"Jackson."

"Yeah?"

"Make sure you're there."

"Count on it."

CHAPTER 87

STARKS MISCALCULATED THE number of men Sanchez would bring to the fight. He'd expected two or three. There were six, plus Sanchez, with Felipe on Sanchez's right. Seven to four. He and Tank were armed, and he was fairly sure Ethan was as well. It might not matter, not with these odds.

Sanchez's men formed a circle around Starks, Jackson, Ethan, and Tank.

"You're one stupid gringo," Sanchez said. "I don't care you killed Crazy D. More *dinero* for me, but Seth is pissed."

"Glad you can see the bright side about Darren. You must be scared, though, if you brought this many men to a meeting."

"This ain't no meeting." Sanchez laughed. He pointed to his right cheek. "This afternoon I'm going to put another blue teardrop right here. First, my soldiers are going to mess all of you up, so none of you can give me any trouble." He grabbed Jackson's arm and pulled him to the side. "Except Jackson. Your soldiers will recover—I want them to join me. But you, amigo, you I'm going to carve like roast *pollo*. Maybe I leave your head attached, maybe not. Maybe I mail it to your children. A present from their papa."

Tank positioned himself next to Starks. Ethan pretended to catch invisible flying things in the air. Jackson moved only his eyes, checking each man in turn.

Starks kept his gaze fixed on Sanchez. "You should look after your men better than you do." He shook his head. "You can forget about getting that teardrop today, or any day." Without shifting his focus, he said, "Felipe, how's the family? They have enough to eat? Is your father as comfortable as possible? Your mother getting some rest?"

Sanchez turned his head toward Felipe. "What the fuck's he talking about?"

Starks answered. "He knows exactly what I'm saying." His eyes flicked to Felipe.

Felipe nodded once. Three of the Hermanos grabbed Sanchez. One man pulled a sock from his pocket and forced it into Sanchez's mouth. The other two Hermanos posted themselves at the entrance. Felipe pulled a wad of thin rubber gloves from a pocket. He handed them to the men and slid a pair on. "Starks, you and your men can leave. Or you can stay. Up to you."

"I'm staying."

"Then you and your men should stand far enough away. Now."

Starks and the other three hurried to the farthest wall. Starks turned to Jackson. "You did well, but you should have given me more information."

Tank and Ethan looked from Jackson to Starks.

"Couldn't," Jackson said. "Sanchez had eyes on me all the damn time. I had to convince him I'd turned against you. Couldn't be seen talking to you, unless I was doing his bidding."

Felipe turned the Cold knob for one of the showerheads on high. Water sprayed down then out as the men positioned Sanchez underneath.

Sanchez's eyes were wild. He struggled, his screams muffled by the sock. Tank stared up at the ceiling. Ethan remained still, watching with an interest that disturbed Starks.

Felipe said, "Turn him to face the wall." He removed the straight razor from Sanchez's waistband, flicked it open, and from behind, slid the blade across his former leader's throat. Sanchez fell limp to the floor.

With a few rapid strides, Felipe reached a drain on the opposite side of the room. He used the razor tip to loosen the screws on the cover, dropped the razor in, putting the screws back in place with a thumbnail.

One of the men pulled a steel wool pad from a pocket. The other man removed a bar of lye soap from his. The four men went to different showerheads, stripped, and scrubbed the blood from their bodies. One of the

Hermanos guarding the door removed spare clothing from the back of his pants.

Felipe asked him, "Anything we need to worry about?"

"No one saw nothing."

Felipe and the other three Hermanos handed their stained clothes to the man. "You know what to do."

Starks pulled Felipe aside. "I wasn't sure how this was going to go down. But I didn't expect his men to side with me. I wasn't entirely certain about you."

"They sided with me. Against Sanchez. I picked men he'd cut more than once. They were eager to pay him back. As for me, as soon as I knew his plans, I figured you'd rely on me to return your favor."

"Tell these men I'll reward them, no matter what their motivation was. In fact, tell every Hermanos they'll get compensation if they join me."

"They're going to ask how much."

Starks glanced at Sanchez's body and at the blood thinned by water disappearing down the drain. "What were they getting from him?"

"Nothing but rep and occasional stingy commissary."

"They'll get more than that from me, and it'll build over time. The better I do the better they'll do."

"What about Seth?"

"I'm not worried about him."

"You should be."

CHAPTER 88

A COUPLE YARDS DOWN the hallway from the showers, Starks said, "Tank, tell the crew the meeting was brief and ended on friendly terms. I don't want them asking any questions." The four of them walked in silence through the corridors and into the yard. Some of the crew sat on the bleachers, cheering other members shooting hoops.

Kane dribbled the ball, threw it, and thrust a fist into the air when the ball dropped through the ragged net. He saw Starks and jogged to the bleachers. "Everything go okay?"

"We resolved our differences. Get back in the game. Looks like you're having a good streak. No point wasting it."

It was only a matter of time before Kane learned the truth. It puzzled Starks as to why he felt guilty about that, almost ashamed. He reminded himself it wasn't his hand that had wielded the razor.

Starks rested his back against the riser behind him and shut his eyes. This was the brief calm before the storm. Once Sanchez was discovered, all hell was going to break loose.

Spencer would more than likely haul him back to the council room. He'd lie. Either they'd believe him or they wouldn't. This time, he didn't have proof of where he'd been. He needed a plausible lie, but the idea of coming up with one was more than he could tackle at the moment, other than saying he'd been in the yard, enjoying the game. His crew would back him up. Guards were another matter. None of the COs on his payroll was pulling yard duty.

Sunlight created a red filter through his eyelids. Like the blood that had been spilled. Most gang leaders would strut and brag about what an accomplishment it was to eliminate two threatening opponents in such a short amount of time. This was one time pride eluded him. So did the relief he'd anticipated. Instead, he had a pounding head and an eddy in his gut.

One person kills.

Someone in turn kills that person.

A cycle is created and perpetuated. Where was the line to be drawn? Who would draw it first?

In that moment, he knew what to do about Trevor.

Although he had no appetite, Starks had to maintain the façade of innocence and normalcy. "Let's hit the chow hall." As one, he and his crew joined other inmates moving through the door.

Inmates in line for trays moved with lethargy that matched their enthusiasm about the food.

Tank said, "Smells like they cooked everything in week-old dishwater."

"Don't think they didn't," Mike replied. "Jackson, what the hell goes on back there?"

"You don't want to know."

The red overhead lights flashed, the alarm wailed.

Stinky said, "Now what?"

To a man, every crew member focused on Starks. "Turn the fuck around."

Lockdown was announced. Inmates left their trays on the table and emptied from the chow hall. News about Sanchez passed among them in whispers, despite guards shouting for them to stop talking.

Back in their cell, Starks waited for guards, for shackles, for accusations, for extended SHU time, for his sentence to be changed to life and the transfer to Red Onion, the worse goddamned prison in the U.S., where he'd serve his sentence until he died. Which would probably be within a week, if that.

The moon crossed the night sky.

The sun rose.

No one came for him.

CHAPTER 89

CO ROBERTS YAWNED as he followed procedure for the count. Starks said, "I'd appreciate a few minutes of your time when you're done here."

"I want to talk with you, too." Roberts moved to the next cell, where there was one inmate waiting instead of two. Starks assumed Jackson had already left for kitchen duty. He hoped that was the case.

Count over, Starks, trailed by Kane, entered the cell and said, "Want commissary for breakfast or chow hall?" He held up a cinnamon roll.

"Whatever you want, Starks."

It was now or never. "I want you to be more independent."

"What do you mean?"

"Anything happens to me, you'll be on your own. Might as well get into practice."

"Is something going to happen to you?" Kane gnawed on a nail.

Starks threw the roll onto his desk. "How the hell should I know? All I'm saying is you need to . . . When that guy grabbed you by the throat, what did you do? You dangled there like a fucking puppet. You could've kicked him in the balls ten times. An altercation can happen anytime in here. If you don't grow a pair and learn how to stand up for and defend yourself, you'll pay the price. That's all I'm saying."

"No one bothers me anymore, because they know I'm with you."

"That's not a guarantee. You're in a fucking maximum security prison. You're aligned with a strong crew, but there'll be times when you're on your own. It's unavoidable. Acting like a skittish animal is going to draw intimidators to you. Any of this making a dent?"

"Yeah." Kane kicked a chair leg. "I get it. I'm a burden you don't want. Fine. From now on I'll stay out of your way."

"That's not my point."

"Might as well be. I'm going to the chow hall. All by myself." Kane, head down, stomped from the cell. He dodged CO Roberts and kept going.

"What's up with him?" Roberts asked.

"He'll get over it. He'll have to."

"Before you ask or tell me whatever, I have to know: were you involved in either or both killings?"

"Why is that when something goes down, people look at me? I'm not the only person those two had issues with."

"I shouldn't have asked. What did you want to see me about?"

"Brunson. Tell him to meet me in the library during my shift this afternoon."

"I'll deliver the message. Anything else?"

Starks shook his head. Roberts left.

He ripped open a sweet roll package and sat in his chair. His hand holding the roll hung at his side. The conversation with Kane hadn't gone well. The words had spilled out, with no forethought. What he'd told the kid was true. Spencer hadn't sent for him, but that didn't mean he wouldn't. Kane could find himself living alone in the cell for a month. Longer. Or sharing a cell with someone who'd take advantage of him every way possible. Sure, the crew could threaten or deal with anyone who bothered or harmed Kane, but would they stay together if Starks was removed?

Footsteps echoed in the corridor, growing louder as they came closer. Tank stopped at the entrance. "Kane's not happy."

"Not my job."

"I hear that. Wanted to tell you some of what's going around."

Starks motioned to the other chair. "Want a sweet roll or something?"

"Thanks." Tank consumed the roll in two bites. "Couple people said Seth's got a bull's-eye on you."

"By now, he should realize it's better for him if he either comes in under me or avoids me altogether."

"I guess we'll see about that. The other thing is Trevor. He's triggering people's tempers. Some of those people saying you should've taken care of him. That Sanchez or Crazy D would've already sent him home in a box to his momma."

"No one gets to decide what I'm going to do to whom and when but me."

"That mean you made a decision about Trevor?"

"Yes."

"Wanna tell me?"

"I'll keep it to myself for now."

Tank shrugged and scratched his ear. "Thought we'd hear more about what happened. Felipe and some of their guys got questioned. Told the council they didn't know nothing. That they were in the gym at the time. I don't know if the council's done asking questions, but it's gone quiet."

"Maybe no news is good news."

"Maybe you got enough guards in your pocket."

"What's enough?"

Tank laughed then grew somber. "If the same kind of shit keeps happening in here, they gonna make our days twenty-three hours in, one hour out. That would piss a whole lotta people off. They maybe blame you."

"I don't think that's going to happen. The biggest troublemakers are gone. Things are going to calm down, at least for a while."

"What about Seth?"

"I'm beginning to think Seth's like the bogey man. A name thrown out to scare people."

"You probably seen him around. Got a lion tattoo on his left arm. He was one of Big Bo's soldiers."

Recollection hit. "I had a couple run-ins with him after Big Bo was killed. Seth wasn't too happy with me when I got him Tasered and thrown into the SHU twice in one week."

"He took over Bo's gang. People saying you need to be scared. In fact, half the people talking to me say they scared shitless of you. Other half think you weak, because of Trevor."

"I can't afford to be overly concerned with what others think of me."

"You sure about that?"

"I know what I'm doing."

CHAPTER 90

THE ANGST HE felt reminded Starks of the first time he'd dropped each of his kids off at school, entrusting his or her care and well-being to strangers. It was irksome to feel that way now about Kane. He needed to find Kane to—what?—apologize, make sure the kid was still breathing? He wanted and needed Kane to trust himself. That meant he had to trust Kane, as well.

Trust someone and you pay for it. Distrust was a necessary pain in the ass.

He glanced at the clock: Ten till eleven. Kane had to come back for the count.

Any attempt to focus on words on a page was futile and had been all morning. Starks put the book away and splashed cold water on his face, stopped himself from standing at the door to watch for Kane. Didn't want to be spotted by the kid or other inmates looking as anxious as he felt.

Three minutes before eleven, chatter filled the block as inmates filed in from wherever they'd been. Two minutes before eleven, Starks's heart thumped hard. He picked at a cuticle until it bled. One minute before eleven, he got up from the chair and stood outside his cell door, gaze fixed on the mouth of the corridor. Kane turned the corner and jogged to his place next to Starks.

"Cutting it close, kid. There's a penalty for being late or missing count."

"Just staying out of your way."

"You're acting like a petulant child."

"What are you gonna do, put me in time-out?"

"You're already in time-out." Starks elbowed Kane.

Kane scowled at him then grinned. The count started; they stopped talking.

Afterwards, Starks said, "Want to come with me to the library today?"

Kane shook his head. "Me and the guys have a basketball game running. You going to chow with us?"

"I'll eat one of my sandwiches here. Think I'll go to my shift early."

"Catch you later." Kane speed-walked away.

If only every disagreement was resolved so easily, Starks thought.

There were still a number to resolve.

And always more springing up at him like a jack-in-the-box.

*

Watching the clock was an unsettling annoyance, but Starks needed Brunson to show. It was only one twenty; two hours and forty minutes until his shift ended. He could count on Roberts to convey the message. No telling what time Brunson would arrive, or if he would. Starks busied himself with every mundane task he could think of.

At a quarter to four, Brunson swaggered in. Starks motioned with his head for the CO to follow him into the office.

Brunson closed the door. "Got the payment. All of it. Your guy works fast."

"Glad it went well."

"Why'd you want to see me?"

"I have what may be an impossible task for you."

"Nothing's impossible if the price is right, except maybe getting you out of prison."

"It's regarding Trevor Morgan."

"I know that little prick." Brunson smirked. "Let's hear it."

CHAPTER 91

A STEADY DRIZZLE KEPT the dust in the yard down and filled the air with an earthy scent. Instead of watching his crew play basketball from the sidelines, Starks joined the game. Plenty of time to shower before his shift started at one.

He was aiming a shot when CO Roberts called out to him. Starks blocked from his mind what the guard might want—like to tell him he was caught and his life was over—and made the throw. The ball went through the hoop. Crew members patted him on the back as he jogged over to Roberts. "What's up?"

"Woman's here to see you. Margaret Hessinger."

Starks stared at Roberts.

"Want me to send her away?"

"No. I wondered if she'd actually have the nerve. Can't help how I look or smell, not that I give a fuck what she thinks." He turned to the players and shouted, "I'm out. There's something I have to take care of."

Starks kept his pace moderate so he could gather his thoughts and tamp down the anger that threatened to boil to the surface. There was no advantage to greeting her with rage. Margaret wanted something from him. He wanted something from her.

The visitation room was nearly empty. Only three tables had people at them. If possible, Margaret's face was even more pinched and pale than it had been at his trial.

He was halfway to her when she saw him. She got up too fast, too clumsily. Her chair fell over, drawing guards' and visitors' attention. Face flush, she righted the chair and held out her trembling hand to him.

Starks glanced at the extended hand and said, "Seriously?" He took the chair across the table from her.

Margaret chewed her bottom lip and stared at him. "I didn't recognize you at first."

"You look the same."

She patted the right side of her thin, lank hair then dropped her hand into her lap. "Thank you for agreeing to see me." When Starks didn't respond, she said, "I'm divorcing Ozy."

"I heard."

"He's trying to persuade me to drop it. He says our children need a stable home with two parents."

"Too bad he didn't feel that way about my children."

Margaret's cheeks reddened. "It wasn't just him your wife was with, and you know it."

"Unbelievable. You're still defending him."

"No . . . I . . . I'm not doing this right."

"What do you want, Margaret?"

"I want to know if there's anything you can tell me to persuade me to go through with the divorce."

"I would have thought hearing Jenny's testimony would have convinced you. Let me remind you that he was fucking Kayla for three years. Promised to dump you and marry her, which he never intended to do, not that that should score any points. Did the nasty with my wife in public, where anyone could have seen them, and did. And there's that whole group-sex thing. How much more convincing do you need?"

"It's not so easy to destroy my family."

"It was easy enough for you to destroy mine." Starks exhaled hard and shifted forward. "Ever wondered what he did while you were away with the kids?"

"He was having sex with your whore of a wife."

Starks snorted. "When you and your children were out of the way, he had sex with Kayla in your house. In your bed, on your dining table, where your children played, inside and out. If there was a surface where they could lie, sit, kneel or stand, it got used. Ozy didn't give a shit about family stability. Or you. Only thing he was concerned about was—"

Almost in a whisper, she said, "In my house?"

"Good. You were listening."

"Oh, God." Margaret's trembling hand went to her bony chest. "I ought to burn the place down with the bastard in it."

"I don't advise it. You might end up in a place like this. You might end up looking like this." He raised his shirt.

Margaret flung her hand over her mouth, her gaze fixed on his scars. Color drained from her face. "I feel sick." She retrieved a tissue from a pocket and held it to her lips.

Starks lowered his shirt. "What a luxury for you that that's all you have to feel about it. You lied about the knife. I probably would have gotten some time in a less severe environment for assault, but not fifteen years in a place that put me into a coma for a few months and scarred me for life."

Margaret looked up. "You were in a coma?"

"Ironic, right? I went to your house that night to tell you what was going on because I figured you didn't have a fucking clue. Your husband attacked me. I fought back. He pulled a knife on me, which he intended to use, and I fought back. No matter how you look at it, everything I did that night was self-defense. And it cost me everything. What I want to know is why you lied."

"I thought I was protecting my family. My children."

"That's something I understand. And yet—"

"We both lost everything that night."

"Wrong. We lost long before then."

Margaret was silent for a few moments. "The night it happened, I didn't believe what you said about Ozy."

"Didn't want to, you mean."

"I was terrified when I saw you beating him. Distraught because my kids saw what you were doing to their father."

"That's the only thing I regret about that night."

"I'm sure if you could go back in time, you wouldn't do it."

"If I could go back in time, I'd do a better job of it and enjoy it more."

"You don't mean that."

"His coma should have been permanent. Then you wouldn't struggle with whether or not to divorce a man who has no respect for you or your marriage, because eventually you'd pull the plug and get on with your life. The question is, Would I get on with mine in here or out there? Would my children still have their father?"

Margaret lowered her eyes and shrugged.

"So," Starks said, "is there anything else you'd like to say?"

"I'm sorry."

"All things considered, Margaret, an apology doesn't cut it. You could say you'll make it right; that you'll leave here and go directly to the police or whomever and admit the truth about the knife."

When she remained quiet, Starks shoved away from the table and left the room without looking back. He could call Parker and tell him what Margaret admitted, but if asked, she could deny it. The admission had to come from her.

All he could do was hope her conscience wheedled her until confession was the only way to silence it.

CHAPTER 92

THE NEXT DAY, when a CO told Starks a woman waited for him in the visitation room, hope filled him. He was certain Margaret had decided to confess and felt it worth another trip to announce this to him. He sped through the corridors, debating whether to thank her or make her grovel for a few minutes.

He spotted his visitor easily, even though she didn't look the way she usually did. In fact, she looked like hell. Starks stood in place, trying to get his tremors to stop. Waited for the hair on the back of his neck to lay flat. Waited for profound disappointment to abate. Reflex caused him to dig his nails into his palms as he waded through the mostly empty tables to where Kayla waited.

She raised her aqua eyes, saw him, and attempted a smile, which she instantly abandoned. He knew his expression was anything but welcoming.

"What the hell do you want?"

Kayla shifted in the chair. "I wish you wouldn't speak to me like that. After all, I'm the mother of your children."

He wanted to call her a liar and state why, but knowing Kayla as well as he was sure he did, it would likely hurt Blake more than her. He quashed that desire and said, "You might be their mother, but you're also a closet slut. Oh, I forgot. That fact has been out in the open for quite a while. Answer me: what do you want?"

Kayla kept her expression contained. "You look different, but you're still the same. Will the verbal abuse from you ever stop?"

"Why don't you just get to the reason you're here."

Kayla pushed her dark hair behind her ears. "I didn't come all this way to trade insults or point fingers. Whatever happened is in the past. It's over. But did you give thought to the fact that changing the child support payments was unfair to the children? That it would affect their well-being?"

"My mother will handle their financial needs fairly. They won't go without."

Through clenched teeth, Kayla said, "Lynn's a witch. There are a lot of other labels I could use, but I'll go with that one, as she *is* your mother. I'm the mother of our children, and I need money to take care of them, without having to wait for your mother to dole out funds for everyday needs."

"You're not fooling me. You want that money—you need that money—to carry on your lavish lifestyle. Fancy trips, spa time, home decorations, and Jaguars cost. Yeah, I heard. Sorry, sweetheart. You want those things you'll have to find a way to pay for them yourself." Starks learned forward and lowered his voice. "Here's an idea. Ask all the men you screwed for free for the money. Back payment for services rendered. Start with Ozy and Bret." He laughed without humor. "What's between your legs is your most valuable commodity. Spread them again. There's no shortage of men, but this time ask for payment first. With the men from your past and any new ones you spread 'em for, you should make a bundle."

"When will you let that go? My God."

"Let it go? You get to go home and enjoy your life and our children. You don't have any fucking idea what my life is like now. Because of you, you selfish, self-absorbed bitch."

Kayla's eyes filled with tears and her face blotched red. "Stop calling me names. You have no right. I'm no longer yours to use and abuse. You blame me for what happened, but it was your actions that put you here. Not me." She brushed tears from her cheeks. "Let's be honest. It was your inflamed, entitled ego that did it. Ego sent you to Ozy's house that night. And for what? I'd ended it with him. You and I were separated, and you were living with Emma."

"You were screwing Ozy years before I moved out."

"I know that's what that jealous bitch Jenny said, but it was a lie." Kayla flung her hands upward. "Believe what you want. You will anyway. But my involvement with Ozy isn't what upset you. Not really. It was the fact that another man could satisfy me. I didn't lie when I said he was better in bed than you. And that's what this is all about: your ever-needy ego."

"All right. You want us to be truthful? Let's put it all out there. Yes, I've had a few women, but I never had sex with them in a car, where people passing by could see. If that's Ozy's *special* treatment, and the way you think women should be treated, you got what you wanted. And for *your* information, the women I had sex with were always better than you. You're mediocre, at best. I stayed with you because I thought you were true to me. What a joke."

A vein pulsed at Kayla's left temple. "I know where you got your example of how to treat a wife: Your damn dysfunctional family. The men cheated and their wives tolerated it. You took it further, though, didn't you? Cheat on your wife, treat her like shit, and then shower her with money and luxuries to cover up your wrongdoings. The women in your family were always doormats for the men to wipe their feet on, and I wasn't like that. I wasn't like your grandmother, who was a prime example. Exactly *how* many women did your grandfather have on the side?"

"You have no right to criticize the women in my family, or any member of my family, especially not my grandmother. You're forgetting who helped support us when we were in school. But you wouldn't stop spending every damn cent that came our way. Your family didn't step up. They were absent and happy about it. You owe every member of my family respect."

Kayla held up a hand in a dismissive fashion. "I can't believe we're still beating that drum. I didn't come here to bicker with you. I came here to discuss the child support matter. And, I want to make peace with you. Let's put everything that occurred in the past behind us. I made mistakes. So did you. No one's perfect."

"Your mistake was getting caught lying your ass off about screwing Ozy and God knows how many other men. How many times did you tell me I was the only man you'd ever been with? And I was stupid enough to accept that, all the way back to the beginning."

"I can't believe you're bringing up Bernard Hazely again. You and I weren't together when I went out with him. Remember? That separation was your brilliant idea. So you could screw around for a while—a vacation from my vagina so you could have more than just our sexual experiences under your belt. Then we got married. As soon as you had enough money, you started with the parties and orgies, exotic strippers, and super models. You thought I didn't know, but Marlin told me everything."

"You seriously believed that loser? For such a conniving woman, your ignorance baffles me. Marlin's never been anything but a jealous ass. He wanted what we had. You think he's your friend? He's like those others you call friend. They don't care about you. You poured your heart out to them—I should say lied to them—and they judged you and talked about you behind your back. They hoped the worse for you, because they were envious of all you had, which *I* provided for you."

"Of course you'd say that about Marlin. But you know everything he said is true. You're no saint, but you're an exceptional finger-pointer. You just never seem to aim that finger at yourself."

"You're wrong. I've blamed myself for some of what happened. But only some of it. I didn't force you to become a tramp. Sure, with the time I've had to think in here, I've wondered if maybe I'd treated you better or given you the attention you wanted—and, I suppose, needed—things wouldn't be the way they are. Then I have to remind myself that your actions demonstrated the truth: You're a common slut. You were giving your body to men before any real issues came up in our marriage. Even before we got married. And I don't just mean Bernard. I'm talking about Phil Wright. In my grandfather's basement."

Kayla's mouth clamped shut.

Starks nodded. "Didn't think I knew about that. Tip of the fucking iceberg of what I know about you."

"Starks, I'm sorry. I'm truly sorry. We each wronged the other. But we also had some good times, meaningful times. Life's too short for us not to make peace. We need to make peace. Please." Kayla's gaze met Starks's. "There's something important I need to discuss with—"

"Keep your fucking peace. You can't fool me anymore." Starks thumped the table with a fist. "We built a life. I worked my ass off to make that happen. Yes, we had good times and bad. My first mistake was to place you on the proverbial pedestal. You didn't deserve that place of honor. You're trash. A whore. You're something to avoid stepping in." He held up his hands. "I'm done with you. Don't show your face here again. Send the kids to visit with someone else, anyone else. Here's another truth: If you died tomorrow, I wouldn't give a fuck."

Kayla reached out for his hand. Tears spilled onto her cheeks.

Starks shook his head and pulled back. "Always the actress. Your tears stopped working on me long ago." He stood and said, "Remember what I told you about coming here again. Don't."

He left her sobbing at the table, with guards, inmates, and visitors staring and glaring at him, and started back to his cell, feeling proud of himself. Kayla was a woman who always had to have the last word. She didn't get it this time. What she got was only a small taste of what she deserved. If what he'd said hurt her, well, it was nothing compared to the hurt she'd caused him. Any pain he caused her was justified—for all the men, for how she'd ridiculed him to them, for the sleepless nights, the depression that engulfed him when he discovered what kind of woman she really was.

So why didn't he feel gratified? Where was the elation he should feel?

His steps slowed. Kayla and Demory were right: He was equally responsible, equally guilty of infidelity. Still, that admission didn't dull his pain and anger.

Kayla had looked bad. And her expression at the end—tortured. He'd wanted to hurt her and had. It had become a habit, an addiction. An attempt to climb above his own wretchedness. But how she'd looked wasn't going to be easy to forget.

Starks leaned against the top bunk and peered out the window.

He'd told Kayla he was done with her, over her.

He refused to believe Emma might be right.

CHAPTER 93

I T HAD BEEN a hell of a night, with Starks bouncing between recriminations and justifications regarding his behavior with Kayla. His final decision was that she deserved it.

After the count and after completing his exercise routine, Starks stood at the small mirror, razor in hand. "Kane, as soon as I'm done shaving, I want to make a private call. Would you mind?"

"No problem, Starks. I told Tank I'd meet him in," he checked the time, "seven minutes. Meet us in the yard after, if you feel like it."

"Sounds like a plan."

At least a couple of things are going right, Starks thought. Kane was doing well with the guys, and his crew was the only one—that he was aware of—that had no real infighting. He hadn't done or said anything extraordinary to accomplish this. Maybe it was a fortunate fluke. He reminded himself that it was early days.

Starks got his cell phone, did a quick corridor check then positioned himself on his bunk.

Jeffrey answered after two rings. "Figured I'd be hearing from you."

"You sound odd. Did I wake you?"

"No."

"I have to be quick. What's happening about the powders? Last thing I need is to run out."

"Mason's been on vacation. Out of the country. Thought it best not to leave a message other than to call me when he gets back."

"When's that?"

"About another week or so. Maybe two."

"It is what it is. I'll just have to be careful. By the way, Kayla came to see me."

"I know. She asked me to meet her for coffee yesterday afternoon. Said the visit with you didn't go well; that you were abusive."

"I reamed her good. I held back, though. There was so much more I could have said. It was obvious she wanted my sympathy. I bet Bret advised her to look as bad as she did so I'd feel sorry for her and put the money back in her control. I left plenty in the accounts. If she's already spent it, that's not my problem."

"Bret's out of the picture, for a number of reasons. For one, he was cheating on her."

Starks slapped his thigh. "Didn't I call it? I said it was a matter of time before the fucking mooch did that. Serves her right. Now I'm convinced her shabby appearance was deliberate."

"How she looks has nothing to do with Bret, and it's not faked."

"Then it *is* concern about the money. Never has enough. Guess I put a crimp in her pampering routine."

"Bro . . . Kayla has cancer. It started in her uterus. That's what terminated the pregnancy. There was no indication of a problem in any prior blood tests she'd had. They found it when they ran tests after the miscarriage. Something triggered the cancer to escalate. It's in her lymph system and major organs."

"She's lying. She just wants you on her side."

"I saw a copy from her medical file. She brought it so I'd have proof."

"So it's the treatments making her look that bad. Soon as she's done with them, she'll get her looks back. And another man."

"Cancer's too advanced. Three specialists told her the same thing. She's got a few months, at most. Decided not to suffer through treatments, since that's all the time she has."

"No wonder Bret got his ass out of there."

"That's all you have to say about it? This is Kayla we're talking about. There was a time when she was the love of your life."

"Hunh."

"Damn, Starks. I never expected you'd . . . She's on her own. I can help her as much as I can, like with the house payments she can no longer make, but I want your blessing."

"I can't tell you what to do, Jeffrey, but Kayla's problem is not my business."

"You don't mean that. You can't."

"I have my own shit to deal with. She's getting as good as she gave."

"C'mon, man. You're better than Bret. Act like it."

"I was better than all of them, but she chose strangers over me. Let her live with that." He barked a laugh. "Or not." Both men were silent. Then Starks said, "Do whatever you want, Jeffrey. I've got to go."

Starks disconnected the call. He didn't move, didn't rush to put the phone away. He knew his response had shocked Jeffrey, probably had disappointed, if not disgusted him. He couldn't help that. Kayla's cancer *was* a surprise. A bigger surprise was that she hadn't contracted STDs.

She'd come to tell him she was sick. Correction—dying. His comments and attitude had stopped her. Too bad.

At least the kids didn't have to live with their mother and her latest boyfriend screwing down the hall from where they slept or out by the pool. Maybe with Bret out of the picture, Kayla would stay home with her children, where she belonged.

The children.

The phone was still in his hand. He could call Jeffrey back, could tell him to take care of everything, including asking the nanny to stay on after Kayla was gone so the kids stayed in the only home they'd ever known.

Without their mother.

Or father.

Starks slammed a fist into the wall. "Goddamn you, Margaret."

CHAPTER 94

STARKS SAT ON his chair, his bunk, paced the constricted space in the cell. He splashed his face with cold water then turned his back on his scowling reflection in the small mirror.

His crew was likely waiting for him in the yard. He should go out there, as though nothing had happened. As though he hadn't talked to Jeffrey. As though his world hadn't once again tilted on its axis.

He stripped his bunk and remade it, tidied his desk and Kane's, refolded their clothes. With a used wet towel, he scrubbed the varnished concrete floor on his hands and knees. After an hour, every surface but the ceiling and fluorescent light fixture had been dusted, cleaned, put in order. It wasn't enough.

One hundred push-ups plus the same number of stomach crunches and lunges later, it still wasn't enough.

No library shift for him on weekends, but the library was the only option that appealed to him. Halfway there, he turned around and went back to his cell.

At ten fifty-five, Kane showed up for the count. He paused at the entrance, running his gaze around the small area. "Whoa. There a contest for the cleanest cell or something?"

"Or something."

"You okay, Starks?"

"I'm fine. Just have a lot on my mind."

"Anything I can do?"

"No, but thanks for asking."

"After the count, the crew's getting a game up. You should come."

"We'll see."

Kane took the hint and stopped talking, which was a relief to Starks. He didn't want to talk. Didn't want to listen to anyone. Didn't want to share space with another person whose head was as filled with thoughts or heart as conflicted as his own. He wanted to think. Especially about his children. Surely, they could see how their mother looked. Had she told them what was going on? Had she told the nanny? What arrangements was she making for their care after she was gone? Or had she relied on discussing this with him when she'd visited?

The count was called. Starks barely paid attention. Afterwards, Kane asked, "You coming with us?"

"What the hell. Let's make a trip to the commissary first."

Starks surprised his crew with sandwiches and beverages. He ate half of his sandwich and gave the other half to Kane. This time he didn't sit the game out. It was a good choice, an obvious morale booster for his guys. They cheered when he made shots and playfully ribbed him when he missed, which were in equal measure. Usually, he missed maybe one out of ten shots, but not today. Today, he couldn't keep his mind on the game.

Kayla was still alive, but was already haunting him, whispering a question repeatedly in his ear whenever he let his guard down: *What am I going to do?*

You screwed up, Kayla. You had everything you could need or want. I made sure of it. And you fucked it all away.

CHAPTER 95

THAT NIGHT, IF Kane asked a question, he got one word, a grunt or a shrug in response. Eventually, Kane stayed quiet, which was what Starks wanted. Needed.

After the ten o'clock count, Starks prepped for bed. He lay in his bunk, praying for sleep, which refused to accommodate him. Instead, Kayla's image insisted he look with different eyes.

Makeup had covered her complexion, but there was no way to hide that her eyes were dull and her usually shiny dark hair lackluster. Usually her attire was too tight, too short, too low-cut. The clothes she'd worn to visit him showed no skin other than her face and hands, as though the temperature outside was crisp rather than sweltering, and hung on her frame like garments on a hanger. He'd been too angry with her about Blake—about everything—to care. She'd brought herself as physical evidence of the destruction taking her life every hour, minute, and second. And he'd ignored the signs. By choice.

Once again, he'd allowed his pride to motivate his actions.

Not feeling so proud now, are you?

Her aqua eyes had captivated him the first time she'd looked at him in English class on the first day of their freshman year. Those eyes had laughed at him, studied him, toyed with him, and eventually gazed at him with admiration, after making him wait two years for any sign of affection. He wanted to believe she'd looked at him with love, but the truth kept him from fooling himself about that. Jenny Hayes had testified at his trial that

Kayla told her she never loved Starks. That he'd promised to give her everything, and that's why she'd stuck with him and eventually married him.

Twenty years as a couple wasn't as easy for him to throw away as it had been for Kayla. They'd been physically intimate teens who delighted in experimenting sexually, a couple who'd moved to Texas then California, struggling each month because their checking account was like a sieve, because of Kayla, who refused to stop spending what they didn't have, refused to be bothered with what was *the man's responsibility*.

And because he could have her, he did what was needed—extra jobs on top of a grueling university schedule, plus cutting back on his own needs so she could have little extras she wanted. Because anytime she got what she wanted, her beauty magnified. Because she demonstrated her appreciation with her body, giving herself to him in whatever way he wanted, as often as he wanted, or had the energy for. Most of the time he was exhausted from all the demands he had to meet, from being the responsible one, from being the one who paced the floor at night trying to figure out how to get them out of another financial hole, or how to smile as though yet another package of ramen noodles for dinner by candlelight—one candle—was fine dining, as long as they were together.

Each year he'd worked harder, longer, to give Kayla and their expanding family a home and life he could be proud of. The more he earned, the more she said was needed for her, for the kids. He'd given her a lot, but in some ways he owed her, if for nothing else, for Nathan and Kaitlin. And, yes, even for Blake.

They'd been happy during those days before the mini-mansion, the expensive cars, and all the luxuries his money allowed them to have. Or, at least, he'd been. Was a woman like Kayla ever truly happy? She seemed genuinely happy when the children were born.

Did she know he wasn't Blake's father?

Jenny said Kayla had a few secrets she swore to take to her grave.

Would he let her take that one?

CHAPTER 96

A T FIVE FORTY-FIVE, first light cast its blue hue through the window. Starks's eyes burned from staring through the night at the bunk above him, at the walls, at the window, and at nothing. He tossed the twisted blanket aside, used the facilities then stood at the cell door, hands wrapped around the bars.

He'd been the biggest damn fool regarding Kayla. Years of practice had made him an expert at it. Despite appearances and outcomes or how anyone would define it, they'd shared a life together. As a family. She'd done her best to destroy it, but he'd contributed to that demise. Their children had suffered because of their stupidity and selfishness. Soon the children would suffer in a way they'd never imagined, should never have to imagine, much less experience. Again. And in part, because of him. They needed support. Someone who loved them needed to let them know they'd be cared for. Jeffrey would help. But it wasn't the same as one's immediate family. That left his mother.

Starks turned and saw Kane, lying on his side, watching him. "Didn't mean to wake you."

Kane kept his gaze fixed on Starks. "I probably slept more than you, but not much. Not with all the tossing and moaning and sighing going on."

"Sorry."

"Something's wrong. You haven't been yourself since yesterday morning."

"Not your concern. Just something I have to work out."

"I'm gonna ask again: are you in trouble?"

Starks exhaled hard and looked away. "When am I not?" He returned to his bunk, drew the blanket up and said, "Try to sleep before we have to get up for the count."

Starks removed the phone from the book. "Kane, I—"

"I'll leave." Kane was quiet a moment then said, "The guys noticed, you know. They're asking me what's with you. When I see them at breakfast, they're gonna ask again. What should I tell them?"

"The truth."

"I don't know the truth."

"Exactly. Go on. They're probably waiting for you at the chow hall."

Starks tucked the phone under his pillow and went to the entrance. Inmates shuffled along the corridor, to breakfast, to a job, to Sunday services. Once the corridor was empty, he went to his bunk and dialed his mother's number.

Lynn Starks answered with, "Who is this?"

"Hi, Mom."

"You should call more often. I don't know how you can treat your mother this way. What did I ever do to you to deserve this?"

"This isn't the time."

"Of course not. If it's not the right time for you, it isn't the right time for anyone."

Starks scrubbed his face with his free hand. "There's something important I need to tell you, and I need you to be quiet long enough to hear me." When Lynn stayed silent, he continued. "Kayla has cancer. It's bad. She's been given a few months to live." He yanked the phone away from his ear, his mother's cackling laugh too loud to bear up close.

Lynn stopped laughing and said, "I've prayed every night for that whore to get the punishment she deserves for what she did to you. I hope the bitch suffers, like she's made us suffer."

"I'm concerned about—"

"She doesn't deserve your concern. You need to worry about yourself and leave her to deal with her fate. Let her boy-toy take care of her."

"He's gone."

"Ha! About damn time. When I think of my grandchildren being in the same house with those fornicators—"

"It's the children I'm concerned about."

"You don't need to worry about that. I'll raise them. In fact, I'll go over there today and pack them up. They can live at my house until the bitch dies. Then we'll move back in, live in *your* house that *you* paid for. And I'll make sure they know exactly what kind of tramp their mother was. I'll rent my house out. I know a good agent I can call."

"For God's sake, Mom, stop."

"Don't you talk to me that way. I'm offering to raise your children the right way, the way I raised you. Do you realize how much I'll have to give up to do that? Who else is going to do it? You certainly can't. I'd think you'd be grateful."

"Listen to me, carefully. Don't you dare say or do anything about this, not until I tell you what to say or do. I don't even know if she's told the kids. They've had enough to deal with, and it's nowhere near over for them. Whatever else you think or feel, their well-being has to come first."

"I'm trying to help."

"It has to be the right kind of help. At the right time. I thought you should know, is all. Promise me you won't do or say anything."

Lynn sniffed. "I promise. But I don't understand why you—"

"I have to go. We'll talk later."

Starks hung his head between his knees and took in several deep breaths. Usually, when his mother railed about Kayla, it satisfied him. Not this time. Worse was that in an excruciating way, it was as though his mother had held up a mirror. The reflection caused his gut to clench. No way in hell would he let her rear his children. No way would he let her feed them her vitriol about their mother. Or, God forbid, push that woman she wanted him to marry on them as someone who'd be their new mother one day.

His mother had always had a temper, had always had to have things her way. He loved her, just like his kids loved their mother, despite whatever she did. But it was too easy to imagine Kaitlin doing something as simple as brushing her hair the way Kayla brushed hers, or looking more like Kayla as she grew into a young woman, and his mother saying, "Just like your whore mother." He'd put the children into boarding school in

Europe before he'd expose them to the environment his mother would subject them to. Maybe his father hadn't been such a bastard, as his mother had insisted. Maybe his father had left her in order to keep his sanity.

Starks dialed Jeffrey's number. "Help Kayla in whatever way she needs. Make the house payments. Pay anything and everything until I can get the child support payments turned back over to you. Sell my Bentley if that'll help. You probably need the space in your garage."

"That's the Starks I know."

"Take her shopping or on a trip, if she wants to go. Make whatever time she has left . . ." Starks's throat tightened.

"I'll do whatever it takes."

"Talk to the nanny. Ask her to stay on, even until I get out. Double her salary. Triple it, if necessary."

"I'll handle everything."

"And for God's sake, do whatever you can to keep my mother away from them."

CHAPTER 97

THE LAST THING Starks wanted was his crew looking at him and wondering what was going on. Or coming out and asking. He wasn't ready to talk about it, not with them. Would they even understand what he was feeling, or would they see him as weak? That concern was too much to deal with on top of everything else. He could fake courage easily enough, but couldn't fake his way out of this torment. Better to stay in his cell and avoid facing them. The hard surface of his bunk was as much comfort as he could or would get.

Kane returned in time for the count at eleven. He didn't leave afterwards, as Starks had hoped.

Silence and tension stretched like elastic between them. Kane said, "What's it going to take for you to confide in me? You helped me. Let me help you, even if it's just to listen."

Starks dragged himself from his bunk and sat in his chair opposite Kane. "I need you to keep this to yourself. I'll talk about it with the others when I'm ready."

"You can trust me." Kane moved to the edge of his chair and waited.

"I just found out my wife . . ." Tears welled in Starks's eyes. His head dropped back and he focused on the ceiling. He swallowed several times and cleared his throat. "'Till death do us part' has new meaning now. Kayla's dying, and soon. Three young children are going to be left without a parent to care for them, or love and comfort them. Their entire lives are about to turn upside down and there's only so much I can do about that while I'm stuck in this fucking place. Children need their mother *and* their father, if both are still alive. If one's gone, they desperately need the other. I'm failing them when they need me most. Again."

Kane's concerned expression altered. He slouched back in the chair, stretched his legs out in front and crossed his arms. "Yeah, they do need you. It sucks being without a father."

Starks's gaze met Kane's. "That's right. You didn't know yours. But you have your mother. She'll come around."

"Don't bet on it. And if you remember what I said, I said my mother forbade me to know him. I always knew *who* he was."

"I didn't realize . . . But you wanted to meet him, get to know him?"

"You can't imagine how much."

"Didn't you ever want to ignore your mother and introduce yourself to him?"

"Sure. But that wouldn't have gone over well. He doesn't know about me."

Starks's surprise was clear. "She didn't tell him?"

"She knew he'd never love her. College antics, you know?"

"Still, your mother should have told him. At least given him the option to do the right thing."

"No point. He had a girlfriend he was serious about. Mom was too angry and ashamed to tell him. So you can imagine why I believed he wouldn't have opened his arms to welcome me."

"I'm sorry, Kane. That had to be painful. For both of you."

Kane focused his gaze out the window. "I read everything about him. He was a successful man, so was often written about in the papers, for one reason or another."

"I still think he should have been given a chance to know about you, even if it was you who told him."

Kane faced Starks. "You sound like you mean that."

"Not only did he have a right to know, he was responsible for you. I hope you'll forgive me for saying this, but you probably wouldn't be here now if he'd been allowed to be part of your life."

Kane's laughter was shrill. He grew quiet then said, "Julie Sandler. That's my mother's name. You remember her?"

"Should I know your mother?"

"You knew her intimately. Once."

Starks sat erect in his chair. "Where's this going, Kane?"

"I think you know. When you pushed pause on your relationship with Kayla, you dated around."

"Exactly. I dated around. Nothing more."

"Except for one night when you went to a party, got drunk, and had sex with my mother. You even called her Kayla. She still resents it."

Starks leaped up. "That's a fucking lie. Why are you doing this? I opened up to you and you're—"

"It's the truth."

Starks walked to the front of the cell and clung to the bars.

Kane said, "Every day of your trial, I sat in the back of the gallery. I was sure they'd let you off. I promised myself I'd tell you then, since I figured you'd be in a good mood, or at least more receptive. Instead, you got sentenced. That's when I saw my chance. To meet you. Talk to you. Be with you."

Starks turned around slowly. "What are you saying?"

Kane shrugged. "The only way to get in here was to commit a crime that would assure it. When you introduced yourself, it was all I could do not to tell you then. Figured it was better if you got to know me first."

"I don't know what your fucking game is, but it isn't going to work."

"It's no game."

Starks aimed a finger at Kane. "You stay the fuck away from me. I may not be able to get you transferred today, but you might as well pack your shit and get ready to go. Until then, spend as much time out of this cell as possible. Don't even try to talk to me."

"I was right. You don't want anything to do with me, despite what you just said."

"Get the hell out of my sight."

"Sure thing. *Dad.*" Kane stopped when he was even with Starks. "I waited a long time to call you that. Doesn't feel as good as I'd hoped."

"Get out. Before I give you the beating you deserve. A word of warning: If you tell your lie to anyone, it'll be the last thing you do."

Starks watched Kane until he turned left at the corridor entrance. He stumbled to his bunk and collapsed onto it. Either Kane was making it up for some inexplicable reason, or the kid's mother needed to put a name to the sperm donor and picked his. No wonder she was adamant Kane have no contact with his father. No wonder she disowned him when he got sentenced to time at Sands. She knew he'd say something, knew the lie she'd told him all his life would out and he'd hate her. He'd feel betrayed, twice.

Julie Sandler. The name meant nothing to him.

The story was ridiculous. Sure, he went to a few parties during the several months he and Kayla were apart, but he never had sex with anyone; his penis wouldn't cooperate—because none of them were Kayla. Instead of good times, he'd been disappointed and embarrassed. Maybe Kane was lying about his mother, to make the lie more believable. But how would either of them know some of the story from that time. The trial, of course. Kane learned enough during that public humiliation to weave intricate details for his deception.

The music and lyrics of "Have You Ever Really Loved a Woman" began to waft through his mind. The song was blasting from speakers at—was it a house or apartment? Bryan Adams had pummeled him with lyrics that reminded him how much he loved and missed Kayla during those months. Reminded him that he *could* see their unborn children in her eyes. Brought home that his idea for a temporary respite from their relationship wasn't as good an idea as he'd imagined.

That night years ago began to come back to him in hazy threads. There was a young woman at the party who had the same hair color and haircut as Kayla's, and a similar figure from the back. He'd thought it was Kayla, and was relieved when he became immediately hard. Was surprised when he staggered to the young woman, tapped her on the shoulder and saw it wasn't Kayla. At first he was disappointed, but the throbbing between his legs wouldn't cease.

He'd said to the young woman, "Any port in a storm." He must have said something else to convince her to have sex with him, or maybe she was as drunk as he had been. That's why he didn't recognize her name. He never knew it. Hell, he hadn't remembered anything about that time until this moment.

That doesn't mean you're my son.

There was only one thing to do.

CHAPTER 98

"I NEED ANOTHER DNA test run. ASAP."

Jim Rogers said, "What the hell's going on, Starks?"

"My cellmate, a kid by the name of Kane Sandler, is messing with me. Says he's mine. From back in college."

"Aw fuck. Any chance he's right?"

Starks sighed and scraped a hand through his hair. "Yes, damn it. But I'm sure as hell not going to take his word for it."

"How am I supposed to get said DNA? It's not like you can hand it over to me."

"Plus, it'll take too long for you to get vetted as a visitor. Only one way to do it. Parker. I'll call him and tell him he needs to get here as quickly as possible. Today, if I can get him to blow off his Sunday. There's something else I need to talk about with him, as it is."

"Good thinking."

"Stay available. I'll call him then call you right back."

"You got it. I'll shoot a quick call to my guy and tell him he's about to earn a grand."

"If he asks for more, give it to him."

Starks dialed Parker's cell phone number. He bit at his cuticles each time the phone rang. "C'mon, Parker. Pick up the damn phone." On the fourth ring, his attorney answered.

"I know it's short notice but I need you to get over here today. I wouldn't ask unless it was urgent."

"Relax, Starks. Margaret Hessinger called me yesterday to confess about the knife. I've already arranged my schedule to see you tomorrow afternoon."

"Glad to hear about Margaret, but I need to see you today."

"I thought you'd have more to say about that. Do you realize what this means?"

"We can talk about it when you get here. Drive over as soon as we hang up."

"What's up?"

"I'd rather talk in private. Please, Mike. I said it's urgent."

"Give me an hour and a half to get there and into a room."

"One more thing. You need to see Jim right after our visit. You can meet up with him or he can find you."

"I can hardly wait to learn what's going on."

"That makes two of us."

The call to Jim was brief.

"It's set, Starks. My guy's on call. Soon as I get Kane's and your DNA, I'll get it to him. No matter what the result is, you want me to check into this Sandler kid and his mother?"

"Not yet. Let me get the result first. Tell your guy I need it—"

"Yesterday. No problem."

"I'll call you after Parker leaves."

"Don't hang up yet. So far, Emma checks out. I even hid cameras in your house, since I wasn't doing round-the-clock surveillance. As for now, she's staying faithful."

"At least something's going right."

Starks put the phone away. He removed Kane's hair from his comb and slipped it into an envelope, which he sealed and labeled. Some of his hair went into a second envelope. Both envelopes were tucked into his underwear.

He returned to his bunk.

Only one thing to do: wait.

CHAPTER 99

CO SIMMONS MADE the announcement Starks was desperate to hear. He accepted the guard's offer of an escort to the private room, but made it plain he wasn't up for chatting.

Parker stood when Starks opened the door.

Starks extended his hand and said, "You didn't have to wear a suit on a Sunday."

"I always prefer to look like I mean business. Now, tell me what's going on. You only use my first name when you're desperate."

"More things at once than I can wrap my mind around." Starks slid the envelopes out and put them on the table. He sat and tapped the envelopes. "Get these to Jim as soon as you leave here. You need his number?"

"It's in my phone. You want to tell me about this?"

"Another time. We have something else to take care of."

"Margaret."

"We'll get to her next. That discussion ties in with this one. I need you to put the child support payments back to what they were before."

Parker studied Starks and said, "The point of changing those arrangements was to keep Kayla from misusing the funds."

"That was then. Kayla's dying."

"Who told you this?"

"Jeffrey. Kayla told him."

"This is one of her tricks, and a cruel one, at that."

Starks shook his head. "Jeffrey saw proof. And, I saw her here a few days ago. She looks . . . I should have realized. I don't want her worrying about money on top of everything else. When things get . . . when she's no longer able to take care of things, I want Jeffrey to take over the financial matters. Get all of it set up tomorrow.

"And that leads me to Margaret. I'm relieved she called you. I didn't know if she would tell someone or if she'd leave me here to rot. Parker, I've got to get the hell out as soon as I can. My kids can't be left without a parent, and I'll be damned if I'm going to let my mother get her hands on them."

"I'm sorry about Kayla. I never expected—"

"Neither did I. What about getting me out?"

"I'm meeting with Margaret tomorrow morning. I'm going to record our discussion and have her sign off on it. Then I'll file for post-conviction relief and follow that with a writ of habeas corpus."

"How long will that take?"

"Filing doesn't take a lot of time. Getting a new trial might. It could take a few months or up to eighteen for a criminal case."

"I don't have even the few months. I have to get out now."

"I understand. And I wish I could tell you differently, but it's best to be straight with you. However, that doesn't mean I can't push like hell to get you remanded into my custody."

"But you can get me out, right?"

Parker tapped his pen on the table. "I can ask to have your sentence reduced to time served. I can also point out what you've been through since you arrived here. But I can't promise anything. Please understand that. We have to pray that Margaret's admission about the knife, which confirms your reaction to Ozy was one of self-defense, is enough to sway whoever makes the decision."

"Do your best. Whatever it takes." Starks slumped back in the chair. "I've given you a lot to take care of."

"I have a large staff of eager young attorneys. Everything will be handled, and as a priority." Parker removed his glasses and twirled them. "I have a question, Starks."

"Ask."

Parker picked up one of the envelopes and turned the labeled front to face Starks. "Who is Kane Sandler?"

"That's what I intend to find out."

CHAPTER 100

STARKS RETURNED TO his cell and stayed there. Kane came back for the count at three and left immediately after, and did so without looking at or speaking to Starks. After the count at six, Kane climbed into his bunk and faced the wall. Starks stretched out on his bunk, with an open book facedown on his chest. Noise and conversations from other cells reverberated in the corridor. Their contribution to the cacophony was silence fraught with daggered thoughts aimed between them. It was Kane who breeched the silence two hours later.

"All day, I kept expecting someone to tell me to get my stuff and move to a new cell."

Starks exhaled hard. "I forgot about that."

"Lucky you."

"What did you expect me to say, Kane?"

"Pretty much what you did. But I'd hoped I'd be wrong." Kane was quiet a moment. "You think it was easy for me to tell you?"

"Why now? Why pick a moment when everything's caving in on me to spew your lies?" Starks heard Kane roll onto his back.

"It's the truth. As for why now . . . because hearing you go on about how your kids need you pissed me off. I've needed you my entire life. I finally get to be with you and you don't want me. And why would you? Why would you want your bastard son?"

"That's yet to be proved."

"My mother's word should be enough. What kind of proof do you need?"

"The kind that's irrefutable."

"Suppose you could get it. Then what?"

Starks didn't know. When no answer was forthcoming, he heard Kane position himself to face the wall again. But what could he say? Nothing. Not until he knew for certain. If Kane wasn't his, it meant the kid had an agenda that started a long time ago. Some sociopathic fantasy that he had no intention of being part of.

If Kane was his . . . well, he didn't have a clue what he'd do about it. Get used to it? How warped could life get where you discover the boy you'd raised wasn't yours. To feel caught between experiencing that gut-wrenching loss, yet still feel a bond, like a cord attached between you. And then learn you have another son.

May have.

What a twisted fucking year, he thought, with four months still to go.

CHAPTER 101

THE LIGHTS BLINKED on at six. Neither Kane nor Starks got out of bed until almost seven thirty. Kane got up first. Starks lay with an arm behind his head, his gaze fixed on the bottom of the upper bunk.

Kane ran the comb through his hair. "You gonna transfer me to another cell today?"

"I haven't decided yet."

"Just get it over with so I don't have to worry about it. I'll worry plenty enough when they put me in with some jackhole or lunatic. But that's not your problem, is it? I'm not your problem."

"I don't think anyone's going to bother you, since you're in my crew."

Kane stopped moving. "You're not kicking me out?"

"Haven't decided about that yet, either. For now, you're still under my protection."

"That's something, at least." Kane climbed back into his bunk, where he sat cross-legged staring out the window.

After Starks's turn at the toilet and sink, he put his energy into his morning exercise routine, all the time feeling Kane's eyes locked onto him. He knew who else needed to see him. He couldn't stay out of circulation any longer, not without creating repercussions. As soon as the count was over, he said, "Let's hit the chow hall."

"I thought you didn't want me anywhere near you."

"For now, we need to keep up appearances, especially with the crew."

"As my mother always says, 'Any port in a storm.'"

Starks lowered his head and shook it. That Kane's mother used that quote often meant nothing. A lot of people used it. And there was still the chance it was all a hoax for the purpose of getting something out of him, probably money. Whoever was behind this farce could forget that.

Unless the DNA proved it was true.

His crew wasn't clear about how to behave. They watched him for clues. Starks acted as though everything was back to normal, even saying it must have been a virus that made him lay low for a while. The lie was accepted, even if not entirely believed, their subsequent conversation and laughter a release from the tension uncertainty brings.

Starks went with them to the yard and stayed on the bleachers, chatting with crew members who took turns sitting near him. This pseudo-occupation was resistance on his part. Nothing stood in his way to make the call to Jim, but he was afraid to hear the result, because either way, something was lost.

He read in his cell after the count at eleven. Kane stayed there as well, until it was time for him to meet the crew for lunch. They didn't speak more than occasionally and made certain it was nothing about what hung between them. At twelve thirty, Starks ate a sandwich. At twelve forty-five, he tucked the cell phone into his underwear and directed his steps to the library.

At two thirty, he closed the door to the small office, kept watch through the window, and called Jim Rogers. "You get the result yet?"

"Man, I've been waiting to hear from you all day."

"This was the best time. And?"

"Kid's yours." Starks said nothing. Jim cleared his throat. "I gotta ask: should I expect anymore surprises regarding offspring?"

Starks cupped his head in his hand. "Not to my knowledge."

"You want me to investigate him and his mother?"

"I'll get back to you about that. I need to let this sink in."

"Need anything else, you know how to find me."

"Be sure to see Jeffrey for compensation."

"Done and done. And before you ask, I didn't tell him what it was for. Not that he asked or would."

Starks ended the call and collapsed back in the chair. Kane was his. Julie—was that her name?—should have told him she was pregnant. He wouldn't have given up Kayla to marry her, but he would have contributed to Kane's care. Like what? He'd been so fucking broke for years.

Who was he kidding? Kayla would have found out. She'd have left him. Maybe that would have saved him from where life with her had taken him. Maybe life with Julie and their son would have been good. Maybe they would have had more children. Maybe, maybe, maybe. Nothing solid ever got built on maybe.

Julie Sandler had told Kane who his father was, and the boy had gone through life yearning to establish connection, perhaps be involved, even if just on the periphery of his father's life. Instead, he'd been denied contact by his mother, who'd raised him alone. He hoped her family had helped. The idea of her struggling to care for his child, his son, was a disquieting burden. He had enough burdens.

He'd told Kane that his father had a responsibility in his regard. All these years, he'd had a son who needed him, needed him so much that he committed a crime to be near him, was brought close to him then rejected when the truth was revealed.

Since January, he'd felt so completely alone at Sands, desolate over the separation from his children. Kane was his son. This was a gift. And although this was the worst damn place for a father and son to be together, they now had the opportunity to get to know each other. Fortunately or unfortunately, they had years to do that.

Then he remembered. If Parker handled everything in an expeditious manner, he'd be leaving. Soon. Leaving his son to years in prison, without his father to protect him.

He'd arrange to pay the crew to look after Kane. He'd hand over the fake thumbs and what they contained to his son. He'd train his boy how to use the toxic powders, how to hide the knitting needle, and he'd keep him supplied with the powders. He'd leave Kane with protection on all sides. And he'd visit him at least once every week. Maybe there was something Parker could do to get Kane out early.

His children would have a lot to contend with in the near future, but perhaps they'd relish the idea of an older brother. Only he would know it was another half-brother. But he'd wait to make that announcement when Kane was released. He'd give him a job at Tendum Enterprises, get him set up for a successful life at his father's side.

He'd make up for all the years his son had been denied his rights.

And he'd start now.

CHAPTER 102

STARKS FELT RENEWED, concerned, excited, anxious. He'd find Kane now and tell him everything was okay. Welcome the boy into the family. Apologize for what he'd said. Apologize for what the boy had endured for nineteen years. Apologize until it wasn't necessary to do so anymore, if that would ever be possible.

He positioned the phone back into his underwear and glanced through the window. Paco bent over the keyboard, his two fingers pecking at speed. Starks left the office and stood at the man's side. "Take over for me. There's something I need to do. I won't be back today."

"That's worth more than a ham sandwich."

"How about a month's worth of commissary?"

Paco said nothing for a moment then grinned. "I thought you were in a hurry to leave."

Starks laughed, patted the old man on the shoulder and exited the library. He knew where he could find Kane. He turned right when he entered the yard and took a seat next to Tank when he reached the bleachers. "How's the game going?"

Tank shrugged. "We back ten points, but we'll catch up."

"How many points has Kane scored?"

"None."

"Sounds like he's off his game today." Starks, feeling responsible for Kane's playing poorly, cupped a hand over his eyes to block the sunlight and searched for his son among the inmates dribbling, throwing, dodging, and running on the hard-packed dirt.

"He ain't scored 'cause he ain't playing."

"Where is he?"

"Said he was gonna do you a favor and do both y'all's laundry."

Starks smiled and said, "He didn't need to do that. I'll go take over that chore so he can get back here and help our team win."

Jaunty steps propelled him across the yard and into the prison. His son was trying to make things right between them. And that's what he was going to call him to his face—*son*. It wasn't prudent to over-anticipate Kane's response to being accepted, being claimed, but he hoped the boy was ready to forgive him, at least as much as he could for now. What was needed was a fresh start for both of them.

What was he going to tell the guys? Maybe nothing. That might be the wisest thing to do for Kane's protection, especially after his own release came through. He'd have to make that clear to Kane, tell him to wait until his own return to the world to make his heritage public, and they'd do it together. He didn't want inmates, guards, or Spencer to hold the son accountable for his father's sins. Starks made a mental note to arrange everything with the guards on his payroll before he left Sands. No, he thought, do it sooner. Better to be safe.

A right turn brought him to the correct corridor, where the laundry room was at the end on the right. Despite how he sped his steps, it seemed to take a week to reach his destination. Then his steps faltered.

Everything is fragile. As Gabe had said, what happens in a moment can change everything. No, he told himself, everything is what it is. It's people who change. The cog slips and you spend your life trying to make the parts fit again so the gear runs as it should. It was something he'd never understood before. Nor had he ever realized how much destruction he'd left in his wake, until now. In his own way, he was no different than his father. He'd sworn to do better than the man who'd abandoned him and his mother, but hadn't. This was his chance to change that.

Yards from the entrance, he heard the spin-dry cycle going on one washing machine. He struggled to contain the grin he wore. Appearing as elated as he felt probably wasn't the way to go.

He stopped just outside the threshold. No one appeared to be in the space. Kane must have started the laundry then left with the intention to return. Maybe he'd gone to their cell. Even though Kane would return to put the clothes in the dryer, Starks didn't want to wait.

He spun around to leave then stopped and turned back. Laundry on the table had been left mid-folding. A cigarette smoldered on the edge of the table. Burning tobacco mingled with the acrid odor of singed Formica and laundry powder, and something else, something he'd smelled before, something that made his stomach roil and his limbs grow weak.

The back of his neck prickled. He didn't want to look where memory prodded him to, but he couldn't avoid it. He stepped into the room and looked left. Red splatters on the wall, on nearby washers and dryers, and on the floor caused him to retch.

Leaden steps inched him toward the corner, where the washers and dryers abutted, where a several-square-foot space existed, where he'd once found something he didn't want to what seemed a lifetime ago, and was desperate not to find now.

It could be anyone.

Please, God.

CHAPTER 103

THE WASHER SPUN to a stop. Starks's shallow, ragged breath was the only sound. He needed to move but couldn't. Every part of him resisted the reality in front of him. A nearly inaudible moan caused him to will numbed limbs to move. His sluggish steps picked up speed across the several yards to the corner. With strength that under different circumstances would have stunned him, he wrenched the washing machine away from the wall: room was needed to hold his battered son in his arms.

Kane cried out when Starks cradled him to his chest. He knew the motion would hurt the boy, but he also recognized there wasn't much time. There were only so many moments left to hold his child. "Kane, it's . . . it's Dad. I've got you now. I've got you, son."

Kane coughed. Blood and tooth fragments sprayed onto Stark's scrub shirt.

"Son, can you talk? Can you tell me who did this to you?"

Kane's eyes were swollen shut. Through engorged, torn lips, he mumbled the word *lion*.

When Starks had found Skullars Bailey in this same corner, he'd used laundry to attempt to stop the bleeding. Skullars had been a large man, and was why he'd believed there was a slim chance his friend would survive despite his horrendous injuries. Even a glimmer of such a chance didn't exist here. Kane had inherited his size, but wasn't as muscular, not that muscles would have prevented the carnage. Seth had beaten Kane hard with something solid, beaten him hard enough to separate flesh from bone, hard enough to break bones now protruding their shattered edges through ruptured skin, hard enough to fracture teeth.

Kane whispered, "Sorry."

A sob caught in Starks's throat. "You have nothing to be sorry for. I'm sorry. I'm sorry about everything. I was coming to find you to tell you . . ." What point was there to mention the DNA test? "I came to find you, to tell you I remembered your mother. She was beautiful, intelligent. And I was a fool to let her go. I had been drinking, but . . . None of that matters now. I know you're my son. I'm so proud that you're mine. Kane, do you hear me? Kane!"

In the stillness of that space, Starks heard the last breath leave Kane's body, felt the release. His son had been denied his father and then denied by his father, and now life.

Now it was his turn. Denied a second chance. Denied the peaceful expression on the departed's face reported by so many. There was far too much damage to Kane's face for that grace to be given to the man who had fathered him. Nor, he felt, did he deserve such grace.

The keening began in hushed tones then amplified as Starks rocked his son in his arms. Head thrown back, eyes squeezed shut, he roared the anguish fragmenting his soul.

CHAPTER 104

"WHAT THE HELL is going on in here?" CO Roberts yelled. He entered the laundry room, followed by CO Simmons. They cursed at first sight of the gore, saw the displaced washer, heard wails come from behind it and rushed to the corner.

Simmons said, "Aw shit. It's Starks's cellmate, Kane something."

Roberts spoke into his radio, ordering a gurney and more guards. He squatted next to Starks. "He's gone, Starks. Put him down."

Starks pulled Kane's body closer. Sobs wracked through him, sometimes silent, sometimes expelled with force.

Footsteps thundered down the corridor, accompanied by the screech of gurney wheels as metal grated against metal.

Roberts tried again. "We need to take over now."

Slowly, Starks lifted his head and looked into the CO's eyes. "He's my son."

It took Roberts a few moments to absorb what he'd heard. To realize Starks's eyes and manner conveyed the truth. "Oh, God." Roberts stood and motioned to the guards to move several feet away, where he talked in hushed tones to them.

Roberts returned to Starks. "Help us lift Kane onto the gurney. You can make sure we do it right."

Starks relaxed his hold and gazed down at Kane's face. Finally, he nodded.

"Let me help you up, Starks." Roberts said in a quiet tone, "Okay, guys, let's move this boy, gently."

The guards positioned Kane's body on the gurney and secured him in place with straps. A wounded moan escaped from Starks when they draped a pale blue blanket over Kane, covering him completely.

Starks walked alongside the gurney. Roberts said, "You should go to your cell and . . ." he averted his eyes from Starks's blood-soaked clothing, "take care of yourself. I'll see to Kane then come back and talk with you about—"

"I'm not leaving him."

"I'm sorry, Starks, but you can't come. Prison rules."

"Fuck the rules!" Starks grasped the side rail of the gurney and hung on.

Roberts took Starks by the arms and turned him to face him, but Starks kept his gaze affixed on Kane. "I'm sorry, Starks, but you can't. I'll stay with Kane. Let us take care of him. I'll see to everything. Wait for me in your cell. Starks, listen to me. It's for the best."

Starks drew the blanket from Kane's face. He ran a hand over Kane's matted hair as dark as his own and kissed his forehead. He stepped back as the blanket was placed once again over his son's face.

Roberts said, "Simmons, take Starks to his cell. Stay with him. If you think he's going to go into shock, get him to the infirmary."

Simmons tugged on Starks's sleeve. "C'mon, Starks. There's a lot to do and we need to let them get on with it." He gave another gentle tug to get Starks moving.

Starks nodded and started forward, occasionally looking over his shoulder at the silent procession following him. When they reached the end of the corridor, he stopped and stayed focused on the guards until another turn into yet another gray *tunnel* removed them from his sight. Simmons propelled him in the opposite direction. He went along without further protest, though, he wanted to scream until there was no sound left in him as much as he wanted to retreat into silence. Once back in his cell, Starks sat on his bunk, feeling more than he could cope with.

It was the simple action of happening to glance at the desk Kane had used, of seeing the sparse items in disarray on its surface, of seeing the half-eaten bag of potato chips that would never be finished that caused Starks to begin his descent into a place for which he had no name.

CHAPTER 105

THREE DAYS BLURRED by in that peculiar way that happens after loss, as though the individual affected stands still on a busy city street while life continues on at its usual pace. There was the time, albeit brief, on Monday spent before the council, with Spencer demonstrating more compassion than Starks imagined the man possessed, aside from the moment he looked askance at him when he said Kane had been dead when he found him and had therefore been unable to learn who had killed him. There was the second time on Wednesday that he was called before the council, when Spencer informed him that Kane's mother was distraught and had said she was going to make the facts of her son's parentage known to the media, to which Starks shrugged.

And afterwards, returning to his cell to see that someone had removed all of Kane's few possessions while he was out. He chose to believe it was meant to be an act of kindness that resulted in wounding him more. He should have expected the removal, should have thought to keep something of Kane's. He hurried to the lavatory, relief flooding him when he found Kane's comb next to his, with a few strands of his son's dark hair intertwined in the teeth. Hair that provided proof they were father and son. Hair that provided proof beyond mere memory that Kane had existed.

There was his crew, bringing him food from their own commissary stock every day, attempting to get him to eat, and failing. Their attempts at getting him to talk failing as well.

Thursday afternoon, Jackson visited Starks in his cell. "Sands officials have acted better than I thought they would. Usually, when a bed opens, they fill it. Nice of them to wait, but you know they're gonna change that soon."

Starks sat on the edge of his bunk with his gaze fixed on his linked hands dangling between his knees. He nodded but said nothing.

"How would you feel about my moving back in, instead of some stranger?"

Starks nodded again and remained quiet.

"There's something you need to know. That bastard Seth strutted around the first two days, bragging that he'd slayed the dragon, because you hadn't done anything to retaliate. Said he'd sent you into your cave to lick your wounds for good, and was taking over. Then word got out that Kane was your son. I gotta tell you that shocked the shit out of all of us. Almost had to sit on Ethan to stop him from stammering about how he was going to take care of Seth for you. Told him what's to be done is your decision. Told that to the crew, too. They're ready to shred Seth and feed him to the birds soon as you give the word.

Jackson waited then continued. "Here's something in your favor. Instead of inmates seeing Seth as the big shit, they're shunning him like he's Amish or something. Even some of his gang's hanging back. Everyone's waiting to see what you're gonna do about him." When no response came, Jackson asked, "Any idea what that's gonna be and when?"

"I don't want to talk about him right now."

"Of course. Sorry." Jackson glanced around the cell. "Trevor's AWOL. The guys are wondering if you know anything about that."

Starks rubbed his face hard. "I did what I thought was best."

"What did you do?"

"For his own safety, I got him moved to the SHU until it can be arranged to transfer him to a different prison. I haven't followed up because . . ." Starks dropped his face into his hands. His shoulders heaved in silent weeping. A few minutes passed before he wiped his eyes on his sleeve.

Jackson gave him a moment. "So you protected the twerp in spite of what he did to you."

"The kid has a mouth on him. He was pissing people off as though he could afford to. I was afraid that if he pissed the wrong someone off, he'd be killed. I didn't want that on my conscience. It's already too cluttered."

"You did what you could for Trevor, not that he's likely to thank you. Problem is, wherever he goes, his mouth goes with him."

"See about getting transferred back to this cell. Talk to Roberts about it. Tell him to talk to Brunson and get it done. Today."

Jackson took this as a dismissal, an end to a conversation Starks wasn't ready to have as yet. He stood and said, "I'll get on it. Anything I can do for you, Starks?" When no answer came, he left.

Starks eased away from the bunk, splashed cold water on his face, briefly studied his reflection in the mirror, not caring about his unshaven cheeks and chin or unwashed hair. He looked into eyes red and puffy from hours of weeping and lack of sleep and knew what he wanted to do. Needed to do.

It was a slim thread, possibly the last one that might keep his sanity intact.

BIN TRAVELER FORM

Cut By: Yolanda C #93 ____ **Qty** 36 ____ **Date** 7-13-26

Scanned By: ____ **Qty** ____ **Date** ____

Scanned Batch ID's

____

Notes / Exceptions

____

CHAPTER 106

STARKS LEFT HIS cell and continued toward the only room that held—what? A way to search for answers that could never repair damages done?

The workroom door was ajar. Starks rapped, entered, and called Gabe's name.

Gabe came around the corner and stopped.

"I'm surprised the door was open," Starks said.

"It's been open for days, ever since . . . I was giving you another day to come find me then I was going to leave my sanctuary and find you."

Starks shut the door but didn't move. Gabe closed the distance between them. He placed his hands on Starks's shoulders, waited for Starks to look him in the eyes and said, "I'm sorry about Kane." He nodded a few times, patted Starks on the cheek then gestured to the chairs. He waited for Starks to speak.

Starks scratched the wooden tabletop with a thumbnail. "You once said when life becomes ashes we need to rise from them like a phoenix. What you forgot to mention was that first, the phoenix bursts into flames. That's happened, and I feel like I'm nothing more than embers dying out. No regeneration to follow."

"Losing a child is an incomparable pain."

"I've lost three. Three sons."

"Mother of God. I thought I knew just about everything about you. You never said—"

"I had a son with another woman, while I was married to Kayla." His eyes met Gabe's. "I took care of him financially, but never acknowledged him. He drowned when he was five." Gabe made the sign of the cross. Starks nodded. "And although Blake is still alive—thank God—he isn't mine. Now, Kane."

Starks gave Gabe the facts he had about Kane's mother, about Kane's decision to be sentenced at Sands, about his caustic denial when Kane told him who he was, and about the proof. "For a brief while, I felt more on purpose and connected to someone than I had for a long time. He came here to be with me and was slaughtered. All he wanted was . . ." Wracking sobs replaced words.

Gabe waited until Starks composed himself then said, "Even though I've gone through similar grief, there aren't any words that make a damn bit of difference other than I understand."

"I feel like I ended their lives myself."

"You didn't."

"I left Kyle and Kane without a father. As for my other children, sure, I was there for them. As long as it was convenient. I all but gave them cash and told them, 'There you go. Now leave Daddy alone so he can make a lot of money and screw a lot of women.' I told myself I worked the hours I did for them. That's one of those self lies you talked about. I did it for me. Had to be a big-shot. I always thought I was so fucking responsible. Look at what I've done to innocent children who deserved better. I've screwed up their lives and mine."

Gabe sighed. "My grandfather always said regret was the only thing to fear. Smart man, my grandfather. Regret is the heaviest fucking burden we ever carry. It's also the hardest one to put down."

"Do you have regrets?"

Gabe barked a non-humorous laugh. "What do you think? Only thing we can do is try to learn from our mistakes and never make them again. Try to anticipate consequences and hope we avoid making worse mistakes."

Starks scrubbed his hands over his new growth of hair. "I don't like what I'm learning about myself. I don't like what it took to get me to look at that."

"Only thing I can tell you is something you already know and will remember when the time's right: You'll come to terms with what's happened." Starks shook his head. "You will. You did it with Kyle. You'll do it about Blake and Kane. Because, my friend, not to, will fuck you up even more than you are right now."

"Come to terms. With what's happened. And with what's about to."

"What's that mean?"

"It isn't over yet."

CHAPTER 107

"IT SEEMS THAT nearly every situation in my life is a no-win," Starks said. "Even when I win, I'm still screwed over by something or someone else. It's like some twisted game where you move around the board and take rewards or licks based on how the dice land."

Gabe edged forward on his chair and rested his forearms on the table. "There's something else, isn't there?"

"Kayla's got a few months to live. She came here to tell me and ask for my help. I never gave her the chance. Instead, I crucified her and told her I never wanted to see her again. I found out later from Jeffrey. And even then I acted like an asshole, which I've since corrected as much as I can." Starks dropped his head into his hands. "I told her I wouldn't give a fuck if she died tomorrow."

"But you do."

Starks used the bottom of his shirt to dry his face. He caught Gabe's fleeting reaction to seeing the scars on his abdomen. "But I still can't forgive her, because I can't forget what she's done. I know I should but I can't."

"You've got that misconception a lot of people have. Forgiveness isn't about forgetting. Unless you lose your memory, you never forget. Forgiveness is about not letting the memory manipulate you like it once did. It's the only way to let go of bitterness so it doesn't destroy you. Had to learn that one the hard way, myself."

"I'm not ready for that yet. It's still too difficult."

"Yeah, it's difficult. What's even harder is forgiving yourself. That one kicks you in the ass and leaves the shoe inside."

A small smile appeared on Starks's lips then left. "I have to hope there's time to make it up to her."

"You said she has a couple months left. Even if she only had a day, you could do it."

"I hope I get out in time."

"What'd'ya mean?"

Starks explained about Margaret's confession. "My attorney thinks there's a possibility he can either get me released for time served or released into his custody. There isn't much I can actually do for Kayla. But I think it would ease her mind if she knew I was there to care for our children. That's if the timing works in my favor. According to Parker, there's a chance it may not."

Gabe whistled. "If you're smart, you'll keep that news to yourself. Anyone in here's got a beef with you, he'll try to end you if he knows you have a chance of getting out."

"Like Seth."

"Word is he's the one who—"

"Kane identified him just before he died."

"I'd heard the opposite."

"That was intentional."

"Like it or not, in here it's kill or be killed. I wish someone could break the loop, but it isn't likely. What are you gonna do, Starks?"

Starks chewed his bottom lip then nodded once, more to himself than to Gabe. His gaze met Gabe's. "I intend to win."

"Win can wear a lot of hats. Which one are you gonna wear?"

"The only one left."